A Ver...
Affair

ABBY GREEN
NINA MILNE
ANDREA LAURENCE

First Published in Great Britain 2017
By Mills & Boon, an imprint of HarperCollins*Publishers*
1 London Bridge Street, London, SE1 9GF

A VERY FRENCH AFFAIR © 2017 Harlequin Books S. A.

Bought For The Frenchman's Pleasure, *Breaking The Boss's Rules* and *Her Secret Husband* were first published in Great Britain by Harlequin (UK) Limited.

Bought For The Frenchman's Pleasure © 2008 Abby Green
Breaking The Boss's Rules © 2014 Nina Milne
Her Secret Husband © 2014 Andrea Laurence

ISBN: 978-0-263-92969-0

05-0617

BOUGHT FOR THE FRENCHMAN'S PLEASURE

BY
ABBY GREEN

Abby Green worked for twelve years in the film industry. The glamour of four a.m. starts, dealing with precious egos, the mucky fields and driving rain all became too much. After stumbling across a guide to writing romance, she took it as a sign and saw her way out, capitalising on her long-time love for romance books. Now she is very happy to sit in her nice warm house while others are out in the rain and muck! She lives and works in Dublin.

This is especially for Margaret, Peter, Jack
and Mary B...not family by blood, but my family
in every other conceivable way.

CHAPTER ONE

As ROMAIN DE VALOIS approached the ballroom he was glad
for a second that the doors were closed. They acted as a barrier
of sorts between him and that world. The thought caught him
up short. *A barrier?* Since when had he ever thought he needed
that? His strides grew longer, quicker, as if to shrug off the unaccustomed feeling that assailed him. And the most curious sensation hit him too at that moment…the desire to have someone
by his side as he approached this set of doors. Someone…*a
woman*…with her hand in his, who would understand effortlessly what he was thinking, who would glance up at him, a
gleam of shared understanding in her eyes. She might even
smile a little, squeeze his hand…

His steps faltered for just a second before reaching the door.
The vibration of the orchestra, the muted raucous chatter and
laughter of the hundreds of people inside was palpable in his
chest. What on earth was wrong with him? Daydreaming about
a woman when he'd never felt the lack of anything before—
much less a *partner*. And one thing was for sure: no woman
existed like that in his world, or even in his imagination until
that second. If he wanted a woman like that he'd be better off
going back to his small French home town, and he'd left that
behind a long time ago—physically, mentally and emotionally.
His hand touched the handle of the door, concrete and real, *not*

like the disturbing wispy images in his head. He turned it and opened the door.

The rush of body heat, conversation, the smell of perfume mixed with aftershave was vivid and cloying. And yet there was a slightly awed hush that rippled through the room when he walked in. He barely noticed it any more, and wondered if he would even care if it didn't happen. His mouth twisted with unmistakable cynicism as his eyes skipped over the looks and the whisperings, seeking out his aunt. The fact was, as head of the fashion world's most powerful business conglomerate, he practically owned every single person who had anything to do with fashion in this huge glittering ballroom, and even some of those who rode on their coat-tails.

He owned all the dresses and suits so carefully picked out with a mind to current trends. He owned the ridiculously expensive cosmetics that sat on the flawless skin of the women, and the lustrous jewels that adorned their ears, necks and throats. They knew it and he knew it.

The crowd shifted and swayed to let him through, and for the first time in his life he didn't feel any kind of thrill of anticipation. In fact what he felt was...dissatisfaction.

He was relatively young, wealthier than any other man there, and he knew with no false conceit that he was handsome. Most important of all, he was single. And here in New York that put a bounty on his head. So he was under no illusions as to what he represented to women in a crowd like this. And those women he'd have taken his pick from before seemed now to be too garish, too accessible. Dismayingly, the ease with which he knew he could pick the most beautiful, the most desirable, now made distaste flavour his mouth. A pneumatic blonde dressed in little more than a scrap of lace held together by air bore down on him even now.

Relief flooded him when he saw his aunt, and he crossed to her side. Focusing on her brought his mind back to the reason he was there at all tonight. To check someone out in a professional capacity—a model he was being advised to hire for one of the most lucrative ad campaigns ever. His aunt was the latest to put pressure on him as the woman in question was one of her own models. He knew well that this woman, Sorcha Murphy, would be like every other in this room. And on top of that she had a history that made her, as far as he was concerned, unemployable. Still, though, he worked and operated his business as a democracy and had no time for despotic rule. He had to play the game, show that he had at least come to inspect her for himself before telling them no...

His aunt turned and smiled fondly in acknowledgment as he approached.

'No.' Sorcha took in a deep patient breath. 'It's pronounced Sor*ka*...'

'That's almost as cute as you, honey...and where is it from?'

The man's beady eyes set deep into his fleshy face swept up and down again with a lasciviousness that made Sorcha snatch her hand back from his far too tight and sweaty grasp. He clearly had no more interest in where she or her name were from than the man in the moon. She managed to say, with some civility and a smile that felt very fake, 'It's Gaelic. It means brightness...

It's been lovely meeting you, but if you wouldn't mind, I really must—'

'Sorcha!'

She looked around at her name being called with abject relief. The need to get away from this oily tycoon from Texas was acute and immediate.

'Kate...' She couldn't disguise that relief as she greeted her friend, and gave her a very pointed look.

Sorcha turned back to the man whose eyes were now practically popping out of his head as he saw the luminous blonde beauty join Sorcha's side. Her best friend merely smiled sweetly at him and led Sorcha away.

'Boy, am I glad to see you. I think I need a shower after that.' Sorcha gave a little shiver.

'I know. He cornered me earlier, and when I saw you with him I knew I had to save you.'

Sorcha smiled at her closest friend in the whole world and gave her a quick, impulsive hug. 'I'm so glad you're here, Katie. These evenings are such torture—do you think we could make a run for it?'

Kate's nose wrinkled in her exquisite face. 'No such luck. Maud is keeping her eagle eye on us, and has already told me that if we scarper early she'll make us pay.'

Sorcha groaned, and at that moment caught the eye of the woman in question—Maud Harriday, doyenne of the fashion industry and head of Models Inc, the agency in New York she and Kate worked for. And who was, for want of a better term, their surrogate mother.

She smiled sunnily until Maud's laser like gaze was distracted by something else, then stifled a huge yawn. They'd both been up since the crack of dawn for work that day, albeit for different catwalk shows.

Kate grabbed a passing waiter and took two glasses of champagne, handing one to Sorcha. She didn't normally drink the stuff but took it anyway, for appearances' sake. Maud liked her models to look as though they were enjoying themselves—especially when they were on show right in the middle of the mayhem of New York's Fashion Week in one of New York's finest hotels, rubbing shoulders with some of the most important people in media, fashion and politics.

Sorcha smiled and clinked glasses with Kate. 'Thanks. I always feel like some kind of brood mare at these functions…don't you?'

Kate was looking around with interest. 'Oh, I don't know,

Sorch…' She affected the broad accents of Maud's famous New York drawl, and repeated her pep talk of earlier. '"This is the one time in the year we get to promote the new faces along with the old."' She nudged Sorcha playfully and said, *sotto voce*, 'At the grand age of twenty-five we're the old, in case you hadn't noticed…' She continued with her strident imitation. '"…and we generate business. These are the people who invest in you, the fashion advertisers who pay your bills, so go out there and look gorgeous."'

Sorcha threw back her head and laughed. 'She'd kill you if she heard you.'

The contrast of their beauty side by side—one blonde, the other dark—drew many gazes in their direction. They shared an easy intimacy that came from a long friendship that had started when Kate had gone to Sorcha's boarding school in Ireland, just outside Dublin.

Kate spoke again, bringing Sorcha's attention back from its wanderings. Her voice was deceptively light. 'Plenty of gorgeous guys here tonight, Sorch…'

A tightness came into Sorcha's face. She was recalling a recent heated discussion with her friend, and she had no desire to rake over the same ground now. No desire to go back down memory lane, where a comment like that was inevitably headed.

'Kate, let's not get into that again, *please*.' The entreaty in her clear blue eyes was explicit. Kate was her best friend—the one person who knew her like no other, who had seen her at her worst. The familiar guilt rose up, the feeling of debt. Even though she knew Kate would never mention it or use it against her. To her relief she saw her friend nod slightly.

'Ok, you're off the hook for now. But it's just…you are one of the most beautiful women I know, inside *and* out. I just wish—'

Sorcha took Katie's hand, halting her words. Her voice was husky. 'Thanks, Katie…but, really, just leave it for now—OK?'

* * *

It hadn't been hard to seek her out in the crowd. From her pictures alone she would have been easy to find, apart from the fact that she stood out effortlessly—a pale foil of beauty next to so much artifice and expensively acquired tan.

He watched the interplay between the two women covertly. He'd heard their laughter before he'd caught sight of her, and had been surprised to find that it had come from his quarry. It had floated across the room and wound its way around his senses. The sparkling smile was still on her face as she talked to her friend. He hated to admit it, but they weren't like the other models, fawning over the men in the crowd. They looked…like two children in the corner, playing truant. Bizarrely, because he wasn't given to such whims, it made him want to be a part of it…

She stood out in every possible way, with long wavy jet-black hair falling below her bare shoulders. In a strapless, high-waisted dress, the pale swell of her bosom hinted at a voluptuousness that was not usual for a top model, and her poise and grace screamed years of practice. The bluest of blue eyes were ringed by dark lashes, and he could see from across the room skin so pale he imagined that up close it would look translucent.

That niggle of dissatisfaction was coming back even stronger. Not usually given to any kind of introspection, Romain ruthlessly crushed it. Still watching the woman, he found his interest piqued beyond what he'd expected to be purely a quick professional once-over to confirm his own opinion…and even more so because she wasn't trying to capture his attention. His mouth compressed. That in itself was unusual.

He'd already decided he didn't want to use her…especially in light of her past notoriety…but, watching her now, he had to admit that on the face of it she would actually be perfect for what they were looking for. His instincts, honed over many years in the business, told him that in a second. Whether she'd contrived it or not, the smiling, sparkling animation on Sorcha

Murphy's face effortlessly held his regard. Usually within these circles models were always so careful to put on some kind of front that any real expression had long been suppressed—either behaviourally or surgically.

He felt an almost overwhelming impulse to see her up close, and before he could control himself it had generated a throb of desire that wasn't usually prompted so arbitrarily. It was a response he couldn't control and which took him by surprise—*again*. It had been the last thing he'd expected to feel when faced with her.

'Beautiful, aren't they? I see that you've found her.'

He started at the low, husky voice that came from his right and was a little shocked at how enthralled he'd become. Had he been that obvious? He quickly schooled his face, but the woman beside him wasn't fooled, and he was thankful that he knew her well—that it was only she who had noticed his momentarily unguarded few seconds. His mouth quirked before he gave her a kiss on both cheeks, and she mock-fluttered her lashes.

'If I was still capable of blushing, my dear Romain, then I'd be red as a beetroot.'

'I'm sure,' he quipped dryly. She was at supreme ease in these gilded surroundings, and he couldn't imagine this veritable woman of steel blushing for anyone or anything.

'So…how are you, *ma chére tante*?'

She patted his cheek with her fan—a trademark eccentric accessory—and smiled affectionately. 'Very well, thank you. We are honoured to have a man of your calibre here. I'm so glad that for once our work interests have dovetailed so neatly as I never see you any more—although I don't imagine that the promise of a room full of beautiful women would have been any incentive?'

Romain tutted. 'First you flatter me, then you show what a low opinion you really have…'

'Hmm,' she said dryly. 'With pictures of you in numerous

magazines courting what would appear to be every single model in Europe, I can see why you might want to seek out new pastures.'

He was used to this affectionate, teasing banter, though he would not have tolerated it in a million years from anyone else. He looked absently around the room. His aunt's words had hit their mark, and he had to curb a defensive desire to tell her exactly how long it had been since he *had* taken a lover. It didn't sit well with him to admit that even that area of his life seemed to be suffering.

Yet Sorcha Murphy stayed in his peripheral vision. It unnerved him, forcing him to say lightly, 'Now, you of all people should know that you can't believe everything you read in the press.'

'I don't know how you keep managing to generate all those billions of yours when you hardly seem to have the time. Always wining and dining—'

'Maud…' he said warningly, but in a completely unconscious gesture his eyes flicked away briefly to seek out Sorcha again. His aunt couldn't fail to notice.

'Ah, yes… So, what do you think?'

He shrugged nonchalantly. 'I'm still not sure…'

Sometimes the older woman was far too shrewd for her own good. And she knew him too well.

She continued blithely, 'Her blonde companion is Kate Lancaster, an old schoolfriend. She's also one of the highest paid models working in the US—originally from London via Dublin.'

Romain kept his expression bland with little effort. Years of controlling his emotions, of never allowing anyone to see inside his head came like second nature and dictated his actions. Affecting acute boredom, he ran his eyes over the friend.

The blonde was indeed exquisite—stunning. A sensual invitation of honeyed, lissome beauty. And… Nothing. No reaction. He had to remind himself his goal wasn't to pursue personal pleasure tonight. Even if catching his first sight of Sorcha Murphy had driven that thought from his mind and body.

He flicked his eyes back to Sorcha and felt his entire insides jolt…again…as though given an electric shock. He shrugged negligently, his hooded eyes hiding his reaction.

His aunt, apparently unaware of his efforts to appear blasé, saw his gaze resting on her. 'So…does she live up to her portfolio?'

'Of course. I wouldn't expect anything less from one of your models, Maud.'

He could feel his aunt preen beside him. She was nothing if not the best in the business for a reason.

'The question remains, however,' he drawled lightly, 'if she's got what it takes for a gruelling campaign, and whether she has in fact reformed from her wild ways…' He could sense his aunt bristle, and looked down into her flashing eyes. If he cast aspersions on one of her girls, then he cast aspersions on her.

'Romain, I won't tell you again. That was a long time ago. Not everyone is like your—'

'Maud…' he said warningly, with more than a hint of steel in his tone this time.

His aunt pursed her lips before saying, somewhat more tentatively, 'I assure you that I've never had a day's trouble with her. She's polite, punctual. Photographers and stylists love her.'

'You forget that I was working in the City in London eight years ago, when the tabloids were full of Sorcha Quinn, *enfant terrible*… The pictures and headlines are easy to conjure up again. It's not so long ago, and this campaign…well, it's sensitive.'

His aunt was beginning to sound exasperated. He knew she'd be coming to the end of her patience any minute now.

'And as I recall you didn't hold back your opinion then either, Romain. If she's survived to be here today under consideration for this job then you at least owe her a fair chance. It's not as if she came out of all that unscathed. It's why she changed her name to *Murphy*—which is how you didn't recognise her straight away when your board suggested her.'

The uncomfortable prickling assailed him again. He *hadn't* recognised her. In fact something in her pictures had reached out and touched him. In a place he'd prefer not to look. Thankfully his aunt was still talking, and it was easy to divert his thoughts.

'That's all behind her, Romain. I have a reputation to maintain too, believe me, and if there'd ever been a hint of trouble she'd have been out. I wouldn't have her on my books otherwise.'

Romain snorted discreetly. No leopard changed its spots so completely. He didn't doubt that quite a few of his aunt's models lived in such a way that if they were ever found out they'd be off the Models Inc register so fast their heads would spin. No. Women like Sorcha Murphy would keep their dirty little habits a secret. And if there was one thing he was fanatical about, it was that he never went near women involved with drugs. Professionally or socially. The very thought made his chest constrict with dark memories.

'I know you, Romain,' his aunt continued, sounding more confident. 'If you were seriously concerned about Sorcha Murphy's reputation you wouldn't have even considered her for this. Your board of directors obviously have no qualms about her past...'

His aunt had a point. And she didn't know that it was largely Sorcha's past and *apparent* redemption that had made them so keen to use her. For him, things weren't so straightforward. He stared across the room, finding it hard to tear his gaze away. Something was keeping him looking. Just as it had with her pictures. Some hint of vulnerability? A quality that many models failed abysmally to recreate for the camera. How could someone who looked so pure, so innocent, have been or—as was most likely—still *be* caught up in such a murky, corrupt world?

Just as he was thinking this, and feeling a surprising feeling of disappointment rushing through his veins, Sorcha Murphy looked across the room, almost as if she could sense the weight of his penetrating gaze. Their eyes locked. Blue and grey. And the world stopped turning.

* * *

Sorcha felt as though she'd just received a punch to her gut. And the only coherent thought she had in her head was: *How did I not notice him before?* There was a niggle of recognition, but she couldn't place him immediately, and the intensity in his eyes was making it hard to focus…

As though incapable of autonomous movement, her eyes could not move from the stranger's gaze. The most unusual steely grey, his eyes were cold…full of something…and she couldn't quite figure what it was. One thing it wasn't was *friendly*. She shivered inwardly, and yet still could not look away. Even though it was his eyes that held her as if ensnared in a web, she was also aware of his phenomenally dark good looks, the way he stood head and shoulders above anyone else, making him stand out in the crowd. Kate was forgotten. Everything was forgotten. Everything was distilled to this one moment and the tall dark man with the mesmerising eyes who kept staring, and staring. As bold as brass.

And then, in a split second of clarity, she read what was in his eyes. Condemnation and judgment. A kind of disdain. Blatantly obvious. A look that had once been all too familiar in most people's eyes—one she hadn't seen for a long time. A tremble started somewhere in her legs, turning them to jelly, and panic seized her insides. Aghast at the strength of her reaction, with a few strangled muttered words she thrust her glass into Kate's free hand and walked through the crowd and out of the room, not even sure what she was running from.

'What on earth happened to you? One minute you were here, and the next you went as white as a ghost and stormed out of the room…'

Sorcha took her glass back from her friend and took a rare big gulp. She'd been in the toilets for the last ten minutes, holding a damp cloth to her skin in an effort to halt the rising tide of a nervous rash that hadn't appeared in years. She was still so stunned and shocked at her reaction to a mere look from that man across the room that she felt shaky. And in no mood to have her far too perceptive friend speculate on the possible reasons why.

One thing was for sure: with that blistering look she'd been transported back to another time. A time she did *not* want to remember. But he'd been with Maud. Surely they wouldn't have been talking about *her*? She hated the irrational feeling of unease it had given her. It had felt as though he'd been able to see right into the very soul of her…

'Nothing, Katie. I just had to go to the loo…'

'For ten minutes?' Katie snorted. 'I know you, Sorcha, and—'

Her friend broke off, seeing something behind Sorcha, over her shoulder, and then her hand was gripped so tight that she gasped. 'Katie!'

'Don't look now, but the most divine man is across the room…he's talking to Maud. He must be this nephew she said was coming tonight.' A look of comic disbelief made Kate's jaw drop. '*My God!* I've just realised who he is. But of course his pictures don't even do him justice… He's looking over here—'

'Katie…' Sorcha groaned, hiding her rising panic. It had to be him—the man she had seen across the room.

When Kate said her next words, they didn't even sink into Sorcha's head straight away because they were said with such breathy awe.

'*He's* Romain de Valois. Maud's nephew is Romain de Valois. It all makes sense now. The girls were talking about him back-stage earlier. He's heading up some huge campaign—not to mention he's even *here*, and easily the most handsome man in New York… Of course they all think they're in with a—'

'*Romain de Valois?*' A horrified gasp made its way out of

Sorcha's throat, which seemed to be tightening up. She'd gone horribly pale. Kate was oblivious.

'Yes…you must have heard of him. Oh, Sorcha, just *look*. He is seriously the most gorgeous specimen—'

'Katie.' Sorcha's voice was urgent, panicked. 'Don't you remember who he is?'

It seemed as though the fates were conspiring to throw her back down memory lane tonight whether she liked it or not.

Her mouth twisted into a bitter line. 'Please tell me you haven't forgotten that piece in the paper…the one that was worse than all the rest of them—the one that caused every other paper, every magazine and every photographer in London to turn their backs on me?'

Kate finally tore her gaze away from the man across the room and looked at Sorcha. Her brow creased for a second, and then her face became horrorstruck—about as horror struck as Sorcha felt.

Kate clutched her hand. 'Oh, God, Sorch…that was *him*. He gave that interview.'

Sorcha just nodded dumbly. Her insides seemed to be shrivelling up. Even eight years ago Romain de Valois had wielded enough influence to crush a fledgling career. He'd made her the black sheep among models. In a scathing interview he had denounced the use of drugs within the fashion world and had held her up as an example. Enough people had been terrified of losing his favour to seriously damage her reputation. Yet her naïve mistake had been far outweighed by the public scandal and the fallout. She'd been cruelly judged and tried for a crime she hadn't committed, and no one had been prepared to hear her side of the story. His power had been too great. And who cared about a skinny teenager? Within weeks there was already a new fresh face. A new lamb to the slaughter.

She'd been well aware of his name over the years, as he'd taken more and more control of the fashion industry and been mentioned more often with the kind of breathy awe that Kate had just shown. But Sorcha had always avoided listening in to conversations about him—had avoided reading about him, looking at pictures. It was a primal reflex to avoid anything that might make her remember that time in her life…and so far, despite his being Maud's nephew, as he was based primarily in Europe their paths hadn't crossed…

It was only the fact that she'd been able to go home to Ireland and start all over again that had saved her. Slowly but surely, with grit and determination, she'd built herself up again. She'd even taken her grandmother's maiden surname in an effort to start over, and so far, apart from a few snide comments, she'd managed to build a successful career. At least until today. Even though Maud knew of her past, and with characteristic aplomb had declared that it didn't matter to her, what mattered was how she behaved *now*, how could Sorcha fight against the poison she'd no doubt hear from her own nephew? Because that was surely what the topic of conversation had been, why he'd been looking at her like that…

'I'm so sorry, hon. I didn't remember…'

Sorcha squeezed Kate's hand. She knew her palm was clammy. 'Don't be silly. How were we to know *he'd* be the nephew Maud was going on about.' Sorcha laughed, and it sounded a little hysterical to her ears. 'After all, she does have about a hundred of them, she's been married so many times. And Romain de Valois wouldn't even remember me, I'm sure.'

Kate smiled weakly, but Sorcha couldn't fail to notice how her gaze gravitated yet again over her shoulder to that man. She looked back to Sorcha almost guiltily. 'Look, it's not as if we have to talk to him or anything…'

Sorcha felt a curious compulsion unlike anything she'd ever felt before, and obeyed some rogue impulse to turn and look, to see again the man who had so carelessly judged her along with everyone else all those years ago. She felt herself turning…only to come eyeball to eyeball with that suddenly familiar light grey gaze across the room—a room that seemed to have shrunk in seconds. And he was now positively glowering at her!

Feeling every part of her rebel at the movement, Sorcha tore her eyes away again and looked back to Kate, who was watching her. Her friend whistled softly, arching one delicate blonde brow. She had missed nothing in the intense look.

'You spotted him before, didn't you? You didn't recognise him, but you shared a look just like *that*…and that's why you ran…'

Kate's words hit far too close to home and made Sorcha's voice uncustomarily sharp—a knee-jerk defence reaction to the riot of feelings and emotions swirling in her breast. 'Katie, I'll tell you right now exactly the sort of person he is. He's a holier-than-thou control freak. A wealthy, empty-headed playboy who turns up at the office only when he's not cavorting on some yacht somewhere, overloaded with silly dim-witted models who don't know their own names. He's lucky we've never crossed paths before, as quite frankly I've matured enough *not* to go over there and land him one, or throw my drink in his face for being such a pompous, bigoted—'

'Well, what's stopping you now…?'

Sorcha stopped dead. It was only then that she registered Kate's stunned look, her mouth gaping open inelegantly on an unspoken warning.

The low-pitched, dangerously accented deep voice came from so close behind her that she fancied she felt a hint of warm breath on her back. *Too late.* She hadn't even noticed. And now he was here, right behind her. And he had obviously heard every word which seemed to hang suspended accusingly in the air.

CHAPTER TWO

AS ROMAIN spoke he felt righteous anger move through him at her insulting words. But he also felt uncharacteristically at a loss. What on earth had possessed him to cross the room so soon? He couldn't even remember forming the wish or the desire to come closer…and yet here he was.

Her back faced him, her skin so pale that he doubted she'd ever been in the sun. And it was very lightly freckled. A true Celt.

It made her even more intriguing, added to her allure. An almost blue-black sheen rippled off her hair as she started to turn around, and when she faced him he sucked in a breath. She was, quite simply, ravishing. Almond-shaped blue eyes ringed with indecently long black lashes. Cheekbones so high and well defined that it was a sin that she wasn't smiling, to make her cheeks full and ripe. And her mouth… Lord, it must have been created by a god of decadence. The lush lower lip was a sensual invitation to touch, feel, slide his tongue across, and on it rested a top lip that was endearing with its slight overbite— an exquisite anomaly in a perfect face, a cupid's bow of tempting irregularity.

Her breathing was rapid, her widening eyes over-bright, the pupils dilated, and her skin flushed under his look. Something hard settled in his chest. He'd been right. He fought a silent battle with himself. Hadn't he just witnessed her little ten-minute trip to the powder room? Where he knew damn well that she and plenty of others like her would have been indulging in snorting a mood-enhancer…the most common kind on this circuit. She hadn't reformed.

He wanted to walk away, wanted to turn around and forget he'd ever seen her. But he also—perversely—never, ever wanted to let her out of his sight again. And he hated himself for it. And he hated *her* for attracting him so effortlessly. Yet he knew he was being irrational. And that fired him up even more.

'Yes…?'

Somehow she managed to articulate a word that sounded English, that made sense. Because one thing Sorcha knew for sure was nothing else made sense any more. Every preconceived notion about this man had fled. He was just a man, a devastatingly attractive man, holding her in some kind of wickedly sensual spell.

Tall, dark and handsome. He was a walking cliché. But no banal description could do justice to the way his hair shone almost black under the glittering lights. The way his hooded eyes hinted at a dangerous sensuality that was so palpable she felt faint. The way his skin shone and glowed with undeniable rude good health, so darkly olive that she fancied he must surely come from the Far East, despite being French. She was tall—almost five foot eleven—but she had to tip her face up to his. She was barely grazing his shoulder in heels.

The bespoke designer suit did little to hide the raw untamed sexuality of the man. Sorcha, from her experience of working with some of the best bodies in the business, knew a good physique when she saw it. His was…perfect. And she'd bet money that it wasn't honed in a gym. This man gave off an air of restless energy that spoke to her, called out to her. As a lover of the outdoors herself, she knew that he would only be content with pushing himself to the max, in the rawest of environments.

What had happened to her? Why couldn't she seem to move? She was vaguely aware that Kate had melted away seconds ago. And he was still looking at her as though he wanted to throttle her! For long moments they stared at each other in silent and heated communication. Finally Sorcha spoke again, more impatiently this time. Who did he think he was to come over and glower at her? She refused to give him the satisfaction of recognition.

'Yes? Can I help you?'

Romain had to focus. Her voice was husky, the accent refreshingly unjarring…melodious…. Clarity rushed back with force when a hapless waiter dropped a glass nearby, shocking him out of his stupor, making her flinch. And then he remembered. And that hardness took hold again.

Say hello, exchange a few words and get out of there—after all, hadn't he come here tonight to meet her? He might have decided to dismiss the notion of using her for the job, but a few words couldn't hurt…

He held out a hand. 'Romain de Valois. I don't believe we've actually met before…despite that flawless character reference.'

Finally some life force returned. She ignored his hand and said, with sweet acidity, 'Nearly as flawless as the one you gave me eight years ago?'

He dropped his hand and looked down at her, cool and unperturbed by her rudeness. 'So you do remember? I wasn't sure if your acerbic comments just now were due to intense dislike on first sight, or if you were referring to that.'

She couldn't hide the bitterness. 'Of course I remember, Monsieur de Valois. It's not every day the press chases a seventeen-year-old out of London, calling for her blood—a press that was spurred on by *your* comments. All you lacked was a pulpit…' Her chest rose and fell and she couldn't disguise her agitation. She could feel her skin heating up under his look.

'Do you forget that you were a seventeen-year-old drug

addict?' he said with harsh inflection. 'Photographed unconscious on the street?'

A pain so sharp that it caused her to stop breathing for a second made Sorcha want to curl inwards. Guilt, shame, and an old, old fear all vied for supremacy. With what felt like a superhuman effort she found some hard brittle shell left. She tossed her hair with studied indifference, and was too wound up to notice the tiny flash in the cool grey gaze.

Her voice was scathing. 'If you've got nothing more to do than come over here like some kind of outdated moral judge and check for track marks on my arms, then please excuse me—' She turned to go, and was taking a step away when her wrist was caught in a strong grip. His touch seared through her whole body like a brand. He slowly and very calmly turned her palm upwards, and made a thorough study up and down the underside of her milky white arm.

'No,' he said musingly. 'No track marks. But then I'm sure you're an intelligent woman. You'd have them well hidden.'

Sorcha finally yanked her arm free and hugged it close to her chest, as though he had burnt her. Her voice was shaking with emotion, and to her utter horror she could feel the sting of tears at the back of her eyelids. 'Mr de Valois, if you would please excuse me? I am here in a work capacity tonight for your aunt. I don't want to cause a scene, but trust me when I say that if you try to stop me leaving again I will scream this room down.'

'There's no need for such dramatics Miss Murphy—or should I say *Quinn*? And if you did anything of the sort I'd put you over my shoulder and carry you out like a child having a tantrum.'

Sorcha gulped, her bravado in short supply all of a sudden. She didn't doubt his words for a second, and the thought of him throwing her over his impossibly broad shoulder... She could feel the heat flare up from her stomach.

She furiously willed a body which seemed to have been invaded by an alien force to obey her silent command to stop reacting to his presence, and gritted out, 'It's Murphy to you. If all you want is to see the tabloid fodder you chewed up and spat out, then have a good look.'

'Oh, I am,' he drawled, and Sorcha mentally castigated herself for her careless words.

She didn't want this man's attention on her…*any part of her.*

'You've certainly grown up…and filled out.'

She sucked in a breath, unaware that her innocent movement caused his eyes to be drawn back to those parts of her body where they had rested briefly in an eloquent accompaniment to his words.

'I was just a teenager—'

'No teenager I knew stayed out till six a.m. every morning, drinking champagne all night, taking cocktails of various drugs to stay awake—'

He glanced pointedly at the glass in her hand. Her knuckles were white on the stem because she gripped it so tightly. Following his glance, and feeling suddenly reckless and rebellious, she tipped the glass to him in a salute. 'Well, I must say it's nice to meet the man who once called me the poison seeping into the industry… Here's to you, Mr de Valois. I wish you luck on your crusade to rid the world of imperfect people!'

And with that Sorcha downed the half empty glass in one go. Very carefully she put it down on a nearby table. And while she still could, feeling sick from the immediate rush of a drink she didn't usually favour, she spun on impossibly high heels and strode away from him, the silk of her long dress billowing out behind her.

More than a few men turned to look as she passed, and Romain couldn't fail to notice, the very strange and proprietorial surge of…something very disturbing. He felt a little shell shocked. He could still see the white expanse of her delicate throat, bared as she had downed the sparkling drink. Her eyes had flashed before putting the glass down.

No woman had *ever* walked away from him like that, or showed such blatant disrespect. Yet, much to his utter confusion, he found himself thinking that his decision to veto her for the campaign suddenly seemed a little too hasty. Watching her walk away had filled him with the almost overwhelming urge to grab her back, strike more sparks, keep her talking.

He hadn't expected this. He'd expected her to be hard, with that smooth shell most models had, yet her vulnerability had hit him straight between the eyes. And he'd been surprised that she'd remembered his comments from eight years previously. His jaw hardened. Despite his aunt's words, and Sorcha Murphy's *apparent* vulnerability, he'd be more than surprised to find that she had given up her old habits.

To be brutally honest, he'd expected that once she'd known who he was she'd morph into exactly the type of woman he'd become immune to. Sycophantic, posturing... But she hadn't. She'd been filled with fire and passion underneath that pale, pale skin. An intoxicating package.

For some men, he told himself angrily, and finally turned away from the image of her slender back walking away from him.

'Well, he can take his job and—'

'Sorcha!' Maud's husky smoke-ravaged voice rang out like the crack of a whip.

It stopped Sorcha in her tracks—literally. She was pacing back and forth in Maud's palatial office that looked out over busy New York streets. Ever since Maud had called her in to tell her that Romain de Valois wanted *her* for his campaign, she'd been feeling jittery and panicky.

She sat down. 'Sorry, Maud, I know he's your nephew—'

'Technically, he's my ex-nephew.' The older woman waved a hand. 'That doesn't matter anyway. Nepotism didn't get him where he is now; that was through sheer hard graft and ingenuity.' Her face softened with unmistakable affection. 'Can you believe even *I* have to answer to him?' She ignored Sorcha's dark scowl, austerity marking her features again. 'The fact is, this is probably one of the most prestigious jobs you could ever be offered—two weeks jet-setting around the world. Do you know how many models were considered? It's so important to him that he's overseeing the whole shoot personally. He's even willing to kick off in Ireland to accommodate your holiday plans—a condition *I* insisted on.'

The thought of even a day with that man glowering down his nose at her, checking up on her every two minutes, caused very contradictory feelings in Sorcha's head...and body. Since that night almost a week ago she hadn't been able to get his dark face and tall, impressive body out of her mind. And she hated it. He was her nemesis—the embodiment of every misunderstanding she had suffered all those years ago.

'Maud...can't you see how difficult this would be? He's not just anyone. He's—'

'I'm well aware of the things he said in London that time. But you have to admit, innocent or not, if you hadn't been caught like that then he wouldn't have had any reason to say anything. His hand was forced by his board. He didn't have the complete control he enjoys now. They couldn't be seen to be taking an easy line on models doing drugs...not when that girl had died so soon before...'

Sorcha felt cold all of a sudden. She was barely able to take in Maud's words, her mind seizing on the girl that she'd mentioned. She had been a young model on the brink of stardom who'd overdosed and died only weeks before Sorcha's own chain of events had unfolded. It always made her feel sick, and impotent with anger and guilt. It was one of the reasons she'd finally followed her heart in the past year and tried to do something about those past events—something concrete...

Maud stood up and came round to perch one hip on her desk. She looked at Sorcha from over her spectacles. 'I'll tell you something else that no one knows…' She sighed. 'It might help you understand…'

Sorcha looked at Maud curiously.

'His own mother was a drug addict. She died of an overdose. So, you see, he has a very personal abhorrence of drugs.'

Sorcha felt a dart of sympathy. But then she remembered the condemnation in his eyes and forced her mind to clear the images she always worked so hard to avoid. She said, somewhat stiltedly, 'Well, his own personal issues aside, I'm sorry for him—but that doesn't excuse his behaviour. When he spoke to me the other night it was obvious he still believes that I'm involved in something. He's not willing to give me the benefit of the doubt. I'm sorry, Maud, but I'm taking my few months out. You know I've been promising this to myself for the past year.'

Her eyes beseeched her agency boss. Maud looked fierce for a second, and then shrugged. 'I think you're mad, Sorcha. I'll let him know, but I warn you—once he's decided on something he's not one to give up easily. He may even try to go through your Irish agency, knowing that you're headed back there. His board of management are adamant about using you…'

Sorcha shot to her feet. 'See! He's been forced into this against his will. He won't push it if I refuse. Please, just tell him and see for yourself. He'll walk away without a backward glance.'

Sorcha closed her eyes and gripped the handrest as the plane took off. She *hated* take-offs. She always imagined the bottom of the plane scraping along the ground at the last moment, and then there was that wobbly bit as it fought for equilibrium in the air—

'Are you all right, dear?'

She opened her eyes and looked at the kind, elderly woman on her right. She smiled weakly, but she could feel the sweat on her brow and knew she must be pale from the concerned look the woman was giving her.

'Fine. Sorry—I just hate taking off. No matter how often I fly, it doesn't get better.'

'Ah, well, sure it's only a short enough flight. We'll be home in no time.'

Sorcha smiled and turned back to look out of the window. *Home*. Ireland. She'd only been back intermittently between jobs in the past year, to work on her project whenever she had the chance, and she'd missed it—missed her apartment. The home she shared with Kate in New York was Kate's. But her place in Dublin was *hers*. Bought and paid for with her own hard-earned money.

The plane was stabilising at last, so Sorcha's hands eased their death grip and she sat back and closed her eyes. It had been ten days since the night of the function in New York, and she hadn't stopped working since then. Every day had been packed to the brim. Even so *that* man—his voice, his face, his air of intense, focused energy—would slip into her consciousness and take up residence.

Just thinking about him made her heart speed up, her breath quicken. And made a whole host of other sensations race through her body. She hated that she could be having this kind of reaction to someone who had so carelessly played God with her life, her career. She forced herself to relax. Hadn't she walked away from him? Yet the look in his eyes when she'd left him standing there that night had been so intense... Maud hadn't had to warn her. She was *sure* that he was a man who would be single-minded in his pursuit of anything...or anyone.

Since leaving Maud's office, only three days before, she'd half expected him to turn up at any moment and demand that she do the job—which she couldn't believe she'd even been considered for, if it was half as amazing as Maud had outlined. There were plenty more models who were far more ambitious, who always got the big campaigns. So why had not seeing him, not hearing anything, led her to feel like a cat on a hot tin roof? Why had she found herself jumping every time the phone rang, only to be in some tiny and very treacherous way *disappointed* when it had just been Katie or her brother?

She'd met the man for mere moments, and he had proved himself to be every bit as arrogant, judgmental and overbearing as she would have expected. Why did it have to be someone like *him* who seemed to be cracking through the armour she'd erected around herself for so long? Why couldn't someone else be making her heart quicken, her breath shorten just thinking of them? Someone nice, unassuming, non-threatening. Someone who would be gentle, kind, sensitive. Certainly not tall, powerful, dark and mysterious…arrogant, overbearing, too confident, too sexual—

'So, dear, were you on holiday in America?'

Sorcha nearly jumped out of her skin—she'd been so intent on listing Romain de Valois's negative attributes to herself.

She shook her head, as much to herself as anyone else, and smiled.

'No…unfortunately not. I've been working…'

With some kind of cowardly relief, she allowed herself to be sucked into inane conversation. Anything to stop dangerous thoughts and images circulating in her head. It wasn't as if she was ever going to meet him again anyway…

Sorcha's mobile was ringing as soon as she arrived at her apartment. She dumped her suitcase and fished it out of her handbag. No number was listed on the screen, but she figured it was because it was either Katie, her mother or her over-protective big brother, checking in to see if she'd landed in one piece, and they were all abroad. She smiled as she answered.

'OK, whichever one of you it is. I'm fine, I've just landed, and the plane didn't crash—although at one stage I seriously thought—'

'Hello, Sorcha.'

Words froze on her lips. Her mouth stayed open. Her throat dried. That voice. His voice. Deep, authoritative, sensual. Disturbingly close. Her hand gripped the phone tight.

'I'm sorry, who is this?'

A soft chuckle made her insides quiver. 'You're pretending to have forgotten me already?'

The conceited arrogance of the man! She knew very well who it was, and hated that he could be *here*, in her space, even if just on the end of a tenuous connection. She felt guilty—as though she'd conjured him up with her imaginings. She would not give him the satisfaction of letting him know that she knew it was him. Even though she burned to know what he wanted.

As if reading her every thought, he spoke with low, seductive deadliness. 'I got your number from Maud, who informed me of your plans to go home. I know you've probably just arrived, but I wanted to get in touch with you as soon as possible.'

Sorcha closed her eyes for a second, knowing it would be futile to pretend ignorance of the power he had. The man was so confidently arrogant that he hadn't even given her time to play dumb.

'Yes, I am back in Dublin now. Thousands of miles from New York. I'm taking a well-earned break—'

'I've got a job proposal to discuss with you.'

Sorcha's mouth opened and closed, a whole host of conflicting emotions see—sawing through her at the realisation that he *was* determined to pursue her for this job. But it would be untenable, unthinkable—surely he could see that?

'I'm afraid I'm not doing any jobs for the foreseeable future. I've been working back to back for the past year—not that it's any business of yours—and now I'm taking time off. As I told Maud before I left, I'm sure you'll find another model who can do whatever it is you have in mind. Thanks for the call, though. Goodbye.'

She was in the act of taking the phone away from her ear, about to switch it off, when she heard a silky,

'*Wait.* You might want to hear what I have to say about the job.'

Reluctantly she brought the phone back to her ear. 'I've already explained—'

'I'm here in Dublin too, actually. I arrived yesterday. Charming city.'

Sorcha nearly dropped the phone in shock, her hand suddenly sweaty. *He was here? In Dublin?*

Feeling very agitated, she walked over to her fourth-floor window and looked down to the street outside—almost as if he might be standing there looking up at her. But the road surrounding her side of Merrion Square was empty, the inner-city rush hour traffic having been and gone. Her heart was pumping erratically.

Trying not to sound panicked, she said lightly, 'That's great. Enjoy your visit, Monsieur de Valois. There are plenty of very good modelling agencies—'

'I had a lovely meeting this afternoon with your Irish agent Lisa. Very accommodating. I've given her the brief for the job, and she agrees with me that you're perfect for what we're looking for.'

Sorcha closed her eyes again and sank into the couch just behind her, under the window. This was exactly what Maud had warned her he might do. It was what she'd been hoping to avoid—at least until she'd booked herself some secluded time away. She hadn't told her Irish agent that she was coming home, knowing full well that she'd have her booked to within an inch of her life before she'd even stepped off the plane. Sorcha was one of their biggest success stories and exports, and Lisa was the agent who had spotted her in the first place. She always felt duty-bound to do as much work for her as she could whenever she came home...as some sort of payback for having defected to the States.

'So, Lisa knows I'm home...' she said dully—as if she even needed to ask.

'She does.'

He sounded so smug that Sorcha sat forward on her couch, anger surging through her veins at the thought that this man, in his stubborn pursuit of whatever it was he wanted, had scuppered her plans for rest and relaxation—not to mention the time she'd put aside to work on the important project that was so dear to her heart. 'Why are you doing this? You can't seriously mean to work with me. You've made your opinion abundantly clear, Monsieur de Valois, and I won't have you watching my every move. Just because you can't handle someone turning you down—'

'Careful, Sorcha.' His voice for the first time sounded hard and lethal.

She stopped despite herself.

'All I'm suggesting is that you meet with Lisa tomorrow. She will tell you what I'm proposing. The decision as to whether or not you want to meet me to discuss the job further will be entirely up to you. No one will force you to do this.'

CHAPTER THREE

NO-ONE *will force you to do this…*

They wouldn't have to, Sorcha thought grimly as she walked the short journey from her agent's office to Romain's exclusive hotel the following day. Lisa had told her where he'd be for their '*meeting*'. She had to hand it to him. He must have walked into the small Irish modelling agency and laughed out loud. It would have been like taking candy from a baby.

She could picture it now: the industry's most powerful head—a person who held the kind of authority that would make anyone dizzy, a man responsible for countless designers and their merchandise and advertising, not to mention his high profile as one of the world's most eligible and handsome men— walked into a tiny basement agency, offered them a deal for one of their models that was in excess of six figures… Well, you wouldn't have to be a rocket scientist to do the maths.

When Sorcha had walked in that morning the place had been buzzing, the excitement palpable. Pretty Woman was not one of the most successful agencies in Dublin, but it was friendly, the girls were lovely, and Lisa had become a good friend to Sorcha. When her career had started to take off in Dublin, and then London, Sorcha had refused to leave Lisa's representation, despite being told it could sabotage her career. And then when the tide had turned against her Lisa had remained loyal in the face of scathing public opinion. Her debt to Lisa was much the same as her one to Katie. Never mentioned, never referred to, but *there*.

Sorcha was well aware that Pretty Woman wasn't doing as well as other agencies. In fact the last time she'd been home Lisa had confided to her that if not for Sorcha the agency might have to close down. So now what was she supposed to do? Romain de Valois had just offered them a massively lucrative job—Lisa had even mentioned that they were hoping to expand their offices on the back of it! The proviso, of course, was that Sorcha had to be the model. Romain had told Lisa that he would not under any circumstances even entertain looking at anyone else.

Seething silently, she made her way through the pedestrian crush on the streets. The air was mild, and blue skies made Dublin look its best, but she barely noticed. Romain de Valois had painted her into a corner and thrown away the brush.

She crossed a busy road and the huge hotel loomed magnificent and ornate just opposite, gleaming in the sunshine. It stood overlooking the main city park, which bloomed with colour. Everything fled her mind as she approached closer and closer. And again she remonstrated with herself. How could such a brief meeting in one night have made such an impact? Why had he pushed her buttons so easily? She didn't want to know, she told herself hastily. And now he was here…controlling her life like a puppet master.

She let the indignation rise. Anything to help block out the far more conflicting feelings—like one in particular, which felt suspiciously and awfully like excitement at the thought of seeing him again.

Romain sat in a high-backed chair at the rear of the main reception room in the recently refurbished Shelbourne Hotel. With his elbows on the armrests, he rested his chin on steepled fingers. He'd positioned himself in such a way that he would see Sorcha arrive before she saw him.

A necessary precaution, as he was suddenly questioning his very sanity. After that night something compelling had taken him over. When further pushed by Maud, who'd assured him of Sorcha's professionalism *again*, and then by his board it had seemed almost easy to give in, to allow himself to be swayed. And now he couldn't remember the last time, if ever, he'd flown halfway across the world to chase a woman. His mouth compressed. He might try to dress it up, call it something else, pretend to himself that his main motive was to get her for this very genuine ad campaign—which he still couldn't believe she'd had the temerity to turn down—but the reality, as he knew well, was that she was the first woman who'd walked away from him.

His mouth twisted. Yet if he could make sure that she behaved, make sure she stayed clean, then perhaps…this could work. After all, he would be on hand every step of the way to ensure things went the way he wanted. He didn't usually consider mixing business with pleasure, but now…He was at a stage in his career where his absolute control meant he could do as he pleased…he was beholden to none. Maybe for once he could relax that rigid control a little. The thought of taming Sorcha Murphy was making that sense of dissatisfaction a distant memory.

And then in an instant she was *there*. That jolt went through his body again, taking him by surprise. His eyes ran over her hungrily, as if inspecting a thoroughbred. From the tip of her shiny black hair, tied back into a low ponytail, to the plain white shirt and casual jacket over worn jeans, all the way to the scuffed runners on her feet. She'd made no effort to impress him—the staid black frames of the sensible glasses perched on her nose said that—and yet her beauty was ethereal and intoxicatingly earthy, just as he had remembered. Unlike other models, who sometimes looked strange in real life, their proportions working for the camera but weirdly not in the flesh, Sorcha looked as good off the page, if not even better, and that was rare. A frisson of excitement ran through him as he saw the concierge point in his direction and their eyes met.

Let the battle commence.

As Sorcha approached Romain, she felt as self conscious as she had her first day on a catwalk. She had that same unsettling reaction she'd had in New York. All of her antipathy, all of her preconceived notions fled as she walked towards him—and then he compounded it by standing with lithe grace. Even taller, broader, more powerful than she remembered. Darker... That hint of Far Eastern lineage struck her again. She reached him, he held out a hand. This time, still in shock to think that he could be *here*, Sorcha let her hand be taken by his. It was firm, cool. His fingers closed around hers and she felt a crazy pulse throb fleetingly and disturbingly between her legs.

'Sorcha.' He indicated a seat opposite and didn't let go of her hand until she sat down. When she finally got it back it was tingling.

She wished for some sanity for reality to come back into her head, which felt woozy. She was determined not to be staying for longer than a few minutes at the most, and perched uncomfortably on the edge of her chair. All previous thoughts of Pretty Woman and Lisa fled in proximity to this man.

'Mr de Valois—'

'I didn't know you wore glasses.'

Sorcha's mouth stayed open. She felt nonplussed until she put up a hand and felt the familiar frames on her nose. She'd been so preoccupied that she hadn't even noticed that she'd forgotten to take them off. Even though her eyes weren't so bad that she needed them right now, she suddenly wanted to keep them on.

'Well, I'm sorry if they're putting you off, Mr de Valois.

I'm afraid, along with my other failings, I'm also slightly long-sighted.'

He tutted and lifted a hand to call for service, before fixing her with that steely gaze again. 'Not at all. They suit you. And please don't put yourself down—'

'Why? Because you'll do that for me?'

For a second there was no reaction, and then a huge smile lit his harshly handsome face, making him look years younger and so gorgeous that Sorcha felt welded to her chair. Wasn't she supposed to be walking out by now? He looked ridiculously exotic against the backdrop of the opulent Dublin hotel, surrounded by the more pale, Celtic-skinned customers. His accent was pronounced, heightening that sense of his otherness in this place.

'As sparky as I remember…that's good.'

Sorcha felt like grinding her teeth. 'I'm not trying to be sparky, Mr de Valois. I'm here to tell you that I'm not interested in your job.'

He waved a dismissive hand. 'Let's order some tea, yes? I believe it is something of a national delicacy…and then we will have lunch.'

'You're not listening to me, Mr de Valois—'

'No,' he said with silken deadliness. 'You are not listening to me. And please call me Romain—after all, we will be working closely together for the next few weeks, and I hate to stand on ceremony…'

Sorcha just looked at him and shook her head. The smooth conceit and downright arrogance of the man was unbelievable.

'*Mr* de Valois, unless you plan on tying me to this chair there is nothing to stop me standing up and walking out of here. I've told Maud and now you that I'm not interested in the job. I'm due to take some holiday—'

She had to stop when a waitress came and delivered the tea. Sorcha couldn't even remember the order having been taken. She watched, disgusted, at the way the pretty young blonde girl blushed a deep shade of crimson when Romain smiled at her and said thank you. The poor girl practically fell over a chair as she left, her eyes glued to what was probably the most stupendously handsome man she'd ever seen in her young life. Romain de Valois, of course, had already forgotten her, and was focusing those long-lashed grey eyes back on Sorcha, with an intensity that threatened to scramble her brains all over again.

Romain was glad of the short distraction of the waitress, because the shaft of pure arousal that had gone straight to his groin when Sorcha had mentioned being tied to the chair had thrown up other images…much more explicit…of her being tied to a bed… He fought to regain some composure, to remember what she had said.

'Which is why we are going to start the campaign here.' He held out a cup of tea, 'Tell me, did you also mention to Lisa that you were not going to take the job?'

The sickening knowledge of how neatly he'd manipulated events brought her some much needed focus back—even though she knew with a sinking feeling in her belly that it would be futile to keep insisting that she wouldn't do the job. She also had to accept the cup he was offering her, or risk causing a scene. She saw a glint of triumph light his eyes, as if he could read her thoughts. He was getting under her skin in a prickly heat kind of way that made her very nervous. It made her voice clipped, arctic. 'In light of past…events—namely your very public condemnation of me—' She stopped as she realised she'd been about to say *at a very painful time in my life*. She knew that she didn't want him to see that vulnerable side of her, so she faltered for a second, her skin heating up. 'I find it hard to see why you want me to do this campaign so badly.'

Romain studied her. She looked about ready to spring off the chair and bolt. And right at that moment all he wanted to do was get up, throw her over his shoulder and carry her upstairs to his suite, loosen her hair, take off her glasses, uncover her body inch by inch, see if those soft swells that he could just glimpse under her shirt were really as voluptuous as they looked… He sat back.

He was not a Neanderthal. He was sophisticated and urbane. This woman might be appealing to the most basic level of his carnal urges, but it was probably because he hadn't had a woman in a while and she was refreshingly different from the cool blondes he usually favoured. He sipped his tea and carefully placed the cup back onto the saucer.

'The fact is, I had decided that we could do without you on this campaign, and was prepared to tell my board so—'

'See?' The relief was evident in Sorcha's voice, in the way her face cleared, and she put down her cup and half rose from her chair. 'That's fine with me. Thanks for the tea—'

'Sit down.'

Sorcha responded to the very explicit threat in his voice, sitting down again before she'd even realised what she was doing. The memory of him threatening to throw her over his shoulder was all too recent. And, as unmistakably urbane as this man was, there was an air of danger about him, a disregard for convention, the niceties.

'But after seeing you in the flesh…'

When he said that his words were loaded with a sensual meaning that was not lost on her. Sorcha's head went so fuzzy for a second that she missed his next immediate words.

'You would be perfect for the job. The only suitable model, in fact.'

She shook her head, trying to clear it, and took her glasses off for a moment to pinch the bridge of her nose in an endearingly personal reflex, something she only ever did when under pressure or stressed.

'Monsieur de Valois—'

'Romain, please.' He smiled, and it was the smile of a shark.

Sorcha gave in. Perhaps this was the way to reach him. She

put her glasses back on and said in her most businesslike voice, 'Very well—Romain.' She ignored the way saying his name made a funny flutter start in her chest. 'I'm sure your board can be persuaded to take on another model to fit their visual concepts. There has to be a million other women out there with my colouring.' She laughed and it sounded strained. 'I mean, all you have to do is step outside this hotel and you'll find hundreds.'

Romain's mouth quirked. She really had no idea how stunning she was. Was she fishing for compliments? But the look on her face was so earnest it made something in his chest tighten.

He shook his head brusquely. 'Not as many as you would think. And none with your unique...past.'

She bristled immediately. 'What's that got to do with anything?'

'It's inspired the whole concept of this campaign. This is no ordinary shoot, Sorcha. Only at its most basic level is it to be a showcase for numerous luxury goods, the season's finest offerings. With the way society is going—the fascination between people and media, the cult of celebrity...you represent someone who was torn down—'

'Thanks to you,' she said bitterly, picking up her cup again with a jerky movement. But Romain ignored her comment, continuing as if he hadn't heard her.

'...and built herself up again. You've shown a tenacity of spirit, if you will. A grit and determination to succeed at all costs. You represent redemption. You've weathered a storm and come out the other side. People nowadays won't buy the image of the virginal prom queen—they resonate more with a fallible person. I'm willing to give you the benefit of the doubt, take my board's and my aunt's word that you *are* reliable. But trust me, Sorcha, if there's a hint of any kind of scandal or drugs I won't hesitate to drop you, and you won't receive a penny. However, as long as I see no evidence of anything...' He spread his hands and shrugged eloquently.

His words made Sorcha reel slightly. She hadn't had her past raked up so comprehensively in years. Or reduced to such succinct devastation. The cup she held in her hand shook slightly, and she put it down with a clatter. She felt as if a layer of skin had been stripped off. 'Well, I'm delighted that someone has seen fit to take the scrap metal of my life and see it fashioned into something that can benefit the greater good of the advertising industry.'

Romain uncharacteristically felt at a loss for words—as if he had somehow made an error of judgment. Sorcha was expressionless. Cold and aloof. Without even knowing how, he *knew* that he'd hurt her—and that knowledge threw him. As it had when he'd seen that vulnerability up close. The hard sheen he'd expected to find hadn't been there. And the vulnerability was there again now—just under the surface.

With what felt uncomfortably like relief, he saw the head waiter from the restaurant approach. He stood and gestured with a hand. 'I've booked us a table for lunch. Why don't we continue this discussion over some food?'

It wasn't a question, and Sorcha felt too shell shocked to argue. Mute, she preceded him out of the reception room and into the restaurant, where gold-coloured banquette seats made their table into a gilded prison of privacy.

CHAPTER FOUR

ONCE seated, Sorcha avoided looking at the unnerving man opposite her. Out of the corner of her eye she could see long brown fingers curled around the edges of the menu, and her heart started to beat fast again. It was some moments before she realised that he was looking at her expectantly. Taking a deep breath, she closed her menu too, having no idea of what it offered.

'So…how long have you needed glasses?' He threw her with such an innocuous question after his last words, which had been so rawly personal. She looked at him warily and was glad of the table between them, and the sturdy frames of her glasses. Perversely, they seemed to give her some protection—as if projecting an image that made her more comfortable in such close proximity to his potent sexuality.

'Relatively recently. Years of late nights cramming for exams have taken their toll—I find I need them for reading, or if I'm tired.'

His brow quirked. 'A hangover from school? Surely it's been some time since you crammed for anything?'

It wasn't really a question, but Sorcha wanted to blurt out defensively that the for the past four years she'd been studying late into the night almost every night. It was one of her most cherished accomplishments—and she'd been about to tell *him*.

Her mouth was still open. Horror filled her at how close she'd come to telling him something so personal. The thought of his reaction if she had made her go cold.

She shut her mouth and smiled sweetly. 'Well, what do you expect? With all the partying I was doing I hardly had time to worry about the state of my eyes, now, did I?'

Her words struck a hollow chord in Romain somewhere. He looked at her intently, but she'd already picked up the menu again. Her whole frame was tight with tension. For a brief second there something so passionate had crossed her face that he'd fully expected her to say something else entirely...but *what*?

'You do seem to live quite the quiet life now, or are you just careful about where and when you're seen, having learnt from past experience?'

The tone in his voice made all sorts of implications about why she might want to hide or not be seen. He was lounging back, at perfect ease, his suit jacket gone, his shirt open at the throat, stretched across his formidable chest. Sorcha sat up straight. She'd let her guard down for one second too many, and the thought that he must have had her investigated in some way made her feel violated.

'If I do take on this job—which it would appear I have very little choice *but* to do—I will not be subjected to this kind of questioning. You know nothing about me or my past. *Nothing*. I will never tell you anything about my personal life.'

He inclined his head with a minute gesture, but Sorcha could see that she'd got to him. His eyes had flashed a stormy grey for a second.

He leant forward and said silkily, 'Never say never...'

She became aware that the waiter was hovering, and Romain, supremely cool again, looked up to indicate that they were ready to order. Sorcha had never felt so many conflicting emotions and sensations before. She very much wanted to run away—get away from this disturbing man whose mere presence seemed to have the power to reach inside her and shine a light on her innermost vulnerabilities.

Romain ordered the fish special, and Sorcha ordered a steak with mash. He reacted almost comically to her order. Sorcha caught his look and read it in a second. How could she forget that she was in the presence of a serial lothario? After that night in New York Katie had been only too eager to fill her in on his reputation, which would have made Casanova blush. Her mouth tightened. He was used to this, of course. Taking models out. Wining and dining them. And no doubt he'd never heard any of them ask for anything more substantial than a lettuce leaf dressed with half a grape.

She caught the waiter just before he left the table and smiled broadly. 'Could you make that a double portion of mash, please?'

When she looked back to Romain she could see what looked suspiciously like a twitch on his mouth. Damn him. Her small childish gesture felt flat and silly now.

They sat looking at each other for a long moment. Sorcha refused to be the one to break her gaze first. And when he spoke she felt light-headed—as if she'd scored some tiny yet triumphant victory.

'Let me tell you a little more about the campaign. I feel that perhaps I didn't give you the full picture before.'

Sorcha's tone was a dry as sandpaper. 'Don't worry—I get the picture. You've got it in for me, and even though I'll be getting paid, it'll be Sorcha Murphy to the gallows again. Although this time with silk gloves on.'

He looked at her for a long moment and felt a surge of something rush through him. Her self deprecation caught him off guard. He wasn't used to women displaying that kind of humour around him. Not ones who looked like Sorcha Murphy.

'To an extent you might perceive that to be the case. And based on what I said earlier I can't blame you. However, it's not an entirely accurate picture…'

Sorcha was surprised to find that he was almost apologising, as if he knew he'd been less than sensitive. She found herself nodding slightly, as if to encourage him to continue, and knew that while she wished she could have walked away well before now, having told him what he could do with his job, another part of her was only too happy to be here, experiencing this man's full wattage up close.

At that moment, before he could continue, the waiter arrived at the table with a bottle of wine. Romain tasted it, and took the liberty of pouring them both a glass. Sorcha felt as though perhaps she shouldn't take any—as if drinking wine might somehow confirm his bad opinion of her—and then berated herself. She wasn't going to change anything for him. She didn't care about his opinion, she told herself staunchly.

He tipped his glass in a mocking salute, and Sorcha took a sip from hers. The cool crisp white wine slipped down her throat like velvet. She thought dimly that it had no right to taste, *feel* so good in such a situation.

His beautifully shaped brown hand played with his glass, distracting her. She felt like clamping a hand over his to stop him, felt annoyed with him for having this power…and then he spoke again, bringing her attention back to his face and his mouth, which was even worse.

'What I was talking about—using you for what you can bring to the campaign in terms of your past…your apparent redemption…quite apart from your undeniable beauty…'

Sorcha went pink. She hated it when anyone made reference like that to her looks. She quickly took a sip of her drink before he could notice. But he frowned slightly, those dark brows drawing together as if she puzzled him. She didn't want to puzzle him. She didn't want him to look any further than Sorcha

Murphy the model, who would stand in front of a photographer and get the shots they required.

'Go on. Please.' Her voice sounded slightly strangled, and she breathed a sigh of relief when the intensity left his face.

'Your past would never be mentioned, never alluded to. What I'm talking about is a...subliminal message, if you will. Counting on the fact that people will see you and may remember, or not, where you came from, what happened...That will elevate the campaign beyond the ordinary, because they will empathise with you.'

'This must be some campaign if you're putting this much thought into it,' she said, somewhat shakily.

He nodded. 'It is very special. Like I said, it *is* to showcase a selection of luxury goods and clothes supplied by my various companies, but it's also going to promote a way of living. It's a move away from the vigorous advertising that is common now—this will be much more...dreamlike...evocative. It centres on two people—a man and a woman—who we follow as they travel all across the world in a romantic game of cat and mouse...'

Sorcha felt for a very uncanny moment as if he might be talking about *them*—but that was ridiculous.

Interested despite herself, she shrugged minutely. 'That does sound...intriguing.'

'And is it killing you to say that?' he asked with a mocking smile.

She shook her head, eyes flashing.

He sat forward then, making her nervous. 'Lisa also mentioned something else to me.'

Now Sorcha was really nervous. Her mind raced... Surely Lisa wouldn't have told him about—?

'The youth outreach centre?'

Sorcha blanched, and Romain saw her reaction. Her eyes were two huge pools of liquid blue, and that damned vulnerability was back.

Sorcha couldn't believe it. How could Lisa have done that? Although, after sitting with the man for less than an hour, Sorcha knew what a physical struggle it was to resist him.

'What did she tell you?' She asked tightly, every line of her body screaming with tension.

'Just that you've been working on it for the past few years, and it's due to open a couple of weeks after we finish shooting…'

Every ounce of self-protection in Sorcha rose up. This was so close to the heart of her, such a treasured secret, that even to be *discussing* it with him was overwhelming. And worse, if he decided to delve any deeper… Sorcha started to shake inwardly. 'Yes. It is. But it's no concern of yours—'

'Or yours either, apparently. Lisa said that you've only been back periodically to oversee the building in the past year.'

The unfairness of his attack made Sorcha reel slightly. She saw spots before her eyes. But she realised quickly that if he thought that, then she could in fact use it.

She lifted one slim shoulder and glanced away, but try as she might she couldn't totally disguise her turmoil. She looked back at Romain and steeled herself. 'Like I said, it's none of your business *what* my involvement is in the outreach centre…' She faltered. She felt as if she was jinxing it just talking about it with him. 'So I'd appreciate it if you don't bring it up again.'

He ignored her. 'Tell me, Sorcha, is it all part of the façade? To make people think you've changed? Did you see someone else, another celebrity, do something similar and think that you'd do the same?' Cynicism twisted his beautiful mouth. 'After all, you can't beat the publicity you'll get on the day. Tell me have you already picked out what you're going to wear as you cut the ribbon?'

Sorcha sat back. A wave of hurt, stunning in its intensity, made her chest tighten. It was as if he had gone inside, to her most inner, secret part and slowly ripped it out to examine. He had *no idea*. And he mustn't. With superhuman effort she drummed up the brittle shell of her composure, and said, 'Why not? I may as well get as much out of it as I can.'

When she saw his look of supreme…righteousness, her anger rose, swift and potent. She leant forward again.

'Tell me, did you walk into that agency and deduct a few noughts from my pay cheque once you saw how easy it would be?' She shook her head, unbelievably hurt and stung, but determined not to show it. 'Men like you disgust me. You don't know when to stop. When it's enough. Like when someone says no they mean no.'

He reached across the table so fast she couldn't escape, and he caught her hand in his. His grip was harsh, and Sorcha gasped as she felt her pulse jump straight to triple time.

'Just as you say about yourself, you know *nothing* about me. So don't presume anything.'

He looked genuinely angry, and Sorcha quailed under his fierce gaze.

'Where I come from it would be unthinkably brutal to force anyone to do anything against their will. This is a job, Sorcha— *that's all*. I've merely used a little leverage to get what I want. Tell me, is it really going to be so hard to pout and pose for a couple of weeks all around the world? To live in luxury and walk away with a few hundred thousand in your back pocket? To see a small agency benefit from the kind of exposure and money only you can bring them?'

She snatched her hand back, shaken to the core. His opinion of her was poisonous. It was tainted. She had to go—get away. She was feeling overwhelmed and seriously out of her depth. Couldn't think straight.

'I…I've lost my appetite.' The thought of eating now was making her feel sick. She stood up, picking up her jacket. Manners ingrained over years meant she couldn't just run out of the door, much as she wanted to. 'Please excuse me.'

And she turned and walked out, an awful urge to cry made

her clench her jaw, lips tight together. She knew her reaction was vastly disproportionate to what had just happened. He was right. She knew that it *was* just a job, that in the end of course she could weather anything for a couple of weeks—especially if it meant her good friend got a cut. But *that* man—

A heavy hand fell on her shoulder just as she reached the doors. She whirled around jerkily, her reaction not from surprise but to his touch.

'Sorcha, I—'

'Look, I'll do your job.' She avoided looking him in the eye, tried to make her voice light to distract him from the fact that she was a quivering mass of confusion and hurt. And to feel so hurt when she barely even knew this man? It just didn't make sense. 'I've no choice, and of course you're right. How can I turn down such a lucrative offer? After all, that *is* what I'm interested in isn't it?'

She couldn't help but look up then, but couldn't read the expression in his eyes. It wasn't what she'd expected. Not being able to read it made her feel even more panicky.

'Sorcha, look, I think we've got off to a bad—'

'Oh, don't say it—please. How could we ever have got off to a *good* start? You're the man who judged me on the basis of little more than hearsay and a grainy photograph eight years ago, who still assumes I'm walking around with track marks hidden on my body. I suppose you wouldn't believe me if I told you I've never touched a drug in my life?' She answered herself with a short harsh laugh. 'Don't bother answering. Of course not.'

She shrugged out from under his hand and moved away, closer to the door. He grabbed her wrist and, loath as she was to leave it there, because that same burning sensation was making her tingle all over, she didn't want him to see how his touch affected her. He was only trying to smooth over turbulent waters. He was a manipulator. There to make sure she toed the line, did as she was told.

She looked at him unflinchingly and her eyes were huge. The glasses were giving her a potent air of subdued sexiness that she was oblivious to. 'Just tell me where and when.'

He didn't speak for a long moment. She fought to appear cool, in control. The past was something that represented her own private hell. She knew there were parts of it, parts of *her*, that she hadn't looked at for a long time, had hoped she'd dealt with. Single-handed, this man was raking up a veritable field of emotional land mines.

'You have a week off. You'll be picked up from your apartment here in Dublin in a week's time—ten a.m. I'll send you over the schedule for the shoot.'

She nodded jerkily, finally retrieved her hand, and backed away through the door. For some bizarre reason she couldn't break her gaze from his until the last moment. Then thankfully the door opened behind her, and she slipped through and was gone.

CHAPTER FIVE

ROMAIN watched her go through the swinging doors, catching fleeting glimpses as they swung back and forth. A whole host of conflicting emotions and desires were battling under the surface of his cool grey gaze. He was watching her walk away *for the second time.*

He vowed at that moment that he would never watch her walk away again. An image crashed into his head of her lying underneath him, her sable hair spread out on a pillow, cheeks pink with arousal and passion. She was looking up, her blue eyes darkened, slumberous, and she was slowly bringing his head back down to hers, where their mouths… His whole body seemed to be igniting from the inside even as he tried to quash the picture. But its eroticism lingered. He wanted her badly. Past or no past; job or no job.

He shrugged mentally. So what if she was the first woman he'd take to bed who didn't like him, or profess to love him? For him that was the kiss of death to any relationship. He was a man who didn't deal in emotions like *like* or *love*. Their mutual antipathy could be transformed into passion. Of that he was sure. It would add an edge that was sorely lacking in his life.

He felt ruthless, almost cruel for making her do this. Then wondered broodingly if it was all an act. That effortless display of vulnerability. The hurt in her eyes when he had speculated on her motives for being involved with the outreach centre. The confusion that had assailed him when she had laughed off the suggestion that he could possibly believe she'd never been involved with drugs.

How could he be feeling in the wrong when he was offering her the kind of contract that any other model would sell their right kidney for? And why wasn't she grateful?

With an abrupt harsh movement he walked back to the table, oblivious to the covetous glances of women as he passed by. Making his apologies to the *maître d'*, he followed the path that Sorcha had just taken and, despite his reasoning to himself, as he took the lift back up to his suite he felt curiously empty. For the first time ever—despite the huge workload ahead of him, and the fact he'd be crossing the world twice in the next few days—the week seemed to stretch ahead into infinity.

The helicopter was coming in low, closer and closer to the lush green land underneath. A mark for landing materialised as if from nowhere, and to Sorcha she'd never seen anything so welcome in her life. The last forty-five minutes had been pure torture. However terrifying she found taking off in a normal-sized plane, her fear had been magnified by one hundred in this tiny machine for the duration of the journey. Her only companion, the chatty make-up artist Lucy, had happily not been able to even try and make conversation. The noise was too loud.

At last they landed. Sorcha's breathing finally returned to normal—only to shoot off the Richter scale again when she looked out of the window and saw a gleaming four-wheel drive with a tall, familiarly dark figure leaning nonchalantly against the bonnet in the near distance, arms crossed over a formidable chest. She gulped. *This was it*. No going back. Long days stretched ahead in which she was going to have to see him every day, every night and hour in between. Even though she hadn't done a location job as long as this before, she'd been away on enough shoots to know what a hothouse atmosphere it was.

As she emerged, feeling decidedly shaky—and not just from the helicopter ride—she slipped on her sunglasses. Early spring on Inis Mór, the biggest of the Aran Islands just off the west coast of Ireland, was brisk and breezy, and rare brilliant sunshine glanced off every surface. The tall figure pushed himself away from the Jeep and strolled towards her. He was even more gorgeous than she remembered, and she stumbled slightly on the bottom step. Thankfully, glasses shielded his eyes too. He was wearing jeans and a casual jumper, making him disturbingly casual, altogether more…*earthy*, *male*.

He held out his hand for her bag. 'Welcome.'

Sorcha held onto it like a lifeline and found that she couldn't utter a word. It was simply too much to be facing him again, and the hurt from their last meeting was still fresh.

His brow quirked over his glasses at the way she held onto the bag. He gestured with a hand. 'It's a beautiful location, no?'

Sorcha knew exactly how lovely it was. Not too far away, at the end of the field, a steep cliff dropped to the Atlantic Ocean, where grey-green swells with white tops battered the cliffs. Thankfully she hadn't noticed how close they'd been to the edge of the cliff, or that would have made the landing even worse. Then she saw his attention divert.

'Ah, you must be Lucy. Welcome. The crew minibus is here to take you to your lodgings. You're the last ones to arrive.'

Sorcha watched him greet Lucy, and saw the inevitable reaction as the younger girl took him in. Unbelievable. As he walked Lucy over to a minibus that Sorcha hadn't even noticed, she followed, assuming that it was for her too.

Just as she was about to get in the passenger seat, she heard a curt, 'No, Sorcha. You're coming with me.'

She turned and found he was very close behind her. She couldn't step back.

'But if I'm staying with the crew then I might as well go with Lucy.'

He shook his head. 'You're not staying with the crew. You're staying with me.'

Panic flared in her belly. 'But—'

His mouth tightened. 'And the cameramen.'

'Oh.'

She looked back for a second and saw Lucy looking from one to the other with a speculative gleam. Knowing the insidious spread of gossip on any shoot, Sorcha didn't want to be giving any fodder within minutes of landing on the island.

She slammed the door shut again behind her and smiled brightly. 'Of course—I should have guessed.' She looked back to Lucy. 'See you in the morning, no doubt…'

'You'll see each other later. We're having a dinner so that everyone can meet and get to know one another.'

And with that he bade goodbye to Lucy, took Sorcha's bag out of her white-knuckle grasp and was soon striding back to his Jeep.

She trotted after him, stupidly incensed that he could walk faster than her, and felt indignation rise at his high-handed manner. When she caught up with him he'd already stowed her bag and was holding open the passenger door. She also hated the fact that she was slightly breathless.

'I would normally stay with the crew. They're going to think it's odd if I'm with you and the photographers.'

'Worried about gossip, Sorcha?'

His disbelieving tone mocked her. After a week of telling herself that she wouldn't let him get to her, already she was failing abysmally. 'Yes, actually. Having me stay with you will be an excuse for them to think—'

'I intend to have my wicked way with you?' That supercilious brow arched again.

Sorcha's stomach clenched down low, and she reacted defensively—as if he had seen her inner turmoil, her helpless attraction. 'Of course not.' She forced herself to stop. He couldn't read her mind. 'That is…I mean, yes—they may think that.' She gave a short, unamused laugh. 'Oh, don't worry—*I* know you'd never taint yourself, touching someone like me. I've no doubt it would turn your moral stomach.'

She could feel her breasts rise up and down with her agitated breath, and hated the fact that she couldn't remain cool and unflappable in the face of his censure, as she had planned. And why wasn't he saying something? He was standing very still, and suddenly Sorcha realised that he was much closer. As if he'd moved without her realising it. Her breath hitched, and stopped altogether when a lean brown hand reached out to cup her jaw.

She felt all at once dizzy, bemused, confused, and a torrent of heat was racing upwards from her belly.

His voice was husky, had a quality that caught her on the raw. 'Actually, you're quite wrong.'

Her mouth opened. She frowned slightly. She couldn't see his eyes. And then he was gone—had stepped back and away as if the last few seconds hadn't even happened. Sorcha had to grab the door for support. She felt adrift. What had he just said? That he *would* want to touch her? Or that he knew the others would think that he wanted to have his wicked way with her? She couldn't think straight.

She heard a door slam, and a cool voice came from the interior of the Jeep. 'Well? Are you going to stand there admiring the view all day?'

Romain strode away from the door he'd just shut, behind which lay the living, breathing embodiment of his sleepless nights for the past week. Sorcha Murphy.

He had to clench his hands into fists. Seeing her emerge from the tiny helicopter less than half an hour before, he'd felt the upsurge of a desire so hot, so immediate, that he had reeled with the force of it. Her obvious reluctance to share his lodgings, albeit with others, had rankled in a way that he really didn't care for. And when he'd cupped her jaw with his hand… She had no idea how close he'd come to hauling her to him and ravaging that soft mouth. Crushing her to him.

He didn't act on basic instincts like that. In fact, although he'd desired plenty of women, not one of them had come close to igniting such forcible desire. He'd had no intention of making his needs so obvious to her, and yet he had. He hadn't ever lost control like that.

A dark, wispy memory struggled up through the threads of his consciousness. At least not since…*then*. And that was so long ago. Would he never be free of that? And *why* was he allowing Sorcha Murphy to even evoke that memory?

Sorcha threw off the knitted shawl she'd been wearing, feeling hot and bothered, and paced the beautifully furnished bedroom with pent-up energy. She'd barely noticed the understated luxury of the old converted farmhouse. The amazing view of green fields and the huge expanse of ocean in the distance went over her head. Even the way the wild garden tapered down to a beach at the back of the house.

She'd hardly exchanged two words with Romain in the Jeep. The tension had been heavy and pulsating between them. She was still going over his words obsessively, and yet nothing in his behaviour since he'd cupped her jaw had led her to think for a second that he *did* desire her. It was as if a switch had been flicked. Once he'd shown her to her bedroom he'd curtly informed her to come back downstairs in an hour, so she could meet the others. They were to give her a briefing on the schedule for the shoot, go through the storyboards.

She sank back onto the bed. Her heart was racing. Two weeks—two weeks of suffering under his condemning looks. Could she do it?

Lisa's face flashed into her head. And also the outreach

centre. In the last week, working intensively with the board at the centre, she'd realised that the money she'd earn from this job could go straight into that and would more than cover the first few months' overheads. It would mean that the centre would have absolutely every possible chance to succeed and flourish...especially as she'd been planning on her involvement being *pro bono*.

She had no choice. She was here now. For better or worse. And she would just have to keep in mind all the people who would benefit from this when things got rough.

'It's a love story...the images will run together almost like a short film.'

Sorcha choked slightly, her attention suddenly and spectacularly brought back into the huge dining room where she sat with Simon, the film cameraman, Dominic, the photographer, and Romain, who sat across the table, his huge taut body lounging against a high-backed antique chair.

The moment she'd walked into the room some minutes before, all her recent rationalising had fled out of the window. Her entire focus had been taken by him—again. She'd noticed in a flash that he'd just had a shower. The clean crisp scent had hit her so strongly that she'd imagined everyone must be able to smell it. His hair was still damp, furrowed from where he'd obviously run fingers through it. And yet when she'd looked at him he'd been practically glacial, those grey eyes as cold as the nearby ocean.

She caught herself and modulated her tone. 'I'm sorry, Simon, can you say that again?'

The cameraman was a nice guy. From London. Good looking, a little cocky, dressed in a very trendily casual way. But he didn't come close to the class that Romain exuded so effortlessly. And she hated that she'd noticed that.

'As Simon said, the stills will run as one campaign and the

film will be shown in a series of thirty-second commercials, the sequence building up the story.'

Reluctantly she looked to Romain, who had spoken. So far the photographer hadn't said anything. But Sorcha knew him well from years ago. He'd been on the periphery of the group she'd hung out with for that brief, yet catastrophic time, and although he hadn't been directly involved she hadn't mistaken the knowing, mocking glance in his eyes. She knew his type, and usually steered well clear. It seemed, however, as if she wouldn't be able to get too far away this time.

She sighed. The weeks ahead were becoming more challenging than she could ever have imagined.

She deliberately focused her attention on Simon, the least threatening of the men in the room at that moment. 'I'm sorry, would you mind explaining a little more?'

He smiled with an infectious grin, which she welcomed as an antidote to the tension she felt. She struggled to concentrate.

'We follow you as you're led on a romantic trail, of sorts, around the world. It'll be a sumptuous, truly global love story. In each place the relationship goes to another level. We see you meet, fall in love, even get married, and it's all going to be shot with a very moody, dreamlike feel. The last shot will show you and your lover with a family.'

Sorcha's head spun. She couldn't look at Romain. For some reason she felt ridiculously exposed—almost as though someone had gone into her deepest fantasies and converted them into a script. And since when had she ever seen herself with a happy family? After the devastation of lies and truths that had followed her father's death, she'd had a cynical and somewhat jaded view of so-called happy families, distrusting anyone who professed to be part of one. As she and her brother could attest, their realities had been anything but happy.

After a few more minutes going over what they hoped to achieve at this location, Sorcha got up to leave, relieved when it didn't look as though Romain was going to follow her. He did, however, remind her that dinner would be held in that dining room for all the crew at eight sharp that evening.

She was breathing a sigh of relief when she reached the door, but it didn't last long when she realised that Dominic was right behind her. He came too close, crowding her as she went through the door, and she automatically stepped away. Everything about him was making some part of her crawl. He wasn't a bad-looking man—in fact she knew that many would find his boyish looks a turn-on—but he left Sorcha feeling cold. He didn't take her hint, and fell into step beside her. She cursed herself for heading outside and not upstairs, to the sanctuary of her room.

'Nice to see you again, Sorch...it's been years, hasn't it? Although I'm sure you remember the good old days... Pity you couldn't handle the pace...'

She deliberately kept her voice light, giving him the briefest of glances. 'Yes, it has been years, Dominic... It's nice to see you too. I'm going to go for a walk, so if you don't mind...'

As she went to walk away, towards the front door, she felt her arm being taken in a none too gentle grip. She whirled around in shock. 'What do you—?'

Dominic was smiling, but it wasn't friendly. 'I *do* remember the good old days. I remember Christian...don't you? I saw him recently. When I told him we were working together he told me all about you.' He looked her up and down. 'I'm looking forward to getting to know you better—and if you're looking for anything...*anything* at all...you know where to find me.'

Sorcha felt disgust and fear fill her belly. She knew exactly what he was talking about. Drugs. She refused to let him bring her back down the path of her dark memories. She pulled her arm free with effort.

'I'd prefer it if you called me Sorcha. And I won't be looking for anything at all. I'm here to work. Now, please—'

At that moment she caught a flash of movement in the hall behind Dominic, and saw Romain coming out of the room. She saw him take in the way she was standing so close to Dominic, and imagined that it must look intimate. Without knowing where the desire was coming from she suddenly wanted to make it very clear that it wasn't. But what could she say or do?

That familiar glower was on his face, and he called curtly for Dominic to come back into the room. Sorcha took advantage and fled out into the sunshine, away from the dark heat of censure in his eyes.

That evening Sorcha looked at the clothes she'd laid out on the bed. Even though tonight wasn't a formal occasion, she itched to put on something that would assert cool professionalism. Romain scrambled her brain, her senses, and she needed all the armour she could muster. She'd been lacking in control ever since she'd come face to face with him in New York, and it had to stop or she'd never get through the job.

She reached for jeans and flat ballet pumps, and a soft cashmere wraparound cardigan. It didn't need anything underneath, but the sensual feel of the fabric—*why did it suddenly have to feel sensual?*—made her team it with a plain white vest top. The deep sapphire colour of the cardigan made her eyes a dark smoky blue. Pulling her hair back and up, she clipped it haphazardly. Stuck on her glasses. She looked at her image, somewhere between a sixteen-year-old cheerleader and a student.

Sticking her tongue out at herself, she ignored the two spots of bright colour on her cheeks and left the room, only to walk smack-bang into a hard, unyielding chest.

CHAPTER SIX

THE wind was driven out of her more as a result of her reaction
to coming into contact with his hard chest than because of the
impact. Sorcha looked up with dazed eyes. Big hands encircled
her upper arms and she could feel his body heat enveloping her.
They were so close that all she'd have to do was stretch up
slightly and her mouth would be close enough to—

With an almost violent movement she pulled free and jerked
away, rubbing her arms. She glowered at Romain, who stuck
his hands in the pockets of his dark trousers and leant against
the doorjamb. A dark shirt made him look dangerous, foreign,
in the gloom of the corridor. The grey of his eyes stood out.

Nervously she touched a hand to her glasses. 'Do you always
lurk outside people's doors? Or were you just afraid I was
turning my room into a den of iniquity?'

A smile quirked his mouth up at one side, making him look
even more rakishly handsome. She wasn't ready to face him—
had been counting on the space, however brief, between her
room and the dining room to gather herself.

'I was merely coming to escort you downstairs. Everyone
is here.'

'I'm quite capable of walking myself down some stairs.'

He fell into step beside her. She wanted to turn away from
his presence but the corridor was old and tiny.

'Prickly, aren't you? I hope this means you're a morning person.'

She scowled at him briefly and preceded him down the stairs.

Romain followed with a thoughtful look on his face. His jaw tightened as his eyes were drawn to the sway of her bottom in the tight, faded jeans. The force of her cannoning into him had shocked him too. Or rather, the feel of her soft breasts crushed against his chest had shocked him—with how badly he'd wanted to walk her back into the room and shut the door behind them.

In the large drawing room everyone was gathered, drinking aperitifs. Local girls in black trousers and white shirts walked through with canapés. Sorcha was relieved to see some familiar faces—and one in particular.

'Sorcha, you gorgeous girl, come here!'

She was grabbed around the waist and lifted high by a tall, handsome man—the hairstylist. When he finally put her down she was laughing and red-faced. 'Val! You nearly stopped the blood supply to my middle region.'

'How is the smartest model in the world?' He pretended to think for a second. 'Now, was it a first, or a second? I can't remember…'

Sorcha punched him playfully. 'It was Summa Cum Laude to be precise, but really it's not that amazing, lots of people got the same mark.'

He looked mock-shocked. 'Maybe so, but you came in the top five of your class, girlfriend. If that isn't—'

'What's this?'

Sorcha's back straightened. For a brief moment she'd forgotten Romain was right behind her. How much had he heard?

Before she could stop him, Val was fluttering his lashes in his campest mode and chattering with scant regard for discretion. 'Our girl here has just graduated with flying colours from—'

'Val, you never showed me your wedding ring.'

Acting on a panicked impulse, desperately counting on Val's extreme yet lovable self-absorption, Sorcha breathed a sigh of relief when he promptly forgot about relaying her news and proceeded to show off the heavy platinum band, regaling them with stories about his recent marriage in London to his boyfriend. This was all punctuated with hot, heavy looks at Romain, who Sorcha could see was completely unfazed. She'd seen other men driven almost to violence by Val's unwanted flirtatious attentions, but Romain was so sure of himself that he was totally at ease, bantering back and forth. It made a funny feeling lodge in her chest.

Val got distracted by someone and walked away just as a bell sounded for dinner. Sorcha already felt wrung out. She made to move, but was blocked by Romain's tall body.

'What did you stop Val telling me?'

She should have known he wouldn't let it go—and she *had* diverted Val with all the subtlety of a brick. Hemmed in between a chair and Romain, she could see everyone filing out to the dining room across the hall and looked after them wistfully.

'Nothing.' She sounded evasive.

'What was he talking about, and why did you distract him from telling me?'

Why was she feeling so self-protective? It wouldn't mean anything if she told him…if anything it might make him respect her more. She opened her mouth. Nothing came out. She didn't want to tell him because she didn't want him to know anything about her. And if he knew this…well, it might make him curious about other things. She needed to keep him at a distance. And then she remembered his scathing response to her involvement with the outreach centre.

She looked up and held her gaze to his, even though it wasn't easy. That intense grey seemed to enmesh her every sense. The room was silent. Everyone was gone, and again it was just the two of them. She willed ice into her eyes and into her veins, which seemed to be far too heated of late.

'He was talking about something that would be of no interest to you. It was personal and private, and he'd forgotten that I'd asked him not to mention it to anyone, that's all. Anyway, how could you possibly be interested in anything about me?'

'Oh, but I am, Sorcha—*very* interested. You're mine for the next two weeks. And you're an expensive commodity.'

Her eyes blazed with sudden fury, and she hated the frisson that had skittered down her spine at the way he'd said '*very* interested'.

'That does not give you the right to pry. I told you before— stay out of my private life.'

His face came close to hers. 'The hell I will—especially if you're thinking of getting cosy with Dominic...'

She reared back. 'What?'

'I saw you two earlier.'

'You saw nothing.'

'I saw—'

'Come on, you two. We're all waiting to eat!'

Sorcha jerked her head round to see Val at the door, with a curious look on his face.

Romain was smooth, as if he got caught in heated dialogue every day. He gestured for Sorcha to precede him from the room, and her legs felt shaky as she did so. She avoided Val's eye, knowing full well that there'd be a very questioning look on his face. He knew her well enough to know that she didn't get into heated debates with gorgeous men.

Dinner provided a brief respite. Sorcha found herself seated next to Lucy, who was as chatty as ever, and Simon. He was busy explaining the logistics of how they would be shooting. She couldn't, however, be unaware of the man on the opposite side of the huge table. Every now and then she'd feel a prick-ling sensation on her neck and look up, only to find that Romain would be deep in conversation with the stylist, Claire, who had grabbed a seat beside him with more haste than grace.

She couldn't mistake the proprietorial manner in which the older woman, who was very attractive with her short blonde bob, was monopolising Romain's attention, and Sorcha sent up silent thanks. But then a little dart of something made her acutely aware of the exact moment when Claire laid her hand on Romain's arm and Sorcha had the bizarrest impulse to go and knock it off, feeling suddenly incensed, as if his arm was *her* personal property. She closed her eyes weakly.

'Are you all right, Sorcha?'

Her eyes snapped open. Simon was looking at her with concern. She smiled quickly. 'Fine. Absolutely fine.' She mustered up a fake yawn. 'Just a bit tired. It's been a long day.'

'Yes. And it'll be even longer tomorrow. They want to try and get a lot done in one day.'

Back in the drawing room for after-dinner drinks a short time later, Sorcha circulated and got to know the group of about eight people. She knew that by the end of the shoot they'd all know each other much more intimately, having been thrust together for hours on end every day.

They seemed on the whole like a nice bunch, and she found to her surprise that she was looking forward to the shoot. The only person she'd avoided, apart from Romain, from whom she'd carefully made sure she was always on the opposite side of the room, had been Dominic. Contrary to what Romain might believe, Dominic had obviously set Lucy the young make-up artist in his sights, and the two had slipped away somewhere. Sorcha was quite happy, wanting to have as little to do with him as possible.

Later that night she lay in the dark, staring up at the ceiling. She'd made her excuses early and had crept away to bed.

This is a job like any other. Be cool, be calm, be professional and everything will be OK.

She kept telling herself that. She could handle anything. Anyone. Even Romain.

But as she turned over and tried to go to sleep, the only image in her brain was the one of his face as she'd left the room earlier. It had held that same intensity when she'd walked away

from him in New York. As if he could see right into her soul…
And that was crazy. He was the last man in the world she
wanted looking anywhere near her soul…

The next day they started early. Simon wanted to get a dawn
shot of Sorcha on the beach. Dressed very impractically, in a
long silk diaphanous dress, she kept a parka on until the last
moment, and tried not to show how cold she was in the chilly
early-morning air.

All the shot called for was for her to walk along the seashore,
find a bottle in the sand and pick it up. The idea was that the
bottle held a message, which she would read and which would
lead her to the next place…and so on.

Standing shivering, waiting for Simon and Dominic to set
up, Sorcha sent up silent thanks that at least on set Dominic
seemed to be professional enough not to allude to anything, as
he had the day before.

'Sorcha…'

Romain.

She'd managed to avoid looking at him, but even so she was
well aware of his location at every moment, and now he was
right beside her. She turned reluctantly.

'Yes?'

Romain looked down at her and his insides contracted. He
didn't think he'd ever seen anyone so gorgeous, cheeks
reddened by the chill wind, long hair loose and wild. Her eyes
shone with a fierce, vivid blue and he almost forgot what he'd
come to say. And that made him feel short-tempered. It also
made him sound clipped.

'We've decided to do a part of the sequence here that we
were going to do in India. It's a shot that includes Zane…your
counterpart.'

Sorcha frowned. Zane was the male model/actor due to
play her lover.

'But Zane doesn't start till we get to New York. He's not here.'

'I'm aware of that fact. But, as Simon pointed out, I'm similar in height and colouring, at least from behind, so I'll stand in for him.'

Alarm bells went zinging off in Sorcha's head, and she looked at him suspiciously, 'What does the shot involve?'

A dark light came into Romain's eyes, confusing Sorcha. Everything around them had faded into the background.

'You and me…' he drawled.

Sorcha fought to contain panic and snapped out, 'Yes, well, even *I* could have deduced that—'

Just then Dominic called for her to step onto her mark. She glared at Romain, who was looking far too smug at her obvious discomfiture.

Sorcha found out more at lunchtime, and she mulled it all over in her head as she took off for a brief solitary walk afterwards. It turned out that the shot Romain had told her about had to be done at sunset, and Claire the stylist had already flown back to Dublin to get the dress required, as it was meant to be part of the wedding sequence. That had made Sorcha's nerves go completely. She'd been too scared to ask what exactly was involved.

Would she have to *kiss him*?

That thought sent all sorts of shivers through her, and not all of them were of disgust…or trepidation. Was he doing this on purpose, just to mess with her?

She berated herself. Now she was just being silly.

CHAPTER SEVEN

A FEW hours later, feeling very nervous, Sorcha stood on the shoreline again, this time in a simple knee-length white broderie anglaise dress from an exclusive designer. It was meant to be a wedding dress. Her hair was up in a loose knot, and a white orchid was tucked behind her ear.

Claire the stylist was muttering as she secured the dress at the back. 'You would not believe the pressure I was under to get back here... And this dress—it's not even been on the catwalk yet. We weren't meant to be shooting it for another week. It had to come from Paris with a courier *and* a bodyguard. And now you're the one that gets to be held in Romain's arms...*honestly*...'

Held in his arms? Sorcha's insides froze. Surely she just meant with his arm around her shoulders as they looked out at the sunset?

And then he was there, striding towards her. He wore a white tuxedo shirt that was open at the neck, a bow tie dangling untied. His black trousers were rolled up to the knee, showing off strong, shapely calf muscles. She felt weak.

The sun was setting over the horizon, and the mood of the crew was getting more frantic, with Simon and Dominic shouting out orders as they worked simultaneously. Romain came and stood before her, slanting a look down her body, taking in her long, slim, very pale legs.

'Very sweet—almost virginal, in fact.'

Sorcha felt a familiar secret pain grip her. She had so much to hide from a man like this.

'Let's just get on with it, shall we?' she bit out.

And in the next instant her world was upended and she was lifted against a broad, strong and very hard chest. Immediately and instinctively her arms had to go around his neck. Wide, surprised eyes clashed with his.

'What the—?'

Romain felt the rigidity in her body. 'Hush. We're meant to be in love.'

'Don't make me sick! And if this is your idea of a joke—'

Simon came over and held a light meter close to Sorcha's face, making her shut her mouth abruptly.

'That's great, guys. Let me know if you need a break, Romain. You'll need to stand there for a while.'

Simon walked away and Sorcha smiled sweetly at Romain. 'I do hope I'm not too heavy for you?'

'Not at all,' he said lightly. 'Like the proverbial feather.'

His arms did feel secure around her—not a tremor. And Sorcha knew well that she wasn't exactly small. She always ate well, but had been lucky enough to inherit a metabolism that burnt off calories quickly. Still, she was no lightweight. The fact that Romain seemed to be holding her so effortlessly made her feel small and feminine, *delicate* for the first time in her life.

She sighed deeply and looked out to sea. But as she sighed, her breasts moved against his chest. She stopped breathing as her nipples reacted and tightened.

His mouth came close to her ear and he whispered softly, his accent pronounced. 'It helps if you breathe…'

She turned her head, and the retort on her lips was quickly forgotten. Their heads were so close together that she could feel his breath reach out and mingle with her own. She saw the deeper flecks of grey in his eyes, the small lines that fanned out from the corners of his eyes, and that suddenly made her want to see him laugh, to see how they crinkled up.

Surrounded in a bubble of sensation, Sorcha couldn't deny it any longer—not when she was held so tight against him. This man had broken through the wall that she'd built around her sexuality. He was smashing it down with what seemed to be little more than that proverbial feather.

Her other hand was somewhere around his shoulder. It had been in the act of pushing him away. But now the feel of his warm skin underneath the shirt was acting like a magnet. Completely unaware of what was going on around them, but perhaps subconsciously knowing that it might be sanctioned, Sorcha's hand moved up of its own volition to his neck.

In a completely untutored and sensuous move that had Romain's heart-rate soaring, Sorcha allowed the back of her hand to drift up his neck, pushing aside the open collar of his shirt. And then, her eyes following the movement as though mesmerised, her hand drifted upwards until her palm rested on his lightly stubbled jaw.

Romain stared down into her face. He willed her eyes to meet his, and as if she could hear him they did. A silken cord had wrapped itself around his every sense and he felt himself tighten and harden. She had become soft and pliant in his arms, her curves moulding to his form like a jigsaw piece slotting into place.

All Sorcha could see was his mouth. Her thumb moved closer, traced the corner of his lower lip. They were so close. And then his head dipped slightly. She felt his breath feather again. Her eyelids felt heavy and started to flutter closed. Every part of her was aching to feel that mouth on hers…

'Very good! And do you know what? We don't even need to see a kiss. I think this works really well…'

Simon's voice cut through the haze of sensuality that had been clouding Sorcha's brain like an alarm going off. She actually flinched—a minor movement, but one which had

Romain gripping her tight to him again. But this time she held herself stiff and would not look at him. *God.* What on earth must he think? They'd been shooting all the time and Sorcha hadn't even noticed!

Romain felt dazed...out of sync as he put Sorcha down until her feet touched the ground. Surrounded by all the crew, he couldn't do what he wanted and keep her close, take that lush mouth as he'd been so close to doing. The way she'd been looking at him just then... He felt limbless. Had he just been taken for a complete fool?

After what seemed like aeons, he put her away from him with two hands. She was very shaky.

His mouth was hard, his face taut. 'You're a good actress.'

She looked up quickly and saw the harshness there, twisting his mouth.

Acting?

Well, if that was what he thought...thank God.

She forced a smile from somewhere and left the protection of his hands. Thankfully she didn't fall at his feet, and with a briskness she certainly didn't feel she said, 'It's my job. What you hired me for.'

And on very shaky limbs she walked over to the others and the protection of the busyness of the crew as they packed up.

The next day they were due to do a couple of quick shots in the morning and then travel to New York in the afternoon. Sorcha had tossed and turned all night, unable to get the memory of being in Romain's arms out of her mind...her body. Giving up at six a.m., seeing the first light of dawn, she got out of bed. She knew what would calm her.

She put on her running clothes—a long sleeved T-shirt and jogging bottoms. Her battered sneakers. She tried to jog wherever she was, finding it to be almost like a form of meditation as well as exercise. She met no one on her way outside, and pulled back her sleep-mussed hair into a ponytail, heading for the beach. The air was crisp and fresh and blue skies promised another beautiful spring day, which in the west of Ireland was an anomaly to be savoured.

Hitting the beach, she found that it was pleasingly much bigger and longer than she'd expected, stretching away a few miles into the distance. After some warming up she set out at a steady pace. The repetition of movement, the control of her breath, all transported her away from disturbing thoughts and images.

About forty minutes later, feeling much calmer and very smug with herself, she came back closer to the house and stopped to rest at the seashore. Impulsively she took off her shoes and socks, wanting to feel the cold sting of the Atlantic on her hot feet. She contemplated going back to get her one-piece, knowing that the initial pain of the icy water would be far outweighed by the exhilarating feeling afterwards. As she stood debating whether or not to go back and get her suit, she looked out to sea and something caught her attention. Someone swimming. Powerful arms scissoring in and out of the water, a glimpse of a strong, olive-skinned back.

Her breath hitched and stopped. It could only be one person. No one else had that physique. And she knew that it would take more than average strength first of all to brave the icy Atlantic and then to swim in it. The currents were sometimes lethal. Mesmerised by his grace and beauty, she couldn't move. And then, too late, she realised that he'd been coming closer all the time. The arms stopped and he stood waist-deep in the sea, water streaming off a perfectly muscled torso. Like some kind of god, he emerged from the waves, and the unreality of it all made Sorcha feel as if she was in some kind of dream.

It was only when he was walking out of the water, showing a broad chest that tapered into a slim waist, dark shorts which clung to powerful thigh muscles rippling under bronzed skin, that Sorcha finally seemed to come to her senses. The sleepless night had obviously taken its toll. She was standing there like some kind of drooling groupie!

With a strangled gasp, she turned and picked up her shoes and socks, about to make a hasty retreat. She hadn't counted on his speed.

'Wait.'

She stopped in her tracks. The serenity of the morning was gone. Her heart hammered anew, and it wasn't from the exercise. She turned to face him and tried to look as blank as possible. It was hard. Romain stood just feet away, hands on hips, chest rising and falling, salt water sluicing off his skin, his hair plastered to a well-shaped skull.

'Enjoying the view?'

She coloured in an instant and Romain frowned. *The outraged virgin?* Where had that come from? Just another aspect of Sorcha's chameleon-like personality. He could see the way she held herself...so stiff...but when he'd been coming out from the water, when he'd seen her first, she'd had a look of something close to exultation on her face.

'Don't be ridiculous. I was out jogging. And I was merely making sure you were OK. I didn't know who was swimming, and the currents here can be strong.'

He picked up a towel from nearby. She hadn't even noticed it. 'Would you have saved me if I'd got into trouble?'

Sorcha snorted inelegantly. 'What do you think?'

He rubbed at his hair, totally unconcerned by her comment. With his face obscured momentarily, she couldn't halt the inevitable slide of her gaze downwards again, seeing how the cold water had made his nipples hard. Her own seemed to pucker and tighten in direct response, and she hurriedly crossed her arms over the thin material of her T-shirt.

'It *was* amazing.' He jerked his head back towards the pounding waves.

Sorcha was distracted for a second, that sexy accent making

her breath hitch again. And she did envy him the experience, knowing well how he must be feeling right now—the rush of endorphins, the tingling sensations as life came back into a body that would be near frozen.

'I know.' She sounded wistful. 'It's been a while since I swam in the sea here, but I remember.'

'Nothing stopping you now. You could go in in your underwear. I can keep an eye.'

The lightness in his voice didn't fool her for a second. And if he thought she was going to strip off in front of him...

She shook her head and watched with widening eyes as he proceeded to hitch the towel around his waist and strip off his shorts underneath. At the last second she whirled away from him.

'Do you mind?'

Romain studied her taut back. Just who *was* Sorcha Murphy?

'I'm decent again.'

Sorcha turned around reluctantly, relieved to see him buttoning up his jeans—although that led her eyes to his hands, and the line of dark hair that snaked up to his chest. A worn sweatshirt abruptly concealed him from view and she felt saggy with relief.

He strolled towards her nonchalantly. 'So, why don't you?'

She frowned, her head feeling muggy, unconsciously backing away 'What?'

'Go for a swim.'

She shook her head again. 'No.' And she struck off up the beach.

He kept pace with her all too easily.

She looked at him sideways, it seemed silly not to admit the truth. 'But you're right...I did think of it. I was going to go back inside and get my swimsuit.'

'Coward,' he called softly.

She avoided his eye, afraid of what she'd see, and looked at her watch. They were at the back of the house, a huge hedge obscuring them from view. 'As I have to be in make-up in less than half an hour, I'm sure you don't want to be encouraging me to be late?'

He spread an arm wide for her to precede him up the path and dipped his head. 'Of course you're right.'

She went to squeeze past him. The narrow gate was too small for two people, and he wasn't budging an inch. Sorcha gritted her teeth, not even breathing, but even so she could feel his chest. She imagined it would still be cold from the sea…and were his nipples still hard?

She felt like screaming inwardly. Until she'd met him in New York, thoughts like this had never entered her head. She didn't know if he was doing it deliberately, just to unsettle her, or because he—

Two arms came round her at that moment, and her heart skidded to a halt.

The feel of her lithe, athletic, yet lush body was too much for him. He was only human, and he couldn't wait any more. Not after the extreme erotic torture of holding her in his arms yesterday and his sleepless night last night.

She looked up, panic-stricken. 'What do you think you're—'

'Something I've wanted to do ever since I saw you across that room in New York, and more especially since yesterday… What we would have done if we hadn't been interrupted.'

His powerful arms held her captive. She couldn't move, and to do so would be to invite a friction between their bodies the thought of which made scorched colour enter Sorcha's already pink cheeks. His words and her own body's reaction scared the life out of her, but something joyous moved through her too, and that scared her even more witless.

She had to do something!

His head dipped, and she tried in vain to push with her hands. 'Aren't you afraid you might catch some immoral disease?' His mouth hovered just inches away… Sorcha knew she should turn her head away—so why didn't she? Her eyes, big as saucers, gazed up into his.

Romain felt his whole body tighten, felt fire blazing a trail along every vein and artery, pumping blood to areas that were becoming painfully engorged. He couldn't even take in her words, or answer with any coherence.

Before Sorcha could move or stop him his head had dipped. The morning disappeared. Mad insanity arrived. Insanity that tasted delicious…like nothing she'd ever dreamt of before. This was a kiss unlike any other she'd experienced. The first press of his lips to hers was benedictory, almost reverent, and then he drew back. She opened her eyes. When had she closed them? And how had her hands crept up to his neck? The stark reality of what she was doing washed through her and she struggled again, but Romain was ruthless. He pushed her back against the gate, trapped her completely with his hard body.

'No, you don't… You want this just as much as me…'

'No!' she panted,. 'I don—'

And this time there was no gentle. He was hard, intrusive, ruthless, and determined to break through her every defence. His tongue forced her mouth open, made a bold foray into her mouth, and though she first had an instinct to bite…it turned quickly into a desire to explore, touch and taste. He tasted of salt water. His hand was on the back of her head, angling her better for his satisfaction. She gave a deep mewl in her throat and her treacherous hands climbed again, finding the way the skin grew silky around the back of his neck, where his wet hair made her think of him emerging from the sea just moments ago. That had a tight spiral of need starting in her belly and rising upwards, consuming every part of her on the way.

Her breasts felt sore, aching heavily against the thin material of her T-shirt and bra. She pressed herself closer, lost in a maelstrom of passion so dizzyingly new and overwhelming that she couldn't even question it. Romain's other hand smoothed down

always made her feel stupidly protected—but she didn't want to draw attention to herself.

As the plane gathered speed down the runway, her heart beat faster and faster.

'What's wrong? Scared of flying?'

The voice came from right beside her ear, and Sorcha jumped, eyes opening wide as she looked to Romain. She couldn't even speak, and just nodded silently. When he saw the truly blatant fear in the blue depths, any teasing fled Romain's mind. He acted purely on instinct and took one of Sorcha's hands in his. It was clenched tight and he had to prise the bloodless fingers apart. Finally he was able to thread his fingers with hers and grip her tight. He saw her other hand go in a white-knuckle grip to the armrest.

Sorcha couldn't believe it. The mind-numbing fear, the awful acrid taste of it, wasn't hitting her as hard as it normally did. The plane left the ground, that awful moment came...and it was still awful, but for the first time ever bearable. It was only then, as the fear began its slow decline, that Sorcha felt the long warm fingers entwined with hers and heat unfurled in her belly. She looked down and could see white and brown fingers in a tangle. A hot, tight feeling made her abdomen clench, and the kiss invaded her consciousness with full lurid recall.

Looking up to Romain with horror, she saw him wincing. Abruptly she loosened her grip, but he didn't loosen his. His face cleared, though, and he smiled.

'Remind me never to arm-wrestle you. I don't think I'd win.'

Sorcha snatched her hand back. She felt acutely vulnerable. She couldn't believe she'd been so weakly transparent.

He settled back comfortably, turning his big body towards her. Sorcha looked resolutely at the back of the seat in front of her.

'So is it just the take-off, or the whole thing?'

She sighed deeply. 'Just the take off.' She looked at him

warily. 'And being in tiny helicopters.' She gave a delicate shudder. 'That trip to Inis Mor…'

'I thought you looked unnaturally pale when you got off. Why didn't you say anything?'

She shrugged, casting him a quick glance. 'What's the point? It's just a silly fear. No need to cause a fuss.'

He felt anger lick through him, but not directed at her. 'So you'd prefer to put yourself through moments of terror like that just to keep people happy?'

'Well, how else would I have got over there—or anywhere, these days?'

He just looked at her broodingly. 'Where did it come from?'

Her head had that fuzzy feeling again. Why couldn't she look this man in the eye for longer than two seconds without her head going to mush? He was going to suspect she was certifiably stupid.

'What?'

'Your fear of flying….taking off…do you know where it comes from?'

Sorcha nodded slowly. Weighed up what it would mean to tell him. He saw the hesitation, and she saw how his jaw tightened.

'I forgot about the embargo on your private life.'

Despite her best instincts, at that moment she perversely wanted to put her hand on his arm. She clenched her hand into a fist again. 'No,' she said tightly, and then, with a small smile that made her feel as if she'd been invaded by a rogue body snatcher, she said, 'It's fine.'

She looked away for a second, and then back, struck by how, even though they were in the plane surrounded by the crew, it felt as though it was just them, in some kind of bubble.

'I was three years old, and we were taking a trip back to Spain to visit my mother's family—'

He looked at her incredulously. 'You're Spanish?'

She hesitated for a split second… *Hadn't she been for*

most of her life? 'Half-Spanish… My mother is. My father is—*was* Irish…'

'He's dead?'

She nodded, and felt herself go cold inside, she knew she was lying about being half-Spanish, but that was a part of her that was certainly out of bounds for discussion and none of his business. That bit of information lay far too close to the truth of everything else.

'He died just before I turned seventeen.'

'I'm sorry.'

Romain saw how she'd changed in an instant from being lukewarm to icy cool. He wouldn't have believed it if he hadn't seen it with his own eyes.

'It was a long time ago.'

'My father died when I was twelve…a heart attack.'

She looked at him, that guarded expression faltering slightly. She remembered what Maud had told her about his mother. 'Mine too…a heart attack, I mean. I'm sorry.'

A moment passed between them, and neither noticed for a second when the air stewardess asked if they wanted anything. Then Sorcha looked up and a guilty flush stained her cheeks. What was she thinking? Getting lost in his eyes, telling him about her father? She saw the way the stewardess practically ate him alive with just a look and welcomed the cold dose of reality.

When they'd ordered water, she could feel him settle back in.

Please, no more conversation…

'So…your fear of flying…'

Sorcha's tone was brisk and almost bored. She didn't see the way Romain's eyes narrowed on her speculatively.

'Like I said, we were on holiday, going to Spain. It's really not that exciting—'

'Indulge me.'

Sorcha gulped, looked at him quickly, and then away again. 'The plane had just taken off, and at the last second something failed and it crashed back down. I didn't have my belt on.' She grimaced. 'I'd managed to unlock it somehow, and when the plane fell back down like a stone I fell and got thrown around a bit...' She shrugged. 'That's it. I told you it was nothing to get worked up about. It's silly to still let it affect me.'

He looked at her for a long, intense moment and couldn't stop the feeling that he was somehow letting her get to him— get under his skin in a way that went beyond physical attraction. He drew back. The shutters came down, his face expressionless.

'If you don't mind, I have an important meeting when we land in New York and I need to concentrate on some paperwork.'

And he promptly shut Sorcha out as effectively as she had shut him out from the start. It threw her. She made the motions of getting a book out of her bag, put on her glasses to read...but the page and the print blurred in front of her eyes. She couldn't relax next to Romain, and her mind was feverishly trying to decipher what had made him clam up like that.

She was intrigued. Suddenly *he* had more facets to him than a mere autocratic and judgmental luxury goods magnate. She recalled how professional he'd been on the set the day before. He'd run it smoothly, fairly...especially when Dominic had threatened to throw a little tantrum when something hadn't gone his way. Sorcha wasn't used to a steadying force on a set. She found more often than not that *she* acted as the peacemaker, the mediator between various hysterical egos.

She sneaked another look, but Romain was a million miles away, immersed in facts and figures, shirtsleeves rolled up, his profile harshly beautiful. And extremely remote. In that moment she had trouble believing that he had ever kissed her with such passion only that morning.

Some time later Sorcha felt a bump and her head jerked up. She'd been asleep on something very soft...it felt like a cushion…only it was no cushion. It was an arm and a very broad chest. She jerked upright completely. Slumberous hooded grey eyes looked back at her, completely unconcerned. Sorcha took it all in in a flash—along with the fact that they were about to land. She must have heard the wheels being lowered.

The seat divide was up, and Romain had leant back into his own reclined seat, pulling her with him onto his chest. The sudden memory of how he'd felt underneath her cheek made a flush spread through her body.

'I…' She couldn't speak.

Romain watched her flounder. She looked sleepy and tousled and flushed and so…gorgeous that he had to shift minutely in his seat. He'd suffered the ignominy of his body reacting against the will he'd tried to impose on it for the past three hours or so, and right now he felt he needed to take a very long, very cold shower. When Sorcha's head had kept drooping in jerks as she'd slept, he'd put down his papers, unbuckled their belts and pulled her into him. Again, he'd been surprised at how her soft curves had seemed to melt into his body, as if made for him. Her evocative scent had drifted up from silky black hair.

Their seats were towards the front, and somewhat screened from the rest of the cabin. And it was that fact now that seemed to be uppermost on Sorcha's mind as her hair swung around her shoulders in an arc and she cast a nervous look backwards.

'No one saw,' he offered helpfully, feeling absurdly annoyed.

She sat back and folded her arms. 'I didn't mean to fall asleep. I must've been more tired than I realised.'

She could see him shrug out of the corner of her eye as he flipped his seat upright, 'The pleasure was all mine.'

She burned. Her insides were on fire. She couldn't even escape and go to the toilet as they were about to land. Buckling her belt again, she busied herself putting her book away—but not before it had fallen out of her hands and into Romain's lap. He picked it up before she had a chance to snatch it back.

'*Man and His Symbols*…Carl Jung…' That imperious brow quirked again.

Sorcha was unaware of the plane touching down, announcing their arrival in New York.

'Yes,' she said tightly, holding out a hand for the book.

He gave it back after a long moment, making sure that their fingers brushed, and drawled, 'I have to admit I'm more a fan of his old adversary, Freud.'

Her fingers burned. The book was hers again. She held it to her chest and said waspishly, 'Now, why doesn't that surprise me?'

'Tell me,' he said equably, which should have had alarm bells ringing in her head, 'would this have anything to do with what Val was talking about the other night?'

She looked at him open-mouthed. And promptly shut it again. She knew if she didn't tell him he'd only ask Val. And if she didn't tell him she risked turning it into something bigger, more…

She sighed inwardly, then outwardly shrugged. She *hated* having to tell him. 'I recently graduated from NYU. I got a degree in psychology.'

He said nothing for a long moment, those eyes assessing, making her nervous. 'Val said you got a first?'

She nodded, amazed at his memory.

'Well done.'

Completely nonplussed, trying to think about what this could reveal, Sorcha just muttered something unintelligible. Too much was happening. Too much of herself was being revealed, and she felt very, very exposed. She did not want him knowing anything about her, and now he knew about the outreach centre, her degree, her fear of flying, *her attraction*…what next?

The hubbub and chatter that surrounded them as people got out of seats and collected bags gave Sorcha an excuse to get away. And she did, with barely disguised panic.

* * *

The next evening Sorcha stood huddled against the wind in her parka jacket on the top of the Empire State Building. This was where they were working for the night. The observation deck was theirs till six in the morning. These were the only shots they had to do in New York.

'So, where's Mr Tall, Dark and Gorgeous tonight?'

Sorcha felt a defensive retort about to spring from her lips and bit it back. Dominic was not the person she should allow to wind her up. So she shrugged nonchalantly, as though she didn't care, and said, 'I have no idea. Why are you so worried anyway?'

Dominic's face contorted into an ugly scowl. 'Because whenever he's around I feel like he's watching me, waiting for me to make some kind of false move.'

Sorcha had to bite back a wry smile. She didn't blame Dominic. Romain did have that ability, and she was glad that it wasn't just her on the receiving end. And, as brilliant a photographer as Dominic was, there was the element of a loose cannon about him.

The truth was, she'd been wondering the same thing herself, her senses on high alert. It *was* odd that he wasn't here, especially as tonight was the first time the other model was involved—her counterpart, her lover. This was where they were to meet for the first time, and she would have imagined that with Romain's apparent love of control he'd be watching Zane like a hawk to make sure he performed.

Sorcha knew Zane well. He was one of the most recognisable male models in the world, and had just broken out to act in a movie. He was a nice guy, easy to get on with. She heard a kerfuffle in the corner. Dominic was having a mini-tantrum about something. She could hear snatches of heated conversation, and he had a mobile clamped to his ear.

'You need to come up here now, because Claire is saying she needs approval for Zane's costume…and if we don't start shooting in the next half hour we're going to jeopardise Simon getting his dawn shots…'

Sorcha's heart started to thump. Silly. It mightn't even be him. Since he was now back in New York, she didn't doubt that he'd have made plans to take some current mistress out to dinner. Wasn't that exactly how men like Romain operated? Ruthless and controlling in business, the quintessential playboy socially—a string of women around the world.

Sorcha couldn't kid herself and think that what had happened between them had meant anything more than a bit of diverting fun for him, and that was why it couldn't happen again. He'd been playing with her—a game of showing her that he was in control.

But some minutes later, as Lucy was touching up her make-up, she saw the observation deck doors open and Romain walk out. The New York night was chilly, and he wore a long black coat that made him look impossibly tall and dark. She hadn't seen him all day and butterflies erupted in her stomach.

He focused on Dominic and Zane and went straight to them. Consulted with Claire. And then, with the issue apparently resolved, and a curt, 'Don't disturb me again unless it's *really* urgent,' he walked back out, not looking her way even momentarily.

It felt like a slap in the face—which was ridiculous when it wasn't even directed at her. She saw the lift doors close, concealing him from view. It was obvious he hadn't appreciated Dominic's autocratic demand at all.

'*He* didn't look happy to be taken away from his date!'

Sorcha looked at Lucy, and ice invaded her veins. 'What?'

Lucy shrugged. 'Well, that's where I bet he was… Why would he want to supervise us up here when he could be taking some beautiful woman out to dinner?' Lucy sighed dreamily.

Sorcha longed to be the gossiping kind just once, so she could ask her if what she'd said was based on fact. But she wasn't, so she didn't. And for the whole night, when Romain didn't reappear, Sorcha couldn't stop imagining him looking into sultry blue, or brown, or green eyes, telling her—*whoever*—that next time they wouldn't be interrupted, with all the passionate conviction he'd used with her, and which she stupidly, treacherously, couldn't get out of her head…

CHAPTER NINE

THE following night they were heading off to India. The next leg of the journey. Sorcha made sure to be one of the first on the plane this time, and chose one of the single seats. She wasn't in the mood to talk to anyone. Last night had made her feel out of control...she'd found herself missing him! As though the set had become a more sinister place without him. Everything had seemed lacklustre... They were barely days into the job and this man was winding her around his little finger with little more than his magnetic presence and one kiss. The thought of which made her squirm in her seat.

She'd tried to see Katie for lunch earlier, but it hadn't worked out with timing. Romain was insisting that they all stay in the same hotels along the way, in order to bond, so she hadn't seen her friend once. And she missed Katie's practical, down-to-earth maternal advice. Although maybe it was just as well that they hadn't met, as when she'd told Katie about taking the job her friend had seemed to think that it was a good thing. She'd probably have encouraged her to jump into bed with Romain, and that was the kind of advice that Sorcha did *not* want to hear.

She plucked her eye mask out of her bag and put it on. At least this way she wouldn't even see if he got on the plane. Because she didn't care. *Liar.* She ignored the mocking voice. And then...as if to mock her further...her heart quickened and she felt herself tremble slightly. The hairs stood up on the back of her neck when an all too familiar scent teased her nostrils. He was *here*. And she knew it without even seeing him arrive. Sorcha knew without a doubt that she was in deep trouble.

Their shooting location in India was the beautiful City of Lakes—Udaipur. It was called the most romantic city in Rajasthan, and Sorcha had to agree, taking everything in the following day as they went by boat from the shore to the Lake Palace. It rose like an eye-wateringly majestic white dream from some Arabian Nights fantasy in the middle of Lake Pichola. She loved the arid heat, the hazy blue sky and the myriad colours everywhere—some so bright that it almost hurt to look at them.

Romain sat beside her on the small seat of the boat, his thigh disturbingly close to hers. In long khaki combat shorts, much like hers, he was managing to look all at once casual and devastatingly attractive. His dark T-shirt clung to hard, defined pectoral muscles that were a wicked enticement to touch and feel. She swallowed.

She'd managed to avoid him on the plane by sleeping most of the journey, and then all the way to the plush, opulent hotel they were staying in on the shores of the lake. But for now she couldn't. She and Romain were in one boat, Simon and Dominic in another. The four were on their way to the Lake Palace to do a recce for tomorrow's shoot. The rest of the crew had the day off, to recover, get over jet lag, and they would too—once this was over.

But she couldn't stop sneaking a furtive glance. Against the backdrop of the ancient Indian buildings he looked like some regal god. And for some reason she felt compelled to speak, her mouth working independently of her brain—because what came out was *not* what she wanted to say at all.

'You were busy in New York.'

She could see his brows pull together and cursed herself. What on earth was wrong with her?

'Is that a question or a statement?' He didn't wait for her answer. 'Actually, yes, I *was* busy. I'm working on a few projects at the same time, and I knew New York would be the last place I'd have any time to spend on them... Tell me, Sorcha, did you miss me?'

She wanted to snort disdainfully, wanted to laugh. Wanted to say something cutting. She opened her mouth, but at that moment all she could see was his eyes. They were luminous in the hazy sunlight, glittering a fierce grey with something so...provocative in their depths that she couldn't say a word. She wondered with awful futility how he had this power to hold her in such a spell...to make her think of things she'd never considered before.

She was helpless, lost in that look. She wanted to blurt out how she'd been tortured with pictures of him on date after date...even though she knew in reality it had only been one night.

'I worked late that night, and then I had to take Maud out to dinner. I missed *you*.'

She couldn't breathe as something awfully exultant moved through her. How was it that he could read her mind? To her utter horror she heard her voice come out shakily, forming words she'd had no intention of saying. 'It didn't seem like that on the Empire State Building.'

A flash of something intense crossed his face, distracting her from her monumental gaffe, and then, as if she'd imagined it, he took her hand, lifting it, bringing her palm to his mouth, where he pressed a kiss to the heated middle. Her fingers curled instinctively, as if to hold the kiss, and all rational thought fled.

'I told you that next time we wouldn't be interrupted, and I meant it.'

Sorcha felt her insides quiver, the blood thicken in her veins. How did he know just what to say to make her forget everything he stood for? Everything he represented to her?

The launch arrived at the Lake Palace, and as it gently hit the small jetty wall Sorcha seemed to come to her senses. But still felt cocooned in some sort of dreamlike haze. Simon and Dominic stood waiting for them. Sorcha clambered off the boat and followed the men around. The breathtaking scenery distracted her momentarily from her churning thoughts and emotions. She gazed in wonder at the beauty of the palace, which had once been built for royalty but was now a five-star hotel.

Finished with discussing the main schedule of shots with the other men, Romain turned to look for Sorcha. She'd disappeared. He walked over to the edge of the terrace, where a complicated lattice design in marble formed a wall. And there she was, just on the level below, down a few steps. He felt that annoyingly familiar punch to the gut. With her hair free, in tousled waves down her back, she stood on the terrace below talking to one of the hotel staff. He was pointing something out to her on a carving, and she was bending down, putting on her glasses to take a closer look.

He knew she wouldn't be faking an interest. And when she turned to look up and smile widely at the man he jealously felt bowled over by her natural beauty. She was dressed simply in shorts, which showed a smooth length of pale, slim leg, and a plain white T-shirt which clung to her breasts far too provocatively for his liking. He vowed to take her, and soon. He couldn't wait much longer, and the sooner he burned himself free of this desire, the sooner he could get back to normal.

Because, as much as he relished the feeling of boredom being gone, he also conversely wanted it back. In these uncharted waters of insatiable desire he felt rudderless. He wasn't used to a woman making him feel like this, and the only other time that had happened he'd been too young to know how to deal with it, or the consequences. Not so any more. This time he was equipped. He would take her and then move on to someone more suitable, *safer*. This was just a temporary madness.

At that moment, as if Sorcha sensed him watching, she turned and looked up. The smile slid from her face and was replaced with a flare in her eyes. Her mouth opened slightly. She wanted him too. He knew it like an immutable truth that stirred in his blood. Though he knew she'd deny it again if he pushed her.

And that was why he found himself tugging her back from getting on the boat as they watched Simon and Dominic go off ahead of them. Now they were alone. No crew around.

Sorcha looked up into Romain's expressionless face. She was very aware of the fact that they were now alone. On a stunningly beautiful idyllic white marbled palace island. Dominic and Simon's boat was chugging away in the distance. Their boatman was looking at them expectantly.

'Have lunch with me here.'

Sorcha's immediate and first reaction was to shake her head and say no. A strong suspicion assailed her, making her quite sure that he was only asking so he could keep her close, could make sure she stayed out of trouble. Romain saw her hesitation. He smiled, and it looked dangerous and far too seductive.

'Don't worry—I won't ravish you. And you have to eat, don't you?'

She opened her mouth, and to her utter horror and chagrin her stomach made a sound like water going down a very big, echoing drain. She promptly shut her mouth and blushed.

'That settles it.' He took her arm and shepherded her back up the steps and into the main open-air foyer of the hotel.

The feeling of unreality lingered as they were shown to a secluded table in the corner of the magnificent restaurant. There were no walls, only columns, open to the warm air, the hazy blue of the sky and the lapping waters of the lake, intricately carved with complicated mosaics which were echoed in the roof above. It was truly the most breathtaking place Sorcha had ever been in her life.

A waiter materialised and she heard Romain order a bottle

of champagne. She stopped him with a brief, light touch on his hand. He looked at her quizzically.

'I'm sorry but do you mind if we don't have champagne? It's just that it gives me a headache...'

She sent a small, hesitant smile to the waiter and then back to Romain, who felt slightly winded.

'If you don't mind...what I'd actually really like is a beer.'

He lifted a brow and felt totally nonplussed. It had been pure reflex to order champagne—his first step in any seduction. And she wanted *beer*? He couldn't remember the last time he'd even drunk a beer, and yet in that instant it seemed to him to be the most desirable drink in the world.

He nodded to the waiter. 'Two beers, please.'

Sorcha felt embarrassed as the waiter scurried away. 'Oh, you don't have to have one just because of me... That is,' she qualified, feeling awkward, 'you don't exactly look like a beer drinking man.'

He sat back. His face was all lean angles, making him look austere.

'Tell me, what *do* I look like?'

Like a man who knows how to make love to a woman...

Sorcha's insides liquefied, and she couldn't believe how a bubble of sensuality seemed to have enveloped them.

She had to control herself with effort. 'You look like a vintage champagne type. Or a thousand-euro-a-bottle of wine type.'

He had actually paid that much and more for wine in the past, and it seemed almost crass now. 'Forgive me. I should have consulted with you before ordering. Though, after seeing you put away half a glass of champagne in one go in New York, I was under the impression that you liked it.'

Sorcha had the grace to smile. 'I actually hate the stuff. I wouldn't have had a glass at all, only for Katie giving me one. Maud likes us to look like we're having a good time at events like that...drinking champagne promotes the stereotype.'

'And you *weren't* having a good time?' he asked easily.

The beers arrived. Romain held his bottle up and Sorcha clinked hers to his. Without breaking eye contact, they both took a long swallow.

Romain closed his eyes for a second. 'I'd forgotten how good it tastes—especially in this climate…' He opened them again, catching Sorcha looking at him with glittering big blue eyes. His body tightened. 'Go on, you were going to tell me why you weren't having a good time…'

She was? She had to be careful. To her consternation, she was finding that he was all too easy to talk to. It would be very easy to let something slip out that she wasn't ready to talk about.

She shrugged minutely. 'Well, you saw what it was like. A room full of movers and shakers. We were there primarily as adornments. People look at us and think: Models—ergo stupid. It's all about seeing and being seen.'

She looked out to the lake. 'In the early days it was all fabulously exciting to be in the same room as the Mayor of New York, or the biggest, newest film star, but really…your illusions get stripped away pretty quickly. Coming from somewhere like Ireland, I think I have a pretty good inbuilt detector for anyone who isn't genuine. And about one per cent of that crowd *are* genuine…'

What she said brought back a niggling sense of *déjà vu*, but before he could dwell on it, pin it down, the waiter returned and took their order. Romain ordered more beers, and Sorcha was surprised to see they'd already been talking for some time. Her eyes took in his relaxed stance, his T-shirt straining across the muscles of his chest. She remembered seeing him emerge from the sea in Ireland. He smiled and she couldn't breathe. The brown column of his throat looked all too touchable.

It felt as if a silken cord of intimacy was wrapping itself around Sorcha.

She spoke to fill the silence which seemed far too heavy and potent for her, seizing on the first thing that came into her head.

'I was here before…' She answered his questioning look, 'On a backpacking trip with my friend Katie, when we were twenty-one. We'd been on a shoot in Delhi, and decided to do a little travelling before going home. We stayed at a tiny hostel just across the water there somewhere. We used to sit in our window, drinking beers. We'd dream about being over here, having a sumptuous meal, fine wine…'

She couldn't stop a sudden giggle from rising, and Romain watched her. She didn't realise how infectious her grin was. She knew part of it was a slightly hysterical reaction to being here in the first place, sharing such an intimate space with this man. At how fast things were moving, changing…

'I'm sorry—it's just that if Katie could see me now, she'd be so horrified…' The giggle crept higher, and Sorcha bit her lip to stop it erupting. But when she saw a twitch on Romain's mouth she couldn't help it spilling out.

'The fact that I'm here in shorts and a T-shirt, fulfilling our fantasy…and drinking *beer*…' A tear escaped from her eye and she had to wipe it away, laughing in earnest now. 'She'd *kill* me!'

A grin broke out on Romain's face, and that sobered her up quicker than anything—the sheer masculine perfection of his features.

Her giggles died away with a little hiccup. 'Sorry…it's just if you'd seen the place we were staying… If Katie was here, she'd be dignity personified…not like me, swilling beer and corrupting your fine palate. Maybe you should have brought her,' she said lightly, too lightly.

Romain shook his head. 'I'm not interested in her.'

Sorcha's heart pounded uncomfortably into the silence.

'Tell me,' he asked, 'you're good friends?'

Sorcha nodded emphatically. This was easy. 'The best. She's been there for me since—' She broke off, stopping her runaway mouth, and finished, 'Since for ever. We've known each other since we were ten…and got discovered at the same time by a scout from Dublin when we were fifteen.'

At that moment their food was delivered. With relief at finding his intense focus off her for a moment, Sorcha tucked into the food, suddenly ravenous. They shared starters of traditional samosas and spring rolls wrapped Vietnamese-style in rice paper. Then Sorcha had ordered a main dish of steamed sea bass, while Romain had opted for a dish unique to the region, *khad khargosh*—wild hare.

When his meal was placed in front of him, and he saw Sorcha wrinkle her nose slightly, he asked, with a quirk to his mouth, 'You don't approve?'

Horrified to be caught like that, she said quickly, 'Oh, no. It's just the thought of the poor little hare…sorry.'

He speared a morsel and ate it, completely unperturbed. 'But you're not a vegetarian. You ordered steak that day in Dublin.'

When she'd fled the restaurant like a bolshy teenager…

She looked slightly shame faced and put her fork down for a moment, lifting her eyes to his. All he could see was their luminosity. Her colouring was exotic against this backdrop.

'I don't normally run out like that.'

He inclined his head slightly in acknowledgement. And felt surprised. He was used to women being petulant, yet that day he knew she hadn't been. Her speedy exit had come from something much deeper. He'd touched on a raw nerve, and he remembered that they'd been talking about her project—the outreach centre. What he'd said then seemed to him to be unbelievably insensitive now. He'd still been labouring under his misapprehension, not believing that she might be different, *reformed*.

And was she?

Introspection kept him quiet. He was thinking about how professional she was. So far she'd been nothing but pleasant, polite, helpful, quiet…not a hint of divadom at all. All qualities his aunt had professed her to have *again* when he'd taken her for dinner. A dinner in which he'd had to focus just to get Sorcha out of his head. That was why he'd largely ignored her when Dominic had called him up to the set in New York. He'd known that seeing her would have the potential to scramble his brain. And he was not comfortable with that at all. He'd known her for less than three weeks, and hadn't even slept with her…*yet*.

With the last succulent morsel of sea bass dissolving on her tongue, Sorcha sat back and dabbed her napkin to her mouth. 'That was…amazing.'

Romain sat back too. 'Yes. And if you want you can tell Kate you had champagne…the works…I'll back up your story.'

Sorcha grinned and held up her bottle of beer to gently clink it with his in collusion. It was only when she took a swallow and saw some kind of triumphant gleam in his eye that her blood ran cold. What was he doing? Acting as if she and he might be in a situation in the future where they would create this little *in joke* to share with Katie…or whoever? Almost as if they were a couple.

And what the hell was *she* doing? This man was the enemy…and yet at this lunch it felt as if he was anything but. She felt shivery and trembly inside. This man was playing with her, that was all.

The plates were cleared away, a clean table lay between them. And then her fears were compounded.

He leant forward, two elbows on the table. Intent. 'I owe you an apology.'

Sorcha tensed slightly. 'You do?'

He nodded. 'That day in Dublin, what I said about your outreach centre, it was unforgivable. I had no right to judge something you've been working on—no right to judge your motivations for doing something like that.'

Sorcha floundered. This Romain was way, way more dangerous to deal with than the autocratic, overbearing Romain.

'Well, thank you.'

Now please drop it, she begged silently.

'Would you tell me about it?'

Sorcha fought against closing her eyes. Her plea had gone spectacularly unanswered. She thought quickly. What harm could it do to tell him just a little? Surely it wouldn't really give away anything? She took a deep breath.

Romain had seen the conflict cross her face, the shadows in her eyes again, the effort it was taking for her to open up to him at all. It made him feel a whole host of conflicting emotions, not least the desire to ask himself, *what does she have to hide?*

Sorcha looked out to the lake, and when she looked back to Romain her eyes were guarded. 'When my father died... Well, we were very close.'

Romain gave a tiny nod of his head, encouraging her to go on. She looked at him steadily, and he was aware at that moment of something powerful passing between them.

'He was my best friend, my confidante.' She shrugged lightly and looked down for a second. 'I was the ultimate daddy's girl. He used to happily tell everyone that he was wrapped around my finger...he'd bring me to his office...everywhere. He died suddenly. No warning—nothing. I got the call from my mum while I was at school. My older brother was away with his family...' She shrugged again, and this time it was jerky, as though she was fighting to keep the emotion down.

'I kind of went off the rails a bit. I left school that summer, and Katie and I had both been offered work in London. Unfortunately I got involved with a crowd of less than savoury characters, and a guy called Christian. I was still very angry about my father's death, and hadn't really dealt with it. At that age there's not a lot of emotional support unless you get it at home...'

Romain stayed very still and quiet, his eyes holding hers, and when she looked at him they seemed to her to be like beacons. Crazy…but very, very seductive. She kept talking.

'I guess that's where the desire came from to do…*something*. For years I've always thought that if there had been some place…somewhere to go…that had offered impartial, confidential advice and support, I might have gone. And I might not have…' She didn't finish, and couldn't look at him any more.

Romain reached across the table and took her hand, covering it with his warmth. Dark against pale. She only realised then that she was shaking.

'Was Dominic a part of that crowd?'

She looked at him. 'How…?'

'He mentioned something at the start about knowing you from years ago. I put two and two together.'

She nodded. 'Christian was his friend.'

'Was Christian your lover?' he asked sharply.

Her sense of danger skyrocketed.

How can I say I'm not sure…? Sorcha thought crazily to herself. She gave a brief, abrupt shake of the head. 'No. I had a crush…it was all quite innocent…'

He seemed satisfied with that, and Sorcha prayed he'd move away from such dangerous waters.

'Is that why you did the psychology degree? So you could work at the centre?' He shook his own head. 'I only realised when you told me about it that you wouldn't have had time to come home for any real length of time…again, I'm sorry Sorcha…'

CHAPTER TEN

SORCHA struggled to stay calm, but she felt like she wanted to get up and run—hide, go away. With every word he was saying he was getting closer, digging deeper, and soon he'd reach the very centre of everything, the place were her desire threatened to bubble out of control.

She pulled her hand back and racked her brain for some way to take the intense spotlight off her.

'And what about you? What are your secrets, Romain?' Her voice felt very brittle, like her control. 'How come you're not married?'

Where had *that* come from?

Romain sat back. At least she'd had the desired effect. His eyes narrowed on hers.

'I was engaged once, actually…'

'You were?' Sorcha's treacherous heart fell.

He nodded briefly, curtly. 'Yes. A long time ago. I was eighteen.' His mouth twisted cynically. 'She was my first true love. But one day I walked into her bedroom and caught her in bed with my older half-brother.'

The words were said without a hint of emotion, but Sorcha could intuit the pain. God only knew, she'd become so adept at hiding her own innermost emotions that she could see it a mile away in someone else. But she knew he wouldn't welcome sympathy.

One big shoulder shrugged with apparent insouciance. 'She'd found out that he stood to inherit the title of Duc. While I too have inherited a title, it's that of mere Comte. He was older, richer, more experienced—and he also stood to inherit the family château.'

He felt familiar satisfaction rush through him when he thought of how he'd bought back that château just a couple of years before. His brother had come to him, begging for aid. And yet, even though it had been a moment he'd waited for a long time, the satisfaction, while still there, hadn't tasted as sweet as he'd thought it would. He'd somewhere along the way lost that all-consuming desire to get back at the brother who had made his life a complete misery from when he was a small child.

'I'm sorry…I didn't mean to bring up something so—'

Before she could say *painful*, and put a word to his feelings, Romain laughed harshly. 'It was a long time ago. She was dead to me a long time ago, and since then—' he made a very Gallic facial expression '—I haven't had the inclination to repeat the experience.'

His face and demeanour said it all to Sorcha. He'd tarred every woman since then with the same brush. His treatment of her said it all too. His obvious ruthlessness in his desire to get her into bed, despite his initial misgivings, which were conveniently dropping away. Which she was allowing him, *helping* him to shed. God, did she want him so badly that she was contemplating letting someone so jaded take her in the most intimate way?

She couldn't read his expression. A tense silence surrounded them and then, as if a switch had been flicked on, he smiled. Jekyll and Hyde. Sorcha shivered.

'I think we've had enough questions and answers—yes?'

She nodded mutely.

'Let's have some dessert…' And he called over the waiter.

Within minutes, he was fast weaving her headlong into the tapestry of desire again, making her forget all her misgivings.

On the boat on their way back to the hotel, the mood was considerably lighter. He made her laugh uncontrollably with funny stories about various fashion designers and their prima donna behaviour. And then she remembered something he had said earlier. 'So you're a count? What does that make you—Monsieur le Comte de Valois?'

He looked at her sharply. He hadn't mistaken the teasing in her tone, even if her face was serious.

He nodded. 'I never use it though. It seems a bit outdated these days.'

'Oh, I don't know.' Sorcha slid him a mischievous glance. 'A count with, I assume, at least one château?' she asked, looking to him for confirmation. He nodded again. 'Well, that's quite the package. In that case I should have curtsied when we met...'

Now she was definitely laughing at him. He couldn't believe it. For a second he felt all the righteous anger and pride of his forebears, and then at the next moment, seeing her mouth twitch helplessly, he had to give in.

'How refreshing—a woman who isn't dropping at my feet with the mention of a title and a château.'

Again he had that split second sensation of thinking, *she's playing me...*

She looked at him from under long black lashes. There was no make-up on her slightly freckled face, and she was so beautiful that his chest ached. But even as he looked he saw something come into her eyes, and she drew back, inwards.

They made the rest of the trip in silence. He could feel Sorcha becoming more and more tense beside him. On disembarking the boat she said a quick brusque thank you and didn't meet his eye, then she fled.

Romain watched her go, a small predatory smile playing around his hard mouth.

* * *

A little later, after a shower, Sorcha gave up trying to have a siesta—too jittery and on edge after that lunch. She felt overloaded with sensations and desires and feelings that confused her. One in particular being that she had to admit to herself that she *liked* him. Really liked him. As for what he did to her body…just thinking about that made her heat up.

She decided to take a walk in the nearby streets to try and calm down.

She ducked into an ornate Hindu temple, feeling for a moment as if she were being followed, and cursed her imagination. Inside, all the different deities were painted in a profusion of bright colours. Little children danced around her, asking for 'school pens', and gave her incense to light. She took some pictures. Those moments, and as she walked through markets, bought herself some clothes, gave her some sense of equilibrium back.

The streets were heaving with humanity, sacred cows and eye-wateringly strong smells. She dodged the rickshaws that held beautiful and mysterious sari-clad women and thought that she was mad to be even *thinking* about anything to do with Romain de Valois. She was no match for him. He just didn't realise it yet.

Returning to the hotel, she was relieved not to have bumped into anyone, but in the corridor on the way back to her room she heard a hissed, 'Sorcha!'

It was Lucy, in the room next to hers. 'Are you OK?'

Lucy looked up and down the corridor and gestured for Sorcha to come in.

She groaned inwardly. She really didn't want to get all girly and chat. But when she got to the door Lucy pulled her inside, shutting the door after her.

'Lucy, I'm really tired—'

'I have something you might be interested in.'

The hair stood up on the back of Sorcha's neck. The young girl held out a small paper packet full of white powder. So stomach fell. She'd encountered this over the years—people mistakenly believing what they might have heard…

'Look, Lucy, I'm really not interested in that stuff. And you shouldn't go waving it around.'

Lucy laughed. 'Oh, don't be such a square. Come on— what's the harm?'

Something hard settled in Sorcha's chest. She made a split-second decision, and behind it was the urge to protect. She grabbed the paper out of Lucy's hand, folding it up carefully.

'Hey—' The girl's face was a picture of surprise and panic.

Sorcha quickly stuck it in the back pocket of her shorts and folded her arms.

'Lucy, how old are you?'

'Twenty-one.'

She looked a little shame-faced, and Sorcha was relieved to see that it didn't look as if she'd taken any of the drug yet. She gentled her tone.

'Look, if anyone else had caught you with this…like Romain…you'd be going home on the next plane. And you'd probably never get work again. Not to mention we're in India. Do you have any idea what the police here would do if you were caught?'

She saw Lucy pale visibly. Sorcha grimaced inwardly. No doubt Dominic had her under his thumb. And she didn't want to scare her.

'I don't care where you got it, because I know who probably gave it to you—' The other girl went red and started to bluster. Sorcha just held up a hand. 'Believe me, I know Dominic from a long time ago, so don't feel you have to protect him. And, Lucy, if you'll take some advice from me, the next time someone offers you drugs don't be a fool and take them. The person you offer to share them with might not be so understanding or get rid of it for you…'

* * *

Sorcha left and went back to her own room next door. It felt as if the white powder was burning a hole in her pocket. She dropped her shopping bag and went straight to her bathroom. She was about to flush it down the loo, when a knock came on her door. Panicking slightly, she stuffed it again into her back pocket.

She opened the door and felt immediately dizzy. Romain stood there, larger than life. And then, without so much as a by-your-leave, he sauntered in as if he owned the place. Sorcha gripped the door handle, loath to shut the door. *What was he doing here? He had to leave!* She could feel herself pale. She could feel the packet, and it suddenly weighed a ton. A cold sweat broke out on her brow. Of all the times!

'Can…can I help you?' she asked, and her voice sounded strained to her ears.

He leant back against the door that opened out onto her patio. His eyes narrowed on her face and Sorcha felt herself flush guiltily. *What was he doing here?*

'Shut the door,' he said quietly.

Sorcha's mind raced even as she did as he asked, not thinking to question it. Could he have seen anything? Overheard anything? He couldn't have… This had to be unrelated. Because if it wasn't… Her blood ran cold.

The door shut behind her, and Romain called softly from across the room. 'Come here.'

Feeling more and more like Alice in Wonderland, slipping down a hole, Sorcha haltingly moved forward. If she could just get into the bathroom -

'You don't need to look like you're about to go to your own funeral,' he drawled, 'It'll be nice, I promise…'

Sorcha looked at him then, and stopped by the bed. He'd cut through the turmoil in her brain even as her insides clawed with guilt. Nice? She shook her head as if that might try and clear it. 'I'm sorry…look…what do you want?'

He pushed himself off the door and strolled towards h

with dangerous intent in his eye. Too late, Sorcha realised what his intention was only when he came so close that she couldn't breathe.

'I told you that next time we wouldn't be interrupted...'

He couldn't mean...

'I want *you*.'

He did. Within a cataclysmic split second Sorcha's world was reduced to Romain pulling her into his arms, chest to chest, and before she could say *stop*, or *go*, or even take a breath, his mouth was stealing every bit of sanity from her.

The rush of sensation and reaction made her forget everything. With shocking ease, her whole being melted into his.

The matter of fact way he'd just come in...the intent in his eyes that reached out to wrap her in a haze of desire...it scrambled her brain so much that all she was aware of was the need to have him kiss her again, to feel his arms around her. That last kiss was seared onto her memory, and now she was coming back to life in his arms.

His mouth moved over hers with insistent mastery. A flame of white-hot desire was racing along every one of Sorcha's veins, and when her mouth opened on a little sigh, and his tongue made contact with hers, her hands reached out and tightened on his shoulders to stop herself from falling at his feet.

Sorcha's two arms twined up around his neck. She stood on tiptoe, couldn't stop the hitched indrawn breath against his mouth when she felt his hand on her back, reaching under her T-shirt to stroke up over the silky skin, moulding the outline of the curve of her waist. An aching wanting grew at the apex of her thighs, and when Sorcha innocently moved her hips, felt his arousal press insistently against her, her heart beat so fast she thought it would burst from her chest.

His arms around her felt so good, so strong, and when one hand moved down to cup her bottom through her shorts, moving her even closer, she couldn't help a little mewl of acquiescence. His hand on her bottom sought to get even closer. She felt him slide it into her pocket—

Sorcha's whole body went rigid in a second. As if ice had just been poured through every artery. His hand was *right there*.

She pulled back and looked up into his face. She couldn't help the look of shock she knew must be there. At another time his reaction might have been almost comical.

He looked surprised at first. Then a small frown appeared and, with deadly, awful inevitability, his fingers closed around the small paper packet and she felt him pull it free from her back pocket. His arms slackened, and all the heat and insanity disappeared as he let her go.

Romain stepped back and a chasm opened up, like an arctic wind blowing between them. Sorcha's eyes closed, her hands were dead weights by her side. She didn't think she was even breathing. The situation was so horrifically awful and unfair she couldn't take in the magnitude of what it meant.

His voice was so cold when it came that it made her flinch.

'Open your eyes.'

She opened them, and could feel the colour drain from her face again. She was freezing.

He held the folded-up paper which had opened slightly, revealing the white powder between his forefinger and thumb, a look of complete and utter disgust on his face—much the same as hers had been only short moments before. Moments which now felt like years.

'I…' Her voice felt scratchy and her lips and mouth still tingled.

'There is not one thing you can say. Not. One. Thing.'

Sorcha's mouth shut. The total and utter immediate condemnation on his face shocked her. He hadn't even a shred of doubt in his mind…and why would he? But it hurt. She bit the inside of her lip so hard she could feel blood. She wrapped her arms around her waist and felt shock set in, felt the shaking starting up, that awful dropping of her stomach—even though she hadn't even done anything wrong!

But one thing she did know, and it was very clear. She could not subject Lucy to this man's wrath. She was just a young girl, starting out in her career. And Sorcha knew she'd look even worse in Romain's eyes if she tried to blame someone else younger, more inexperienced.

Having made the decision to take the blame, or at least protect Lucy, Sorcha felt a kind of calmness wash over her. After all, what did she really have to lose? Wasn't this what he had expected all along?

The shaking subsided.

Romain saw her chin tilt up minutely, her shoulders straighten. A light of defiance come into her eyes. And as the awful, betraying disappointment rushed through him he felt himself get cold and hard inside. *Fool, fool, fool.* And yet even now, in the midst of this, he was taking in her huge blue eyes, the delicate pale column of her throat, the way her breasts pushing at the thin fabric of her T-shirt made him think of the way they had just pushed against his chest. And, much to his abject horror, his body reacted to that image, that thought.

He moved towards her, and all Sorcha's paltry bravado disappeared. He took her arm in a harsh grip and half-dragged, half-walked her over to the bathroom.

He was curt and harsh. 'You know what to do.'

He thrust the folded-up parcel at her as if it was contaminating him, and Sorcha felt like crying, laughing and screaming all at the same time. What would he say if she told him that this was exactly what she had been about to do before being interrupted?

With shaking hands she emptied it into the toilet, flushing the offending drug away. The sound was magnified unbearably in the tense atmosphere. With legs shaking so much that she'd fall if she didn't sit, she sank back onto the side of the bath. She looked at the ground. She had to try something.

'Romain—'

'I don't want to hear it.'

She looked up, her eyes huge, beseeching, and quailed at the coldness she saw in his face. It was nothing like she'd ever experienced.

She tried again. 'It's not what you—'

He laughed harshly, arms crossed against his chest. Arms that had just now held her so tight she'd never wanted him to let her go. She ached inside.

'*Think?* That's original. No wonder you were in such a hurry after lunch. Tell me…' he said, and he relaxed back against the sink, one hip propped up. But the lines of his body screamed anything *but* relaxed. 'Was the whole purpose of your little walk just now to get drugs? Is that why you were so eager to get away? Because you needed a fix? Did you have someone lined up before we even got here? I'm interested to know how this would work. Do you call ahead. Or is it—'

'Stop it!' Her hands gripped the edge of the bath as she tried to make sense of what he was saying, the barrage of questions. 'I… How do you…?'

'How do I know you took a walk?' he asked. 'Because I was taking a walk myself, and saw you go into the temple.'

His mouth twisted as he remembered following her. Being captivated by her.

He looked unbearably harsh. 'Charming picture. Playing with the kids…taking photos…lighting incense.' He shook his head. '*Dieu*…what a fool I am. You were on your way to pick up your stash. I actually thought—'

He cut himself off. His eyes were so glacial that Sorcha felt as if a layer of her skin was being peeled off slowly. But she couldn't take her eyes from his.

'I lost you, though…after the market where you bought that *salwaar kameez*. That's obviously when you went off to find your little…contact.'

She shook her head miserably and stood, legs still shaking. 'I promise you…it's not what you think.'

'Promise me? That's rich.' He stood upright and towered over her in the small space. 'To think that in Dublin when you asked if I would believe you'd never touched drugs I actually thought about it…considered it…I would have believed it if I'd heard nothing but your chain of lies today. But only a mere hour after telling me breathlessly about the outreach centre, how important it is, you're—'

A look flashed across his face, and as if he'd said too much he cursed in French and strode back out into the bedroom.

Sorcha followed him, stood at the door of the bathroom. He had his back to her, looking out of the patio doors. She didn't know where to start, what to say. She could see exactly how he would construe events…words…and could only watch his taut, unrelenting back helplessly. And even in the midst of this the memory of how it had felt… He turned and fixed her with those cold eyes, and immediately her skin flushed guiltily. As if he could see her shameful thoughts.

'What are you going to do?' she asked bravely, and steeled herself.

He looked at her for a long moment. She could almost see the cogs whirring in that sharp brain. And then, as if having come to a decision, he strolled nonchalantly towards her. His face was unbearably cold, but the look in his eyes was full of desirous intent. His demeanour spelt absolute danger. Sorcha instinctively grabbed onto the wall beside her as he came close. She looked up helplessly. Ensnared.

And suddenly she thought of something.

Without passing it through the filter in her brain, she found herself blurting out, 'Look, I know why you're reacting like this. I know what happened with your mother…'

CHAPTER ELEVEN

HE STOPPED dead in front of her, and immediately she knew she'd made one of the biggest errors of her life. He froze. His face became a mask of non-reaction, his eyes glittering jewel-hard shards of icy grey. He spoke after what felt like aeons, and his words dripped with disdain and disgust.

'What do you know?'

It was a question but Sorcha wasn't foolish enough to open her mouth again.

'Maud told you. It can only have been her. What did she tell you?'

This person before her was someone Sorcha had never seen. Even at his most dismissive, judging…this *cold* creature hadn't existed. A thousand miles gaped between this man and the man who'd taken her for lunch, the man who had kissed her.

He moved closer, and Sorcha tried to move back but the wall was in her way. She wanted to apologise, wanted to tell him that he was scaring her.

'Did Maud tell you that my mother was addicted to opium since she was a child growing up in Vietnam?'

Sorcha, horribly mesmerized by his nearness and eyes, just shook her head.

'Did Maud tell you that she lived her whole life in a drug-fuelled haze?'

Again she shook her head, horror spreading through her. He came even closer. She could feel his body now, his chest moving up and down against hers, and to her utter self-loathing she could feel herself respond, her nipples tightening.

'Did she tell you that she only came out of it long enough to have me and my older half-brother? To make two unhappy marriages?'

Sorcha couldn't do anything. He was so close now that she could feel his breath. His head came close and a hand was cupping her jaw, angling her head up to his. *Please*, she wanted to beg. *Stop.*

'Did she tell you that at the age of seventeen I found her dead body? Bloated and almost unrecognisable from an overdose?'

An ache clogged Sorcha's throat, and her eyes stung. With his hand cupping her jaw she couldn't move her head. She opened her mouth to try and say something, to reach him, and he took advantage, driving his mouth down on hers, full of pent-up aggression and anger.

Sorcha's hand had come up to his, to try and take it away, but in her shock she left it there. His words were swirling in her head, but all she could feel was him, wrapping his arms around her again, his tongue dancing erotically with hers. He was relentless, a master of her senses, and she could do nothing but succumb even as she felt a tear trickle out from under one eyelid and down her cheek.

After a long, long moment Romain pulled back with a jerky, violent movement and looked down at her. He shook with reaction—to what he'd just revealed, to what he'd found on Sorcha's person, and most of all to the way she was making him feel. To the way she held his body in her spell. He could see wetness on her cheek, where a lone tear had left its mark, but instead of inciting concern, he welcomed the hardness that settled in every bone. She was looking up at him with those big eyes. Lips trembling, plump from his kiss. And he would have her. Even though it went against every moral principle he'd held dear. Even though he'd hate himself. Because he couldn't *not*.

'You asked what I'm going to do, Sorcha…well, this is what I'm going to do. I'm going to take your delectable body when I'm good and ready. And I'm going to sate myself with you, burn myself free of this desire I feel.'

Sorcha swallowed painfully, her head and insides in absolute chaotic turmoil. 'But…you mean…you're not going to send me home?'

He shook his head and a cruel smile touched his mouth. 'No way. At this stage that would cost me money…' He trailed a finger down her cheek and around her jaw. 'And cost me my sanity. You're going to finish the job…as my mistress…'

Long after he had left the room, with nothing more than a curt reminder to be ready to leave for the set at five in the morning, Sorcha sat on the bed in a daze. With a weird, bizarre calmness that she knew was shock, she was thinking of all the advances she'd had from men over the years.

She'd inevitably found their attentions unwelcome, jarring, and very unsexy. As a result, she was vastly inexperienced when it came to men and sex. She had an ongoing fear that somehow she was *cold*, or *frigid*. More than one man had hurled those words at her. But, any man who'd tried to touch her with any kind of intimacy had left her feeling cold. And yet Romain was making her feel anything but frigid. Even when subjecting her to his ice-cold disdain.

Why, oh why, did it have to be him? She lay back, rolled over, and curled up into a foetal position. She could never be intimate with someone who was judging her so harshly, even though she knew she couldn't blame him for this latest development. She had chosen to protect Lucy, and he'd had all the ammunition ready and lined up for just such a situation. And mentioning his mother? She squeezed her eyes shut, the pain of his words still sinking in like knives. She concentrated her breathing and forced her mind away from it, from the sympathy that still gripped her.

In turmoil, she thought of his autocratic assurance that he would make her his mistress. She knew that he wouldn't have to do much. He'd pretty much established that just by looking at her she turned to jelly and was his. It was pathetic.

She couldn't stop her mind going back… Eight years ago something had happened to her. And even to this day she wasn't sure *what*. How could she explain that to someone who was the least likely to believe her explanation of how she'd ended up in that awful spiral of events? She'd always expected that the moment she decided to let someone be totally intimate with her would be the moment she revealed herself fully. She'd never done that with anyone. Not even Katie or her brother—and they were the only people she trusted in the world.

How could she sleep with someone…with *him*…when she didn't even know for sure if she was a virgin? She grimaced painfully. She was sure on an intellectual level that she was. But on some other level, deep down, enough doubt that had been placed in her mind to question herself…and that was a torture she only wanted to share with someone gentle enough, sensitive enough to handle it. She knew well how awful it would sound if she tried to explain, as though. As though—

She couldn't even go there with herself.

She buried her face in the bed, as if to block her predicament out completely. She wasn't successful.

Sorcha moved from behind a leafy palm and stepped into the glittering white of the inner courtyard. It was dusk. A shimmering pool in the middle offered up reflections of the surrounding intricately carved walls. A bird of paradise flew through in a quicksilver flash of colour. Lotus flowers sat on the water like flowering jewels. And there, on the other side of this oasis of beauty, stood her lover, waiting for her. She walked slowly, as if in a dream, felt the silk of her long dress moving like liquid satin against her legs. She reached him. A stunning portrait of handsome perfection in a black tuxedo. He pulled her into his arms and kissed her.

Simon's voice rang out. 'That's great, Sorcha and Zane. We'll do it one more time, and then it's Dominic's turn.'

Sorcha smiled at Zane as he let her go. It was a brittle smile, and hid the aching hurt in her throat and chest. It had taken Lucy a lot longer today to do her make-up, after her sleepless night, and it hadn't been helped by the girl's monosyllabic bad mood. Sorcha couldn't feel bad as she was the one who had acted on a reflex, taken the drugs from her and decided to protect her.

She had refused to acknowledge or look to where she knew Romain stood behind a monitor, watching proceedings as they were filmed. Except just now, walking over to Zane, trying desperately to act her heart out, she'd found a lean, autocratic face coming into her mind's eye, superimposing itself onto Zane's features. And it was actually only six-thirty a.m. They were pretending it was dusk. There was a whole lot of day left to get through.

By midday, Romain was pacing like a caged tiger. Seeing Sorcha at the crack of dawn in a dress that was breathtakingly *indecent* was testing his control to the limit. Along with the fact that she hadn't acknowledged him once, and skittered away if he came near her. Right now she was seated on the corner of the set. She was a picture of contradictions that made his head swim. And the inarticulate rage from yesterday was still close under the surface.

The long, flowing silver-grey dress clung precariously to the soft swells of her breasts. A diamond clipped just under her bosom was the only feature, and the dress fell from there to the floor in a swirling symphony of silk. What had made his trousers feel tight all morning was the fact that it had an artful thigh-high slit. So when she walked one long, lithe and luscious leg peeped out in all its lissome glory.

His decision, his announcement to her that he would take her as his mistress, was making it hard for him to rein in the desire. He cursed himself again for not just taking her last night. Why had he left her alone?

Uncomfortably, he knew why. Because too much had happened, too quickly. He'd reeled with the shock of coming face to face with her duplicity, with the hard evidence...the image of that white powder still made his stomach contract. Reeled at the fact that all along she *had* been playing him, with what he'd revealed about his mother, and reeled at how, even after all this, he could *still* want her. Even more. It burned him up inside.

He couldn't take his eyes off her. With her hair piled high, exposing a long graceful neck, she looked like a teenager playing dress-up. Her shoes were off, her legs were crossed, one small bare foot peeping out from under the folds of silk. Her brow was creased over her glasses in concentration as she read her book.

Who was she trying to kid?

After lunch, Sorcha waited for them to get the next set-up ready. She was congratulating herself on having managed to avoid Romain all morning, but every time she saw where they'd had lunch the previous day, on the other side of the courtyard, she felt ill. Clammy and sweaty.

She heard Dominic call for her impatiently. He had it in for her today, and she could only imagine that Lucy must have told him what she'd done. She prayed that he wouldn't make an issue of it. She should have guessed that things wouldn't be going her way...

Hours later everyone was crabby: a mixture of the dense, heavy heat and the jet lag which some were still suffering from. Dominic had become so unbearable that Sorcha felt compelled to go over to him and say something—anything, to get him to lay off. She'd even seen Romain raise a brow at one stage, when he'd been sharp to the point of rudeness. When she confronted him he turned on her, making her blanch, and real fear struck her. It was only then that she realised they were cut off from everyone else, behind a huge plant.

He gripped her arm at the elbow, drawing her further into seclusion, and Sorcha bit back a retort.

'How *dare* you play almighty God with Lucy? It's none of your business what—'

Sorcha refused to let the fear rise, to be bullied, and she rallied back. 'It *is* my business when it's offered to me, Dominic. And what are you doing, giving her that kind of stuff anyway? She's barely out of her teens.'

He smirked, and it was ugly. 'Yet she pleasures me every night like an adult.'

Sorcha felt bile rise, and tried to wrestle her arm away—but his wiry strength was too much.

'But you know, Sorch, I'd much prefer to taste your sweetness. Christian told me all about you…how sweet you taste…'

A black hole threatened to consume Sorcha. Her deepest, darkest fear was being articulated out loud, *here*, by this odious man.

'Come on, Sorch, just a kiss…'

He pulled her into his wiry body, and she struggled in earnest now. This was a nightmare. What had possessed her to think she could reason with someone like this?

Bending away so far that it felt her back might break, she still felt hot breath on her neck. Panic gripped her. She pushed against him. 'Dominic—*no!*'

'Come on…just pretend it's lover boy…'

His mouth touched her skin. She felt teeth. A wave of dizziness washed over her, and then in an instant he was gone, pulled back so brutally that she went forward with him, and would have fallen if Romain hadn't caught her, an arm holding her steady away from Dominic.

'This is not the time or place.' His voice was so chilling that Sorcha was reminded of the previous day. 'Now, go back out there and finish the job you've been paid to do.'

Dominic just nodded, a mottled flush on his cheeks, his eyes overbright. Sorcha couldn't believe it. He was high! How had she not even noticed?

When he had gone, Romain turned Sorcha to face him. She was shaking all over. He didn't allow it to move him. He was still hard and unrelenting.

'We'll talk about this later.'

He had a hand under her arm and was leading her back outside. Her neck still stung from where Dominic had practically bitten her, and she still couldn't believe it. Did Romain really think that he'd interrupted them lovemaking?

Forcing herself not to let a wave of self-pity engulf her, Sorcha called on all her professional pride and somehow got through the rest of the day. When they wrapped she stuck close to Val, and made sure she was on a boat with him. Dark shades covered her bruised eyes. Her mouth was a grim line. When she got off the boat and she heard a familiar voice behind her she stopped, but didn't turn around. Her slim shoulders were rigid with tension.

Romain came and stood in front of her. She could see the rest of the crew walking away towards the hotel.

'You can avoid me all you want, Sorcha, but ultimately you won't be able to. You know that, don't you? And you *will* tell me what was going on with Dominic.'

She said nothing. Didn't move. If she had looked she'd have seen his jaw clench angrily at her stony silence.

Romain could see her throat work. Dark shades covered her eyes, and he nearly moved to take them off but at the last minute didn't. Almost as though he was afraid of what he might see...?

Instead he cupped a hand around her jaw, felt the delicate line and saw a pulse jump in response.

'Be down in the lobby for dinner at seven.' His voice was silky, deadly. 'And if you're not I will come and get you.'

That evening Sorcha stepped out of the lift at seven on the dot. She was dressed traditionally in a *salwaar kameez* with her hair pulled back, plain hoop earrings, and she had her glasses on. Protective armour.

Romain watched her approach and felt the familiar tightening happen in his body at the way the black material clung and curved around her body, the tight trousers under the tunic making her legs look long and slim. *Tonight* he would have her. Make her pay.

To Sorcha's intense relief she saw the rest of the crew and remembered that they were all going for dinner together. A reprieve. She made for Val, seeking protection but Romain blocked her before she could get to him.

He could see the frustration on her face, but he took her arm, and unless she wanted to create a scene Sorcha would have to leave it there. He made a joke with Simon, and then led the way down the street to a beautiful restaurant on the shores of the lake.

When Sorcha saw that Romain meant to have her sit next to him, and that Dominic looked likely to be on the other side of her, it was too much. She didn't care. She reacted on pure, desperate impulse and grabbed Romain's hand, making him look at her with surprise, his dark brows drawing together.

She entreated with her eyes, with all she had. It was the first thing she'd said to him all day and her voice sounded unbearably husky. 'Please. I don't want to sit next to him.'

She couldn't stop a shudder running through her, and Romain's frown drew even deeper as he noticed the minute movement. He looked to his side and saw Dominic taking a seat. For some reason, and not wanting to look too closely at why, he just nodded perfunctorily and let himself sit between Dominic and Sorcha.

An hour later Sorcha was pushing food around her plate. It was still heaped high with food that she couldn't touch, because her insides were churning so much.

'Smile, Sorcha, you look as if you're going to the gallows. And you haven't eaten all day. You should make some effort.'

She cast a quick glance to Romain on her left. 'Don't tell me you're concerned?'

'Not at all,' he said easily, and draped an arm along the back of her chair, making her pulse trip predictably. 'You're going to need your energy for later…that's all.' And he took a studied sip from his wine glass.

Sorcha gripped the napkin that was on her lap and twisted it.

He got caught in a conversation with Simon across the table, and Sorcha turned with relief to Val, who was on her other side. He was looking at her with a concerned face.

'What's up, Sorch? Every time I look at you you're either flushed like you have a fever or deathly pale…'

She forced a smile. 'Nothing. Just tired, I guess.'

Val jerked his head in the direction of Romain. 'Well, he's been about as subtle as a dog marking his territory.'

Sorcha's spine straightened. 'I don't know what—'

Val snorted. '*Please.* From day one he's marked you as his.' He took her hand under the table and said in a serious voice under his breath, 'Sorch, I mean this in the best possible way, but you are not like the women he goes for. I've seen the casualties of that man dumped by the wayside, and it's not pretty.'

Sorcha felt hysteria not too far from the surface. 'Val—'

'Just…be careful. That's all I'm saying. I don't want to see you get hurt…'

As Val gave her hand a quick squeeze and turned away, Sorcha had to swallow painfully. *Too late for that.* If Romain had his way she'd become his mistress tonight, and be well on the way to becoming his next casualty.

With an abrupt movement she stood up. Romain seized her wrist in a lightning-fast grip. Nobody else seemed to have noticed, but she glared down at him. 'What do you think you're doing, Romain?'

'Where do you think you're going?'

'The toilet—if I may?' She arched a brow.

He glowered up at her, but finally released her and watched her every step of the way as she left.

When she came back he looked at her suspiciously. The reality was so far from what he obviously imagined it was laughable, and she wondered just what she was really doing protecting Lucy. Was the thought of Romain being antagonistic somehow easier to deal with than Romain charming her to seduce her? An uncomfortable prickling assailed her, and she knew she didn't want to look at that.

A splitting headache made her temples throb, and she knew it was from the tension and stress.

Romain looked at her as she pinched the bridge of her nose. He felt irritation rise. Big, wary blue eyes snagged his then, and his breath caught for a second in his throat. God, but she was beautiful.

Sorcha met his grey fathomless gaze head-on. She had to at least try. 'I'm going to go back to the hotel. I'm tired and I have a headache.'

Romain used every bit of will-power to control the carnal urge to just carry her off then and there. He would not let her reduce him to such base behaviour. He shook his head. 'You're not going anywhere until I say so, and I am not ready to leave.'

Sorcha leant in towards him, agitated. His gaze dropped to the shadowy line of her cleavage under the V of the top. His body hardened in anticipation.

'I'm not a prisoner, you know.'

He looked at her intently. 'No…there's another word for what you are…'

Sorcha sagged back and fell silent.

An hour later Sorcha looked around her in dismay. Somehow someone had persuaded everyone to go to a small bar not far from where they were staying, and even though she dreaded going back to the hotel, and hadn't really contemplated what would happen when she did, she wished she was anywhere but there. With everyone getting drunk around her—apart from Romain, of course, who was in complete control, and disconcertingly as at home here as he had been in five-star surroundings—Sorcha felt absurdly sober.

He was talking to Simon at the bar. The laughing and shouting was grating on her nerves. And a jukebox had started up playing Bollywood songs. Normally she loved them, but right now they sliced through her head. Dominic and Lucy were messing with the playlist, and Sorcha had just about had enough.

She got up and went to leave, not caring any more what Romain might say. Sure enough, just as she was about to walk out, she felt a firm grip on her hand. It set little fires racing up and down her arm.

'Look, Romain, I've had enough. I've got a splitting headache.'

The noise *was* intense with the music playing. Romain was about to say something, but just as he opened his mouth to speak the song on the jukebox finished. And before he could say a word, into the brief silent interlude between that and the next song Dominic's voice sounded across the small bar, clear as a bell and loudly indiscreet.

So drunk or high that he was unaware of the music stopping, he was shouting into Lucy's ear. '…can't believe the stupid bitch took that coke off you and gave you a lecture. Who does she think she is? Holier-than-thou cow. Surprised she didn't go running straight to lover boy to dob you in…'

Dominic kept talking, totally oblivious to the fact that everyone had gone completely quiet and was privy to his conversation.

As if in slow motion, Sorcha watched Romain take in the words, the expressions crossing his face. With a strangled cry she pulled her hand free and ran.

CHAPTER TWELVE

'SORCHA, let me in.'

Sorcha stood in her room, arms around her belly, her breath still harsh. She'd run all the way back to the hotel. When his knock had come on her door, she'd jumped. Maybe if she just—

'Sorcha, I know you're in there. And if you don't open the door I will knock it down.'

She could hear it in his voice. He would. She walked slowly towards the door and inexplicably felt as if shifting sands were beneath her feet. Her mind raced. What did this mean? Did he believe what he'd heard? Her headache pounded with a vengeance.

With a deep, shaky breath, her heart pumping, she slid the bolt back and opened the door. Romain loomed tall and dark and powerful. Sorcha stepped back. She couldn't take her eyes from his, they were staring at her with such intensity.

Romain came in and shut the door behind him, resting his tall frame against it. His face was implacable. He folded his arms across his chest. In dark trousers and a dark shirt he was overpoweringly sexy and dangerous to Sorcha. She backed away, further into the room.

'Why?' was all he said at first.

Sorcha fancied for a moment that she'd missed the first part of his question. When her mouth opened but nothing came out, he stepped away from the door.

He spoke again. 'Why did you do it? Why did you protect her?'

Sorcha's head swam. He *believed* her?

'I... I...' She shook her head. It was too much to take in.

He started pacing back and forth, and the tension in his form radiated out from his body and enveloped her. She felt the bed behind her and sagged onto it, looking at him helplessly.

He stopped in front of her and she had to look up.

'Sorcha. Please tell me why you would protect Lucy. Why didn't you just tell me that *she* was the one with the drugs?'

Something desperate in his voice caught on her insides and twisted them. She shook her head again and gave a tiny shrug.

'I'm sorry...' Her voice came out faintly. 'I just...'

He came down on his haunches before her. Sorcha gulped at the light in his eyes. With just one low lamp on in the room, all the lines in his face were thrown into sharp relief.

'It looked so bad. And I thought...I didn't think you would believe me. Not after...not after everything else. I didn't want her to get into trouble. She's just a kid.' Sorcha shrugged again and said huskily, 'I guess I felt I had nothing to lose.'

He looked at her for a long moment and then stood again, hands on hips. 'I can't believe you let me think that... *Why* would you do it? Why wouldn't you defend yourself?'

Why would you let me believe that about you? The words resounded in Romain's head, compounding the awful clawing guilt he felt. The shock from hearing Dominic's careless words still reverberated through his body. The awful sinking in his belly when he'd confronted the pair as soon as Sorcha had left the bar. He'd known the truth as soon as he'd really focused on them. The scene with her and Dominic earlier flashed into his head, and the other man's behaviour all day...it all took on a new light. He felt sick.

Sorcha stood then too, and paced away from him, agitation

marking her jerky movements. She turned and faced him. 'Admit it, Romain, catching me with a gram of coke in my back pocket is something you've imagined could be a possibility from the start—isn't it?'

He looked uncomfortable for a second, and nodded briefly, tersely.

She threw her arms wide and laughed harshly. 'See? I knew how bad it looked, and I *knew* what had happened—never mind how it looked to you! And what if I *had* blamed Lucy yesterday? How would that have appeared on top of everything else? To be blaming someone as young and innocent as her…'

His mouth twisted. Who is anything but…'

Sorcha smiled a little sadly. 'Lucy *is* just young and silly. Dominic has turned her head, and in this business it's all too easy to follow someone's lead.' Sorcha's voice grew hesitant. 'What are you going to do with them?'

Romain ran a hand through his hair and looked very weary all of a sudden. 'They're in no state to be coherent now. I'm going to fire Dominic…' He shrugged. 'And give Lucy the option of staying on or going. As you say, she is young, and thanks to you she didn't actually take anything. Is that OK with you?'

'That's fair, I think,' Sorcha said quietly, a little stunned that he was giving her any say. 'Dominic was the real problem, not her, and maybe this will teach her a lesson.'

He moved closer to her and Sorcha's breath snagged. The energy in the room became heavy with *something*.

'When you asked me that day in Dublin if I'd ever believe you'd never touched drugs…'

Sorcha held her breath.

'You haven't, have you?'

There was a huge black hole opening up under Sorcha. Somewhere she'd avoided visiting for a long time. And for the first time she knew she couldn't avoid it. Very slowly, she shook her head, her eyes never leaving his. She saw some strength in them, something to cling onto. Defied telling herself that it was *him*.

He came closer. 'So what happened in London?'

A bubble seemed to surround them. The outside world didn't exist. Sorcha was looking into grey eyes so intense that she was losing her soul.

'I told you about what happened after my father died…'

Romain nodded, coming closer again, not breaking eye contact. Not letting her be distracted.

And in that moment, all of a mere split second in time, Sorcha made a subconscious decision.

'It wasn't as simple as that.'

'Go on.'

Her hands twisted in front of her. 'After my father died I found my birth certificate in his study at home. I found out that my mother…the person I'd always known as my mother…was in fact *not*.'

There. It was out. And Romain was still looking at her, moving ever closer. Soon he would be able to reach out and touch her. That made Sorcha speak again, as if to keep him back. Space.

'My real mother was in fact my father's secretary. Irish, not Spanish. She had no other family and she died in childbirth with me. When the hospital called looking for her next of kin, who she had listed as my father, my mother found out what had been going on. *She* hadn't been able to have any more children after complications with my brother's birth, so she decided to take me in as her own.'

Her face was so pale it looked like alabaster in the dim light. 'The pain of not being able to have more children far outweighed the pain of her husband's infidelity.'

Romain was so close she could breathe in his smell, and she felt dizzy. Even dizzier when he took her hand and led her over to the couch in the corner to sit down. Sorcha only noticed then how shaky she was.

'And that day in London? When the photographers found you unconscious in the street?'

Sorcha felt numb. The words came out, but she wasn't really aware of saying them and knew that she had gone inwards somewhere.

'That day...was the last straw.' She couldn't look at him. Couldn't launch straight into a bald explanation without going back a little first.

'I'd felt so all over the place, and Katie had done her best to try and comfort me, but...' She looked up then, and Romain had to take in a breath when he saw the pain in her eyes, 'Can you imagine what it was like to discover that you hadn't been who you thought you were? I spent my whole life believing that woman was my mother—that I was half-Spanish...' She gave a strangled half-laugh. 'I mean it's ridiculous. If you saw my brother he looks more Spanish than Irish, and me...' She gestured with a shaking hand to herself.

She took a shuddering breath and went on, too far gone to stop now. 'I shut Katie out. Completely. She was my best friend and I ignored her for weeks. She knew those guys were bad news. And so did I, underneath it all, but I was just...so angry, so confused. I can see now that it was a cry for attention. My crush on Christian was all the kick I needed to be led astray. But, despite my brave show of rebellion, I was terrified of them, really. Of that world, the hedonistic way they behaved.'

'What happened...?'

'We were at a party in another model's house.' Her eyes beseeched him. She wanted him to understand. 'I felt so lost in my desperation to feel part of *something*—anything. I'd managed to convince them I was one of them...but in reality I was hiding drinks, throwing them into plants, pretending to get drunk...If they took drugs I'd act all blasé like I wasn't in the mood. As if they bored me. I hadn't slept with Christian, and was feeling more and more uncomfortable with it all…*him*…and he was getting increasingly pushy.' She took a deep breath. 'At the party, I overheard him tell a friend about how he'd spiked another girl's drink, and then…' she shuddered minutely '…what he'd done to her. I knew right then that I wanted out. It had gone too far. But, as if he *knew*, he came and handed me a drink. He stood there…wouldn't leave until I'd drunk it. By then, I was really terrified. I could feel the effects straight away. I pretended I had to go to the loo and called Katie…'

Sorcha sighed deeply and felt a calmness move through her whole body, as if telling this was somehow exorcising something within her. Romain was still looking at her intently. She seemed to draw strength from it, from him.

'When Katie came I was unconscious in a bedroom…on my own. Somehow she managed to get me outside. She had to leave me for a minute, while she looked out for the ambulance… The paparazzi knew the house as a hangout for models, and they were lying in wait—especially so soon after that other girl—'

'I remember,' he said grimly.

She looked at him warily. 'That's it…That's the sordid and very sad truth. I was naïve, silly—'

Romain put a finger to her mouth. 'No. You were reacting to extreme circumstances. They merely offered you the comfort you thought you needed. But all along, Sorcha, you stayed true to yourself.'

She looked at him and felt like crying. To distract him and herself from the rising tide of emotion, she got up and went into the bathroom.

Romain watched her go, his whole world imploding from the inside out.

She returned and held out the small bottle of pills. He frowned and took them, looking at her warily.

'Homeopathic tablets for prickly heat rash. I take them whenever I go to a hot country because I react to the sun. That's the sum total of my drug use—apart from perhaps paracetamol. I've never even smoked a cigarette.'

He handed her back the bottle and stood stiffly. He'd never felt at such a loss. Had never been in this situation.

His accent was pronounced. 'Sorcha…'

Suddenly she couldn't bear to see him like this. She was just as much to blame. 'Romain, it's fine—'

'It's not fine.' His hand slashed the air. 'If I'd known these things…'

'You didn't know because I didn't tell you—or try to defend myself.'

He looked at her darkly. In a way it had been so much easier yesterday, when he had believed her guilt, to take her in his arms and tell her that he was going to take her as his mistress. But now…things had shifted. Were different. Or were they?

He reached out a hand to tuck some hair behind her ear. He saw how her body tensed, her breathing changed, her eyes widened. Stepping close to her, breathing in her own evocative scent, he could feel it wrapping around his senses, making his body tight with need. His hands lifted and he took off her glasses.

Sorcha's hands came up automatically, but Romain was too quick. The glasses were gone. On the couch beside them. Then his hand was at the back of her head, threading through her hair, unravelling the strands, taking out the elastic band. She put a hand on his to stop him—and that was a mistake. Because she felt the strong bones, the hairs on his skin, felt the pulse thundering. Like her own. Her mouth felt dry.

'What are you doing?' she croaked out.

With a fluid, easy move he pulled her into his body. He stared down into her eyes with an ardour that made it hard to concentrate, that drove everything out of her mind. And she found herself clinging onto it.

She asked again, 'What are you doing?'

His answer was to pull her into him even more, tight against his body, where it felt as if they were joined at every conceivable point.

He bent his head and his breath feathered close to her ear, making her skin tingle all over. 'I told you I'd take you as my mistress…though I meant it as a form of punishment… I still want you, Sorcha…but this time it'll be purely for pleasure.'

And before she could emit a word or a sound he'd taken her mouth with his, and nothing existed but this—the physical reality of Romain de Valois kissing her as if she was the only woman on the planet. Everything was in that kiss. The apology he hadn't articulated, the pent-up passion that had existed since the moment she'd seen him across the room in New York.

Sorcha felt her insides melt and come back to quivering life. The enormity of what she'd just shared was too much…too cerebral. She needed the physical, *welcomed* the physical. Her arms went up and twined around his neck. She imagined that not even a feather would pass between them. And *there*, against the apex of her thighs, she could feel him, hot and heavy and hard.

'Oh…' she breathed, her own body reacting with spectacular swiftness. She could feel herself grow damp, and colour scorched her cheeks.

He pulled back and brushed a tendril of hair off her cheek. '*Oh*…is right…' he said huskily.

And then, as if answering some plea she wasn't even aware of articulating, he bent his head and his mouth met hers again. There was no hesitation, no thought other than *this*. Now. Here. This man. This insanity where all rational thought flew out of the window.

She groaned deep in her throat when she felt him pull her even tighter, deeper. Cradled in his lap, she moved her hips in a minutely experimental gesture. He pulled back, breathing raggedly.

'Do you know what you're doing?'

She looked up, mute, her lips feeling plump and bruised, tingling. She longed to taste him again.

With one move he'd taken her into his arms and walked over to the bed which was highlighted by the moonlight streaming into the room. He laid her down and she watched as he undid the buttons on his shirt, then his torso was revealed, and even though she'd seen it before she took an intake of breath at the sheer perfection.

'Now you... I need to see you...'

Sorcha felt like a twig in a burning rapid. Something was trying to impinge on her consciousness, but she couldn't let it. Mustn't let it.

Very reverently, Romain came down beside her and started to lift the tunic of the *salwaar kameez*. Sorcha shifted her hips and lifted her arms, and it slipped over her head. Now her torso was bare, apart from her black lacy bra. Her skin looked incredibly white against the material. Romain was staring at her, and she felt her nipples tighten painfully.

He ran a hand over her stomach, to rest it under the curve of one breast. Her breath was growing more and more ragged. Keeping his hand there, he bent his head again, and when their lips met she strained upwards, her tongue finding and meeting his, tangling and tasting in a feverish dance. And when his hand moved up to cup her breast, to run a thumb-pad over one engorged tip, she almost cried out. She had *never* felt this before. And it was here, with this man, where her awakening was taking place.

With those thoughts reality intruded.

Romain's mouth was blazing a trail of hot kisses down her neck, down to where she wanted nothing more than for him to find that tingling point, suck it into his mouth. And she knew if he did that she'd be lost.

Going against every cell in her body, with weak, ineffectual arms, she started to push at Romain's formidable shoulders. For a moment he did nothing, his mouth still making its way ever downwards and Sorcha despaired of getting him to move. She just knew he had to…she wasn't ready for this yet. There was no doubting where this was going to end if she didn't stop it now.

'No… *No!* Romain—stop, please…'

One hand was around her ribs, just under her breast, and his mouth was a breath away from one aching hard nipple. She could have wept with frustration—but there was too much at stake and if they went any further she'd have to explain…the worst bit of all…

CHAPTER THIRTEEN

'WHAT—what is it?' His voice was hoarse, his breathing jagged. She could feel his bare chest rise and fall against her side.

She turned her head, fighting back sudden tears. Then she pushed his hands away and sat up, moving back, taking her top and putting it over her breasts. Her hair fell around her shoulders.

What the hell was going on? Romain couldn't figure the lightning-fast change and went to reach for Sorcha again, his fingers itching with the need to touch, caress. He was on fire.

She scooted back even further, her eyes huge in the dim light. 'No! Don't touch me.'

Such panic laced her voice that Romain jackknifed off the bed and switched on another lamp, coming to stand with hands on his hips. He looked angry and aroused and very intimidating. Sorcha swallowed miserably.

'I'm sorry…I just can't do this. With you.'

He ran a hand through his hair. 'What are you talking about Sorcha? If not me then who? I don't see you burning up for anyone else's touch.'

And the thought of her doing this with anyone else made him almost incandescent with rage.

She closed her eyes for a second to block out his potent image. Of course she didn't *burn up* for anyone else. There never had been anyone else, and at this moment in time she couldn't ever imagine feeling this way about anyone else. But he couldn't know how deeply he'd drawn her into his web of seduction.

'I just can't…'

Romain was pacing up and down. His shirt was flapping around his chest and Sorcha wished he'd stop and do it up— anything so that she wouldn't have to look at him and get heated up all over again. He went and leant against the patio door, arms crossed, muscles bunching in a way that made him even more provocative. Sorcha avoided his gaze, holding her top in front of her like a lifeline.

He stepped out of the shadow and he saw how Sorcha shrank back into the bed ever so slightly. He also saw the flare in her eyes, and the way they ran hungrily down his chest. Her hands were shaking. But, as he came closer he saw the shadows in those clear blue depths. That vulnerability hit him square between the eyes—*again*.

'Why, Sorcha? Just tell me why?'

Sorcha looked at him then, and fire lit her eyes. She felt so transparent at this moment, and she hated that this man had done it to her. Somewhere along the way he'd morphed from arch nemesis into…something else, and the thought of what that might be made her very scared.

'Why do you have to know everything about me?' she asked jaggedly, conveniently forgetting her own eager response just moments before. 'Can't you just let me be?'

He came down on the bed beside her, and held her with one arm when she would have scooted away. It was warm and heavy against her skin. She could already feel how her body was responding—the tightness in her belly, her lips tingling in anticipation of his touching hers again—and she didn't just want him to kiss her mouth. She wanted him to kiss her…*everywhere*.

She closed her eyes weakly. Tonight seemed to be the night when some god had determined that she would be torn down and built up again, and she knew that somehow some very cowardly part of her had clung to his bad opinion of her, had taken Lucy's guilt on as her own in order to avoid this... Because if he suspected the worst, then he'd never see the real her.

She opened her eyes. His face was too close, but she knew he wouldn't be moving anywhere.

'Dites moi pourquoi...?'

Tell me why...?

Sorcha turned her head away. She felt as bared as she'd ever been, because what she was about to tell him *no one* knew. Words came out in a rush. Her voice was none too steady

'Because...I haven't done this before...and I don't even know...if I'm a virgin.'

She felt tears spring into her eyes and shut them tight. Her jaw wobbled. She'd heard his swift intake of breath and then nothing. Maybe he'd go? Leave? Maybe taking a virgin was a step too far for someone like—?

A warm hand came to her jaw and pulled it round gently. She kept her eyes squeezed shut.

'Sorcha. Open your eyes.' His voice was husky.

She opened her eyes and knew they must be swimming as he was a blur in her vision.

He was looking at her with that intense ardour again, and it confused her.

'Do you want to tell me why you think you might not be a virgin?'

She shook her head.

He came up closer, dwarfing her body with his own, and her eyes followed him helplessly.

'I think it's time you told someone. It might as well be me.'

His words were so matter-of-fact that they actually distracted her. Sorcha looked at him, as if searching for some hidden meaning, and finally she realised that he was right. Sooner or later she would be in this situation again and right now her body was burning up for a fulfilment that only he could provide.

She took a deep breath before she spoke her next words. 'When I came to in the hospital when the drug had worn off, I knew that I'd blacked out for a bit before Katie got to me. I tried to stay awake for as long as I could.' She shrugged. 'I never said anything…but just…always had a fear that Christian, or someone, might have done something to me and I didn't know…'

He looked at her for a long moment. She couldn't read his expression, but at least it didn't have the horror in it that she'd always imagined she'd be faced with. But then he moved back, and Sorcha felt so bereft it was like a pain cramping her belly.

He got off the bed, his face all shadows and harsh angles in the light. Powerful arms folded across his chest. Driven away again.

Sorcha's body still throbbed and pulsed. But she had to concede the thought of her being a virgin was obviously too much. *She* couldn't even take in all of what she'd just told him, or how wantonly she'd acted… Her whole brain seized up in embarrassment at the thought. Awkwardly she slipped her top back on and stood up from the bed too.

'I'm sorry,' she said stiffly. 'I should have told you before we let things…'

Romain stepped out of the shadows that had concealed him. He'd needed some kind of protection to hide the extent of the pain he knew must be etched on his face at having to stop, his arousal not having abated one bit. And to hide the shock…the need he'd had to comfort her. To think that she was a *virgin* made his blood fizz and jump. The urge he'd had to press her back down and subdue her fears with kisses had been almost overwhelming. But how could he do such a thing after everything she had just told him?

For the first time ever he was putting a woman's emotional needs first, and it made him reel.

He strolled towards her doing up his shirt. She looked so vulnerable and so damned beautiful that his fingers shook on the buttons. He stopped in front of her and willed the heat in his body to cool. He tipped her face up to his and had to stifle a groan. 'Sorcha. I think you've been through a lot.' His mouth twisted. 'Much of it at my hands. Why don't you get some rest?'

That was about all he could manage—because if he didn't leave right now, then he'd tip her back and take her, ready or not. With that in mind, and staying well away from any erogenous zone, he pressed a swift kiss to her forehead.

Sorcha watched him walk away. Bereft didn't even come into it. She felt as if he were tearing out her heart and carrying it with him. Again she had that feeling of needing the physical to counteract the mental...If he walked out through that door, the bubble would burst—whatever *thing* it was that had just happened to make her tell all. To trust him.

He was at the door, and Sorcha felt something fierce and elemental run through her. Needing what she knew only he could offer her, emboldened by everything she'd just shared, she called his name softly. So softly that he didn't stop. His hand was on the knob. But then, as if her call had wound its way through the air between them and reached out to him, he halted for a second.

'Romain...' she said, more strongly this time.

He turned and looked at her. She saw the lines on his face, as if he was making a supreme effort, and she prayed it was what she thought. She'd already revealed so much she felt a little invincible. Bold.

'Don't you *want* to make love to me?'

He turned around and rested his whole body back against the door. He made some kind of inarticulate sound. And then he said, very hoarsely, 'More than you can imagine.'

'Then don't leave.'

'Sorcha...' he said helplessly.

She gripped the bedpost. 'Please, Romain. Don't leave. I need you to...make love to me. I need *you*.' Aghast at her nerve, she said, 'If I could move I'd come over there, but I'm afraid if I do I'll fall down...'

Her heart-aching honesty reached out and grabbed him by the scruff of the neck. As if he'd even stood a chance when he'd heard that soft *Romain*… A heated urgency moved him, a deep throbbing in his veins, and he pushed off the door and within seconds was *there*—Sorcha in his arms, mouths fused, her hands wrapped tight around his waist. He could feel her whole body tremble against his.

He pulled back and looked down for just a moment. He tried to will some sanity into the situation. 'Sorcha…are you sure?'

She just nodded, then reached a hand up and around the back of his head, pulling him back down to her. 'I've never been more sure of anything in my life.'

That was it. He was gone. Had just been given licence to sate the burning ache in his loins. Before he could even think about it Sorcha had reached down and pulled off her top, dropping it to the floor.

Romain undid the buttons on his shirt, his eyes never leaving hers. With his shirt gone, he pushed her gently back onto the bed. His hand moved down her shoulder, taking her bra strap with it, his other hand taking the other one. He reached under and behind, undid the clasp, and then the wisp of material was gone.

He hovered over her like a Greek god and said, 'Sorcha…just trust me. I won't hurt you.'

She nodded jerkily and fought back tears. His words made a faint alarm go off somewhere, but it was drowned out in the heady clamour of her pulse. This was so far removed from what she had envisaged this moment to be like. Nowhere to be seen was the vaguely insipid man she'd always imagined; gentle, un-assuming, sensitive. Instead it was *this* man, who had all those qualities but packaged so much more dynamically. He was larger than life and he had turned her life upside down and inside out. In the space of what must in reality have been just an hour, she'd bared her soul—and now she was about to bare her body completely.

The moment was so huge that she felt faint. To drive it away she reached up and pulled his head down to hers, her mouth searching blindly and finding his, their tongues meeting and meshing. And soon the only thing she could think about was the need that was building inside her that had to be assuaged—*now*.

She felt him undo the tie of her trousers and slip them down her legs. She kicked them off. Then he dealt with his own trousers. And briefs. As he came back down alongside her she caught a glimpse of the visible evidence of his arousal and her insides contracted.

Somehow her pants were gone. She couldn't even remember if she had slipped them off or if Romain had. Their mouths clung. His hand smoothed its way down over her heated flesh, over the swell of her breast, fingers teasing the turgid tip. She rocked against him, seeking and finding that hardness. Hesitantly, she drifted a hand down between them, revelling in the feel of his smooth, silky skin. It felt hot to the touch.

She reached round and felt his behind, one taut, perfect globe, and then one muscled strong thigh. When she felt a hand exploring her belly, going lower, her breath and her wandering hand stopped. With infinite gentleness Romain's fingers threaded through the hair that hid her sex and delved into that place which was moist with her desire.

Her head fell back and he watched her face as his fingers sought and found the secrets of her body. Unconsciously she moved against his hand, seeking more. His thumb rubbed against her clitoris, fingers thrusting in and out. Her hand gripped his thigh and brokenly she begged him. 'Please... Romain...'

So he did. He brought her over the edge. Felt the uncontrollable spasms of her body around his fingers. She trapped his hand with her legs, her body suddenly acutely sensitive and looked up, her cheeks flushed.

Romain smiled and took her hand, brought it down to touch

him. Her eyes widened as, with his hand over hers, he let her encircle the hard shaft. 'See what you do to me?'

Heat. All Sorcha could think of was heat and molten blood running through her veins. The desire was building again, spiralling, tightening every part of her. Romain came over her, one thigh between her legs, opening her up to him. Her hand fell away from him as he moved over her fully and the potent heat of him lay between her legs. Where her universe seemed to end and begin.

He pressed a kiss to her lips, a lingering one, and as he did, with his chest against hers, he slid into her tight opening. Sorcha gasped against his mouth. But he didn't break the kiss, and slid a little deeper. Although there was no physical barrier to impede his entry, it was clear that no one had penetrated her like this before now. A fierce, elemental wave of pride and ownership washed through Romain. He finally took his mouth from hers and looked down. He wanted to see her face when he took her, when he was so embedded within her that she wouldn't be able to think of anything else, *anyone* else.

He felt her hands on his back, her legs come up, and with that movement he couldn't help himself sinking deeper. A brief spasm crossed her face and Romain halted immediately, his heart hammering. 'Are you OK?'

She nodded and smiled. 'More than OK... You feel... amazing.'

And then he surged forward again and was there. At the core. At the centre of everything. Sheathed completely in a hot velvet glove of tightness. Holding back from pulling out and driving in again as hard as his body demanded, he controlled his movements. There would be time for that later. When he took her again. At the thought of that, unbelievably his body hardened even more. It made his head spin.

With steady thrusts he pierced Sorcha's flesh again and again. Until she thrashed beneath him. Until her hands pulled at his arms, his shoulders. Until her head was flung back and her chest thrust up and he felt the ripples along his length that told him of her fast-approaching release.

And, because it had taken more strength than he possessed, for those few final moments he gave in to the elemental waves building in his own body. When she cried out her release his own body contracted and then spilled its life seed into her. He slumped over her, breathing harshly.

When Sorcha woke, some hours later, the light of the rising dawn was stealing into the room. She couldn't move. She'd never felt so heavy. Never felt so at peace. Never had a naked man wrapped around her back before, with one big hand cupping her breast…. She felt an inordinate feeling of well-being rush through her. She moved her bottom a little and heard a sleep-rough growl in her ear.

'Stop that. You're going to be sore today…and if you keep doing that I won't be able to stop myself.'

Her cheeks flooded with warmth. Already she could feel his erection pressing insistently against her.

So she turned and faced him. Sleepy grey eyes regarded her with heavy-lidded sensuality. Emotion welled through her like a tidal wave, and she had to stop her hand from reaching out and tracing every line of his exquisite face. It looked even darker, shadowed with a little stubble.

How had they got here? Sorcha coloured again. Well, she knew how they had got *here*, but she had a flash of memory back to New York, remembering the intense attraction and also the intense antipathy. His extreme arrogance. Another wave of tenderness made her feel dizzy for a second, and in that moment she knew it was a much bigger emotion.

It was *love*.

She loved him. He had been witness to her ultimate capitulation. And her redemption. He had made her whole again—given her back her sanity. She now knew that eight years ago *nothing* had happened without her knowledge, and that made her feel giddy with love for this man. It also made her reach out, despite her best intentions, and curl a hand around his neck, bringing his face close to hers.

'Sorcha, what are—?'

She pressed a sweet kiss to his mouth.

And then, so suddenly that it felt almost violent, he pulled back, those grey eyes coldly expressionless. And in a split second he was out of the bed and walking towards the bathroom.

Sorcha lay frozen. The chill in his eyes just now had made a direct hit into her very bones. Snatches and snippets of the previous night sank heavily into her consciousness. She heard the hiss of the shower. Could imagine that tall, lean, finely honed body standing underneath the spray, water sluicing down…

What was she doing? Daydreaming, mooning… Did she want to be lying here like some kind of lovestruck groupie when he got out? There had been no tender words this morning—nothing to indicate that this was anything but normal practice for him. The morning after for him was something he was used to. He'd merely done what he'd set out to do—taken her to bed. Hadn't he asserted his intention to do that *no matter what*?

Lying there, stricken, she had to recall with abject horror how she'd told him…*everything*. Absolutely *everything*. There wasn't a part of her, mentally or physically, that this man didn't know. She recalled her rush of love just moments ago and cringed. She'd projected so much more onto their union than he had.

She heard the shower stop. And, with a reflex action so swift she surprised herself, she leapt out of bed, put on her clothes, and was about to leave the room when, with her hand on the door, she realised she was in her own room.

'Going somewhere?' a mocking voice drawled from behind her.

CHAPTER FOURTEEN

SORCHA turned around, her cheeks burning. She felt stiff—literally and emotionally. Nakedly vulnerable.

'I'd like you to leave, please. I have plans for the day, and I have to pack and get ready for Spain.'

She avoided looking at him as he was dressed in nothing but a tiny towel. Baring everything except… Her cheeks burned again as he quite calmly dropped the towel and started to pull on his clothes. He didn't seem to be fazed by her coolness. And that only confirmed her worst fears, suspicions.

He dressed and strolled towards her. But when she would have turned the knob and opened the door he stopped her hand with his. Snaking his other hand around the back of her head, he tilted her head and dropped his mouth onto hers, stealing a kiss that was hot and made her yearn to lean into him, her body already remembering, wanting, aching all over again. But then…he let her go. She opened dazed eyes. His were cool, alert. It almost seemed as if last night had never happened—as if she'd dreamt up Dominic's timely confession, as if the physical had been the only thing.

'As it happens, I have to go on to Madrid ahead of the crew for meetings. I have my private jet waiting at a nearby airfield. Come with me.'

At that moment, as if she'd even needed it, Val's words came back to her like an insidious poison. She was another casualty. Maybe not right at this moment, but any day now.

She shook her head vehemently. 'No. I've booked a day trip. I'll travel with the crew tomorrow.'

He regarded her, and she focused on a point just over his shoulder. She was immovable, tense, waiting for his insistence—which she was sure was coming.

Romain still regarded her. He knew he could persuade her but at that moment something flashed into his head and he went cold.

Sorcha sensed it and looked up, her eyes wary. Guarded.

'We didn't use protection last night.'

Sorcha saw the horrified expression on his face. Felt guilty even though she'd been the innocent one. She couldn't believe she'd let him take such a liberty without even noticing herself. But then, she hadn't been aware of much…

She feigned all the insouciance she could muster. 'Well, I'm assuming that you're clean. And I'm due my period…' She faltered because it inexplicably hurt to admit it. 'Today, actually…' She fought down the bizarre emotion that ripped through her and tossed her head. 'So you don't have to worry…'

Romain was implacable. He just bit out a curt, slightly haughty, 'Of course I'm clean. And that's good…about your period…'

With the atmosphere humming tensely, he opened the door and left. No kiss. Nothing.

Sorcha sagged back when he'd left. His eagerness to leave had left her slightly stunned. The man had her upside down and inside out. And how *could* she have been so remiss as to forget about one of the most basic fundamentals—protection?

Romain looked out of the tiny window by his seat in the luxurious Learjet. In his hand he cradled a glass of neat whisky. The ground dropped away beneath him and he felt numbed, removed from everything. One thing concerned him. One thing consumed him—his body and his mind.

Sorcha Murphy.

He still couldn't believe how wrong he'd got it. *And how right*. He still hadn't really allowed the enormity of what she'd shared with him last night to sink in. The enormity of how he'd contributed to her awful pain eight years ago. How philosophical she'd been, how little anger she'd held…when she had every right to rant and rail. It shook him to his core. And then to find she'd been a virgin…and that he was her first—

His hand clenched around the glass even tighter, knuckles white. He fought to control the intense desire that made his body react like an over-eager teenager. What little control he might have possessed around her before had long gone.

When she had pressed that kiss to his mouth this morning two things had driven him from the bed so fast his head had spun. The first was that he'd never woken wrapped around a woman, *aching* to have her again and again. And the second was that he'd seen something in her eyes that had made him feel something he hadn't felt in a long, long time. Something he'd recognised. Because once he had been the one who had bared his soul, shared his secrets, shared his dreams with someone—and they had not trod softly on them…in fact they had ground them out and used them against him.

But he pictured her face as she had stood by the door…when she'd given him her assurance that she wasn't likely to become pregnant. Sorcha Murphy had looked anything but delicate, fragile, vulnerable. With any other woman he had clarity, he was removed, objective, never so lost in the passion that he became careless.

His hand clenched tighter on the glass. He stopped the churning in his mind but couldn't control his body, which ached to possess her again. His head throbbed.

Sorcha was bone-weary. Everyone was feeling it—along with the long transatlantic journey they'd just made the day before.

Today, in Madrid's main square, a huge crowd had turned up to watch them filming. It was a sequence in which she and Zane joined in with old people waltzing in the square. They were doing it for the last time, and again Sorcha couldn't help her eyes searching…seeking…looking for one person. She felt empty inside. She'd known he was due to be at meetings but still, she had expected—didn't want to say *hoped*—he'd turn up. Was he already off with another woman? She had it bad, and Val's warning kept sounding in her head like a claxon.

'OK, guys—that's a wrap in Madrid. Well done. Travel day tomorrow to Paris. We're leaving at midday sharp.'

Sorcha breathed a sigh of relief and smiled tiredly at Zane. The atmosphere on set had been a million times better since Dominic had disappeared, and a new photographer had arrived to meet them here in Spain. Lucy had obviously had her dressing down from Romain and decided to stay. She'd apologised to Sorcha the previous day, coming to her room not long after Romain had left.

The cars took them back to their sumptuous hotel on a quiet street nearby, and Sorcha took a long, relaxing bath. At least she had something to look forward to for the evening. She pushed all thoughts of Romain out of her head.

An hour later, dressed in a knee-length silk flowery dress and a cardigan, with flat shoes, her hair still damp, and dark glasses, Sorcha emerged from the hotel armed with her guidebook and a map. As she turned to her left and began to walk she didn't see the sleek car pull up, or Romain uncoil from the back seat, see *her* and, with his brows pulling into a frown, dismiss the car and start to follow her.

The tiredness he'd been feeling in every bone had vanished as soon as Romain saw Sorcha emerge from the hotel before him. But she hadn't seen him. She was engrossed in a map and guidebook. It made him feel pettishly impotent. He was used to women looking out for him, waiting for him...*welcoming him*. So he'd decided to follow her—and he didn't look at how this behaviour was such an anomaly to his normal *modus operandi*. It had been too long since India, and the way her hips swayed in the silk dress was making his body react with an annoying degree of uncontrollable arousal.

He caught another man do a double take as she passed him, and he had to fight the urge to go and claim her, take her hand...

As he struggled to regain control he had to reason with himself. He'd been with women who were more beautiful. Women who were sleek, sophisticated, *experienced*. but there was something—*many things*—about Sorcha that he couldn't figure out. Was that it? Maybe she was just playing him as he'd never been played before? Maybe he was the one who was looking like the complete fool, despite her comparative innocence?

That thought made him stop in his tracks for a second, and he realised he was following a woman like some mad, deranged stalker. When she disappeared from view he fought an intense battle...and let her go.

That night, however, Romain found himself sitting in the dim light of the hotel foyer. He'd knocked on Sorcha's door. She hadn't been there. She was obviously still out. Feeling more and more agitated, kicking himself for not following her earlier, Romain now nursed a stiff whisky and waited.

And then, with that husky laugh preceding her, he saw her walk in through the open doors. But she wasn't alone. She was with a man. A tall, dark, very handsome man. Recognition hovered on the periphery of Romain's stunned brain, but Sorcha looked up into the man's face and laughed again, looking so *happy*, and then *he* looked down at her as if—

Romain had jerked his body out of the seat so fast his head swam, and the movement brought Sorcha's eyes to his. They widened. Her mouth opened. Her cheeks flushed.

He closed the space between them so fast that Sorcha felt dizzy.

'Romain…' Her heart leapt with a joy she tried to crush. She took in his features as avidly as if they'd been separated for weeks, not just a couple of days.

The man beside her took her arm out of his and Sorcha's focus came back. She saw how Romain transferred his gaze to glare at him. They matched each other height for height, build for build.

A dryly amused, deep voice spoke from beside her. 'Sorch, do you want to introduce me to this gentleman who looks as if he wants to kill me?'

Somehow she found her voice.

'Romain de Valois, please meet Tiarnan Quinn…my brother.'

The rush of relief that ripped through Romain nearly floored him. Tiarnan must have seen something, because he deftly manoeuvred the three of them over to a couch and ordered a round of drinks.

Moments later Romain still felt a little shaky, and sipped at his drink with studied carefulness. Of course he knew Tiarnan Quinn. Who didn't? The man was a multibillionaire—an entrepreneur who had made a name for himself as someone who tore down countless companies only to build them back up again. Sorcha's words came back to him. That was why they looked so different. Her brother had inherited his mother's Spanish genes. But she'd never mentioned just *who* he was.

That caught Romain up short too. In his experience if people knew other people with power, not to mention were *related* to them, they invariably used it shamelessly—and Tiarnan Quinn was one of the most recognised, powerful people in the world.

Tiarnan stuck out a hand, making a proper introduction, and the tension dissipated, Sorcha watched as the two very Alpha males bonded in true male fashion. Recognising each other's pedigree. As only men in their rarefied circles would. It would have amused her if she hadn't still been getting over the shock of how she'd reacted to seeing Romain.

After a conversation she couldn't even remember, everything still a blur, Tiarnan got up to leave. Sorcha held onto him in a tight hug, as though loath to let him go. He looked down at her with concern in his eyes, and she forced herself to smile as if nothing was wrong. He'd already spent too much time worrying about her, feeling guilty for not having been there for her all those years ago. And he had a difficult nine-year-old daughter. She didn't want to add to his burdens.

When he'd gone, Sorcha ignored Roman and walked resolutely to the elevator. He was right behind her. When the door closed, the space seemed unbearably intimate. She determined not to give any indication of her bone-deep response to seeing him.

Think of his attitude that morning. Think of his attitude, his coolness—

Romain hit the stop button and the lift juddered to a halt. Sorcha's eyes flew to his.

'What do you think—?'

He reached for her, and against her volition she found herself in his arms. He bent his head to hers and took her mouth with such sure mastery that she didn't have a hope of pretending this wasn't what she wanted too.

Things escalated with scary swiftness. There was no hesitation. The temperature in the small enclosed space soared. Sorcha's hands dragged off his jacket, searched for and opened buttons on his shirt, pulled it out of his trousers. She needed to feel flesh, and when she did her hands ran round his back, her legs weakened.

Romain's own hands ran urgently wherever they could. The silk material of the dress slipped and slid through his fingers, thwarting his efforts. With a guttural moan he lifted his mouth from hers and with very little finesse tackled the offending buttons, just managing to hold back from ripping them open. Eventually he could see a pale swell, and like a man starved of water he pulled down the lace of her bra. Her breast sprang free and he bent his head, taking the puckered tight peak into his mouth.

Sorcha's hand was on his head, his fingers clasped tight around his skull. She sagged back against the wall of the elevator with her eyes half open. And what she saw in the mirror opposite served as a harsh wake-up call.

Romain's dark head at her breast, her eyes feverish with brightness, a flush extending from her chest and up, her dress half off, his own shirt flapping open, his jacket on the ground. She felt his hand snake down and reach under her dress, moving up her leg, and with an abrupt move she pushed him back and stood away, breathing heavily. Everything in disarray.

'Stop… We can't…'

Fiercely aroused grey eyes glittered down at her. Her mouth felt swollen and plump. She could feel the wet aching heat between her legs—knew she was so ready that all he'd have to do would be to strip off her panties, lift her up against the wall—

'And why would that be, when it seems to be an inevitability between the two of us if we're alone for more than a second?' His voice sounded harsh, taut with need. And it echoed through her, making a lie of her words.

Weakly she shut her eyes and started to do up her dress. Thanked God for divine intervention. 'We can't because I have my period…I *told* you.'

And you were relieved—don't you remember?

Sorcha looked at him almost accusingly.

Romain ran a hand through his hair and had to feel relief that some kind of sanity had broken through, because he knew that if she hadn't stopped them right now they *would* be making love in a lift. And he had to realise too that, yet again, he was without protection. And that it most likely wouldn't have stopped him this time either…

'Yes. You're right.' With a calm he didn't feel, he started to do up his own clothes. And then, when they were ready, standing almost like two strangers, he pressed the button for her floor and the lift ascended again. The moment of insanity gone.

Romain remonstrated with himself. He couldn't go on like this. It was too...out of control. Seconds in a lift and he'd been pawing at her like some lust-crazed schoolboy!

He was back in time to a place he thought he'd shut out for good. *Again.* In the presence of *this* woman.

That time—the only other time he'd felt the same sensation of being out of control—he'd got it back by shutting off his heart. He liked his life just the way it was. He could cope with a certain level of dissatisfaction. Because the alternative if he pursued this—pursued *her*—He shut down that line of thinking.

Sorcha Murphy could *not* be the only woman he would desire ever again...and he would prove it.

When the bell pinged softly, Sorcha flinched. She got out without even looking at Romain. Her insides churning, her belly tight. And he said nothing. The door slid shut again behind her.

Back in her own room, Sorcha stripped and crawled into bed. She felt cold. The intense white heat that had consumed them from nowhere in the lift had gone and left her aching with unfulfilled desire. She had stupidly imagined, *hoped*, that the rush of love she had felt in India after sleeping with Romain had been just an extreme response to having shared so much of herself. To baring herself so completely.

But seeing him tonight—the way she'd reacted then...the way she'd gone up in flames in the lift—all that told her that her response had been all too real. She buried her head in her pillow to stop the weak, silent tears. She hadn't learnt a thing. The first person to come along and make her open up and she'd fallen for them like a devoted puppy.

Silly and naïve all over again.

To go and fall in love with Romain de Valois, of all people. The one man in the world who would not, *could* not, love her back.

CHAPTER FIFTEEN

'OK, SORCHA, now look at him as if you really love him.'

Sorcha was doing her best. In a street full of extras, in the middle of Paris, she was looking into Zane's eyes. But instead of blue all she could see was grey. And all she could feel was those grey eyes boring into her from the other side of the street.

'OK, and now, Zane, take her in your arms and kiss her.'

Zane pulled her into his arms, his consummate professionalism making it smooth and graceful, but Sorcha felt as stiff as a board. And when Zane pressed his lips to hers she was glad that the camera was favouring him, because she could feel a wave of revulsion come over her.

Romain watched from behind the monitor. A red mist had descended on his vision as he had watched Sorcha laughing and joking with Zane. And now she was kissing him. Did she have to look so good in his arms? Did he have to grab her so close? The thought of Zane feeling her curves pressed up against him had Romain ready to call out, the job forgotten, the reason they were even there forgotten. But just then Simon did it for him and told them to cut. Romain trembled slightly. Still out of control for this woman, despite his best efforts.

They'd been in Paris for almost four days. They were running behind schedule because of a problem with some of the clothes not being available, and then a problem with the specialised camera that Simon was using. But this was it—the last shot.

When they finally agreed they were happy with everything, they called a wrap and released all the extras. Everyone started packing up, and Sorcha disappeared to her dressing room in a nearby hotel with Zane and the stylist.

She and Zane had done a sequence of shots earlier, with a one-year-old baby girl and a five-year-old boy. It had affected Sorcha far more deeply than she would have thought, bringing up a hitherto non-existent biological clock, and she'd found herself very studiously avoiding Romain's laser-like gaze. Kate was the one who'd always wanted a family, not her. What was wrong with her?

'Are you staying around for the party tomorrow night, Sorch?'

She looked at Val, arching her brow. Her whole body ached with tiredness. And ached with the knowledge that Romain had obviously decided he'd had enough of their…whatever it was. He hadn't made contact once since arriving in Paris. She was already a casualty.

'They're throwing a wrap party to say thanks, and they're inviting some bigwigs to see a very rough cut of what we've shot.'

Sorcha shook her head. She couldn't imagine anything worse than hanging around for longer than absolutely necessary. And she had to get home for the opening of the outreach centre in two weeks' time.

'No…I'm going to try and get a flight home in the morning.'

'So things didn't—?'

She halted Val's words with a quick, curt, 'No.'

The last thing she wanted too was to see an I-told-you-so look on anyone's face.

When Sorcha got back to the hotel a little later she was so tired all she wanted to do was order Room Service and crawl into bed. She had a shower and felt a little better, putting on a soft voluminous robe and wrapping her hair in a towel. When the knock came, she went and answered, assuming it to be the food she had ordered.

The breath whooshed from her body when she saw Romain on the other side, one arm leaning on the doorjamb, the other stuck in his jeans pocket.

She went to slam the door on a reflex, but Romain stuck his foot in the way.

'Excuse me,' she said as coldly as she could, her insides a mass of quivering nerve-ends. 'I'm expecting Room Service and then I'm going to bed. So if you wouldn't mind moving your foot…'

'Of course.' He obliged happily, but instead of moving it and stepping away from the door, he moved it and stepped inside.

Sorcha gaped at his audacity and crossed her arms over her chest, glad of the huge robe which concealed how her body was responding.

'I meant for you to leave.'

He leant against the back of the door and his eyes raked her up and down. 'I've missed you, Sorcha…'

Sorcha snorted, and words trembled on her lips, her mind swirling with confusion. Even though she was doing her best to act cool and insouciant, to push him away, she was hurting badly—and that largely had to do with something someone had left out for her tin the dressing room. It rose up and she spoke without thinking.

'Could've fooled me. We've been in Paris for four days now. If you've missed me so much, maybe you should have taken *me* out to dinner last night instead of Solange Colbert.'

Romain tensed. 'How did you hear about that?'

Sorcha cursed her runaway mouth. Would she never learn? And she cursed whoever it was again for leaving that paper just where she'd see it, with all the subtlety of a brick. And then she felt too angry to care.

'Romain, please don't insult my intelligence; she's one of France's most famous models. It's all over the French press today. Very cosy pictures.'

'My relationship with her is none of your business.'

'Well, evidently,' Sorcha spat out.

He advanced towards her with silky deadliness. Sorcha backed away. 'Don't come near me.'

'Why?' he taunted. 'Because you can't trust yourself?'

'Don't be ridiculous. I trust myself fine. I'm just not interested in another woman's cast-offs.'

'And if I told you nothing happened?'

'I wouldn't believe you.'

He shrugged, still advancing, 'Well, then, I'm afraid you're just going to have to believe what you want.'

Sorcha's knees hit the back of the bed and she staggered slightly.

'Get away from me.' But her voice was breathier this time. He filled her vision, her senses, her mind—and, God help her, she wanted him to fill her body.

'I haven't seen you since we got to Paris because I've been caught up in unavoidable work meetings...and in wrapping up this job.'

A voice mocked him. *Liar...you tried to stay away and it didn't work...*

Sorcha tilted her small chin defiantly. 'You don't have to explain yourself to me. I don't care.'

He continued as if she hadn't spoken. 'Then Solange called me yesterday and asked me out. *Asked me out.* And I went. Do you know why?'

Sorcha shrugged. She couldn't take her eyes off his. He was so close now that she could touch him if she wanted to, and her hands itched.

He sounded almost angry, and the intensity of his tone was doing something intense to Sorcha's insides.

'Because *you* are everywhere I look. You're in my head, my blood, and it's like a fever. I've never felt this way about anyone and I don't like it.'

'Well, I'm…sorry.'

And then something elemental moved through Sorcha, and she stepped forward so her nose was within centimetres of Romain's chest.

She poked him with a finger and he swayed back slightly. 'Actually, do you know what? I'm *not* sorry. And do you know why? Because I never asked for this. From the word go I told you I didn't want to do this job, but you insisted because you always get your own way. I never asked to be attracted to you. I never asked for you to take me to bed. I never asked to spill my guts. Well, I've had enough, Mr High and Mighty—Mr Confused who doesn't know what he wants—'

'What did you say?' he asked incredulously.

Sorcha was past caring—past being really aware of what she was saying. Her blood was on fire and she was afraid that if she didn't keep talking she'd jump on Romain and beg him to take her right there and then, standing up against a wall.

He stopped backing away and Sorcha looked up, at a loss for words for a second. The air sizzled around them. And then, with a sudden swift movement, Romain had pulled open and yanked down the top of her robe, so she was bared to him from the waist up. Sorcha gasped in shock and outrage, but just as swiftly Romain grabbed her close, taking both of her hands with one of his and anchoring them behind her back.

She struggled fruitlessly, about as effective as a fly on its back, and any more gasps or words of outrage were silenced as his mouth came down on hers and a violent explosion of need erupted in her belly and between her legs.

He lifted his head for a brief moment and said, 'You're wrong. I know exactly what I want, and it's right here in my arms. *Et maintenant, je n'en peux plus…*'

Sorcha opened her mouth to speak, but he stopped any words with his own mouth again. She had a moment of wanting to struggle, but then she became aware of how her breasts were crushed against his chest, the friction of his shirt making her nipples taut and tight with need. The towel had slid off her head and her hair was wet against her back, where his hand was threading through it to the back of her head, urging her closer, angling it for his benefit. Any thought of struggle fled. Instead she wanted to feel him, flesh to flesh. She struggled to get her hands free but he was so strong, so ruthless. His other hand moved down her back, skimming under the robe, loosening it even further until it hung treacherously on her hips. And then with a brief flick of his fingers it fell to the floor completely, and she was naked in his arms, captive to his onslaught.

His hand urged her against him, and she could feel the heated evidence of his desire through the fabric of his jeans. The friction against her own deeply sensitised body was making her tremble. And then his hand moved up over her waist and higher, around the front, over her belly to the swell of one breast. He still hadn't released her mouth, his tongue and teeth nipping, tracing her full lower lip. Sorcha was dizzy with needs that clamoured through her blood and body like waves pounding against a shore.

When his hand closed around that breast, and his mouth finally left hers to make a sensual passage ever downwards, her legs couldn't hold her up any more. She would have sunk to the floor if not for Romain's arm supporting her. His mouth closed over the tight, turgid peak with an almost savage intensity, and Sorcha couldn't stop herself from crying out. She ached with the need to touch and caress. Her hands being imprisoned was too much of a torture.

'Please…Romain…please…' she begged brokenly, hating the weakness in her voice.

'Please, what?'

'Please…let me go…'

'Never.'

His eyes glittered with glowing silver flames. He did finally release her hands, but only briefly, to carry her over to the bed. He laid her down, stripping off his clothes with indecent haste, and she didn't have time to formulate a word or a thought. He stood before her, a tall, lean bronzed specimen of thrusting male potency. He reached for something in his jeans pocket. *Protection.* He smoothed it on. Even that reminder couldn't cool her blood. Watching him stroke it on made her even hotter.

All she could think was for this moment he was *hers*. She opened her arms to him and he fell on her. They kissed and touched and stroked and smoothed and writhed. Their bodies were slick with sweat. Breath intermingling, short and rapid.

And then he was there, thrusting more deeply than he had done before. Sorcha's whole body arched up to his and her legs wrapped around his waist, taking him even deeper into a spiral of ecstasy too urgent and immediate to question. Driven by a force he'd never encountered before, Romain looked down into Sorcha's clear blue gaze, saw how her cheeks were hectic with colour, how she bit her lip to keep her moans back. He kissed her mouth to stop her biting it, unaware of the tender nature of his gesture.

And then he felt her bite his shoulder in direct response to the way her body was starting to contract around him—so powerfully that he could feel every spasm as it clenched around his shaft, urging him on to a deeper and more intense orgasm than he'd ever experienced. When it came, he actually blacked out for a second, and then the world came into focus again, his body still pulsing, still releasing.

After a long moment he pulled free and pulled Sorcha close into his chest, for that was the only thing he was capable of doing. And he knew in that moment that everything he'd thought or believed before had gone out of the window. But he was in no state to try and rationalise what that meant right now…

* * *

'I want to go home to Dublin, Romain. I have things to do there.'

Sorcha looked out of the window to the busy Paris street outside. Her whole body seemed to be one big, aching mass of fizzing nerve-ends. They'd made love all the previous evening and into the night. When she had commented on how Room Service had never arrived, Romain had informed her that he had asked that they were not to be disturbed. So then they had ordered Room Service again. And a bottle of wine.

As if too much personal history had been shared, they had been careful not to stray into those waters. They had spoken of general things, drunk the wine and eaten. And then afterwards they had made love again, long and languorously, until the dawn light had tinged the sky outside with pink.

He was dressing behind her. She could hear him pull up jeans, close the button, pull on his shirt… She closed her eyes and swallowed. Her body was reacting to just hearing him. God, she didn't even have to see him to want him. Her heart ached so much that it was like a physical pain.

The tenor of their relationship had changed so much since it had become physical. Romain was harder, more distant. The lightness that had existed between them, however briefly, at lunch that day in India was gone. Once he'd achieved what he'd set out to do the gloves had come off. And now the job was over and he was sating himself while he could. It was horrendously obvious. But though she knew *he* would be able to walk away, was used to this, she wouldn't. But she'd have to.

He came close behind her and she willed him away. But of course he didn't obey her silent plea. He pulled her hair aside at the back of her neck and pressed a kiss there, to the tender skin. A shudder of arousal ran through her. To stop it, she turned around.

'You *have* to come to the party. People will expect you to be there.'

'Romain, I—'

He felt a surge of anger move through him. Why did she have to be so stubborn?

'Sorcha, the job isn't officially over until after this party.'

She paled under his gaze, and he could see the shadows under her eyes. He felt his chest constrict. But something bigger motivated him, and he didn't want to look at what that was.

'Are you ordering me to go?' she asked quietly, her heart breaking a little more. Because, despite all the intimacy they'd shared, not one word of tenderness had been spoken. Even now, if he'd been asking her to come *with him*, because he wanted her there, then she would have gone without question. And castigated herself afterwards.

Romain stood stock still and thought silently to himself, *If that's what it takes.* Instead he shrugged. 'If you want to leave—leave. But you are expected to be there—to show a united front with myself, Zane…the rest of the board and the crew.'

She felt a little dead inside—cut off from everything around her. If she made a big deal and left, he might suspect something of her feelings for him. It would kill her to stay for one more night, but she would. Anything to avoid that penetrative gaze, that questioning mind.

She fixed her attention on something on the wall above his shoulder. 'Very well. There's an exhibition I wanted to see before I left. It won't make any huge difference if I leave tomorrow, I guess.'

Romain felt something suspiciously like relief flood him even as he reacted to her nonchalant tone.

'Good. I'll pick you up at seven.'

Big blue eyes caught his. 'I can go with—'

'*I'll* pick you up at seven.'

He pressed a swift kiss to her mouth, and she watched as he strode from the room.

The door shut behind him and Sorcha sank back onto the

window seat behind her. For the first time since he'd arrived the evening before, her whole body sagged. Her mind was thankfully a little numb.

CHAPTER SIXTEEN

A LITTLE before seven that evening, Sorcha stood in much the same position as she had earlier, looking out of the window. She felt very still and serene inside, but she knew it was just the calm before the storm. The storm which was going to come when she would walk away from Romain and never see him again.

A knock sounded on the door and she jumped. That brief moment of tranquillity was gone. This evening was it—the last time she'd be with him, see him, experience him. So whatever fantasy she had in her head would have to be lived out tonight. She walked over to the door and opened it.

The breath left her body as if she *hadn't* already seen him in a tux—first in New York and now here again. She reacted as if it were the first time. He looked resplendent. Too gorgeous for words. His heavy-lidded sensuality was overwhelming.

Jerkily she gestured for him to come in. 'I just have to put on my shoes, then I'm good to go.'

She went into the small dressing room and pulled out shoes from her open case. Coming back out into the bedroom, she saw he was looking at her strangely. She hopped from one foot to the other, pulling the shoes on. Not feeling like smiling at all, she managed to quirk a small one and ask, 'What's wrong? Have I got something on my nose?'

She went to look in the mirror, to check her reflection.

Romain came and stood behind her, hands on her shoulders, and she could feel her body react just to that impersonal touch.

'You have no idea how stunning you are, do you?' he asked.

Sorcha blushed and tried to turn around, but he wouldn't let her. She refused to look at herself, mortified. 'Romain, I'm well aware that I'm lucky enough to have good genes that make me photogenic, but really there are a million women more stunning—'

He turned her almost savagely in his arms and tipped her chin up with a finger. 'You're the most beautiful woman I've ever seen.'

Inside and out.

She shook her head in denial. His mouth bent to hers, stopping any words. And when he broke away he whispered, 'Yes. You are.'

He reached into his pocket then and took something out—something in a long box. He flicked his eyes down to her shoes and his mouth quirked. 'This should match what you're wearing...'

Unaccustomed to receiving gifts from men, Sorcha didn't know what to do or say, so she took the box and opened it. A huge ruby glowed up at her from velvet folds like a living, breathing thing. Before she could articulate a word Romain had lifted it out and deftly fastened it. It hung on a long chain around her neck. Bare of any other jewellery, with her hair smoothed back behind her ears and falling down her back in a sleek black curtain, she did look perfect.

'Romain, I can't wear this. It must have cost a fortune.'

'Cost doesn't matter,' he dismissed arrogantly. 'Wear it for me. Please?'

She felt torn, all her instincts shouting at her to take it off. But she just gave a small nod.

He took her hand in his and led her from the room. She grabbed a small black bag and wrap as she went.

When they stood in the lift as it made its descent, Romain's eyes couldn't stray from Sorcha. He'd never seen her look more stunning. Her simple black silk dress had a deep vee halter neck, and was completely backless, showing off her pale skin, unblemished and silky smooth. It fell in soft swirling folds to her knees, and deep red, almost scarlet high heels added a splash of colour. But wasn't that her? She always surprised—never did the completely conventional thing. The ruby glowed and shone as it swayed with the movement of the lift, nestled between the firm globes of her breasts.

The trip to the venue for the party—a very well-known hotel right beside the Place de la Concorde—was made largely in silence. The air that surrounded Sorcha seemed to hum with some indefinable energy. She was aware of Romain on the seat beside her, and his every minute movement seemed a thousand times bigger, more momentous. At one stage he reached across and took her hand. Pressed a kiss to the inside of her palm. It was the third time he'd kissed her like that, taking her breath away. To look into his eyes so deeply was torture, and yet she couldn't look away.

The car slid to a smooth halt and they got out, Romain helping her with a firm hand. Suddenly Sorcha was blinded by the sudden flashing of a thousand cameras. Shouts and incoherent questions were hurled their way.

'Romain—*Romain*!'

He hurried her through the crush and into the foyer, and when they got in she couldn't stop the uncontrollable shaking that had taken over her body. Those few seconds of flashing cameras had taken her back in time as if it was yesterday.

Romain made a gesture to someone that Sorcha didn't see, and led her over to a quiet corner. He sat her down on a seat and bent down on his haunches before her, looking up into her too pale face.

'Are you OK?'

She half nodded and shrugged, feeling his strength wrap itself around her. His two hands held hers and the heat was beginning to seep through, the chill leaving her body. She nodded again, more forcefully this time.

'I'm sorry. I just got a fright. I'm not used to that kind of reception—or at least I haven't been since…'

Romain looked grim. 'I'm sorry, I should have warned you. Come on, let's go inside. I'll get you a brandy.'

He pulled her up and, keeping a firm hold on her, walked her to the closed doors that led inside. For a second he stopped and looked down at her, to check if she was OK, and when he did she looked up at him. She gave a small smile and squeezed his hand gently, telling him what he needed to know with her eyes, and the sense of *déjà vu* that washed through him made stars dance in front of his eyes. This was the moment—*this* was what he'd been imagining in New York…

Sorcha, thinking he was waiting for her, tugged at his hand, and they went inside to a huge room which was already thronged with what looked like all of Paris. She wasn't aware of the slightly shell shocked look that had crossed Romain's face. She was fighting against the urge she had to sink into his side, clutch his hand for ever. She'd never had this level of protection before, and it felt far too seductive and irresistible. She had to remember that after tonight she wouldn't have it any more.

In the lavish ballroom, Romain didn't let Sorcha out of his protective sight. She chatted and joked with the crew, and other people she knew who'd been involved in the campaign, but her heart felt as heavy as a stone.

Some hours after arriving, close to the end of the evening, Romain grabbed her hand in a fierce grip. She stifled a gasp and looked up to his face. He was ashen, and looking at something, or someone, she couldn't see.

'What is it?'

He didn't even seem to be aware that he was crushing her hand in his.

He muttered something unintelligible, and Sorcha asked again, 'Romain, what is it?'

'My brother,' he said, so faintly that she had to strain to hear him. 'My brother is here.'

Now she understood. She recalled what he had told her. Before Sorcha could speak again, or ask any questions, he muttered something, let her hand go and strode off into the throng.

Left alone for a moment, telling herself it was silly to feel so bereft, Sorcha went to the bar to get some water.

They had shown a rough cut of the commercial and Sorcha had to admit that it wasn't like anything out at the moment. It was whimsical and dreamy, and the shots from India looked fantastically exotic.

Sipping at the water, Sorcha turned when she felt a tap on her shoulder. A very beautiful blonde woman stood there, as tall as Sorcha, in a red gown which plunged daringly low, showing a more than generous cleavage. Sorcha could see immediately that she'd had work done—her face looked a little too perfect. Her eyes were blue, and glittered with a hard light. Her red lips curved in an unfriendly smile, and Sorcha's own immediate smile faltered.

'You are Sorcha? The latest woman in Romain's life?'

Sorcha flushed deeply at the woman's rudeness, at the nerve she'd struck. She knew without doubt that she meant nothing good.

'I really don't see that that's any of your business.'

The other woman looked her up and down. 'Ah, but you see it is. Because if it wasn't for me you wouldn't be here tonight with him.'

Sorcha made a move to get away. Feeling as vulnerable as she did, the last thing she wanted was to deal with some ex-lover of Romain's.

The other woman stopped her by planting herself straight in front of Sorcha. Hemmed in by someone at her back, she couldn't move.

'Please excuse me.'

The woman arched a brow. 'You're not even curious as to who I might be?'

'Not really,' Sorcha answered, her eyes searching for and finding Romain. She found him easily enough. He was with a smaller man. They looked quite similar, and she realized that the man must be his brother. The other woman's face came close, and Sorcha could smell spirits on her breath. She shrank back.

'That man that he's with. That's his brother. My husband.'

Sorcha looked again, despite herself. The other man's face was fleshy and mottled. She could see that from across the room. And middle age hadn't been kind to him. He had a definite paunch, and his hair was thinning on top.

'Not as handsome as Romain, is he?'

Sorcha flushed again, and tried to move.

'The ironic thing is, you see, I chose Marc over Romain. All those years ago Marc was the handsome one, the one with the prospects. As I'm sure you know, they had different fathers, so my full title is Duchesse de Courcy. Romain could only have offered me the title of Comtesse, and I was greedy…'

Sorcha went very still. The woman looked at Sorcha again, and utter hatred was in her eyes. Years of bitterness. Anger. Sorcha could see it a mile away—and she had an awful feeling she now knew exactly who she was.

'You…you were Romain's fiancée, weren't you?'

The woman laughed. 'He told you about me? How sweet. Did he tell you how heartbroken he was? How when he came in and found me on top of his brother he went white and proceeded to get blind drunk for a whole week?'

Sorcha was beginning to feel sick. But the woman was relentless.

'I ruined him for anyone else. *Me.* I may never have him now, but at least no one else will either—'

'Martine. Your husband is looking for you. I think it's time to leave.'

Romain materialised out of thin air and practically frog-marched Martine over to his brother. Someone escorted them out of the room.

On legs that felt none too steady, Sorcha went to find her bag and wrap. Two hands encircled her waist, bringing her back into contact with a hard, familiar body. She twisted around in his arms and looked up at him accusingly.

'You told me she was dead.' Hurt made her voice husky.

He shook his head. 'I said she was dead to me. I had no idea they would be here. But my brother heard about it on the grapevine and needed another hand-out…'

'That woman is poisonous, Romain. How could you have ever—?'

'Believe me, I ask myself that question every time I see her.' His face was carved from stone.

Sorcha felt cold inside. 'Your whole life, Romain…You do this…pursue beautiful women…it's all to get back at her, isn't it? Some sort of petty revenge?'

'Don't be crazy.'

Sorcha shook her head. Her insides were crumbling. 'It's not crazy. She said that because she'd rejected you, you wouldn't let anyone else have you—and it's true.'

Sorcha could feel the tension in his frame as he held her. His mouth was a slash of a line.

'Don't try to psychoanalyse me, Sorcha. And you're completely wrong. I look at that woman now and she fills me with disgust.'

'Yes, perhaps. But that doesn't stop how you allow her to keep affecting your behaviour.'

Her words hung in the air between them. They cut close to

the bone. But Romain didn't want to poison the air with thoughts of Martine now. He pulled Sorcha close—close enough so that she could feel his arousal press against her.

Like a well trained mechanism, her body leapt into joyful response, totally going against the will her head was trying to impose on it.

One more night…that's all you have and then he'll move on. But for tonight he's yours…

Fighting an internal battle so strong that for one brief moment she thought she did have the strength to walk away, Sorcha quickly knew that her weak side had won out. The weak side that wanted, above all else, one more night with this man. So she allowed him to pull her even closer. And stared up into his eyes.

'Let's get out of here.'

The following morning, very early, Sorcha slid from the bed. Behind her, amongst the rumpled sheets, lay the languid and relaxed form of Romain's body. A sheet strategically hid the powerful centre of his manhood. His face looked younger in repose. Relaxed. Lashes curling darkly onto dark cheeks.

Sorcha's heart twisted so much in her chest that she almost made a sound. He shifted slightly and she held her breath. And then, when he didn't wake, stealthily she picked up her things and crept from his room back to her own, down the corridor…

CHAPTER SEVENTEEN

Two Weeks Later

'AND it's with great pleasure that I now declare this Dublin Youth Outreach Centre…' Sorcha bent and cut the blue ribbon over the door with a flourish '…open!'

It was amazing, really, she marvelled, how the human body and mind could conceal pain from everyone around them. Everyone was clapping and cheering, party poppers were going off, flashbulbs were flashing, TV cameras were whirring. This was a moment of great personal joy. She had done this single-handedly, with no help from anyone except herself—not even a penny from Tiarnan—so why was it all she could think about was the lonely ache in her heart?

'Sorcha, well done! You've done such a brilliant thing…and what a coup, getting the Prime Minister to launch it with you!'

Sorcha smiled as people filed past her into the centre, where the champagne was already flowing, giving their congratulations along the way. She'd got a call from Tiarnan that morning, to say good luck and that he was sorry he wouldn't be able to make it. Sorcha hadn't been surprised, but still it *hurt* that she had no one here to share this with her. Even Katie had had to cancel her flight at the last minute, as Maud had begged her to take on a job which, with her usual dramatics, had meant life or death.

She greeted the last person to go in. The news crews were packing up gear to bring it inside. So what if she was alone again?

Something across the road snagged her gaze…Sorcha's breath stopped right there in her throat as she watched a tall, dark man uncoil his body from a parked car across the road.

She had to be imagining things… Was she so distraught that she was hallucinating?

But as she blinked and watched it was unmistakably, without a doubt, Romain de Valois crossing the road. And the first thing that happened was that a huge lump in came to her throat. Of all her loved ones she'd want here, it had to be her *unrequited* love who came.

By the time he had crossed the road she had herself under some kind of control. When he stopped in front of her, she looked up and couldn't read his face. It was expressionless, and his eyes were hidden behind dark glasses, making him look even more mysterious, handsome. A dark suit and blue shirt made him look austere, formal. Her heart hammered like a piston.

He gestured with his head, as if he were looking her up and down behind those shades. 'Very demure…for a woman who leaves a man in the middle of the night without even a note.'

His voice and that accent caused such an immediate reaction in her blood that she almost swayed. He must be referring to her outfit. She'd dressed relatively conservatively today, knowing that some elements of the press would be out to get her. In a grey pencil skirt, white high-necked blouse, her hair tied back in a ponytail and her glasses on, her only concession to fashion or frivolity were the black fishnet tights and eye-wateringly high black heels.

Her chin tipped up, her eyes clear, belying the whirlpool her stomach had become. 'It was the morning, actually, and I thought you'd prefer a clean break.'

One brow arched up. 'Oh, did you, now? How considerate.' He took the glasses off and finally she could see his eyes. But they too were cool, expressionless. Even so, joy at seeing him again ripped through her and held her captive. She hoped the extra make-up she'd had to put on covered the shadows under her eyes. She was so pale she couldn't get away with anything.

'Now is not the time or place to discuss your leaving. I believe you have a speech to give?'

Her speech!

She'd forgotten everything—where she was, what she was doing.

Romain took her lightly under the elbow and led her into the centre, where everyone was chatting loudly. The TV crews had set up and were indeed waiting patiently for her to speak. Nerves threatened to attack her, and for a brief moment Romain wasn't the centre of her universe. But knowing that he was there emboldened her. She didn't care about how or why he was there—just drew on his strength because she needed someone.

When she stood up, her voice faltered at first. But then she saw Romain at the back of the room. He nodded at her, telling her without words that she was OK, that she could do this. And she did. She made a very impassioned speech, telling a little of her own history, how lost she'd felt as a young person. There was a long moment of silence when she finished, and then huge, raucous applause.

For some time afterwards she was swept into interviews and photos and conversations. And every time she looked for Romain she saw him chatting to someone different. He wasn't brooding in a corner, as she might have expected. At one point she looked over and he was throwing his head back, laughing at something someone had said. It made her heart swell and soar.

And she had to be very careful. Because if he had come just to pick up their physical relationship, then she wasn't interested. And she was quite sure he wasn't interested in anything else.

* * *

'So. What *are* you doing here?'

They were walking out of the centre. It had turned dark outside. Sorcha's heels sounded loud in the quiet of the empty city street.

He didn't answer. 'I'll give you a lift home.'

'You don't know where I live.'

'You should know by now that I know everything.'

Sorcha gave in wearily. His arrogance was by now wholly usual. He led her to his car and, much to her chagrin, he did know exactly where she lived. He drove there as if he knew the city better than herself. When she got out, he got out too, and followed her to her door. She turned as she slid the key in the lock.

'Look, if you've come here just to—'

'I've come here to talk to you.'

Silly flutters made her heart jump, and she furiously clamped them down. He was probably peeved that she'd walked out without saying goodbye, that was all.

When they got up to her apartment, which was at the top of the house, she realised that she'd never had a man in her flat before. Or at least not a *lover*. She felt self-conscious at the thought of him seeing her inner sanctum, and busied herself turning on lamps and going into the kitchen, opening and closing doors. She turned around to ask him what he'd prefer and he was right behind her, holding two bottles of beer.

'But how did you...?'

'One in each pocket. I know you don't like champagne, and I knew you'd want to celebrate today...'

Stupidly, Sorcha felt tears threaten. She reached up and pinched her nose, taking off her glasses on the pretext of cleaning them. Romain put the beers down and took her glasses out of her hands, tipping her face to his.

Her eyes were swimming, her throat working and her lips trembling. It was all he could to not to take them, touch his lips to hers...but now was not the time. Instead he pulled her into his chest and held her tight, rocking her as she wept and made his shirt wet.

After a while Sorcha pulled back, feeling silly. Two minutes in her apartment and she was weeping all over Romain like some hormonal teenager. She avoided his eyes, knowing she must have mascara everywhere. She rubbed at her cheeks and her eyes felt raw and puffy. 'I'm sorry. I don't know what came over me.'

'It's OK,' he said gently. 'You felt lonely. I know, because I've felt like that for a long time.'

She looked up at him warily and rubbed at her cheeks. 'You?'

He nodded and took her hands away, rubbing at her cheeks with his thumbs, his big hands around her jaw.

His voice was husky. 'I'm very proud of what you did today.'

'You are?' she said, knowing she must sound like some kind of parrot. She was completely bemused and confused as to why he was here, what he wanted.

He nodded and, taking the beers, led her out into the sitting room, making her sit down. He expertly flipped open the beer tops and shucked off his overcoat, sitting down beside her. His scent, his presence, overwhelmed her, and Sorcha took a big swig of beer just to try and counteract the shock.

'Why did you leave like that, Sorcha?' His eyes pinned her to the spot.

Feeling agitated, she stood up. Somewhere between the door and the kitchen she had kicked off her shoes. She hugged her arms around her and went to stand by the window. She firmed her inner resolve. 'Because I thought you'd prefer it like that.'

She couldn't help but recall how close she had been to turning around and going back. It had been at that moment, in the cab, on the way to the airport, that she had noticed the morning paper. A photo of her and Romain, leaked from God knew where had been splashed across the front page. Her in his arms on the beach on Inis Mor. And inside more pictures of him with ex-lovers, and the one of him dining with Solange Colbert.

And a huge discussion about which woman was the new one in his life, and the pros and cons for each. It had been hideous. And it had made it very easy for Sorcha to keep going straight to the airport.

'And what gave you that impression?' He sat back, as at home as if he lived there, one arm across the back of the couch. Relaxed. Debonair. Disconcerting to her equilibrium.

Suddenly Sorcha felt angry at the way he'd swanned back into her life, threatening to turn it upside down all over again. She conveniently blocked out the fact that she'd only felt half alive for the past two weeks.

'Oh, I don't know, Romain! Maybe it's something to do with the fact that you have a reputation that would make Casanova blush... I mean, what *did* you want?' She threw her arms wide.

He stood and was immediately dangerous. 'You, Sorcha. I wanted you and I still want you. I decided to give you the benefit of the doubt. I would have thought, Well, she must do this with every lover. But I knew that I had been your first—so unless you're planning a lifetime of having sex and walking away then maybe it's not something that came so easily.'

His words flayed her. This was it. This was where she had to protect herself. He was advancing, and she knew that if he so much as breathed near her she'd turn to mush. So she squared her shoulders and said cuttingly, 'Well, that's exactly it. You *were* my first lover, Romain, but I don't expect you to be my last. So if it's closure you're looking for, then this is it. I meant to leave you like that. I knew it was coming to an end. You obviously didn't.'

And somehow, as if invaded by some alien force, she kept going, the words spilling out in a stream of consciousness, all designed to protect herself. 'Was it because it happened to you? You had your heart broken by the person you entrusted your secrets to? So you felt bad for me—wanted to make sure I was all right? Well, I'm fine. You can see I'm fine. Now, please, if all you wanted was to salve your conscience I'll save you the bother, because I'm fine.'

Romain looked as if she had just slapped him in the face. His mouth compressed to a thin line of anger.

'You said "I'm fine" three times. I get the point. I'm not welcome.'

He picked up his coat and carefully, too carefully, put it over his arm.

Sorcha was already feeling the effects of her words on her body. An out-of-control shaking starting up in her legs.

Romain turned and walked to the door. Sorcha's vision blurred, and for a second she thought she'd faint.

He turned then and looked at her. Through her. He smiled, but it was harsh and didn't meet his eyes. 'Do you know the really funny thing? I've let history repeat itself. All these years I've been so careful to avoid getting emotionally involved...and within minutes of meeting you in New York, when I knew you were tempted to throw that champagne in my face, I was already more emotionally involved with you than I'd ever been with anyone in my life. When I woke up that morning two weeks ago and realised you had gone—*left*...the pain was indescribable. The only thing that gave me the courage to come here today was a misguided belief that I had seen something in your eyes that might lead me to believe...' He shook his head and opened the door.

Sorcha couldn't move she was in so much shock.

Before leaving he turned back one more time and smiled sadly. 'It would appear that I am destined to play the fool in love. For you, Sorcha, have my heart—whether you like it or not. Perhaps that's my punishment for judging you so cruelly—not once, but twice. I didn't lose my heart to Martine all those years ago. It took seeing her with you in the same room that night to realise that. All I lost was my head and my pride. But this...*this* is much worse, and I can see exactly why

I protected myself for so long if not being loved brings this level of pain. *Adieu*, Sorcha, I hope you find happiness and love in your life.'

When he had gone, and the door had clicked quietly shut behind him, Sorcha's hands went to her mouth as she stifled a sob that wouldn't emerge. She was frozen. Couldn't move. She heard the main door slam. She heard a car door open. Close. And finally she was galvanised into action. She didn't think, she moved. Like lightning. Sprinting down the stairs, taking two at a time, until she got to the heavy front door. She was all fingers and thumbs opening it, but finally it sprang free.

The rain had arrived. It was lashing. She saw Romain's car pulling out of the parking space, into the road, about to drive off.

'No!' she shouted, her voice hoarse with emotion. 'Romain…come back…*come back!*'

He started to drive away, and Sorcha ran down the steps in her stockinged feet, heedless of the rain and the wet pavement. She had to hitch up her skirt in order to run after his car.

'Romain, wait! *Wait!*'

The car was driving away, too far, too fast, and she faltered, her steps slowing, a sob rising. It was too late. Already she was thinking of what she could do—where she could go to find him, track him down, Maud must know where he lived—and then she saw that the car had stopped, red brake lights on.

Almost hesitant to walk forward, in case he sped off again, Sorcha walked tentatively. When she saw that he wasn't going anywhere she sped up and ran the last few feet. She pulled open his door. She was saturated, hair plastered to her head, clothes stuck to her. Rain ran in rivulets down her face.

She was crying, big racking sobs, tears mingling with the rain on her face.

'You big idiot. Of course I love you. I love you so much I can't eat, sleep or think. The only reason I left that morning was because you gave me no indication that I meant anything to you except an a...a...affair. You said you just wanted a mistress...'

He stepped out of the car and she thumped him on his shoulder. He wrapped his arms around her waist so tight that she couldn't breathe and lifted her up, feet off the ground, head buried in her neck. She pressed kisses wherever she could find a spot, and when he could he pulled back and let her down gently. The rain coursed over them but they were oblivious. He grabbed her close again and drove his mouth down onto hers, taking and giving no quarter, passionately demanding her promise again, and she gave it, stretching up, her whole body arching into his.

'God, Sorcha...' he breathed finally when he lifted his head, his breath coming harsh and swift. 'Don't ever do that to me again.'

She hit him again on the shoulder. 'Well, don't shut me out again.'

He smiled. 'Deal.'

And then he got down on one knee, still oblivious to the weather. Sorcha felt her heart about to burst from her chest.

Romain looked up, so heartrendingly tender that she caught her breath. 'I just got you a temporary ring for now...on the way over here. I didn't want to tempt fate by getting the real thing, and I know you'd probably like to choose it yourself anyway...'

Sorcha smiled and hiccupped as he took her hand.

'Will you please marry me and make me a sane man, before I go crazy with love for you?'

She nodded immediately. He held out a cheap silver Claddagh ring, and Sorcha thought she'd never seen anything more lovely. He slid it onto her finger and she looked at it. She held out her hand to him. It was shaking.

'It's on the wrong way.'

'What?'

'If we're...' she looked down at him shyly, 'In love the heart should be facing my heart, and even on this finger, some might consider us already married.'

He stood up and took the ring off her finger, carefully turning it round so that when he slid it on again the heart faced inwards.

'Then as of this moment and until we make it official, we are married. You have my heart...always.'

'As you have mine,' she promised, gazing up into his eyes, her hand tracing his jaw.

He bent his head again and kissed her, long and deeply, and it was only the honking of a horn that broke them apart. An irate taxi driver was waiting behind Romain's still running car, his head sticking out of the window.

'Would the two of you just get a room?'

Much later, as the moonlight broke through stormy clouds outside and bathed Sorcha's room with milky light, she held Romain's head to her breast and stroked his hair.

'You know...' he said musingly, as his hand ran up and down her arm.

'Hmm...' she said, too blissfully tired to make it a question.

'When I stopped the car that time, I hadn't seen you behind me. I stopped because I was determined to come back and make you see that you loved me, whether you liked it or not. It was killing me to think that I had been your first lover and yet you wanted to experience others, so I was going to come back and make love to you till you begged for mercy. Then you appeared at my door, soaking, like an avenging angel, telling me you loved me. I thought I was dreaming...'

'So you mean I went out there and ruined my tights and got soaking wet for nothing?'

He flipped up and hovered over her, his big body gleaming in the light, his eyes blazing into hers, telling her of his love.

'But it was fun drying off...no?'

She twined her hands around his neck, 'Oh, yes…that was definitely fun…'

They kissed long and luxuriously.

'You know, I want lots of children, with jet-black hair and blue eyes,' Romain said as he kissed his way down Sorcha's neck.

Joy surged through her.

'I think blue is a recessive gene to grey.'

'Not in our children,' Romain declared arrogantly.

Sorcha shook her head and smiled fondly. 'No, they wouldn't dare.'

He came over her then, imprisoning her body with his, making her very aware of his newly aroused state. Sorcha's hair rippled onto the pillow behind her like black silk. Her cheeks were flushed. Her eyes were slumberous, like a cat's. Romain realised that this was the exact image he'd had in his head all those weeks ago in Dublin, the day she'd walked out of the restaurant. As confident as he had been then that he could make it come true, he hadn't counted on the journey it would take him on, or the wealth of experience this woman would bring into his life, enriching him emotionally beyond anything he could have ever dreamed. He felt love surge through him again. Strong and true.

He smoothed the back of his hand across one flushed cheek and smiled down into blue eyes darkened with passion, burning with love.

Sorcha locked her arms behind his head, bringing her breasts up and into close contact with his chest. She looked serious. 'Romain…you do know I couldn't give two hoots about becoming a countess, or the château…or anything? All I care about is you… I love *you*…'

He sank into those blue depths. He'd truly found the one person in the world who loved *him*…who knew him completely. As he knew her.

'I know…' he said huskily.

'Good.' She smiled cheekily. 'Then hurry up and make love to me. I'm not getting any younger, and if you want lots of babies…'

'It would be my pleasure…for ever.'

And it was.

BREAKING
THE BOSS'S RULES

BY
NINA MILNE

Nina Milne has always dreamt of writing for Mills & Boon—ever since as a child she discovered stacks of Mills & Boon books 'hidden' in the airing cupboard. She graduated from playing libraries to reading the books, and has now realised her dream of writing them.

Along the way she found a happy-ever-after of her own, accumulating a superhero of a husband, three gorgeous children, a cat with character and a real library...well, lots of bookshelves.

Before achieving her dream of working from home creating happy-ever-afters whilst studiously avoiding any form of actual housework, Nina put in time as both an accountant and a recruitment consultant. She figures the lack of romance in her previous jobs is now balancing out.

After a childhood spent in Peterlee (UK), Rye (USA), Winchester (UK) and Paris (France), Nina now lives in Brighton (UK), and has vowed never to move again!! Unless, of course, she runs out of bookshelves. Though there is always the airing cupboard...

For my parents, for believing in me.

PROLOGUE

Dear Diary

My name is Imogen Lorrimer and my life is in a less than stellar place right now.

For a start there is every possibility that my temporary new boss is about to fire me. His name is Joe McIntyre and, just to really mess with my head, he has taken to appearing in my dreams.

Naked.

Last night was particularly erotic. I won't go into detail, but we were in his office and let's just say various positions were involved...as were varying bits of office furniture...glass-topped desk, red swivel chair...

Obviously I know this is thoroughly unprofessional and utterly inappropriate.

In my defence he is gorgeous.

Think sexy rumpled hair—dark brown, a tiny bit long, with a few bits that stick up. Think chocolate— the expensive kind—brown eyes. Think a strong but not too dominant nose. A long face, with a sculpted jaw and clearly defined chin. Oh, and a body to die for—Joe McIntyre is a long, lean fighting machine.

Problem is, however much I appreciate the man in my dreams, the real live clothed version of Joe McIntyre is a ruthless corporate killing machine. He is a troubleshooter who has been called in to overhaul Langley Interior Design and we are all in danger of losing our jobs.

In fact there is every chance he will fire me on the spot tomorrow—especially given my recent screw-up.

I cannot let that happen. I cannot afford to lose my job. Not on top of everything else.

To be specific I am:

Homeless—my scumbag boyfriend, Steve, of three years has just dumped me for his ex—Simone—and thrown me out of the flat we shared. So I am currently living with my BFF—and, whilst I love Mel like the sister I never had, I can only sleep on her pull-out bed for so long. I think I'm cramping her style.

Heartbroken—Steve ticked all the boxes on my 'What I am looking for in a Man' list. I thought he was The One.

Broke—I blew my savings on a romantic holiday for Steve and me. And, unbelievable though this may sound, he is now taking Simone. How humiliating is that?

It's no wonder that I am fantasising in my dreams. My real life sucks.

Time for some ice cream, methinks!
Imogen x

CHAPTER ONE

JOE MCINTYRE LEANT back in the state-of-the-art office chair and picked up the CV from the glass-topped desk.

Imogen Lorrimer. Peter Langley's PA for the past five years.

She of the raven-black hair and wide grey-blue eyes.

Faint irritation twanged Joe's nerves; her looks were irrelevant. 'No Mixing Business and Pleasure'. That was an absolute rule. Along with 'One Night Only' and 'Never Look Back'. From *The Joe McIntyre Book of Relationships*. Short, sweet and easy to use.

Joe gusted out a sigh as his eyes zoned back to his emails. Leila again. Shame the manual didn't tell him how to deal with a blast-from-the-past ex-girlfriend from a time he'd rather forget. But this was not the time to open *that* can of worms—his guilt was still bad enough that he had agreed to attend her wedding, but there was no need to think further about it. Right now he needed to think about this interview.

Imogen Lorrimer had snagged the edge of his vision the moment she'd entered the boardroom two days before, when he'd called an initial meeting of all Langley staff. He'd nodded impatiently at her to be seated and been further arrested by the tint of her eye colour as she'd perched on her chair and aimed a fleeting glance at him from under the straight line of her black fringe. For a fraction of a second he'd faltered in his speech, stopped in his tracks by eyes of a shade that was neither blue nor grey but some-where in between.

Since then he'd stared at her more than once as she scuttled past him in the corridor, dark head down, clearly reluctant to initiate visual contact.

But he was used to people being nervous around him. After all he was a troubleshooter; people knew he had the power to fire them. A power he used where necessary—had in fact already used that morning. So if firing Imo-gen Lorrimer would benefit Langley Interior Designs he wouldn't hesitate. However attractive he found her.

As if on cue there was a knock at the open office door and Joe looked up.

Further annoyance nipped his chest at the realisation that he had braced himself as if for impact. Imogen Lor-rimer was nothing more than an employee he needed to evaluate. There was no need for this disconcerting aware-ness of her.

For a second she hesitated in the doorway, and despite himself his pulse-rate kicked up a notch.

Ridiculous. In her severely cut navy suit, with her dark hair pulled back into a sleek bun, she looked the epitome of professionalism. The least he could do was pretend to be the same. Which meant he had to *stop* checking her out.

'Come in.' He rose to his feet and she walked stiffly across the floor, exuding nervous tension.

'Mr McIntyre,' she said, her voice high and breathy.

'Joe's fine.' Sitting down, he nodded at the chair oppo-site him. 'Have a seat.'

Surely a simple enough instruction. But apparently not. Astonishment rose his brows as Imogen twitched, stared at the red swivel chair for a few seconds, glanced at him, and then back at the chair. Her strangled gargle turned into an unconvincing cough.

Joe rubbed the back of his neck and studied the apparently hypnotic object. As might be expected in an interior designer's office, it was impressive. Red leather, stylish design, functional, comfortable, eye-catching.

But still just a chair.

Yet Imogen continued to regard it, her cheeks now the same shade as the leather.

Impatience caused him to drum his fingers on the desk and the sound seemed to rally her. Swivelling on her sensible navy blue pumps, she stared down at the glass desktop, closed her eyes as though in pain, and then hauled in an audible breath.

'Is there a problem?' he asked. 'Something wrong with the chair?'

'Of course not. I'm sorry,' she said as she lowered herself downwards onto the edge of the chair and clasped her hands onto her lap.

'If it's not the chair then it must be me,' he said. 'I get that you may be a bit nervous. But don't worry. I don't bite.'

Stricken blue eyes met his as she gripped the arms of the chair as though it were a rollercoaster. 'Good to know,' she said. 'Sorry. Um…I'm not usually this nervous. It's just…obviously…well…' Pressing her glossy lips together tightly, she closed her eyes.

Exasperation surged through him. This was the woman Peter Langley had described as 'a mainstay of the company'. It was no bloody wonder Langley was in trouble. Perhaps he should end this interview here and now.

He'd opened his mouth to do just that when she opened her eyes, gave a little wriggle in the chair, and—*wham!*

An image zigzagged across his brain—a picture of Imogen Lorrimer, standing up to wriggle her way right out of that navy skirt, shrug off the jacket and slowly unbutton the pearl buttons of her white shirt. Before shaking that dark hair free so it tumbled to her shoulders, then sitting back down on that damn red chair and crossing her legs.

A hoarse noise rasped from his throat. What the hell…? *Why?* Where on earth had *that* come from?

It was time to get a grip of this interview—*and* the conversation. A sigh escaped her and for a second his gaze focused on her lips. Hell, this was *not* good. 'Never Mix Business and Pleasure' was a non-negotiable rule. His work ethic was sacrosanct—the thought of jeopardising his reputation and ruining his business the way his father had done was enough to bring him out in hives.

So this awareness had to be nixed—no matter how inexplicably tempting Imogen Lorrimer was. His libido needed an ice bath or a night of fun. Preferably the latter—a nice, relaxed, laid-back evening with a woman unconnected to any client. Someone who could provide a no-strings-attached night of pleasure.

In the meantime he needed to concentrate on the matter in hand.

What had Imogen said last? Before she'd frozen into perpetual silence.

'It's just…obviously…what?' he growled.

Imogen caught her bottom lip in her teeth and bit down hard; with any luck the pain would recall her common sense. If it were logistically possible to boot herself around the room she would, and her fingers tingled with the urge to slap herself upside the head.

Enough.

She had had enough of herself.

It was imperative that she keep her job. For herself, but also because if she were here she could do everything in her power to make sure this man didn't shut Langley down.

Peter and Harry Langley had been more than good to her—the least she could do was try to ensure this corporate killing machine didn't chew up their company and spit it out.

Instead of sitting here squirming in embarrassed silence over last night's encounter with a fantasy Joe McIntyre.

Time to channel New Imogen, who fantasised over gazillions of hot men and didn't bat an eyelid.

She moistened her lips and attempted a smile.

Brown eyes locked with hers and for a heartbeat something flickered in their depths. A spark, an awareness—a look that made her skin sizzle. The sort of look that Dream Joe excelled in.

Then it was gone. Doused almost instantly and replaced by definitive annoyance, amplified by a scowl that etched his forehead with the sort of formidable frown that Real Joe no doubt held a first-class degree in.

Straightening her shoulders, she forced herself to meet his exasperated gaze. 'I apologise, Joe. The past few weeks have been difficult and the result was an attack of nerves. I'm fine now, and I'd appreciate it if we could start again.'

'Let's do that.' His words were emphatic as he gestured to her CV. 'You've been Peter's PA for five years—ever since you came out of college. He speaks very highly of you, so why so nervous?'

OK. Here goes.

There was no hiding the fact that she'd screwed up and, given that Joe had been on the premises for two days, there was little doubt he already knew about it. So it was bite the proverbial bullet time.

'I'm sure you've heard about the Anderson project?'

'Yes, I have.'

Stick to the facts, Imogen.

'Then you know I made a pretty monumental mistake.' Her stomach clenched as she relived the sheer horror. 'I ordered the wrong fabric. Yards and yards of it. I didn't realise I'd done that. The team went ahead and used it and the client ended up with truly hideous mustard-coloured

curtains and coverings throughout his mansion instead of
the royal gold theme we had promised him.'

A shudder racked her body as she adhered her feet in
the thick carpet to prevent herself from swivelling in a
twist of sheer discomfort on the chair. 'Mistake' was not
supposed to be in the Imogen Lorrimer dictionary. To err
was inexcusable; her mother had drummed that into her
over and over.

'It was awful. Even worse than...' She pressed her lips
together.

His eyes flickered to rest on her mouth and a spark ignited in the pit of her tummy.

'Even worse than what?' he demanded.

Nice one, Imogen. Now no doubt Joe was imagining a
string of ditzy disasters in her wake.

Tendrils of hair wisped around her face as she shook
her head, sacrificing the perfection of her bun for the sake
of vehemence. 'It doesn't matter. Honestly. It's nothing to
do with work. Just a childhood memory.'

Joe raised his dark eyebrows, positively radiating scepticism. 'You're telling me that you have a childhood disaster that competes with a professional debacle like that?'

He didn't believe her.

'Yes,' she said biting back her groan at the realisation
she would have to tell him. She couldn't risk him assuming she was a total mess-up. 'I was ten and I came home
with the worst possible report you could imagine.'

Imogen could still feel the smooth edges of the book-
let in her hand; her tummy rolled in remembered fear and
sadness. *Keep it light, Imogen.*

'Having lied through my teeth all term that I'd been
doing brilliantly, I'd pretty much convinced myself I was
a genius—so I was almost as upset to discover I wasn't
as my mum was.'

The look of raw disappointment on Eva Lorrimer's face

was one that she would never forget, never get used to, no matter how many times she saw it.

'Anyway…' Imogen brushed the side of her temple in an attempt to sweep away the memory. 'I had the exact same hollow, sinking, leaden feeling when I saw the mustard debacle.'

Joe's brown eyes rested on her face with an indecipherable expression; he was probably thinking she was some sort of fruit loop.

'But the point about the Andersen project is that it was a one-off. I have never made a mistake like that before and I can assure you that I never will again.'

Whilst she had no intention of excusing herself, seeing as the word 'excuse' also failed to feature in her vocabulary, she had messed up the day after Steve had literally thrown her onto the street so his ex-girlfriend could move back in. She'd reeled into work, still swaying in disbelief and humiliation. Not that she had any intention of sharing *that* with Joe; she doubted it would make any difference if she did. She suspected Joe didn't hold much truck with personal issues affecting work.

Panic churned in her stomach. The Langleys wouldn't want Joe to fire her. But Peter was in the midst of a breakdown and Harry was stable but still in Intensive Care after his heart attack; neither of them was in a position to worry about *her*.

Leaning forward, she gripped the edge of the desk. 'I'm good at my job,' she said quietly. 'And I'll do anything I can to help keep this company going until Peter and Harry are back.'

Including fighting this man every step of the way if he tried to tear apart what the Langley brothers had built up.

For a second his gaze dropped, and his frown deepened before he gave a curt nod.

'I'll bear it in mind,' he said. 'Now, let's move on. According to Peter this is a list of current projects and obligations.' He pushed a piece of typewritten paper across the desk. 'He doesn't seem very sure it's complete and he referred me to you.'

Imogen looked down at the list and tried to focus on the words and not on Joe's hand. On his strong, capable fingers, the light smattering of hair, the sturdy wrists that for some reason she wanted so desperately to touch. Those hands that in her dreams had wrought such incredible magic.

Grinding her molars, she tugged the paper towards her. 'I'll check this against my organiser.' She bent at the waist to pick up her briefcase. And frowned. Had that strange choking noise been Joe? As she sat up she glanced at him and clocked a slash of colour on his cheekbones.

Focus.

Imogen looked at the paper and then back at her organiser. 'The only thing not on here is the annual Interior Design awards ceremony. It's being held this Wednesday. Peter and Graham Forrester were meant to attend.' She frowned. 'Could be Peter forgot. Or he's changed his mind because the client can't make it. Or he's too embarrassed to face everyone.'

Joe's forehead had creased in a frown and his fingers beat a tattoo on the desk—and there she was, staring at those fingers *again*.

'Tell me more about it.'

'It's a pretty prestigious event. We won in the luxury category for the interior of an apartment we did for Richard Harvey the IT billionaire. He commissioned us to create a love nest for his seventh wife.'

Joe's brows hiked towards his hairline as he whistled. '*Seven?* The man must be a glutton for punishment.'

'He's a romantic,' Imogen said. 'You've got to admire that kind of persistence.'

'No.'

'No, what?'

'No, I *don't* have to admire it. It's delusional. Sometimes dreams have to be abandoned because they aren't possible.'

Easy for him to say—it was impossible to imagine a lean, mean corporate machine having *any* dreams.

'Some dreams,' she agreed. 'But not all. I truly believe that if you persevere and try and you're willing to compromise there is a person out there for everyone.'

After all, she had no intention of giving up finding a man to match her tick list just because she and Steve had gone pear-shaped.

'Richard has just had to try harder than most. And,' she added, seeing the derisory quirk to his lips, 'he and Crystal are very happy—in fact they are in Paris, celebrating their meetiversary.'

'Excuse me?'

'The day they met a year ago. Richard has whisked her off to Paris for a romantic getaway. That's why they can't attend the awards. I hope Richard and Crystal get to celebrate *decades* of meetiversaries.'

'Good for you. *I* hope to show Richard that we value the award we won for decorating his apartment. So, tell me more about the project. Who worked on it?'

'Peter, Graham and me. Peter often lets me get involved with the design side of things as well as the admin stuff.'

Joe's brown eyes assessed her expression and his fingers continued to drum on the desk-top. 'How involved were you on the project?

'I designed both bathrooms.'

'Could you show me?'

'Sure.'

Trepidation twisted her nerves even as she tried to sound calm. Maybe Joe would use this to make his final decision on her job. Or was it something else? There was something unnerving about his gaze; she could almost hear the whir and tick of his brain.

'I'll get the folder.'

Once she'd pulled the relevant portfolio from the filing cabinet at the back of the room she walked back to the desk.

Placing the folder carefully on the glass top, she leaned over to tug the elastic at the corner. *Whoosh*—an unwary breath and she had inhaled a lungful of Joe: sandalwood, and something that made her want to nuzzle into his neck.

No can do. Newsflash, Imogen: this is not a dream—it's for real.

She needed to breathe shallowly and focus—*not* on the way an errant curl of brown hair had squiggled onto the nape of his neck but on demonstrating her design talent.

'The spec was to create something unique to make Crystal feel special.'

'Tough gig.'

'I enjoyed it.'

Back then she'd been living in Cloud Cuckoo Land, absolutely sure that Steve was about to propose to her, and throwing herself into the spirit of the project had been easy. She had enjoyed liaising with Richard over the plan and ideas—loved the fact that the flat was to be a wedding surprise for his wife.

'These are the bathrooms.'

She pointed to the sketches and watched as he flipped through the pages.

'These are good,' he said.

His words vibrated with sincerity and she felt her lips curve up in a smile, his approval warming her chest.

'Thank you. The hammock bath is fab—big enough for two and perfect for the wet room.'

Imogen and Joe, lying naked in the bath... Just keep talking.

'I went for something more opulent for the second bathroom. All fluted pillars and marble. With a wooden hot tub, complete with a table in the middle for champagne.'

Her breath caught in her throat. *Imogen and Joe, playing naked footsie... Move on, move on.*

'And this was my *pièce de résistance*. I managed to source sheets threaded with twenty-two-carat gold for the bedroom.'

Oh, hell. Time to stop talking.

Closing the folder, she moved around the desk, willing her feet not to scurry back to the dratted chair.

'Anyway, Graham can take you through the rest of the project.'

'Not possible.'

'Why not?' Imogen studied Joe's bland expression and the penny clanged from on high. 'Have you *sacked* Graham?'

Joe shrugged. 'Graham no longer works for Langley.'

'But...you can't do that.' Outrage smacked her mouth open and self-disgust ran her veins. How could she possibly fantasise over a man who could be so callous?

He raised his eyebrows. 'I think you'll find I can.'

'Graham Forrester is one of the best interior designers in London. He's Peter's protégé. Why would you get rid of him?'

'That is not your concern.'

Her hands clenched into fists of self-annoyance. She'd let herself relax, been *pleased* that he had approved of her work. Taken her eye off the fact that he had the power to take Langley apart.

'Graham is my friend and my colleague. I went to his wedding last month. He *needs* this job. So of course it's my concern. And it's not only me who will say that. *Everyone* will be concerned. We're like a family here.'

'And that's a good thing, is it?' His tone was dry, yet the words held amusement.

Anger burned behind her ribs. 'Yes, it is.' A wave of her hand in the air emphasised her point. 'We're the interior design version of *The Waltons*. And sacking Graham is the equivalent of killing off John-Boy.'

His lips quirked upwards for a second and frustration stoked the flames of her ire. He could at least take her seriously.

'You *have* to reconsider.'

The smirk vanished as his lips thinned into a line. 'Not happening, Imogen.'

'Then I'll…'

'Then you'll what?' he asked. 'I think you may need to consider whether your loyalty lies with Graham Forrester or with Langley.'

'Is that a threat?'

'It's friendly advice.' Rubbing the back of his neck, he surveyed her for a moment. 'Peter described you as an important part of the company—if you walk out to support Graham, or undermine my position so I'm forced to let you go, the company will lose out.'

Dammit, she couldn't let Peter and Harry down—however much she wanted to tell him to shove his job up his backside. If she were still here maybe she could do something to prevent further disaster…though Lord knew what. Plus, on a practical note, she couldn't add unemployment to her list of woes.

'I'll stay. But for the record I totally disagree with you letting Graham go.'

'Your concerns are noted. Now, I need you to reinstate Langley's presence at the awards ceremony. We're going.'

'What?' Imogen stared at him. '*You* can't possibly mean to go.'

'Why not?'

'Because it will look odd for Graham not to be there. And you being there is hardly going to send out a good message; it's advertising that Langley is in trouble.'

He shook his head. 'It's *acknowledging* that Langley is in trouble and showing we're doing something about it. The head in the sand approach doesn't work.'

The words stung; she knew damn well from personal experience that the head in the sand approach didn't work. 'My head is quite firmly above ground, thank you.'

'Good. Then listen carefully. Whether you believe it or not, I am good at my job. Me being at these awards will reassure everyone that Langley is back on its feet and ready to roll.' He leant back and smiled a smile utterly devoid of mirth. 'So we're going. You and me.'

Say what? Imogen stared at him, her chin aiming for her knees.

Joe nodded. 'You worked on the project, you liaised with the client—it makes sense.'

CHAPTER TWO

IMOGEN PACED HER best friend's lounge, striding over the brightly flowered rug, past the camp bed she was currently spending her nights on, to the big bay-fronted window and back again. 'Makes sense!' She narrowed her eyes at Mel and snorted. 'Makes sense, my...'

Mel shifted backwards on the overstuffed sofa, curled her legs under her and rummaged in her make-up bag. 'Imo, hun... You need to calm down. Joe is in charge and you have no choice.' Holding up two lipsticks, she tilted her blonde head to one side in consideration. 'It may even be fun.'

'Fun?' Imogen stared at her, a flicker of guilt igniting as her tummy did a loop-the-loop of anticipation. 'Fun to spend two hours working late with Joe and then going to an awards ceremony with Joe. That's not fun. It's purgatory.'

Mel raised her perfectly plucked eyebrows. 'Imo! Imo! Imo! Methinks you protest too much. Methinks you fancy the boxers off the man.'

There was that fire of guilt again. How could she be so shallow as to have the hots for such an arrogant, ruthless bastard?

'Youthinks wrong,' Imogen said flatly. 'And why are you looking at me like that?'

'A) Because you couldn't lie your way out of a paper bag and B) because I'm hoping you aren't planning to go to the awards ceremony looking like that.'

Imogen looked down at herself. 'What's wrong with

this? I wore this to a big client dinner with Steve a few months ago.'

'Exactly.'

'What is that supposed to mean?'

'Imogen, sweetie. That dress is *dull*. It's grey and it's shapeless and it's boring. It's how Steve liked you to dress because he was terrified you would run off—like Simone did.'

'That's not true. I chose this dress because...' She trailed off. 'Anyway, it will have to do. In fact with any luck no one will notice me. I mean, it's wrong to go to the awards ceremony when Graham did most of the work.'

Mel frowned. 'It sounds to me like you did your fair share. Plus, Graham can't go because he doesn't work for Langley any more. Plus, you said that Joe said he would still be credited.'

'Humph...' Damn man had an answer to everything.

'So you are going to this ceremony to display to the world that Langley is alive and flourishing. If you go dressed like that everyone will think Langley is on its last legs and you've bought a dress for the funeral.'

'Ha-ha!' Imogen exhaled a sigh as she contemplated her best friend's words. Mel knew all there was to know about clothes, and she had a point. 'OK. How about my little black dress with...?'

'It's more big black bin-bag, Imo. I have a way better idea. You can borrow one of *my* dresses.'

'Um...Mel. You know me. I really, really don't want to be...'

'The focus of attention? Yes, you do. And I've got the perfect outfit. Wait here a second.'

Imogen exhaled a puff of air—of course she wanted to do the right thing for Langley, but she knew Mel, and her friend's fashion taste was nothing like hers. Imogen's taste was more...

More what? In a moment of horror she realised she didn't know. In all her twenty-six years she'd always dressed to please others.

Eva Lorrimer had had very firm ideas about what a young girl should wear, and at her insistence Imogen had obediently donned plain long skirts and frilly tops. It had seemed the least she could do to make her mum a little bit happy. Plus, anything for a quiet life—right?

Then Steve... Well, was Mel right? *Had* she let him dictate what she wore? Steve had always said he hated women who flaunted or flirted when they were in a relationship. He had told her how Simone had always done exactly that. So she'd worked out what he approved of and what he liked and taken care to shop accordingly. Because it had made her happy to make him happy. Plus, anything for a quiet life—right?

Mel waltzed back into the room. 'What do you think?'

Imogen stared at the dress Mel was holding up. If you could even call it a dress. For the life of her she couldn't work out how she would get into it, or where all the lacy frou-frou would go, or even how it could even be decent. The only thing that was clear was the colour—bright, vibrant and sassy.

'It's very...red.'

OK. It wasn't what *she* would choose. But if she had the choice between something in her wardrobe chosen by her mum or Steve and something chosen by Mel, right now she was going with Mel's choice.

'I'll wear it.'

Mel blinked. 'Really? I was prepared for battle.'

'Nope. No battle. Though you may have to help me work out how to put it on.'

'I'll do better than that—I'll lend you shoes and do your make-up as well.'

'Perfect. Thanks, sweetie. You're a star.'

Surprise mixed with a froth of anticipation as to what this New Imogen would look like.

An hour later and she knew.

Staring at the image that looked back at her from the mirror, she blinked, disbelief nearly making her rub her eyes before taking another gander. Her mother would keel over in a faint, Steve's lips would purse in disapproval—and Imogen didn't care. She looked....*visible*.

'You look gorgeous. You look hot. Joe McIntyre won't know what's hit him.'

'I'm not doing this for Joe.'

Liar, liar, pants most definitely on fire.

Squashing the voice, she gave her head a small shake. The butterflies currently completing an assault course in her tummy were nothing to do with Joe.

'I'm doing it for Langley.'

Mel dimpled at her. 'You keep telling yourself that, Imo,' she said soothingly. 'Have fun!'

Joe glanced around the office and gusted out a sigh. Not that there was anything to complain about in the surroundings; he'd sat in far worse than this mecca to interior design and it hadn't bothered him. The problem was that wherever he was sitting he'd never had this level of anticipation twisting his gut.

Irritation stamped on his chest. Anticipation had no place here. The awards ceremony would go better for Langley if Imogen Lorrimer were there. She had worked on the Richard Harvey project, knew many of the people who would be there, so it made sense for her to attend.

Joe snorted and picked up his cup of coffee. Listen to himself. Anyone would think he was justifying his decision because he had an ulterior motive in taking Imogen. When of course he didn't. Or that he was looking forward to taking Imogen. Which was ridiculous. The woman couldn't

stand him, and he had the definitive suspicion that she was
planning some sort of rearguard action against him in the
hope that he'd change his mind about Graham Forrester.

She was probably running a Bring Back John-Boy Campaign.

Yet in the past two days he had more than once, more
than twice, more than...too many times...found himself
looking for Imogen or noticing her when there'd been no
need to. Caught by the turn of her head or a waft of her
delicate flowery perfume.

Exasperation surfaced again and he quelled it. Just because her appearance had somehow got under his guard
it didn't mean there was a problem. He knew all too well
the associated perils of letting personal issues into the
boardroom. That was what his father had done and the
result had been a spiral of disaster—a mess bequeathed
to Joe to sort out.

So there was no problem. All he had to do was recall
the grim horror of working out that his family firm was
bankrupt and corrupt. Remember the faces of the people
he'd been forced to let go, the clients whose money had
been embezzled.

Enough. The lesson was learnt.

His computer pinged to indicate the arrival of an email;
one glance at the screen and he groaned. *Another* email
from Leila. Every instinct jumped up and down—he was
no expert on the intricacies of relationships, but he was
pretty damn sure it wasn't normal for an ex to suddenly
surface after seven years, invite him to her wedding and
then email him regularly to give him advice he hadn't
asked for.

Resisting the urge to thump his head on the desk, he
looked up as the door rebounded off its hinges and Imogen entered.

No. She didn't enter. It was more of a storm... A vivid

red tornado of gorgeous anger headed straight towards him and slammed her palms down on the glass desk-top.

'Something wrong?' Joe asked, trying and failing to ignore the sleek curtain of hair that fell straight and true round her face and down past her shoulders to the plunging V of her dress. Surely there was more V than material?

Continuing his look downward, he took in the cinched-in waist and the flouncy skirt that hit a good few centimetres above the knee. Her legs were endless, long and toned, and ended in a pair of sparkly peep-toe sandals.

Stop looking. Before you have a coronary.

He tugged his gaze upward to meet a fulminating pair of grey-blue eyes.

'Yes, there *is* something wrong.'

Her breath came in pants and Joe clenched his jaw, nearly crossing his eyes in an attempt to remain focused on her face.

'I know I shouldn't say anything. I know I shouldn't put my job on the line. But I've just come from seeing Harry and Peter in the hospital and they told me that you've got rid of Maisey in Accounts and Lucas in Admin. How could you? It's *wrong*.'

The fury vibrating in her voice touched a chord in him, aroused an answering anger to accompany the frustration and self-annoyance already brewing in his gut.

'No, Imogen, it isn't wrong. It's *unfortunate*. Streamlining Langley is the only way for the company to survive. I'd rather a few people suffer than the whole company collapse.'

She huffed out air and shook her head, black hair shimmering. 'But don't you care?' she asked. 'It's like these people are just numbers to you.'

The near distaste in her eyes made affront claw down his chest. 'I do my very best to minimise the number of people I let go and I certainly don't take any pleasure in it.'

She stood back from the desk and slammed her hands on her hips. 'You don't seem to feel any pain either.'

Her words made him pause; sudden discomfort jabbed his nerves. It was an unease he dismissed; feeling pain sucked, and it didn't change a damn thing. This he knew. Hell, he had the whole wardrobe to prove it. So if he'd hardened himself it was a *good* thing—a business decision that made him better at his job.

Aware of curiosity dancing with anger across Imogen's delicate features, he shrugged. 'Me sitting around crying into my coffee isn't going to enable me to make sensible executive decisions. I can't let sentiment interfere with my job.'

'But what if your executive choices hurt someone else?'

'I don't make choices to hurt people.'

'That doesn't mean they don't *get* hurt. Look at Graham. I happen to know he has a large mortgage, his wife is pregnant, and now you've made the choice to snatch his job from under his feet. Doesn't that bother you?'

'No.' To his further exasperation he appeared to be speaking through clenched teeth. 'The bottom line is I do the best for the company as whole. Overall, people benefit.'

'Have you ever watched *Star Trek*?'

Star Trek? Joe blinked. 'Yes, I have. My sisters are avid fans.' Repeats of the show had been a godsend in the devastating months after their parents' death; Tammy and Holly had spent hours glued to the screen. Blocking out impossible reality with impossible fiction.

'Joe? Are you listening to me?'

'For now. But only because I am fascinated to see what pointy-eared aliens and transporters have to do with anything?'

'You know how it works—they *say* they believe in sacrificing the few for the many. But they don't really mean it—somehow in real life they end up knowing that it's wrong and they go back to rescue one person, risking everyone, and everything is OK.'

Was she for real? 'The fatal flaw in your reasoning is right there. *Star Trek* isn't real life. It's *fiction*.'

'I get that—but the principle is sound.'

'No. The principle sucks. If you run around trying to please everyone, refusing to make tough choices, then I can tell you exactly what happens. Everyone suffers.' He'd got another wardrobe to prove *that*. 'In real life Kirk would go down, and so would the *Enterprise*.'

'That is so…'

'Realistic?'

'Cynical,' she snapped. 'I don't understand why you can't see reason. The main reason Langley is in difficulties is because of Harry's ill health. He's the one who understands finance. Peter doesn't. Once Harry's on his feet everything will go back to normal. Surely you should be taking that into consideration? Trying to think of some way to salvage everyone's jobs.'

The jut of her chin, the flash of her eyes indicated how serious she was, and although he had no doubt his decisions were correct, it occurred to him that it was a long, long time since anyone had questioned him, let alone locked phasers with him. Apart from his sisters, anyway…

It was kind of…exhilarating.

Even more worrying, his chest had warmed with admiration: Imogen was speaking out for others with a passion that made him think of a completely different type of passion. His fingers itched with the desire to bury themselves in the gloss of her dark hair and angle her face so that he could kiss her into his way of thinking.

For the love of Mike… This was so off the business plan he might as well file for bankruptcy right now.

Curving his fingers firmly round the edge of his desk, he adhered his feet to the plush carpet and forced calm to his vocal cords. 'My job is to make sure that Harry has a viable company to come back to. I am not out to destroy Langley. That's not how I operate.'

'That's not what your reputation says.'

Disbelief clouded her blue eyes with grey and the disdain in her expression caused renewed affront to band round his chest.

'Imogen, there are some companies that even I can't salvage. But if you study my track record you will see that most of the companies I go to sort out get sorted out. Not shut down. My reputation is that I'm tough. I'll make the unpopular decisions no one wants to make because they let sentiment and friendship cloud their perspective. I don't.'

A small frown creased her brow. 'So you're telling me you're cold and heartless but you get results?'

'Yes. Peter and Harry wouldn't be able to let Graham go. I can. They, you and Captain Kirk may not like my methods, but I *will* save Langley.'

Annoyance at the whole conversation hit him—talk about getting overheated. Who did he think he was? The corporate version of the Lone Ranger? He'd spent the better part of the past half an hour justifying his actions, and he was damned if he knew why. Anyone would think he *cared* about her opinion of him.

'Now, can you please sit down so we can get some work done?'

At least that way the bottom half of her would be obscured from sight and his blood pressure would stay on the chart.

Imogen dropped down onto the chair. Joe's words were ringing in her head—and there was no doubting his sincerity. So, whilst she saw him as the villain of the piece he saw himself as the hero.

She chewed her bottom lip—was there any chance that

he was right? Then she remembered Harry Langley's pale face, blending in with the colour of his hospital pillow. His slurred voice shaking with impotent anger as he vowed to put things right.

She thought of the size of Graham's mortgage, his pride that his wife could be a stay-at-home mum if she wanted... of Maisey's tears when she'd phoned her on the way here from the hospital...

All those people suffering because of the man sitting opposite her.

Yet a worm of doubt wriggled into her psyche. His deep voice had been genuine when he'd spoken of the necessity of his cuts, the bigger picture, his desire to save Langley.

But, hell, that didn't mean she had to *like* him. Nonetheless...

'Imogen.'

His impatient growl broke into her reverie.

'Did you hear a word I said?'

'Sorry. I was thinking it must be hard to always be seen as the villain,' she replied.

'Doesn't bother me.' A quizzical curve tilted his lip. 'You starting to feel sorry for me now?'

'Of course not.'

The idea was laughable; Joe McIntyre didn't need sympathy. He needed to be shaken into common sense and out of her dreams.

'Well, tonight we need to at least call a truce. You acting as though I am some sort of corporate monster will do more damage to Langley than I can. So you need to play nice.'

Wrinkling her nose in a way that she could only hope indicated distaste, she nodded. Instinct told her a truce with this man would be dangerous, but he was right: they could hardly attend the award ceremony sparring with each other.

'As long as you know I am playing. As in pretending.'

'Don't worry,' he said, his voice so dry it was practically parched. 'Message received, loud and clear. The truce is temporary. Now, can we get on with it? I've ordered a taxi to take us to the hotel at seven, and I want to go through Peter's client list with you before then.'

An hour later Imogen put her pen down. 'I think that's it,' she said.

Flexing her shoulders, she looked across at him. Big mistake. Because now she couldn't help but let her gaze linger on the breadth of his chest under the snowy-white dress shirt and the tantalising hint of bare skin on show where he hadn't bothered doing up the top buttons.

Looking up, she caught a sudden predatory light in his brown eyes. A light that was extinguished almost before she could be sure it had been there, but yet sent a shiver through her body.

'You've done a great job.' Pulling at the sheaf of paper she'd scribbled on, he glanced down at her notes.

'Thank you. I'll type those up for you first thing tomorrow. The notes indicate what each project was, how many times they've used us, and a few personal bits about them. Not *personal* personal, but...'

Babble-babble-babble. One probably imagined look and she'd dissolved into gibberish.

'Things that show I'm not delivering the same spiel to each client,' he said. 'Exactly what I need.'

He stared down at the paper and cleared his throat, as if searching for something else to say. Could he be feeling the same shimmer of tension she was?

'So...according to this, you've done a lot of actual design work.'

'Er...yes... I told you I help out.'

'I didn't realise how much. Why haven't you put all the project work you've done on your CV? Or, for that matter, why haven't you put things on a more formal footing? I'm sure Peter would agree to sponsor you so you could go to college.'

'That's not the way I want my career to go.'

It was a decision made long ago. What she prized above all else was security—a job she enjoyed, but not one that would rule her life. She'd seen first-hand the disastrous consequences of a job that became an obsession, and she wasn't going there.

'Why not? You've got real talent and great client liaison skills. Everyone I've spoken to so far has only had good things to say about you—even Mike Anderson.' He nodded at the paper. 'From everything you've written there, it seems clear they'll all be the same.'

Imogen couldn't help the smile that curved her lips as she savoured his words, absorbed them into her very being. 'Everyone? Even Mike Anderson? For real?'

'For real.'

He smiled back and, dear Lord above, what a smile it was. Instinct told her it rarely saw the light of day—and what a good thing *that* was for the female population. Because it was the genuine make-your-knees-go-weak article.

The moment stretched, the atmosphere thickening around them, blanketing them...

'So what do you think?' Joe asked.

'About what?' *Focus, Imo.*

'Changing career? Within Langley if it remains a viable option. Or elsewhere.'

Forcing herself to truly concentrate on his question, she let the idea take hold. New Imogen Lorrimer—wearer of red dresses and trainee interior designer. *Yeah, right.* There was no version of Imogen who would leap out of her comfort zone like that.

And she was fine with that. More than fine. The whole point of a comfort zone was that it was *comfortable*.

'Not for me, thank you. I'm very happy as I am.'

End of discussion; there was no need for this absurd urge to justify herself.

Glancing at her watch, she rose to her feet and pushed the chair backwards. 'Look at the time. I need to get ready before the taxi gets here.'

An audible hitch of breath was her only answer, and she looked up from her watch to see dark brown eyes raking over her. Without her permission her body heated up further—a low, warm glow in her tummy to accompany the inexplicable feeling of disappointment at a decision she knew to be right.

'You look pretty ready to me,' he drawled.

Was he flirting with her? Was she dreaming?

An unfamiliar spark, no doubt ignited by the sheer effrontery of the dress, lit up a synapse in her brain. Hooking a lock of hair behind her ear, she fought the urge to flutter her eyelashes.

'Is that a compliment?'

'If you want.'

There was that look again—and this time she surely wasn't imagining the smoulder. Even if she had no idea how to interpret it.

'It's also an observation.'

As he rose to his feet and picked up a black tie from the back of his chair Imogen gulped. Six foot plus of lean, honed muscle.

'So,' he continued, 'seeing as you had a bathroom break a quarter of an hour ago, my guess is that you're avoiding this discussion. True or false?'

Mesmerised, she watched his strong fingers deftly pull the tie round his neck before he turned and picked his jacket up.

'False...' she managed.

Right now she needed to get away from the pheromone onslaught—she *wasn't* avoiding the discussion. Much…

'If you say so.' Slinging the jacket over his shoulder, he headed towards her. 'And, Imogen? One more thing?'

'Yes?'

Oh, hell—he was getting closer. Why weren't her feet moving? Heading towards the door and the waiting taxi? Instead her ridiculous heels appeared superglued to the carpet as her heart pounded in her ribcage. A hint of his earthy scent tickled her nostrils, and still her stupid feet wouldn't obey her brain's commands.

His body was so warm…his eyes held hers in thrall. Hardly able to breathe, she clocked his hand rising, and as he touched her lower lip heat shot through her body.

A shadow fleeted across his face and he stepped backwards, his arm dropping to his side.

'Don't forget to smile,' he said.

CHAPTER THREE

IMOGEN DUCKED INTO a corner of the crowded room, needing a moment to breathe after an hour of smiling, socialising and being visible. The set-up was gorgeous—worthy of the five-star hotel where the event was being held. Glorious flower arrangements abounded, in varying shades of pink to fuchsia, layered with dark green foliage. Chandeliers glinted and black-suited waiters with pink ties appeared as if by magic with trays of canapés or a choice of pink champagne and sparkling grapefruit juice.

Surreptitiously she slipped one foot out of a peep-toe, six-inch heeled shoe. Flexing it with relief, she let her gaze unerringly sift through the crowds of beautiful professionals, slip over the fabulously decorated room, heady with the fragrance of the magnificent spring flower centre-pieces that adorned each table, and found the tall figure of Joe McIntyre.

If it really was Joe and not some sort of clone.

Because ever since they'd walked through the imposing doors of the hotel Joe had undergone some sort of trans-formation. It had been goodbye to her taxi companion, Mr Dark and Brooding, and hello Mr Suave as he networked the room, all professional charm and bonhomie, not a single frown in sight.

But worst of all had been his closeness, the small touches as he'd propelled her from person to person, dis-pensing confidence in Langley and an insider knowledge of interior design that was impressive.

Little surprise that he had gathered a gang of female groupies who were now hanging on to his every word adoringly.

'What's wrong, Imo? That's a pretty hefty scowl. Contemplating the man who'll bring Langley down?'

Shoving her foot back into her shoe, Imogen turned and plastered her best fake smile to her face. *Great!* The man she'd been avoiding all night: head of IMID, Langley's chief competitor.

'Evening, Ivan. How are you?'

'I'm fine. Bursting with health. Which is more than can be said for poor old Harry and Peter. How *are* they?'

Imogen's skin crawled as Ivan Moreton's grey eyes slid over her with almost reptilian interest. Ivan had no principles or scruples, and had engaged in so many underhand schemes to undercut and undermine Langley that she'd lost count.

His methods were unscrupulous, but legal. So to hear him stand there, full of spuriously concerned queries as to Peter and Harry made her blood sizzle. Especially when he looked as though he could barely stop himself from rubbing his hands together in glee.

'Firmly on the road to recovery, thank you, Ivan. I'll be sure to tell them you were asking as a further incentive to get them back into the office.'

To wipe that smug smirk off your face.

'If, of course, they have an office to return to,' Ivan said, with a wave in Joe's direction. 'Could be that Mr McIntyre will have sold it off.'

'Joe wouldn't do that.' Imogen clamped her lips together; had there been a note of *hero-worship* in her voice? Please, no...

Ivan's eyebrows rose. 'Don't be deceived by those rugged looks, Imo. Joe McIntyre will do what it takes. Though even *he* makes mistakes. You see, Graham Forrester now works for me—and he's one very angry designer. Imagine offering him a salary cut. Graham said he's never been so insulted in his life.'

Imogen blinked as she tried to process that little snippet of information.

True, Graham couldn't afford a salary cut—but Peter had given Graham his first break, shown faith in him, showered him in pay rises. Shouldn't loyalty count for something? At least enough for Graham not to feel insulted and maybe not go straight to Langley's biggest competitor?

Or perhaps everyone else in the world got it except her? Were all capable of making executive decisions without sentiment?

Imogen took a step backwards, uncomfortably aware that whilst she had been thinking Ivan had stepped straight into her personal space. Enough so that now the coolness of the wall touched the bare skin on her back. If he came any closer, so help her, she'd either punch him on the nose or—better yet—take a step forward and pinion him with her heel.

'Joe won't be selling off the offices because there will be no need to,' she stated. 'Langley is still alive and kicking—and hopefully we'll be kicking *your* sorry behind for a long time to come.'

'Dream on, Imo. But I like your style.'

His cigarette-infused breath, tinted with alcohol, hit her cheek and she turned her face away.

'When I buy Langley out I'll put in a special bid for you.'

Ewwww. No one would thank her for creating a scene, but enough was enough. Imogen lifted her foot.

'Sounds like you need to be talking to *me*, Ivan.'

Imogen expelled a sigh of relief as she heard Joe's drawl, and then she looked up and saw the glint of anger in his eyes. She spotted the set jaw and something thrilled inside her.

Get some perspective, Imo.

For a start she was quite capable of looking after herself, and had had a perfectly good self-defence plan. Plus, Ivan was planning a Langley buy-out—*that* was what she needed to be thinking about. Instead of going all gooey because Joe was being protective.

The interior designer spun round and held his hand out. 'Joe. My friend. How are you doing? Imogen and I were just—'

'I can see exactly what *you* were just doing, Ivan, and I'd appreciate it if *you* didn't do it again.'

Ivan's grey eyes flicked from Imogen to Joe. 'You calling dibs, my friend?'

Imogen gave a small gasp. *Please let it have sounded like outrage, not hope.*

'No.' Joe stepped forward, his lips curling in a smile that held no mirth whatsoever. 'But if you want to talk about Langley deal with me. Not anyone else.'

The interior designer gave a toss of his dyed blond hair and stepped backwards. 'I'll do that. I'll get my PA to call your PA and set something up. I'm *very* interested in a buy-out.'

With that he turned and walked away.

'You OK?'

'I'm fine.' Imogen waved away his look of concern. 'Ivan Moreton is a sleazebag, and if you hadn't turned up he'd have been on his way to A&E with a stiletto through his foot.'

This time Joe's smile was real, and Imogen's stomach rollercoastered, all focus leaving the building.

'It's time for the presentations,' Joe said.

So not the moment to discuss the impossibility of an

IMID buy-out; plus, it would best to do that out of Ivan's range.

'I'll text Richard.'

'Why? What happened to the romantic Parisian get-away?'

'Nothing. He wants to show his support so I've arranged for him to be video conferenced in.'

'Great idea? Yours?'

There was that warmth again at his words... She needed to stop being so damn needy of people's approval. Just because praise had been a rarity in her childhood it didn't mean she had to overreact to it.

'Thanks,' she said, as coolly as she could, and quickly bent over her phone to hide the flush of pleasure that touched her cheeks.

A minute later her phone vibrated and she glanced down at it and blinked. Read the words again and gave a small whoop under her breath.

'Good news?'

'Yup. Look. That's Richard. He and Crystal have bought a place in Paris and they want us to pitch for the job of doing it up.' She continued reading. 'He wants us—you and me—to meet him in Paris on Friday.'

Joe and Imogen off to Paris. Be still her beating heart.

Polite applause broke out around them as the first speaker mounted the podium.

'That's excellent news. You'd better book some tickets on the Eurostar, then.'

Was that all he had to say? Was she the only one all of a flutter here? Of course she was. After all she was the one with the dream problem.

Turning away from him, Imogen stared resolutely at the speaker and tried to focus on his words. For the rest of the evening she would focus on interior design. *Not* on the man sitting beside her.

* * *

'Paris?' A pyjama-clad Mel stared at her in sheer disbelief. 'You are going to *Paris* with Joe McIntyre?'

'Yes.' Imogen snuggled back on the sofa and cradled her mug of hot chocolate. 'Ironic, really. I practically begged Steve to take me there, but he wouldn't. Said it held too many memories of Simone.'

She took a gulp of hot chocolate and pushed away memories of just how much time she had spent choosing a cruise that didn't contain any locations holding any memories of Simone. There was *real* irony for you. Because right this minute now Steve and Simone were on that luxury cruise, paid for with *her* hard-earned money, creating new memories.

'I'd rather go with someone hot like Joe than Steve,' Mel said musingly.

'That's plain shallow,' Imogen said. 'Heat level isn't everything in a man, you know. There are other attributes that are way more important.'

The sort of traits *she* looked for in a partner: kindness, stability, loyalty, security. More irony—how had she misjudged Steve so badly?

Mel shook her head, blonde curls bobbing. 'Not if you're on a jaunt to Paris.'

'It's not a *jaunt*. It's a business trip. We're not even staying overnight. Joe is out of the office tomorrow, I'm meeting him at St Pancras Station on Friday late morning, then we're coming back straight after our meeting.'

'*Tchah!* Why don't you book the wrong tickets by "mistake"? Then you could end up staying in a romantic hotel and...'

'I'd end up fired.'

Though for one stupid, insane moment her imagination had leapt in... She could see the hotel silhouetted on the Parisian horizon...

Imogen drained her mug. 'I'm for bed.'

'Oh!' Mel gave a gasp. 'I was so gobsmacked by Paris I forgot to tell you. Your mum called—she said it was urgent. Not *that* sort of urgent,' she added hastily, seeing panic grip her friend as she imagined the worst. 'But she did say you needed to ring her back, no matter what time it was.'

Imogen sighed. This wasn't what she needed right now, but Eva Lorrimer hated being made to wait.

Grabbing her mobile phone from the floor, she dialled her mother. 'Hey, Mum. It's me.'

'Finally.'

'Sorry. The awards ceremony finished late.'

'I only hope you going means you'll keep your job, Imogen. You make sure you impress Joe McIntyre. *Somehow.* Good PAs are two a penny, and now you've managed to lose Steve you will need to support yourself and—'

'Mum. Mel said it was urgent?' Surely reciting all Imogen's shortcomings couldn't be classed as imperative at past midnight. Even by Eva's standards.

'It *is* urgent. Steve has proposed to Simone on that cruise he's taken her on. They're getting married.'

Breath whooshed out of her lungs; surely this was some sort of joke. 'How do you know?'

'Clarissa rang me with the news.'

Better and better—Imogen bit back a groan. Clarissa was Steve's mother and one of Eva's old schoolfriends. If you could call her a friend. No doubt she had rung up to gloat.

'It's all over social media too,' Eva continued. 'Simone even put out a message thanking you for providing such a wonderful setting.'

Excellent. Now she'd be a laughing stock to everyone who knew her. Humiliation swept over her in a wave of heat that made her skin clammy.

Eva gusted out a sigh. 'That could have been *you* if you'd played your cards right. *You* could have a man to rely on—a man to support you and keep you secure. You should have done more to keep him, Imogen.'

Like what? She'd done everything she could think of to make Steve happy. Obviously she'd failed. Big-time. Steve himself had told her that she wasn't enough for him.

But instead of the usual self-criticism a sudden spark of anger ignited in the pit of her stomach. The bastard had actually proposed to another woman on the cruise *she* had paid for using her hard-earned savings. What would he do next? Send her the bill for the engagement ring?

'Actually, Mum, maybe I'm better off without him.'

'Steve was the best thing that ever happened to you, Imogen. Yes, I'd have preferred a fast-track banking career for you, but the next best thing would have been marrying a man with one...'

As Eva's voice droned on Imogen ground her molars and waited for the right moment to intercede.

'Mum. I understand how you feel.' That her daughter had let her down yet again. 'But I'm exhausted. We'll talk more tomorrow.'

Imogen disconnected the call and resisted the urge to bang her head against the wall.

Joe glanced at his watch, and then around the busy Victorian-style St Pancras station. Men and women tapped onto tablets, sipped at coffee or shopped in the boutiques. But there was no sign of Imogen. Where the hell *was* she?

Ah. There she was: striding across the crowded lounge, briefcase in one hand, cup of coffee in the other, dove-grey trouser suit, hair tugged up into a simple ponytail.

'Sorry I'm late,' she stated as she came to a halt next to him.

Joe frowned; her tone indicated not so much as a hint

of sincerity. In fact it pretty much dared him to comment. Imogen seemed… He glanced at her coffee cup as she tugged the lid off. Full. Yet she seemed wired—there was a pent-up energy in the tapping of her foot, an unnecessary force as she dropped her briefcase onto a chair.

'No problem. We've still got three minutes till we need to board.'

'Good.' She took a gulp of coffee. 'Then I have time to grab a *pain au chocolat*. Get myself in the mood.'

Because what she *really* needed right now was sugar on top of caffeine.

Joe swallowed the words. As a man who had brought up twin sisters, he knew exactly when it was best to keep his opinions to himself.

Clearly something had happened in the day and a half since he'd last seen her. But equally clearly Imogen's private life was nothing to do with him.

So he was *not* going to ask her what was wrong; he was going to stick to business.

Focusing on her back, he followed Imogen through the departure lounge to the ticket barriers, where they were smiled through by a svelte member of Eurostar staff. They moved along the bustling platform and onto the train.

He waited until she'd tucked her briefcase next to her and sat down opposite him, her eyes still snapping out that 'don't mess with me' vibe.

'So, could you brief me on our meeting with Richard Harvey? Has he told you anything about the project at all?'

'Nope. All I know is that it's a place in Paris. He's also said he's giving Graham a chance to pitch for it as well, because it seems only fair.' She frowned. 'My guess is Graham got on the phone and guilted him into it with a sob story about how you had brutally thrown him out.'

Joe raised his eyebrows. 'I thought you agreed with him?'

'I do, but…' Her slim shoulders lifted in a shrug and her

eyes sparked. 'If you must know Graham rang me yesterday, and he was really vindictive. Not only about you but about Peter too—and that's not fair. It's not as though *Peter* sacked him. And even *you* offered him a reduced salary.'

'You told me yourself about his mortgage and his wife; you can't blame him for accepting a more lucrative offer and now being loyal to Ivan.'

'I can blame whoever I like for whatever I like.'

Joe blinked at the sheer vehemence of her tone.

'Anyway,' she went on, 'Ivan is an out-and-out toad.' The description brought a small quirk to his lips until she said, 'And you aren't going to let him buy out Langley, are you?'

Damn. He'd hoped she'd forgotten that, but maybe this was why she was on the warpath.

'That's not something I can discuss with you.'

'But…you can't be seriously thinking about it. It would kill Harry off.'

'If a buy-out is offered I have to consider it.'

She opened her mouth as if to argue but inhaled deeply instead. 'OK. Fine. Clearly you don't have a better nature to appeal to, so tell me what I can do to help avert a buy-out.' Her fingers encircled the plastic table's edge and her nose wrinkled in distaste. 'Because I'd rather starve in a ditch than work for Ivan.'

He could hardly blame her; a sudden wave of aversion washed over him at the very thought. Irritation with himself clenched his jaw. If the buy-out was best for Langley that was the road he'd take. Full stop.

'That will be your choice. My decision will be based on what's best for Langley as a business.'

Eyes narrowed, she tapped a foot on the carriage floor. 'If we win this Paris project will that make Langley safe from Ivan?'

'Depends on the full extent of the project. But, yes, it would help.'

'So you're fully on board with going all out to win it? You haven't already decided that the buy-out is the way to go?'

Joe resisted the urge to roll his eyes. Why didn't she get that the decision was nothing to do with her?

'Can we drop the subject of the buy-out and concentrate on winning the Richard Harvey project? What else can you tell me about Richard and this meeting that will help our pitch? Is he bringing wife number seven?'

'Yes. I've told you her name is Crystal—and obviously don't make a big deal of her being number seven.'

Joe snorted. 'Well, gee, Imogen—thanks for the advice. *My* plan was to ask for a rundown of each and every wife along with a view of the wedding albums.' He gusted out a sigh. 'I'll happily avoid the entire topic of marriage.'

Imogen shook her head. 'Richard likes talking about marriage. Like I said, he's incurably romantic—which I suppose is why he's bought a place in Paris. As far as he is concerned he has finally fulfilled his dream—he's found The One. So probably best *not* to share your "dreams should be abandoned" theory.' Her eyes narrowed. 'Even if I'm beginning to wonder if you're right.'

'Me? Right? Wonders will never cease.' Curiosity won out over common sense. 'What brought that on?'

Opening her mouth as if to answer, her gaze skittered away as she clearly thought better of it and shook her head. 'You know, the daft dreams we have when we are young. I once thought I'd become an artist—had some stupid vision of myself in smock and beret, sketching on the streets of Paris or attending the Royal Academy, studying the masters in Italy, exhibiting in Rome—' She broke off. 'Absurd.'

Yet the look in her eyes, the vibrant depth of her tone, showed him that the dream had been real.

Lord knew he could empathise with giving up a dream. For a second he was transported back to a time when the world had truly been his oyster. He could smell the sea spray, taste the tang of salt in his mouth, feel the thump of exhilaration as he rode a wave. The incredible freedom, the knowledge that he would win the championships, would get sponsored, would...

Would end up dealing with bereavement, loss and responsibility.

Whoa. There was no point going there, and guilt pronged his chest because he had. The decisions he had made back then had been the right ones and he had no regrets about making them. His sisters had needed him and nothing else had mattered. Then or now.

Shaking off the past, Joe focused on Imogen—on the dark tendrils of hair that had escaped her ponytail and now framed her oval face. On the blue-grey of her eyes, the straight, pert nose and lush, full lips.

'So what happened to those dreams?' he asked quietly. Had they crashed and burned like his?

Picking up her cup, she rested her gaze on his mouth. 'Common sense prevailed. Bills need to be paid...security needs to be ensured. Starving in a garret sounds very romantic, but in real life I like my food too much. So I ended up opting for a PA role. I'm more than happy with that.'

Coffee splashed onto the table as she thunked the cup down, the black droplets pooling on the plastic. Instantly she grabbed a napkin to absorb the liquid.

For a moment Joe was tempted to argue. She didn't look that happy to him. But that really was nothing to do with him.

'Good,' he said instead. 'If you think of anything else to do with Richard let me know. Anything that could give us the edge.'

'I can tell you more about him, if that would help. He's

very generous—almost too much so. He likes throwing his money around and it can come across as a bit in your face, or as if he's showing off. But it's not like that. I think he thinks he has to buy friendship. Reading between the lines, I think he had a pretty rotten childhood. So, yes, he's generous. On the flip side of that he *does* have a bit of a chip on his shoulder, and that can make him take offence easily. He's also a touch eccentric—there's a story about how he actually locked three rival advertising executives in a room together and gave them an hour to come up with a snappy slogan. Said he was fed up with long meetings and endless presentations and statistics.'

Joe drummed his fingers on the table. Clearly the two of them had got on—that would be an advantage. What else could they use?

'Have you been to Paris before?' he asked.

'Nope.'

'Has Graham?'

A frown creased her forehead. 'I'm not sure... Oh, yes, actually he has.' An indecipherable expression flitted across her features. 'He proposed to his wife atop the Eiffel Tower.'

Was it his imagination or was there a quiver of bitterness in her voice?

'Is that the sort of thing that will impress Richard Harvey?'

'Yes, but I don't think there's much we can do about that. Unless, of course, you...?'

'No. I've never proposed to anyone in Paris.'

For a second the memory of his one and only proposal entered his head and he couldn't prevent the bone-deep shudder that went through him. The humiliation of being on bended knee, Leila's look of sheer horror, the violin faltering to a stop in the background... *Whoa. Not going there.*

'But,' he said. 'I *do* think we need to do something to impress Richard. Something that will appeal to his eccentricity more than a lengthy proposal.'

'Such as...?'

'What time are we meeting him?'

'Six p.m.'

Joe looked at his watch. 'So we'll have a few hours when we get there. Let's go to Montmartre.'

Confusion furrowed her brow further. 'Why?'

'Because it will appeal to Richard's sense of the romantic as well. We can tell him we've soaked in the ambience, walked the streets of a place where great art has flourished. And...' He shrugged. 'For a few hours you can live your dream.'

The words sounded way too significant.

'I'll even buy you a beret.'

Live your dream.

Imogen followed Joe across the bustling train station, revelling in the sound of French being spoken around her and inhaling the aroma of croissants and baguettes that was being emitted from patisseries and *boulangeries*. No matter what, she wasn't going to let Steve's actions spoil the next few hours and her chance to see a bit of Paris.

The chance to *live her dream.*

Oh, God. Her eyes snagged on the breadth of Joe's back as he strode through the crowds He had no idea what he was suggesting; if she lived her X-rated dreams she'd be arrested.

Her head whirled as a flutter of nerves rippled her tummy, her thoughts running amok as they made their way through the bustle of the Métro.

Joe hadn't so much as flirted with her, and yet...there was something. Something in the way his eyes rested on her that sent a shiver through her. Something...just something that was making her overheated imagination leap and soar.

Something that was mixing with the anger at Steve that continued to burn inside her…something that was making her want to be different.

Deliberately, she reached up and pulled the pins out of her hair, ran her fingers through it so that it rippled free to her shoulders. She felt Joe stiffen by her side, saw his hand clench around his broad thigh. Astounded by her own daring she oh, so casually allowed her leg to brush against his, revelling in the solid muscle. Then surprise shot out a tendril as a tremor ran through his body.

What if…what if Joe was *attracted* to her? Even a little bit?

Stop it, Imogen.

That way lay madness. Joe McIntyre was a ruthless businessman and her temporary boss. Moreover he was responsible for sacking her friends and colleagues. Worst of all he was considering a buy-out by Ivan Moreton. Joe McIntyre was the enemy, and she'd do well to remember it.

'Our stop,' he said.

They emerged into the late summer sunshine and Imogen tipped her face up and let the rays warm her. It was glorious, and the feel of the cobblestones through her sensible flat navy pumps seemed to send Parisian history straight to her very soul.

Glancing up at Joe, she wondered if the surroundings were affecting him. Somehow he looked different—his mouth a touch less grim, his whole body more relaxed. His sleeves were rolled up and her eyes snagged on his forearms and she gulped. A sudden crazy urge to capture his toned muscular glory on canvas touched her. Montmartre—home to so many artistic greats—must be getting to her.

'OK. Where first?' Joe asked.

She swivelled to look at the imposing outline of the Sacré Coeur, looming on the Paris skyline in its sugar-white beauty. Considered the cemetery where so many *artistes* were buried. Then there were all the shops, the *tabacs*, the boutiques, the Moulin Rouge, the...'

Yet right now all she could focus on was Joe.

Think, Imogen. Focus.

'Let's get lost in the alleyways—randomly explore. And I've heard of a wonderful fabric shop that is here some-where—maybe we'll find that. Richard would appreci-ate that. If we can I'd love to go the Sacré Coeur as well.'

'Sounds like a plan,' he said as he tugged his dark blue tie off and shoved it into his jacket pocket, then freed the top button of his shirt.

To reveal the bronzed column of his throat.

Licking suddenly parched lips, Imogen knew they had to get moving before she threw her arms around him and pressed her lips to the warmth of his skin. Yet the danger-ous attraction tilted through her, urging her to throw cau-tion to the wind. Be shocking, be different.

Make a total arse of herself.

Any minute now Joe was going to sense how she was feeling, see her quiver with desire, and then mortification would consume her. She'd made enough of a fool of her-self over Steve to last a lifetime.

'This way,' she said brightly, and plunged into an al-leyway, barely aware of the bright colours and bustling crowds.

The key was to keep talking until she'd got her head on straight. Dredging her brain for any information she had on Montmartre, she kept up a flow of conversation. 'Such an amazing place... Did you know there are so many art-ists who lived and worked and are buried here...? Not only artists... Have you heard of Dalida...? Iconic singer...but so tragic... Amazing how many artists are tragic, really...

My father was a big fan of Degas…and Zola… Isn't it so wonderful to be here…? I really feel we are getting the real Montmartre vibes—'

'Imogen.' Joe's deep voice broke into her words. 'Are you OK?'

'Of course. I'm just making conversation.'

'I think you'll find you're making a monologue,' he said.

'Yes, well. It's so super…'

Super? Really, Imogen?

'To be here. We're getting the real Montmartre vibes. I guess I'm a little overexcited.'

'Hardly surprising, really,' he said, and now his rich voice was laced with amusement. 'This is definitely the essence of Montmartre, all right.'

'Huh…?'

Foreboding raised the hair on her arms as she looked round. Oh, crap. Crap. Crappity-crap. Garish neon signs vied with more artistic depictions, but it was abundantly clear exactly where they were.

The entire street was filled with sex shops.

CHAPTER FOUR

NOW WHAT?

Soon enough she'd be able to boil a kettle on her cheeks—not that a kettle would be easy to come by in a sex shop.

This was the stuff of nightmares; they couldn't just have found a street full of museums, could they? Or artists sketching people? Oh, no! Or this couldn't have happened when she was with Mel. Or on her own. With *anyone* other than Joe McIntyre.

Her nerves jangled with irritation as he looked round with an interest he didn't even bother to hide before turning his gaze back on her.

Damn the blush that still burnt her cheeks, and damn her prudish upbringing that had left her believing that sex was something dangerous.

Not that she blamed her mother; Eva Lorrimer had fallen prey to lust and then fallen pregnant—an event that had thoroughly derailed her life. She'd ended up married to a penniless artist she'd had nothing in common with—a man she'd considered beneath her socially and intellectually whom she had never forgiven. Any more than she'd forgiven herself.

Little wonder she'd drummed into Imogen the need never to let herself be dazzled by looks or taken in by 'the physical side of things'. Her mother would have hustled her out with here, hands over her eyes. But Eva wasn't here.

Plus it was ridiculous, really—this insane feeling of awkwardness. Looking round, it was more than clear to her that no one else was embarrassed. Couples strolled with their arms wrapped round each other's waists, stopping to look into windows. A group of women whose pink bunny rabbit outfits indicated that they were without doubt on a hen party laughed raucously, the noise carrying on the afternoon air. Chic single women, debonair single men, groups of chatting tourists all smiled, sauntered on completely at ease. Whereas *she* stood here like some prim and proper maiden from Victorian times.

The amused look that Joe gave her didn't help one bit, ruffling her self-annoyance into a desire to…to…to what? Kick him. *Very mature, Imo.*

'I take it you didn't plan on visiting this particular bit of the district.'

'No.'

'Come on, then. I think if we double back down that alleyway there we should hit a *different* type of shop and then it shouldn't be difficult to find the Sacré Coeur.'

Imogen hauled in a breath and stiffened her spine. 'Now that we're here I think we should check one out.'

Joe's brown eyes glittered with surprise and something else—perhaps a flash of discomfort. *Ha!* Maybe he wasn't as man-of-the-world as he appeared to be.

'You sure?'

Double *ha*! She was right. His body was ever so slightly rigid and his voice had a hint of clenched jaw and gritted teeth about it.

So now she knew that he was feeling awkward too, the sensible thing to do would be to get the hell off this street.

Sensible.

The word grated on her soul.

She was sick of being sensible. She had oh, so sensibly picked an oh, so sensible man—using her über-sensible tick list—and look where it had got her. Well, stuff it. Sensible Imogen could take a hike. Not for ever, but just for a while. Temporary New Imogen was going to take over and things were going to be different.

The unfamiliar spark of rebellion took hold and took over her vocal cords.

'Of course I'm sure. Why shouldn't I be? There's nothing wrong in having an interest. A *healthy* interest in… you know…' Imogen closed her eyes in silent despair. Had she said that?

'I do know,' he said, and suddenly the atmosphere thickened. The buzz of French chatter, the sound of the church bells all dimmed. Everything faded and all Imogen was aware of was the look in Joe's eyes as he stepped towards her. So close that she could smell that tantalising male aroma, the underlying sandalwood. So close that if she lifted a hand she would be able to place her fingers on the width of his chest and feel the beat of his heart.

Whoa!

They both stepped back at exactly the same second and Imogen gave a slightly shaky laugh, horribly aware that her legs were feeling more than a touch jellified.

Joe rubbed the back of his neck and his face was neutralised, all emotion cleared. 'Lead the way,' he said.

Joe knew this was a bad idea; he was having enough issues keeping his attraction for Imogen leashed. Entering through the portals of a sex shop with her probably wasn't going to help—not so much because of the merchandise but more because he sensed that Imogen was bubbling with…*something.* She had been all day and certainly was now; there was undoubtedly an emotional maelstrom brewing and he wasn't at all sure he wanted to be caught up in its wake.

'This one,' Imogen said, pointing towards a large well-lit store that looked like an emporium or even a supermarket.

Joe followed her through the doors into the spacious

shop and nearly crashed straight into her back as Imogen came to an abrupt halt. Moving next to her, he glanced down at her and saw her eyes widen, but before he could say anything a shop assistant crossed the floor.

In his forties, the man had a discreet charming smile, dark blond hair and an urbane manner. *'Bonjour,'* he said courteously. *'Anglais?'*

Joe nodded. *'Oui, monsieur. Je parle français, mais—'* He broke off. Maybe Imogen did speak French. 'Do you speak French?' he asked.

A shake of her head served as her answer; evidently the merchandise was still rendering her speechless.

The man smiled. 'It is not a problem,' he said. 'I speak English. My name is Jean and I am here to help. Is there anything in particular the two of you are looking for? Something to spice up—?'

Imogen's head snapped round. 'We aren't together.'

'Apologies. You just have the look of—'

'Colleagues,' Imogen intercepted. 'We are here to… research…for a friend…who is…um…writing a book on erotica.'

Jean swept his gaze over them. 'I comprehend completely,' he said, his voice smooth. 'You are enquiring for a friend. Many people do that. So, you must let me show you around to make sure your…friend…gets a proper overview of passion. I shall show you items that can enhance pleasure.'

Joe felt a shudder run through Imogen's body and wondered what she was thinking. Was she imagining herself in the throes of passion—? Oh, hell—*her* thoughts weren't the problem here. His, however, were. Images branded his retina. His body wasn't interested in anything that this shop could offer—his body knew that all it needed was Imogen's touch. In fact any enhancement and he'd probably go up in flames.

So perhaps a guided tour was preferable to walking round just with Imogen.

'*Merci*, Jean. Much appreciated.'

'This way.' Jean stepped forward.

'Why did you agree?' Imogen whispered.

'Why did you say we were researching for a friend? If that were true we would *want* a tour.'

No way was he explaining *his* need for a chaperon.

'Now, here we have the lingerie. Come closer—touch... feel.'

Jean motioned to Imogen and after a second's hesitation she stepped forward and fingered the deep midnight-black confection. 'Oh...'

Joe bit back a groan at her reaction. Her gasp was soft, yet so appreciative as her slender fingers stroked the material.

'It's so sensual,' she murmured. 'Is it pure silk or...or a mixture?'

For a second Jean looked surprised, and then his face cleared. 'Ah, you are a woman who likes texture and feel. This is a blend of silk and satin, but we also have other fabrics. Cashmere...soft suede. Perhaps for you the blindfold would be a good thing?'

Imogen dropped the lingerie and jumped backwards. 'Um...I'm not sure...'

But Jean was in full swing as he led them inexorably over to a section that was devoted to an extensive range of blindfolds. 'You see, to be deprived of sight lifts the anticipation and allows the other senses to come into play.'

The audible hitch of her breath, the flush that tinged her high cheekbones, told Joe all he needed to know. Imogen was wondering exactly what it would be like to be blindfolded—and, heaven help him, *he* wanted to be there when she explored that particular fantasy.

'I am sure,' Jean said smoothly, 'that your friend would be interested in this.'

'Friend?' Imogen flushed even redder and then nodded. 'Yes, absolutely. This is all very helpful. Isn't it, Joe?'

There was a certain part of his anatomy that would undoubtedly disagree.

Her elbow in his ribs prompted his vocal cords and demonstrated exactly how close they were standing. 'Yup. Our friend will be very interested in all this.'

Jean beamed. 'Then let's keep going. Down here is the costume aisle. You have the nurse costumes, the superhero, the...'

Aisle followed aisle, until finally Jean came to a halt. 'So this has been helpful?'

Joe stepped forward. 'Amazingly so. Thank you, Jean.'

'We'll be sure to recommend our friend visits here,' Imogen chimed in.

Minutes later they exited the shop, and Joe inhaled the Parisian air as they started walking in the late-afternoon sun, heading towards the Sacré Coeur.

Imogen stared down at the ground as she walked, presumably shell-shocked by the mass of information she had accrued.

'I can't believe we did that,' she said.

Neither could he. What had he been thinking? Checking out a sex shop was hardly a work-related activity, however he spun it. Time to regroup.

'Let's stop for coffee and check out a map to find that fabric place you mentioned.'

'OK. Good idea.'

He led the way into a small café and sat down at a scarred wooden table. A few minutes later, espresso in one hand and a map in the other, he expelled a sigh of relief. Control restored.

Until he glanced at her, took in the way she twirled a tendril of hair round her finger as she gazed at him almost speculatively.

'What?' he said.

'I'm not sure I can ask,' she said.

He snorted. 'We just spent half an hour in a sex shop with a man extolling the virtues of a Power Stallion vibrator. Right now you can ask me anything.'

She stared at him for a moment and her lips tipped up in a smile. 'I wish you could have seen your face when he said it still wasn't quite the same as the real thing.'

He grinned. 'I imagine my expression was pretty much a mirror image of yours when he explained what a g-wand does.'

Imogen giggled—a full-on, proper fit of giggles—and as he watched her features scrunch up in mirth he couldn't help himself. A sudden chuckle fell from his lips and developed into laughter. The kind that came straight from the belly. The sort of laughter he hadn't experienced for a while—not since his sisters had taken off travelling.

'I can't believe it really happened,' Imogen said breathlessly. 'Poor Jean. We should have bought something, really.'

Lord—she looked so beautiful when she laughed. Her face was so alive, her dark hair highlighted by the sunshine filtering through the window. An intense spike of desire pierced his chest, and the urge to lean across the polished wood of the table and cover her delectable mouth with his own was almost overwhelming.

Gripping the edge of the table, he forced himself to remain still, all inclination to mirth gone.

Her blue-grey eyes met his and her laughter ceased abruptly.

The silence thickened and her lips parted as her breathing quickened. Joe's brain was scrambled. Conversation—he had to find something to say before sheer momentum tilted him towards her.

'So, what were you going to ask?'

Imogen blinked, as if his words were reaching her through a haze of desire. 'It doesn't matter. Really.'

'No, go ahead.' Surely she grasped that they *had* to talk—use their lips to form words, not anything else.

'All those things in the shop... Do you think they're important in a relationship?'

OK. This wasn't the topic he'd been hoping for. Damn it, couldn't she have been wondering about the weather, or French politics, or his opinion on the socioeconomic state of Britain or something?

'Would you like your girlfriend to come home dressed as Wonder Woman, wielding a whip?' she continued.

'I don't have a girlfriend.' As answers went it was a cop-out, but as questions went hers hadn't exactly been social chitchat.

'Hypothetically?'

'Not hypothetically either. I'm not really a relationship type of guy.'

'So you're celibate?' Imogen raised a hand to her mouth as pink stained her cheeks. 'Hell. Sorry. I really did *not* mean to say that.'

'Don't worry—and, no, I'm not celibate. I just don't do relationships.'

'So what *do* you do? One-night stands only?'

For a moment he was tempted to duck the question, but a strange defensiveness tightened his grip around his coffee cup. 'Yes.'

'Oh. So, then...um...would you mind if your bedroom partner was into all that stuff?'

'I wouldn't have a problem exploring the idea of using some of the things Jean showed us, but I certainly don't expect or want all my bedmates to come accessorised with a whip or a latex uniform.'

'But would you *prefer* a partner who wanted to explore those ideas?'

'If we're going to have this conversation—' and heaven only knew why they were '—then I need to know why we're having it.'

'It's…' For a second she stared down at her coffee. 'Research.'

'Research for what?'

'I was wondering if I should…well…maybe pick up a few items from Jean's arsenal.'

'That's something you would need to discuss with *your* bedroom partner.'

'Given my current bed partner is a cuddly rabbit that's seen better days, that's probably not going to work. That's why I'm asking you. For a general opinion.'

'I don't think turn-ons can be boiled down into a general formula, Imogen. Everyone's rules of attraction are different.'

Imogen sighed. 'I guess I've just never thought that sexual attraction was particularly important in a relationship.'

Joe frowned. How could a woman so clearly made for the bedroom think sexual attraction was unimportant?

'That probably explains the rabbit situation,' he said.

Clearly not the right thing to say.

Imogen's eyes narrowed. 'You're saying I'm single because I don't believe sex is the be-all and end-all to life?'

'I'm saying sexual attraction is a key component to a relationship.'

'What makes *you* an expert? You just said you don't do relationships.'

'I don't. But I *do* do sexual attraction, and I can vouch for it being an important thing.'

'Sure. But there are other things that are way more important. Kindness, loyalty, shared goals, a sense of humour, being good parent material. They all rate way higher than sexual attraction on my tick-list.' Her voice vibrated with absolute belief.

'Tick-list?' *She had a tick-list?* 'You have an actual, for real list of requirements? Manly chest? Sizeable bank balance? A yen to walk down the aisle.'

He was honest-to-God fascinated.

'Chest size irrelevant,' she said.

Though he couldn't help but notice her gaze linger on his pecs with perhaps a hint of regret.

'Moderate rather than sizeable savings account to demonstrate that security is important to him. And, yes, I need him to be pro marriage. And kids. I want financial security and whilst I'm happy to share my salary I need a partner who pulls their weight.' Her voice had a steely ring Joe usually heard in a corporate boardroom not a bedroom. Any minute now she'd give him a PowerPoint presentation. 'I want a man who wants children, who will be a wonderful dad who puts his children before himself.'

'So what do you do? Sit every eligible man down, ask for a copy of his bank statement and make him write an essay on his opinion of a white picket fence?'

'Of course not.' Against the odds her eyes narrowed further. 'But, yes, I do need to know whether we have long-term compatibility. So of course I do an assessment.'

'You don't think that's a bit clinical?' To say nothing of a touch kooky.

'No more clinical than only having one-night stands to serve a bodily function.'

The disdain in her voice touched a nerve.

'A one-night stand is about way more than bodily functions.'

'If you say so…'

Her nose wrinkled in distaste and defensiveness rose within him.

'I do. It's about passion and chemistry and spark.'

He allowed his gaze to linger on her mouth, heard her breath catch in the slender column of her throat.

'When the scent of the other person turns you on, when the idea of touching them becomes consuming, when all you want to do is pull them into your arms and kiss them.'

Her tongue snaked out to moisten the bow of her lips and his willpower snapped. Maybe he could show her what she was dismissing with such contempt.

'A bit like now,' he growled.

And in one movement he hitched his chair around the curve of the wooden table and cupped her jaw in his hands, expelled a sigh at the silken texture of her skin beneath his fingers. He ran his thumb over the fullness of her lower lip, saw the quiver run through her body.

As he covered her lips with his own, Joe was dimly aware that this was a bad, *bad* idea—but then Imogen's taste, her scent, her warmth eradicated all vestige of thought. All he wanted was to plunder the softness of her coffee-scented lips as they parted to allow him access.

Her tongue tentatively stroked his, and as she moaned into his mouth he was lost. He tangled his fingers in her smooth glossy hair as she twined her arms around his neck; her fingers brushed his nape and desire jolted through him.

'Closer,' she murmured, and he slid his hands over her shoulders and down, spanned her slender waist and pulled her onto his lap.

Who knew how long they remained, lips locked, lost in sheer pleasure? Until the clink and clatter of plates, the whir of the coffee machine penetrated his brain. What the hell was he doing? Melded against someone tantamount to being an employee. Someone whose job he had the power to take. Someone who could be trying to influence him to protect not just her own job but other people's as well.

Hell and damnation.

Pulling backwards, he broke the kiss and she gave a small mewl of protest, her eyes pools of desire clouded with confusion.

Her breathing as ragged as his, she scrambled off him and stood, one hand gripping the table for support. 'I…I…'

Joe hauled in air and willed his pulse-rate to slow down and his brain to move into gear. Imogen did not look like a woman out to seduce him for gain; she looked as shell-shocked as he felt. Surely that couldn't be simulated?

Regardless… 'That was a mistake,' he said flatly.

Yet she looked so damn desirable still, with her hair dishevelled, her lips swollen from his kiss, that it took all his willpower to remain seated.

Chill, Joe. It was a kiss. One kiss. Even if it had been the kiss of all kisses it was not a deal-breaker. 'Never Mix Business with Pleasure' was still Rule Number One.

Yes, he'd erred; he'd let the line between professional and personal fuzz. Given Imogen a few hours to live the dream, agreed to visit a sex shop, shared laughter, discussed sex. Time to redraw that line in permanent marker. Of the fluorescent kind.

'A mistake that we need to put behind us.' He glanced at his watch. 'We've got a couple of hours. Let's put them to good use and visit some places that will impress Richard Harvey.' As opposed to a sex shop.

Imogen nodded, tugged the edges of her jacket together and smoothed down her trousers, visibly pulling herself together. 'I think we should find the fabric shop, visit the cemetery and go to the Sacré Coeur.'

'Done.'

Imogen walked up and up and up the calf-wrenching steps towards the top of the glorious domed cathedral. She welcomed the pain—welcomed even more the legitimate reason for her heart to pound against her ribcage.

As the sun struck the blinding white of the travertine walls she was dazzled—not just by the rays but by the sheer dizzying possibilities of life.

She knew how she *should* be feeling: thoroughly ashamed with herself. She'd kissed a man who was her boss, her enemy, the wrecker of her friends' and colleagues' lives. Joe had spoken the truth: the kiss *had* been a mistake.

But it had also been earth-shattering. She'd never experienced one like it and her body still fizzed with the sheer joy of it. Apparently lust trumped principles. But who would have thought a kiss could be so incredible? How could she regret a kiss like that?

Apprehension prickled her skin. *Take care, Imo.* Perhaps this was how her mother had felt all those years before—beguiled by Jonathan Lorrimer's looks and charm. And look what had happened there.

Not that Joe was remotely charming, nor making any attempt to beguile her. In fact he appeared to have erased the kiss from his memory banks.

Their whole trip around the fabric store and their entire tour of the museum had been achieved civilly enough—Joe had asked intelligent questions about the fabrics, observed the paintings in the museum with genuine appreciation—but gone was the man who had laughed with her and wreaked such magic with his kiss. *This* man was the consummate professional, with his tie back round his neck as if that could restore professional equilibrium.

Currently Imogen would have settled for any sort of equilibrium. Even now the nape of her neck tingled. Every molecule of her body was hyper-aware of the strength of him just behind her on the narrow stairway as they approached the summit.

Her breath caught as she looked down over the awe-inspiring vista of Paris. The Eiffel Tower jutted above the rooftops of thousands of differently shaped buildings, all glinting in the late-afternoon sun. It made her feel dizzy, different, infused with wonder.

'It's incredible...'

'Yes.'

Had his gaze lingered on her face for a heartbeat before he'd turned to stare out at the panorama?

Ridiculous. He was talking about the view, for heaven's sake! She had to get some perspective. They'd shared a kiss. Big deal. Now they had to return to normal. Joe equalled Big Bad Boss. Imogen equalled Employee. She needed to concentrate on her job.

'Have you seen it before?' she asked. There. Perfect. Normal civil conversation.

'Yes.' As if realising the brevity of the syllable, he continued, 'I came with my sisters once.'

'Really?' It was strange to imagine Joe in family mode.

'Really.' A smile touched his lips—a genuine one. 'I'm not sure they appreciated the glory of the scenery. They were fourteen and more interested in the glory of French boys.'

His lips pressed together, as though he regretted sharing even that much personal information.

A glance at his watch and, 'We need to go.'

Guilt prodded her as she scuttled after him through the tourist crowd. She'd completely lost track of time—hadn't given work a single thought since they'd got on the Métro. All she'd thought about was Joe. Oh, and sex. In conjunction.

As their taxi screeched and sped through the Paris traffic Imogen squeezed her hands into fists and focused. The hours for living the dream were over and it was time to concentrate on reality and the need to wow Richard. If only her body would stop with the snap, crackle and pop...

The taxi glided to a stop and she climbed out, stood on the pavement whilst Joe paid the driver. The street teemed with chicly dressed chattering women and casually dressed men. Elegance mixed with gesticulation and passion, and for a minute Imogen wished with all her heart that she was in Paris with a lover.

Joe.

Delusional, Imo.

'Let's go,' she said, and they wended their way through the throng into the warmly lit interior of a bar.

Small and intimate, its tables glowed golden in the muted light from retro lamps and the candles that dotted the embrasures in the wax-dripped wall.

A bar curved down one side of the room, behind which there was a bewildering array of bottles and an old-fashioned cash register that evoked images of a Paris of decades before. The soft strains of jazz filled the evening air, reminding Imogen of the sheer thrill of being in the romantic capital of the world.

'Over here.'

Peering through the throng, Imogen spotted Richard and Crystal sitting in a corner booth, a pitcher of delicate pink liquid on the table in front of them.

Happiness was evident in the glow of their smiles, the linking of their fingers as they both rose to their feet. Richard looked younger than she remembered, his salt-and-pepper hair longer, his whole stance more relaxed.

No doubt that was Crystal's influence. In her late thirties, she radiated a serene timeless beauty and her glance at her husband was soft with love. For them Paris was a truly romantic getaway, and envy tugged at Imogen's heartstrings.

Forcing a smile to her face, she stepped forward and greeted the couple, introduced Joe.

'Good to meet you, Joe,' Richard said. 'Sit—order whatever you like. On me. I recommend the Vieux Carré cocktail. Cognac, sweet vermouth, rye and Benedictine, with a dash of Angostura bitters.'

'Sounds good to me,' Joe said.

'Me too,' Imogen agreed.

Once they were seated, with their drinks in front of them, Richard smiled at Imogen. 'Isn't Steve accompanying you on this trip? I thought you'd take advantage of the chance for a romantic getaway?'

Next to her Joe stiffened for a second, his movements jerky as he picked his glass up.

'Maybe give him the opportunity to pop the question if he hasn't already, eh?'

Mortification encased her body as her cheeks heated to no doubt a tomato-red. Memories came of how she had gushed to Richard about her belief that she and Steve were so suited, so compatible, so together.

She had been truly delusional.

Now she would have to admit that Steve had left her for his ex and was going to marry her. Well, call her a great fat fibber but she couldn't do it—couldn't bear to see the pity in Richard Harvey's eyes.

'He couldn't make it,' she said, ignoring the snap of Joe's head, sure she could feel his look boring through her temple.

'That's a real shame,' Crystal said. 'We were hoping to meet him.'

Richard turned to Joe. 'Did *you* bring a significant other half with you?'

'No. *I'm* a single man.'

The older man sighed, and then shrugged. 'Then I suppose the best thing will be for you both to stay in the apartment.'

Huh? The words of confession Imogen had been preparing withered on her tongue. Trepidation tiptoed down her spine as she picked up her glass and forced herself to sip rather than gulp.

'What apartment would that be?' she managed.

Richard smiled. 'Well, as you know, Crystal and I have

bought a place in Paris and want it done up. I could go to someone over here, but I'd prefer to use either you or Graham. So I've come up with a plan.'

Oh, hell; this plan was going to be a Harvey Humdinger—Imogen just knew it.

'Sounds intriguing,' Joe murmured.

'I've rented two romantic Parisian apartments,' Richard explained. 'One for Graham and his wife and one was meant to be for Imogen and Steve—though now it's for you two. You stay there tonight. Then on Monday morning I want a two-page proposal on how you would design the interior of a four-bedroom, three-bathroom Parisian apartment. I'll make my decision based on that.'

'How does that sound?' Crystal asked.

'That sounds like a challenge Langley will be more than happy to accept,' Joe said.

Come on, Imogen. She could do the whole gibbering wreck thing later. Right now wasn't the time.

Raising her glass, she summoned a smile that she could only hope denoted calm, professional confidence. 'I'll drink to that.'

'Excellent,' Richard said. He reached into his pocket and pushed a set of keys across the table. 'Here are the keys to 'Lovers' Tryst.''

Of course. What else could it be called?

Joe and Imogen—off to Lovers' Tryst for the night. Dear Lord.

Panic bubbled in her tummy, and yet a thoroughly misplaced anticipation strummed her veins.

CHAPTER FIVE

IMOGEN SWEPT A sideways glance across the limo that Richard had insisted they use and shifted on the seat, nerves jangling. Joe's whole body pulsed with contained anger and had done ever since they had said their goodbyes to Richard and Crystal. It wasn't her fault that Richard had come up with this mad idea, so she could only assume that his irritation was at the situation—not her.

Sod it. The brooding silence was getting old. 'So,' she said brightly, 'isn't it generous of Richard to say he'll pay for any clothes and things that we need to purchase? And to have booked us a table at one of the poshest restaurants in Paris?' She glanced down at herself. 'Do you think this is all right to wear to eat in a French restaurant? Probably not.'

'It doesn't make any difference to me whether you wear a sack,' he said, the words rasping in the regulated air of the limo. 'So don't waste your time or Richard's money on a seduction outfit.'

'What?' Confusion tangled her vocal cords. 'I don't understand.'

'I don't like being played, Imogen.'

'Still not with you.'

'I don't trade business favours for sexual ones.'

'*Excuse* me?'

'The kiss.'

Her neck cracked as she swivelled on the plush leather seat to face his grim expression. The dusk had harshened the angles of his face further. 'Are you for real? You think that was for *business* reasons?'

'You wouldn't be the first to try it. You said yourself you would do anything to save Langley. Maybe you're hoping to persuade me to drop the buy-out plan, give your friends their jobs back.' He leant back against the padded leather. 'So if you had seduction plans for later cancel them.'

'Believe me, Joe, I'd rather seduce...' Hell she couldn't think of anyone low enough. 'Ivan...'

'Maybe that's your plan B. Though I can't help feeling sorry for that poor sap of a boyfriend you've got at home, waiting to propose. The man who satisfies your crazy tick-list. Does Steve *know* you go round kissing people in cafés? Sitting on their laps and—'

'Stop!'

Imogen wondered if it were possible to explode with rage. If so, she damn well hoped she took Joe with her. Anger ignited, heated her veins. How *dared* he?

'You arrogant, stupid schmuck! For your information, Steve and I split up six weeks ago.'

He snorted. 'More lies, Imogen? Why didn't you tell Richard?'

'Because I felt such a damn fool. I raved about Steve to Richard, about him being The One. I was too embarrassed to admit I was wrong.'

As the limo glided to a stop outside a shopping mall tears of sheer rage and mortification threatened. How could Joe tarnish a kiss that had made her blood sing and her head spin? Made her feel attractive and desirable and wanted? Palliated the sting of Steve's parting words?

Now it turned out he believed she had engineered that kiss because she was a gold-digger, a spy or a cheat. Good grief—if she wasn't so furious she'd laugh. Because one thing she knew: Joe had been just as much into that kiss as she had.

'I think you're forgetting something, here. That *you* kissed *me*!'

'Imogen…'

'Just leave it, Joe.' She shoved the car door open, nearly tumbling the chauffeur over as he waited to open the door for her, and set off across the car park, her rage spiking further as she marched, feet pounding the tarmac, and realised he wasn't damn well even going to follow her.

Fine.

Anger heated her veins, seethed and simmered as her brain formulated a plan.

She'd show him. She'd show him exactly what he was missing. There wasn't a cat's chance in hell she'd seduce him, but she was damn well going to make him wish she would.

Sanity tried to point out that maybe Joe had been a little misled by the fib she'd told Richard. But that wasn't the point! He could just have *asked* her before jumping to such insulting, stupid conclusions.

An hour later Imogen stared at her reflection, relieved that rage still buoyed her because she knew otherwise there was no way in heaven or hell she would be able to carry this off.

The dress was…outrageous. In a good way. It managed to scream seduction whilst hollering elegance. Black see-through gauze featured, fluttering to mid-thigh and covering her chest, whilst allowing tantalising glimpses of the black corset-like bit underneath. Shells striped the dress in a fun, flirty line, and the whole look was complemented by the strappiest high-heeled shoes imaginable. Delicate leather lines crisscrossed her feet, cool and seductive against her skin.

'*C'est magnifique!*' the sales assistant exclaimed, clapping her hands together.

'*Merci bien.*'

To her own surprise she didn't feel even a smidgeon of self-consciousness as she walked through the mall. Instead she fizzed with a sheer intoxicating vitality, every sense heightened and fuelled by the attention she garnered.

Joe was leaning back against the limo, arms folded, the breadth of his shoulders somehow accentuated by the length of the car. His white shirt had been swapped for a black one, with the top button undone to reveal a triangle of tanned skin that tantalised her gaze. He was intent on his phone screen, and a frown slashed his forehead.

Anticipation whispered in her stomach as she neared him and he looked up. The temptation to punch the air at his expression nearly overwhelmed her but she restrained it. Instead she savoured every second of his dropped jaw, every shade of heat that glittered in his brown eyes as they swept over her, lingering in appreciation as he stepped towards her.

Her brain gave out conflicting orders—*step towards him, move backwards, turn and run*. Grinding her molars, she adhered her stilettoed feet to the tarmac of the car park and faced him. He was so close she could smell the tang of masculinity, the scent of arousal. Her muscles ached with a need to reach out and touch him, to trace a finger along that V of skin, to unbutton his shirt and...

No! The plan was to show him what he was missing—not to offer herself up on a plate, thereby confirming all his insulting, overbearing assumptions.

'You ready for the restaurant?' she asked, keeping her voice casual with a supreme effort of will. 'I figure it will be pretty upmarket, so I want to look my best. You never know. As you're not available I may get lucky and find some loaded French sex god to seduce instead.'

She slapped her palm to her forehead.

'Oh, yes. I forgot. I'm *not* here with some cunning plan

to seduce anyone. I'm here to work. To come up with a proposal for Richard and Crystal.'

Joe stepped backwards, leant against the car and raised his eyebrows. 'You can hardly blame me for jumping to the conclusions I did.'

'Wrong. I can *totally* blame you. You could have asked first. You know—like, *Imogen, I'm a bit confused. Who is Steve?*'

'OK.' Folding his arms, he met her gaze. 'Imogen, I'm a bit confused. Who is Steve?'

'I told you. He is my *ex*-boyfriend. I am a free agent, and that kiss earlier wasn't about me being out to get anything or me being unfaithful to anyone.'

'So what *was* it about?'

'You tell me.'

His heated gaze swept over her body and then he straightened up, the glint in his eyes doused. 'It was a moment of insanity,' he said. 'And I apologise. For being so unprofessional. How about we put the whole episode behind us and move forward? Truce?'

What could she say? His voice was sincere, his gaze direct. 'Truce,' she agreed.

The twitch of his lips was a surprise as he gestured towards her. 'I take it that dress was chosen with the express purpose of torturing me?'

'Absolutely. Is it working?'

'Yes.'

Why, oh, why did he have to smile? A devastating smile sinful enough to make her hair curl. Oh, God. Perhaps this whole idea hadn't been so brilliant after all—especially as Joe wasn't playing the part she'd allotted him. Her tummy churned as she tried to work out what the hell was going on. Wondered if Joe had any idea either.

He opened the limo door for her and she slid inside, pulling her stomach muscles in so as not to so much as brush against him before scooting all the way across the leather seat.

Clamping her knees together, she shoved away the realisation that short and see-through, whilst effective, was also...well, short and see-through. From somewhere she had to muster the light sabre of professionalism. Hadn't she said she was here to work? Now would be an excellent moment to do exactly that.

'So,' she said. 'What do you think about Richard's idea of a two-page proposal?'

'I think you were right. Richard Harvey is a touch eccentric. But his idea has its merits. We'll have a quick decision for the minimum outlay of time.' He paused. 'I do realise he's thrown you in at the deep end, though. I'm thinking about calling Belinda off a project so that she can come and look at the apartment.'

Joe's words were as effective as a bucket of ice, dousing elation in reality. How stupid was she? It hadn't even occurred to her that *she* wouldn't be the one to put together the proposal. Forget stupid and substitute nonsensical. Her job at Langley was as a PA—sure, she'd dabbled in interior design, but Belinda had proper qualifications and expertise and was the obvious choice to go up against Graham.

Richard had asked for her presence, but he hadn't specified that Imogen worked on the proposal. She was just a point of contact and she should have realised that herself. If she hadn't been too busy living in some sort of fantasyland.

All too aware of Joe's gaze on her face, she looked out of the window, not wanting him to read the hurt or the sheer embarrassment that was no doubt etched there, relieved when the limo pulled to a stop.

'I'll text Belinda from the restaurant.'

It was all for the best. Did she *really* want the responsibility of going up against Graham? Having to face Peter's disappointment and the knowledge that she'd let Langley down if or rather *when* she didn't succeed? Far better to stay ensconced in her comfort zone.

'She's perfect for the proposal.'

Tension pounded Joe's temples as he followed Imogen into the restaurant and nodded automatically at the *maître d'*, who swooped towards them majestically, his gold-braided jacket a perfect fit with all the grandeur of the baroque theme.

Not that Joe cared about the gold and gilt that abounded, or the ornate mirrors on the stone walls, or even the wrought-iron chandeliers that glinted with the ambience of wealth.

Right now he was too busy questioning the swirl and whirl of emotions that Imogen had unleashed inside him. Anger at himself rebounded against a small and unfamiliar sense of panic. There was the ever growing problem of their attraction, not helped by the tantalising torment of her dress. But worse than that was the way his chest had panged at the quickly veiled hurt in her eyes when he'd suggested Belinda.

Realising that the *maître d'* still hovered, he shook the thought away. 'We have a reservation. Made by Richard Harvey,' he said.

The *maître d'* smiled his dignified approval and gestured to a black-suited waiter with a gold tie. 'This is Marcel. He will look after your table. Marcel, please take Miss Lorrimer and her companion to the table Mr Harvey requested for them.'

Joe gave in to temptation and placed his palm on the small of Imogen's back to steer her, his flesh tingling with warmth and an unexpected sense of possession. Just what he needed—more unfamiliar emotions that didn't make sense.

He eyed the table and further misgivings tingled his already frazzled nerve-endings. The table was… The word *intimate* sprang to mind. The kind of table for lovers, not colleagues—the type where you sat at adjacent angles so your knees pressed together, so it was easy to place your hand on your partner's thigh, indulge in a little footsie. The handy pillar would allow or even encourage canoodling.

He suddenly remembered that the gleaming candlelit table had been originally intended for *Steve* and Imogen.

Bloody wonderful.

Marcel seated them and then beamed. 'Mr Harvey has made a selection for you, but he's asked me to tell you first in case you have any allergies.'

Joe allowed the list of exquisite dishes to wash over him; the only relevant thing here was the length of the damn menu. They would be here for *hours*. On the other hand that might well be better than whatever Lovers' Tryst had to hold.

Right now it was time to get a handle on the situation, get a grip of said handle and start steering. Whatever the menu, this was a business dinner.

'That sounds fine. But I'll stick to water rather than wine.'

'It sounds *incredible*,' Imogen interpolated. 'Please make sure that you let Mr Harvey know how much we appreciate all this. And water for me as well, please.'

The waiter bowed, turned and glided across the restaurant floor, leaving them alone. No, not alone. Yet despite the fact that the restaurant was full, and the hum and buzz of conversation filled the air, Joe had the ridiculous impression that he and Imogen were in their own private space.

Imogen darted a glance at him and then reached down for her bag. 'I'll try Belinda now.'

'Is that what *you* want to do?' he asked, rubbing the back of his neck.

A frown creased her forehead as she moistened her lips. 'It makes sense.'

As he forced himself not to linger on her glossy lips it occurred to him that *nothing* made sense—and that was the problem. She'd got him so damn distracted that he'd let the personal and the business line fuzz. *Again.* He couldn't tell whether he wanted Belinda to come and look at the apartment because it was best for Langley or because Belinda would provide them with a chaperon. Didn't know if he wanted to allow Imogen to do the proposal because that was the right thing for Langley or because he wanted to assuage the hurt that had flashed across her eyes.

Enough.

Time to apply logic.

'I'm not sure it does,' he said as he drummed his fingers on the snow-white tablecloth. 'The impression I got was that Richard wants *you* to do it. I also believe that you understand how his mind works. We're up against a time limit. And Belinda is flat-out on other projects.'

There was a pause as she looked down at the bread roll she was crumbling into tiny pieces. 'But I'm a PA. I have no qualifications in interior design—or advertising and marketing.'

'But this is coming up with a concept. Isn't that exactly what you did for Richard's bathrooms?'

'Well, yes. But that was after we'd won the contract. And if Peter hadn't liked my ideas he'd have nixed them. There's a whole lot more riding on this.'

'Is that what's scaring you?'

Her fingers stilled, her head coming up as her eyes narrowed. 'It was your idea to bring in Belinda.'

Joe shook his head. 'I acknowledged that Richard was asking you to take on a lot and said I was *thinking* about bringing Belinda in. I haven't made a decision.'

'Oh.'

'So, do you think you can pull this off?'

She hesitated, her features creased into worried lines as she manoeuvred the crumbs into a line. 'It's just such a big responsibility. What if I let you down?'

Watching the play of light over her features, he was gripped by the urge to reassure her, to tell her that of *course* she wouldn't, to reach out and cup the delicate curve of her jaw.

Instead, 'There are no guarantees, Imogen. It's the risk you take. For what it's worth, I think you have a better shot at it than Belinda.'

'You do? You think I can pull this off?'

'Yes.'

'For real?'

'For real.'

Her face lit up and her lips curved in a genuine smile that constricted his lungs.

'I've seen your work and I've seen your rapport with Richard. I think that's key. So, yes, I think you can do it. But if you feel more comfortable calling in Belinda that's fine too.'

With a swoop of her hand she swept the crumbs into a small pile and nodded. 'I'll do it. And I'll give it my very best shot. I promise.'

Joe lifted his glass as relief trickled over him—they were back in *business*. His gut told him that using Imogen was the right decision.

'It's a plan,' he said.

'Thank you…'

Leaning forward, she placed a hand on his forearm, her touch sparking awareness. A citrus burst of shampoo, a tendril of black hair tickled his nose as she placed her lips in a fleeting caress against his cheek.

'For believing in me.'

CHAPTER SIX

BIG MISTAKE. FROM the second she slanted her body so close to his Imogen knew she might as well be juggling dynamite. His toned forearm tensed under her fingers and as her lips brushed the six o'clock stubble of his jaw need shivered through her.

The sensible thing to do would be to pull away, but the urge to nuzzle his skin, to take the opportunity to inhale that Joe scent, was nigh on overwhelming. Adrenalin swept through her tummy in a wave—this man wanted her as much as she wanted him, he believed in her, and he was so damn close that suddenly it seemed mad to fight this attraction. In this second she couldn't even remember why they were.

His body stilled, and then with a murmured curse he pulled back. 'Jeez, Imo. You are messing with my head.' He shoved his hands through his hair and nodded towards the centre of the restaurant. 'We're in public—in Richard Harvey's favourite restaurant. When Richard asks Marcel how we enjoyed our meal I'd like Marcel *not* to say we spent it in a clinch.'

Heat flushed her cheeks as she tried to quell the elation. She was messing with his head—who would have thought it? But...

'You're more than right. Here isn't the place. But—' She broke off as Marcel approached the table with a genial smile.

'Here we have a selection of dishes. The *amuse-*

bouches. Lemon, nuts, grapefruit and celery in a potato net. Haddock soufflé. And tuna in squid ink. Along with the best baguette in Paris.'

'It looks fabulous, Marcel. *Merci*.' Her words were spoken on automatic. Not even the scrumptious aroma that wafted up from the plate could distract her from the buzz her body radiated, the tingle of her lips where she'd brushed his cheek.

Once Marcel had gone, she met Joe's gaze.

'We have a problem,' he said. 'So I suggest we have a look round this apartment and then book separate rooms—preferably on separate floors—in a local hotel.'

'What about Richard? Staying there is part of his plan.'

'I'll come up with a reason if he asks. I doubt he will. The important thing will be the proposal. Whatever it is going on with us, I think distance is the key solution.'

'Or we give in to it.'

The words were blurted out without thought, spring-boarded to her brain from her instincts.

His body stilled and then he shook his head. 'No. Bad idea. We work together so that is not an option.'

'I get that—and, hell, I'd normally agree. But in this case the business is done. You've already made a decision about the proposal. And I swear to you I will give it my all. I am excited about the opportunity to do this for Langley. But I'm not propositioning you out of gratitude or because I want anything else.'

'So why *are* you propositioning me?'

'Because I've never felt like this before. And once, Joe—just once in my life—I want to succumb to lust. To say sod the rules. Not to be sensible. For one night.'

Hell, it wasn't too much to ask, was it? That for once she could ride the wave and not do the right thing? Sure, there was a part of her brain that was covering its eyes, unable

to look, *shocked* by the sheer effrontery of this version of
Imogen Lorrimer. But, damn it, she was going to ignore it.

'That's what you do, isn't it? One-night stands?'

'I thought they weren't your thing.' Joe picked his glass
up and put it back down again, his eyes dark with desire.

Her lungs seemed to have forgotten how to function;
breathing was problematic. 'I've changed my mind.'

A moment's pause during which his brown eyes bored
into her expression. 'You're sure? One night? No strings?
Because I can't offer anything else, Imogen.' He raised
his hand before she could protest. 'I don't mean job-wise.
I mean emotionally or time-wise. I don't tick your boxes.'

'One night is all I want as well, Joe. I'm not in the
market for a relationship right now.' She needed time to
regroup, update her tick-list. 'I've just come out of one.
Plus—' She broke off. There was no need to explain to
Joe that she didn't trust this whole insane attraction, that
she would never risk letting it control her. That was the
beauty of a one-night stand. 'I promise you this is all about
the sex.'

A long moment and then he gusted out a sigh, his expression unreadable, before he smiled—the toe-curling,
hair-frizzing version. 'Then let's eat and get out of here.'

How was she supposed to eat? Her appetite for food
had legged it over the horizon long ago. All she wanted
to savour right now was Joe; her nerves stretched taut
with need.

But somehow she made it through the exquisite combination of tastes: the bite and tang of roast lobster fla-
voured with lemon and ginger, the intensity of a seafood
bisque complemented by seaweed bread. But all the time
she was oh-so aware of the solid thickness of Joe's thigh
next to hers, the pressure of his knee under the table, the
plane and angle of his strong jaw, the way the chandeliers
glinted over the dark spikes of his hair.

The promise in his eyes made her tummy swirl in anticipation. Until finally—*finally*—they had eaten the last bite of a superbly light pistachio soufflé, had exchanged compliments with Marcel and could exit the restaurant.

Imogen welcomed the cool evening breeze on her face, though she couldn't help a small shiver as it hit her sensitised skin. Without speaking Joe shrugged off his jacket and placed it round her shoulders. Warmth encased her inside and out.

'Thank you.'

His hand clasped hers in a firm grip. 'No problem. The apartment isn't far.'

'Good. I'm...' *Burning. Yearning. Desperate.*

He looked down at her. 'Me too,' he said, with a sudden low chuckle that rippled into the breeze and tugged her lips into an answering smile.

Half-walking half-running, they wended their way along the pavement.

'It should be just down this alley,' he said, already digging in his pocket for the keys.

They reached a navy blue wooden door—he shoved the key into the lock and thrust the door open.

And came to an abrupt halt.

She could see why: the room they had stepped into was...*sumptuous*. Decadent. Luxurious. With warm red walls, rugs and throws that begged to be touched, deep crimson and gold curtains that would cocoon the room and its occupants against the outer world.

Then she saw the mural on the wall directly opposite the door.

A man and a woman entwined together, their naked bodies sinuous and beautiful. The pose intense, passionate, vivid.

Imogen swallowed, and then moistened her lips to relieve her parched mouth as her awareness of Joe further heightened. But with awareness came worry, and a sudden shyness tensed her body. What if she didn't come up to scratch? Surely this apartment was meant for women who were more...more beautiful, experienced, sexy?

Then Joe moved behind her, his body heat warming her as his fingers massaged her shoulders.

'You OK?' he murmured.

'My heart is beating so damn hard it's like I'm consumed—and yet I'm scared that I'll mess this up.'

Disappoint you.

'Not possible.'

His fingers continued to wreak their magic and she wriggled in sheer appreciation.

'But if you've changed your mind...'

A last lingering doubt snaked through her brain and she quashed it ruthlessly. This was her chance to experience something she might never experience again. Yes, lust was dangerous—but it was a danger she was fully aware of and had no intention of falling prey to.

As for the risk of disappointing Joe... Every molecule in her body told her that they'd work it out. This was *her* night and she'd regret it for ever if she didn't take it.

'No. I haven't changed my mind.'

'Good,' he growled as his hands slid to her shoulders, glissaded down to her waist.

He nuzzled her neck and at the touch of his lips she shivered, arched to give him better access. As she did so her gaze fell on the mural and she saw it in a new light— a picture of two normal people who were following their instincts, engaged in something natural and beautiful.

The realisation sent a thrill through her, and suddenly she needed to see Joe—see the man who was already giving her such pleasure.

As if he felt the same he stood back and turned her, so she was flush against the hard plane of his chest. The light scent of sandalwood mixed with sheer Joe assaulted her senses. Imogen looked up at him and her breath caught in her throat at the sight of the raw desire that dilated his pupils.

Standing on tiptoe, she looped her arms round his neck, buried her fingers in the thick brown hair. Joe's broad hands curved round her waist and his mouth covered hers. Imogen savoured the tang of pistachio and the flavour of mint leaf as his tongue swept the bow of her mouth and she parted her lips. Sensations rocketed through her as his tongue stroked hers, sliding and tangling and tormenting, and she matched him stroke for stroke.

She pushed against him, desperate to be closer, for more, pressing heavy breasts against his chest. His hands plunged down from her waist to cup her bottom, and she moaned into his mouth as momentum built and strummed inside her.

Breaking their kiss, he stepped backwards and sank down onto the deep crimson sofa, pulling her onto his lap, the strength of his thighs hard under hers.

Her clumsy-with-need fingers fumbled at the buttons of his shirt and tugged the silken black edges apart. Then *finally* she touched his skin, ran her hands over his packed chest.

Joe found the zip of her dress and tugged it down in one deft movement, gliding the gauzy material over her shoulders and down her arms, freeing her breasts.

'Jeez…' he breathed. 'You are gorgeous, Imogen.'

His large hands cupped her breasts and as he circled her standing-to-attention nipples. Imogen arched backwards in ecstasy. Then in one smooth movement he lifted her off his lap and laid her down on the expanse of the sofa.

'I need to see all of you,' he said roughly as his hands pulled her dress down.

Lifting her hips, she felt the material slide down and

off into a pool on the floor, followed by the lacy wisp of her knickers.

Joe's heated gaze glittered over her. 'So beautiful...' he murmured

Imogen allowed her gaze to run down his body, saw the impressive bulge that strained the zipper of his trousers. A quiver of anticipation thrilled through her.

'Joe?'

'Yes.'

'I think you need to take your clothes off. Things seem to be a little out of balance at the moment.'

'Your wish is my command, beautiful.'

In one lithe move he stood on the plush carpet and shucked off trousers and boxers to stand before her in glorious naked splendour.

Unfamiliar exultation shimmered over her that he could be so aroused by her body. Propping herself on her elbows, she let her gaze absorb every glorious millimetre of him— the light sheen of his sculpted torso, the ripped abs, the thick muscular thighs—and she shivered, imprinted the memory on her brain.

He smiled at her. 'Seen your fill?' he asked with a delectable quirk of his eyebrow.

'I could look at you for hours.'

It was nothing but the truth, and the knowledge that she'd love to draw him, to try and capture his arrogant male beauty on paper, crossed her mind. *No way, Imo.*

Instead, 'But I can think of other things to do right now.'

'As I said, your wish—'

'Then come here,' she said.

CHAPTER SEVEN

JOE PULLED THE fridge door open and welcomed the stream of cold air that hit him as he inspected the contents. As he'd suspected there was everything he needed for an impromptu midnight picnic—he wouldn't expect anything less from Lovers' Tryst. And he wanted Imogen to know that she deserved champagne and caviar and strawberries and cream, even if they weren't sensible.

Though the real reason he was here in the kitchen wasn't only food and drink—he needed a moment to regroup. The past hour had been sensational, and yet his body still hummed with desire. As if it was greedy to make the most of every hour of this night.

But he wanted this to be special for Imogen—more than just for the sex. Her words from the restaurant echoed in his ears. *'Because I've never felt like this before. And once, Joe—just once in my life—I want to succumb to lust. To say sod the rules. Not to be sensible. For one night.'* There had been wistfulness in her voice, along with the certainty of what she wanted—and it had called to something in him.

Convinced him to just once break a rule. There was no harm in it. Imogen had been right—he'd made the decision to let her run with the proposal and that decision had been made with no ulterior motive in mind. They were here for a night. From tomorrow morning it would be all about work, and soon he would leave Langley and move on. Rules Two and Three were still in place. 'One Night Only'. 'Never Look Back'.

The thought brought a certain relief as he loaded a tray and pushed the fridge door closed. He exited the kitchen and made his way down the corridor to the bedroom.

Breath whistled between his teeth as he took in the opulent splendour. An enormous circular bed with a curved wooden barred headboard dominated the floor and mirrors mastered the wall space.

Imogen sat cross-legged on the bed, dressed in a thick white towelling robe. 'It's a little unnerving to see myself from all angles,' she said. She gazed at the tray and her face lit up. 'I can't believe I'm saying this, but I'm ravenous.'

'It's all the exercise,' he said as he stepped forward and lowered the tray onto the bedside table. 'Champagne?'

'Yes, please.'

Minutes later they had plates balanced on their laps and a glass of bubbles in their hands.

'Thank you for this. It's incredible,' she said. 'I can safely say I've never eaten caviar in bed at midnight before. I've never eaten caviar at all.' The glance she swept at him was a touch shy. 'I thought one-night stands were just about the sex.'

Her words sent a small cold shock straight to his chest; when had he ever contemplated a midnight picnic before?

'No need for thanks. All I did was open the fridge.' *But you went looking*, a small voice pointed out. 'Seemed a shame to waste the contents.'

Imogen paused, a caviar-spread cracker halfway to her lips. 'Don't sweat it, Joe,' she said. 'I meant what I said. I don't want any more than a one-night stand. I'm just happy that it's turning out to be a definite once-in-a-life-time experience.'

Since when had he been so readable? 'So you still don't believe in one-night stands?'

Her slim shoulders lifted in a small shrug. 'I can't see the point in them.'

'Really? Then I must have done something wrong.'

For a second she looked discomfited, her lips forming the cutest circle, and then she chuckled. 'You know damn well you did everything completely right. But it wouldn't feel right to do this on a regular basis. Like I said, I want a lot more than sex from a relationship and I won't risk getting blindsided by lust.'

'I thought we did pretty good on the lust front. Don't you agree?'

'Yes.' Her lips curved up in a sudden sweet smile. 'This has been totally amazing. But in a long-term relationship there are other things that are way more important.'

'Fair enough. But why not go for it all? Security, shared goals *and* great sex.'

Imogen blinked, as if the idea had never even occurred to her as a possibility, and then she shook her head and sipped her champagne. 'Honestly? I think a dynamite attraction would fuzz my brain and my perspective. I don't want physical desire to affect how I think and reason, or cause me to make stupid decisions. I've seen how that works out. My mother married my father because she fell in lust—and, believe me, their marriage is *everything* I don't want mine to be.'

The vehemence in her voice twanged a chord of empathy in him. 'Yet they've stayed together, haven't they?'

Perhaps Imogen knew the answer as to why two unsuited people stayed together despite every reason in the world to separate. An image of his own parents came to his mind and he felt the familiar gnarling of emotions in his gut. Frustration, confusion, anger, bewilderment.

Max and Karen McIntyre—good-looking, rich and devoted to each other. Or so they had appeared to Joe. Because he'd seen what he'd wanted to see or what they'd wanted him to see? Little wonder that he'd been sent to boarding school—he could only imagine the strain the pretence must have cost his parents.

'Yes,' Imogen said. 'They have. I think it's because in some dreadful way they've become codependent. So used to the shouting and the arguments and the bitterness they can't imagine leaving. They've made a mess of it and I don't want that—I certainly don't want that for my children. So I think I'll stick to my tick-list and keep sexual attraction off it. It's not a big deal.'

Given her earlier responsiveness, her sheer uninhibited enjoyment, that was hard to believe. And anyway… 'Don't take this the wrong way, but clearly the tick-list didn't work with Steve.'

'Noooo. But the principle is still sound. All I need to do is amend the list to make sure I avoid men who are still hung up on a previous girlfriend.' A small sigh escaped her lips. 'You'd think that would have been obvious, wouldn't you? Instead I was sure I could be the one who'd help him get over her—be there for him, build up a relationship. *Hah!*'

Joe frowned as he considered her words. 'You're telling me Steve left you for his ex?'

'Yup. It's even worse, in fact.' Her hands clenched round a fold of red sheet.

'What happened?'

Jutting out her chin, she gazed at him almost defiantly, her blue-grey eyes daring him to feel pity. 'I gave Steve tickets for a cruise for his thirtieth birthday a few months ago. He took Simone instead of me and proposed to her on the cruise. They're getting married in a couple of months.'

'For real?'

'I don't think you could make that up.'

'Well, I'd like to say I'm sorry. But I'm not. The man sounds like an absolute tosser and you're way better off without him.'

Imogen's lips curved up in a sudden smile. 'So no sympathy?'

'Nope.' He topped up their glasses and raised his. 'I think it's more a cause for celebration. To a new start.'

The chime as crystal hit crystal was oddly significant, and as if feeling it Imogen wriggled backwards to lean against the graceful curve of the headboard.

Shaking away the emotion, Joe took her empty plate from her. 'You done?'

'Yes.'

'Good. Because I have some excellent ideas for what to do with the strawberries and cream.'

She moistened her lips. 'Care to share?'

'Oh, yes. I have every intention of sharing. Now, come here. And drop the sheet.'

Batting her eyelashes at him in an exaggerated fashion, she pushed the sheet down in one fluid movement. 'Your wish is my command,' she murmured, and the hot rush of desire swept away all other thoughts.

Imogen opened her eyes and for a heartbeat confusion fuzzed her brain—until the twinge of hitherto unused muscles brought back a flood of glorious memories. Memories that culminated in finally falling asleep wrapped in Joe's arms, her cheek nestled against the smattering of hair on his chest.

Rolling over, she realised her only bedmate now was the finger of light that filtered through the slats of the blinds to hit the rumpled, cold red sheet.

A sense of bereavement socked her, and Imogen gritted her teeth. *No!* The night was over and waking up naked in bed together was not the way forward for the professional day ahead. Joe at least had had the sense to realise it.

Yet how could she erase those memories that still buzzed through her veins and exhilarated her body. Surely she wouldn't be human if she didn't regret the bone-deep knowledge that she'd never plumb the depths of lust as deeply again? For the first time ever she truly understood exactly how her parents might have got carried away by a tornado of passion. How they might have believed that if their bodies were so in tune so must their minds be.

Well, Imogen knew differently, but it was probably just as well not to put that knowledge to any further test.

So...no regrets. Instead it was time to haul herself out of bed and start to concentrate on work.

Entering the bathroom, she did her very best to look at it with the eye of an interior designer.

But how could she when her skin tingled as it relived the memory of leaning back against those glittering mirrored tiles, water jetting down, Joe soaping her, his muscles under her fingers smooth, hard, delectable as she returned the favour. The memory made her dizzy her and she clenched her hands around the cool edge of the sink.

Come on.

Lists. That was the way forward. As she showered she focused on the minutiae of the bathroom. Mirrored tiles, wet room, scented candles, exotic shampoos...

Shower over, she tugged her hair into a ponytail, pulled on the simple jeans and striped T-shirt she'd purchased the day before and pushed the bedroom door open.

This was fifty shades of awkward—and her nerves tautened as she approached the kitchen. The aroma of strong coffee tickled her nostrils as she entered and walked across the marble floor to the open French doors.

She put one hand to the side of the door for balance as she took in the scene.

Joe sat at a circular wrought-iron table—damp from the shower, hair spiked up, jeans and navy T sculpting the toned strength of a body she knew by heart. There was a cup of coffee in front of him, his laptop was up and running, his phone was to his ear. So gorgeous... The temptation to grab him by the hand and drag him back to the bedroom had her tightening her grip on the doorjamb.

Moving on. Maybe she should concentrate on the exotic plants that hid the patio from the street, on the hum of traffic, the sunlight striping the verdant leaves. Anything but Joe.

He nodded as he spoke. 'May the best man win. I'll see you on Wednesday.'

He dropped the phone onto the table and suddenly Imogen knew she couldn't face him just yet.

Coffee. The world would come into focus with the help of caffeine.

Hurriedly she turned and headed towards the coffee machine. She just needed a minute to regroup—*breathe in, breathe out and repeat*—then, coffee cup in hand, she headed outside to join him.

Joe was intent on his laptop, his conversation over, a frown creasing his forehead.

'Morning,' Imogen said, and foreboding weighted her stomach. Joe looked formidable—a far cry from the man she'd had a midnight picnic with in bed.

'Good morning.'

Fighting the urge to turn and run, Imogen forced her unwilling legs forward, pulled out a chair and sat down.

What now? For the first time since they had entered the apartment Imogen wondered if she had screwed up monumentally by sleeping with Joe. 'Um...'

His gaze was unreadable, his expression unyielding as he looked across the table at her, and Imogen felt the heat of embarrassment curdle her insides. This was not the expression she'd wanted to see.

Come on, Imo. What did you expect? The night was over and Joe was back in ruthless businessman mode—there was no reason for him to look at her with warmth.

Yet surely what they had shared last night had to mean *something*?

'So how does this work?' she blurted out. 'This is uncharted territory for me. I don't know the etiquette of the morning after. What usually happens?'

'Breakfast and goodbye.' He picked up his coffee cup. 'Unfortunately not an option in this case.'

'Unfortunately?' Hurt crashed into anger and created fury.

For a second she thought she saw emotion flash across his face, and then the guard was back up, his jaw set, the outline of his mouth grim.

'Come on, Imogen, let's be grown-up about this. I could write a whole tick-list of my own with reasons why last night should not have happened.' He closed his eyes and grimaced. 'I can't believe I said that. I meant a list—not a tick-list.'

Imogen forced herself not to flinch. She'd shared something important with him last night about her parents' disastrous marriage and her need for a tick-list, and now he was mocking her.

'I'd rather have a tick-list than some sort of cold, emotionless relationship avoidance criteria.'

A sigh gusted through the air as he pushed his chair back over the paved stones. 'And this is exactly why last night was a mistake. We need to work together—not sit here trading *emotional* insults.'

Imogen opened her mouth and then closed it again, focusing on the backdrop—the terracotta pots and the mosaic patterns of the outdoor tiles

Joe was right. This was about Langley. About keeping Langley safe from Ivan Moreton by winning the Richard Harvey project.

Imogen frowned as Joe's earlier words echoed in her ears. *'May the best man win. See you on Wednesday.'*

'Who were you on the phone to earlier?'

His fingers drummed a tattoo on the table. 'Ivan Moreton.'

'You're going to see Ivan Moreton on Wednesday?'

'Yes.'

'But…'

'But what?'

There was no quarter in his voice or expression; any minute now she'd see icicles form as he spoke.

'Did you think last night would affect my buy-out decision?'

'No!'

What *had* she thought? She'd foolishly, erroneously, stupidly thought the man she'd shared a bed and so much more with last night wasn't capable of selling off the company to a douchebag like Ivan Moreton.

Cold realisation touched her with icy fingers—she'd done the thing she'd sworn she wouldn't. Let lust—the way Joe had made her *body* feel—affect her judgement. Joe had never claimed to be Mr Nice Guy—Imogen had repainted him to suit herself. Just because he could make her body achieve the heights of ecstasy, she'd rewritten his personality.

Idiot. Idiot. Idiot.

Shame coated her very soul when she remembered how she'd spilled her guts about tick-lists, her parents' marriage, Steve and Simone. And what had he shared in return? Zilch—a great big zip-a-dee-doo-dah zero. Humiliation jumped into the mix. Maybe he hadn't even been listening—maybe all his women experienced the urge to confide in him post-orgasm and he just tuned them out until he was ready for the next round.

'Well?' he rasped.

'I have no expectations of you whatsoever.' Hauling in breath, she dug deep, located her pride and slammed her shoulders back. 'There is no need to worry that last night will make any difference at all to us working together.'

She'd made a monumental error and slept with the enemy—forgotten her work obligations and where her loyalty lay. It was time to make up for that. So she'd use what he'd given her—channel the fizz and the buzz, take the memories and turn them into creative vibes.

'*I* care about Langley and I will create a kick-ass proposal that will beat Graham's hands-down. And, yes, I do hope that influences your decision about selling out to Ivan Sleazeball Moreton.'

His email pinged and he glanced down at the laptop screen. For a second Imogen saw irritation cross his face.

'Trouble?' she asked. As long as it wasn't anything to do with Langley she damn well hoped that it was.

'Nothing I can't deal with.' He lifted his gaze. 'So, any ideas yet?'

'Give me a ch—' Just like that an idea shimmered into her brain, frothed and bubbled. 'Actually, yes, I do.'

He gestured with his hand. 'Go ahead. I'm listening.'

Imogen hesitated—right now she didn't even want to share air space with the guy, let alone tell him her idea. But, as she had so spectacularly forgotten last night, Joe McIntyre was the boss.

'I need to show Richard and Crystal that Langley can create an apartment that is essentially French—a place that combines fantasy and reality, a place where they can feel at home and on holiday all at the same time. A home with a sexy edge, with glitz and glamour, but somewhere to feel comfortable. For example—look at this kitchen. It's very minimalist…not really the sort of kitchen you could imagine cooking in. So I'd design a kitchen that conveys the chicness of croissants and coffee, the sexiness of caviar and champagne, but also the hominess of cooking a romantic boeuf bourgignon together. Then on the proposal I'd sketch all those elements.'

To her own irritation she realised she was holding her breath, waiting for Joe's opinion. *Please just let it be a need for the professional go-ahead. Nothing more.*

His fingers tapped on the wrought-iron of the tabletop as he thought.

'Sounds good. Come up with an idea like that for each room and I'll come up with a cost mock-up. Let's get to work.'

CHAPTER EIGHT

'DONE.' IMOGEN DROPPED the charcoal pencil onto the sheened mahogany Langley boardroom table and blew out a sigh. Exhaustion made her eyelids visibly heavy, and dark lashes swept down in a long blink as she reached for her cup of coffee. 'Here.' She pushed the piece of paper towards him. 'If you hate it don't tell me.'

Joe shook his head. 'I haven't hated anything yet.'

Far from it—over the past two days Imogen had produced some truly exceptional sketches. Perplexity made him frown yet again at her genuine inability to see her own talent. Instead doubt often clouded her vision and caused her to chew her lip in a way it was nigh on impossible not to be distracted by.

Not that he had given even the whisper of a hint of said distraction. After the sheer stupidity of his behaviour in Paris he'd made sure to keep to strictly professional boundaries. As for Imogen—once she'd got immersed in the project it had been as if she'd entered a world of her own.

'I know you haven't. But I'm worried neither of us can see straight any more—we're too knackered.'

She had a point; they'd worked round the clock. They'd worked in the apartment, worked on the Eurostar and come straight to Langley, where they'd set up shop. Grabbing only a few hours' shut-eye on the boardroom sofa.

'And,' she continued, 'this last room is pretty crucial—the master bedroom is meant to be the *pièce de résistance*.'

Full marks to her, he thought. Although a flush tinged

the angle of her cheeks, her voice and gaze were steady. Yet he knew she must be remembering their own bedroom interlude. He glanced down at the sketch and his heart thudded as images filtered across his brain. Imogen had taken the bedroom at Lovers' Tryst and delivered to it her own unique twist. No longer circular, the bed seemed suspended in the air.

'It's a floating bed,' she said. 'It's different and romantic. I know it may be more expensive, but...'

'I'll check.'

'No!' Her face paled as she nodded at the clock. 'Look at the time.'

'It's eleven.'

'Eleven *p.m.*'

'Oh, hell.' The impact of her words hit Joe with a sucker punch. 'Richard said first thing Monday morning and it's an hour until midnight. Do you think we need to get this over there now, rather than at nine a.m.?'

'I think Richard is quite capable of disqualifying us if we don't meet the exact letter of his instructions.'

'So we'd better get it couriered across right now. I'm on it. You get it packaged. We'll email it across as well.'

Anger spiked inside him, along with a surge of adrenalin—he should have spotted that midnight trap right from the get-go. Instead of pondering over Imogen's lack of self belief. Instead of interspersing working flat-out with his fight to sever the bonds of attraction that had him so distracted.

Imogen nodded and raced across the boardroom, and he pulled his phone out of pocket—this proposal would get to Richard Harvey on time if it killed him. No way would he let Langley down—that would *not* be acceptable. If he didn't know a courier service would get it there more quickly he'd take it himself.

Fifteen minutes later Imogen stared at him, worry painting creases on her forehead. 'It *will* get there, won't it?'

'Yes. I've used Mark before—he whizzes round London faster than the speed of light. And Richard's offices aren't that far away. Plus, we know the email made it. So we're covered.' He nodded. 'Well spotted, Imogen.'

'I should have thought of it before,' she said. 'But now I'm worried we've sent a proposal that's not as good as it could be. I thought we had a few more hours to polish it.'

'Don't be so hard on yourself. I didn't think of it at all.'

'You don't know Richard as well as I do.' She paced the room, long jean-clad legs striding the length of the boardroom table. 'I *want* this contract.'

Her smile was tremulous, and for an insane moment he wanted to pull her into a hug, slide his hand down her back and utter soothing words. Shock rooted him to the deep-pile carpet that covered the boardroom floor and he tried to school his features into professional support mode.

'So do I. I promise you it's a damn fine proposal and it's got a really good chance. You couldn't have done more than you did.'

'Huh. That's what I used to tell myself after exams. *You've worked really hard, Imogen, maybe this time you haven't messed it up.*' Her hand covered the slight curve of her tummy. 'Ugh. It makes me feel queasy.' Pressing her lips together, as if to stop the flow of further information, she resumed pacing.

Her words triggered a memory of Imogen in his office just a week before, telling him about her ten-year-old self bringing a report home and her mother's disappointment. He recalled her words in the Michelin-starred restaurant, her fear of undertaking the proposal, and a pang of understanding hit him.

Instinct prompted the words he had used so many times with his sisters. 'You have given this your all and no one can ask more than that. Including yourself. If we don't win this proposal you haven't let anyone down.'

'That's easy for you to say,' she said, coming to a stop in front of him 'If I lose and Graham wins there's a bigger chance you'll sell Langley to Ivan. For you that's just business—another day on the job. But for me… I will have let Peter and Harry down. They will be devastated, and in their state of health that will have a knock-on effect. And I will always wonder if I should have called Belinda in.'

He shifted backwards slightly—not a good plan to have the lush curve of her breasts in his line of sight. 'That was my call, and no matter what happens I stand by that decision. You are taking too much on yourself. Both Peter and Harry have seen this proposal and they love it.'

'That doesn't guarantee I'll win. And if I don't, Langley is one step further to ending up in Ivan's hands. That's a fact, isn't it?'

To his own surprise Joe felt a prod of guilt, even as he forced his features to remain neutral. No way could he let emotional reasoning affect a business decision.

'Yes.'

'There you go, then. *My* responsibility. My bad if it goes wrong.' Her hair shielded her expression as she continued her relentless striding across the room.

He rose and strode towards her, blocked her path as she paced. 'Stop.'

This was important enough that he would force himself to ignore the way her delicate scent enveloped him, would allow himself to get close to her.

'It will *not* be your fault if Langley ends up in a buy-out situation. You will *not* have let Peter down—or Langley. Promise me you get that.'

Her chest rose and fell, her blue-grey eyes were wide as she stared up at him, and suddenly he felt all kinds of a fool. What was he doing, overreacting like this? If only she wasn't so beautiful—ink-stains, smudged eyes, creased T-shirt and all.

Stepping backwards, out of temptation's way, he forced himself to sound casual. '*I* will be making the decisions as to Langley's future—no matter what happens you can absolve yourself from blame. In fact I'll provide you with a life-size photograph of me and a set of darts. How's that?'

'It sounds like a plan.'

A thoughtful frown creased her brow—almost as if she were trying to figure something out. *Join the club.*

'Joe?'

'Yes?'

'I'll still be throwing those darts, and I'm still a bit of a wreck, but…you've made me feel better. Thank you.'

'No problem.' Embarrassment still threatened and he shrugged it off. 'In the meantime, if you want to head home now I'll call you a taxi.'

Imogen shook her head. 'I don't think I'll be able to sleep—I'm too wired on coffee and adrenalin. And what if Richard gets back to us now? I'll stay here—but you don't have to stay as well.'

As if he'd leave her in a deserted building at this time of night. Hell, call him old-fashioned, but he wouldn't leave *any* woman in that situation. Anyway…

'I want to hear Richard's decision too.'

It was no more than the truth—he did want Langley to win this bid as a stepping stone on its way to recovery. And he did also want to be with Imogen when the verdict arrived—to see her lips curve into her gorgeous smile if they won or to offer comfort if they hadn't. That was fair enough. They'd worked incredibly hard for this proposal— had bonded *professionally*.

'Why don't you order a pizza? I don't think we remembered to eat today.'

'Sounds like a great idea,' she said.

His tablet pinged to indicate the arrival of an email. He glanced down and supressed a groan. Leila again. This was now officially out of hand and he had no idea what to do about it.

'Your mystery caller again?' Imogen asked. 'The one who makes you sigh every time you get an email?'

Nearly choking in an attempt to inhale a puff of air, he shook his head. 'She's *not* a mystery caller.'

For a nanosecond Imogen's shoulders tensed, and then she turned the movement into a shrug. 'If she isn't mysterious why don't you tell me who she is?' She hesitated. 'It may help to talk about it.'

'No.'

He regretted the curtness of the syllable as soon as it dropped from his lips, but the thought of explaining the Leila situation in full had moisture sheening the back of his neck.

With an expressive upturn of her palms she rolled her eyes. 'Fair enough. It was just a thought. I'll go and order the pizza.'

Joe watched her as she picked up the phone and then dropped his gaze to the email. Incredulity descended, causing him to reread the words in the hope that he'd got it wrong. *Now what?*

His gut informed him that he was seriously mishandling Leila, his actions being dictated by the sear of guilt. His eyes veered up to Imogen—could it be time to acknowledge that he needed some help, here? Every bone in his body revolted at the idea, but as he read the email again panic roiled in his stomach.

There was no choice—he couldn't afford to mess this up and, like it or not, he was way out of his depth.

Imogen placed the order, trying and failing not to watch Joe. It didn't look as if the email was giving him joy. In fact she was pretty sure he'd groaned—and she didn't think it was because she'd ordered him an extra-hot pepperoni, double on the chillies.

His mystery woman was none of her business. Joe had made that more than clear and he was right. It was personal stuff, and she and Joe had already got *plenty* up close and personal. Heaven knew what impulse had even made her offer to help—perhaps it had been the way he had clearly wanted to help *her*?

Tucking her phone back into her jeans pocket, she marched over to him, pulled out the seat opposite and plonked herself down. 'Pizza won't be long.'

'Great.' Thrusting his hand through his already spiky hair, he inhaled audibly. 'Um…now I've read the email, if you're still up for that offer of help, I could do with a little feminine insight.'

Surprise made her raise her eyebrows; it must be bad, because it was clear from the way he had squeezed out each word that the request had been made with total reluctance.

'You *are* a little pale about the gills.'

'I'm feeling a little pale about the everywhere.'

Imogen flicked a glance at Joe's screen and curiosity bubbled to the surface. 'OK, then. Tell me how you can use a female point of view and I'll give it a shot.'

Joe gestured at the email. 'The mystery woman is Leila. She's an ex-girlfriend from seven years ago. I hadn't heard from her since the split, then three weeks ago she emailed me an invitation to her wedding. Which is less than two weeks from now. You may have read about it—her fiancé is Howard Kreel.'

Imogen blinked. 'Your ex-girlfriend is Leila Wentworth? The woman who is engaged to the son of one of the planet's richest men?'

She and Mel and most of the country had discussed the wedding, marvelling over Leila's blonde beauty and the entire rags-to-riches Cinderella story, with an element of superhero thrown in. Howard had rescued Leila in an alleyway, where she had been on the verge of being robbed, and their relationship had grown and flourished from there—to the point where now they were planning a three-day wedding extravaganza in the Algarve.

'Wow.'

'Yeah, *wow.*' The sarcastic inflexion was accompanied by a lip-curl.

Obviously Joe was less than entranced by the prospect. In which case...

'It is kind of weird that she has asked you, but maybe she has literally invited everyone she has ever known. If you don't feel comfortable my advice is not to go.'

Difficult to believe he hadn't worked that out for himself.

Joe shook his head. A faint colour touched his cheekbones and a shadow fleeted across his eyes. 'There's more to it than that. It's...' He drummed his fingers on the table. 'I need to go.'

'Why?'

'It doesn't matter why.'

'Even though you don't want to?'

Impossible to believe that Joe would attend any function he didn't want to. Confusion along with a hint of foreboding threaded through her tummy.

'I don't have a problem going. The problem is that Leila has started sending me emails on a daily basis.'

'Saying what?'

Joe expelled a sigh, and for a moment he looked so bewildered she felt an irrational misplaced urge to lean over and smooth the creases from his forehead.

'Saying how important love is and how I must learn to embrace it—how important it is to find the person of your dreams. Pages and pages of it.'

'So how have you replied?'

'I tell her that my life is very happy as it is, but thanks for the advice. But the emails keep on coming.'

The woman sounded unhinged—which begged the question: why was Joe going along with her?

'I'm not getting this. What happened to being ruthless? Tell her to get knotted and say that you have your love-life perfectly under control.'

'I can't do that.' Joe shifted in his seat, discomfort clear in the set of his jaw and in the frown that slashed his forehead. 'This is important to her—I just need to figure out why.'

Realisation dawned with a sense of inevitability that stuck in her craw. Joe was hung up on an ex-girlfriend. What was it about her that attracted men who held ten-foot torches for old lovers?

'You OK?' Joe asked.

'I'm fine.'

What else could she say? All she'd wanted from Joe was a great night between the sheets. He'd given her that—it made no difference if he'd harboured feelings for an ex whilst he did so. Yet somehow... Damn it, it did. Bad enough that he regretted the night—now the attraction was even further sullied. But that wasn't Joe's problem. It was hers. She'd offered her insight and she'd make good on that.

'Absolutely fine. What did today's email say? Obviously she's upped the ante or you wouldn't need my input.'

'Today's email informs me that Leila has lined me up with a series of potential girlfriends because she wants me to—' he hooked his fingers in the air to indicate quote marks '—"find true love and embrace the peace and inner tranquillity that this true love will bring".' He snorted and pushed away from the table. 'Little wonder I'm a bit green about the gills.'

Imogen frowned—why on earth would Leila want to

set Joe up with a friend of hers? Come to that, why was she so worried about Joe's love life?

Joe exhaled a sigh. 'No way do I want to face a line-up of women, all trying to bring me to a sense of inner tranquillity. Come to that, it would hardly be fair to them. I'm not on the looking-for-love market.'

'Just don't go. That way the line-up can't get you.'

'It's not that's simple, Imogen.' He tipped his palms in the air. 'If Steve and Simone ask you to their wedding will you go?'

'That's different.'

'Why?'

'For a start my mum and Steve's mum are friends—or at least they went to school together. So no doubt my parents will go, and Mum will want me to go so that everyone can see that I'm OK. And Steve and I were together only recently—we share lots of mutual friends and I guess I'll want to show them that I'm not licking my wounds somewhere. So it's a matter of parental pressure and pride. That's not the case for you.'

'But it is important to you that everyone thinks you're OK?'

'Well, yes…'

'It's important to me to see that Leila is OK. And I need her to believe that *I* am OK.'

The words shouldn't hurt as much as they did—yet each one impacted her chest with meaning. Joe was still in love with Leila, but he was willing to stand aside and watch her go to her true love. Leila knew Joe still loved her and was doing her best to get him to move on. Any minute now Imogen would need a bucket.

'If it's important to Leila that you find love then I guess you'd better find a woman, fall in love and take her to the wedding.'

Then perhaps as a finale everyone could watch a herd of flying pigs perform a musical.

'Don't be sil—'

Joe broke off, leant back in the stylish boardroom chair, and surveyed her with a thoughtful expression that set alarm bells off in her mind. The last thing she wanted was for Joe to suspect her state of mind—hell, she wasn't sure she understood it herself yet. She just knew she was sick and tired of hearing about men and their love for their exes. Been there. Done that. And it was getting old.

To her relief the intercom buzzed to herald the arrival of the pizza.

Joe lifted a hand. 'Just give me a second. I'll grab the pizzas.'

'OK.'

Imogen had no intention of taking this conversation further. Joe would have to figure this one out on his own. Maybe he should storm the wedding and declare his love. After all, surely he wasn't the sort of man to stand aside and let the love of his life marry someone else without a fight.

It was nothing to do with her. Yet the insidious feeling of *yuck* still made her skin clammy. It seemed every which way she was doomed to being second-best.

CHAPTER NINE

JOE HANDED SOME money over to the pizza delivery boy and balanced the boxes on both hands as he strode back to the boardroom, his brain whirring as he analysed his idea from all angles.

He pushed the door open and glanced round. Imogen sat at her laptop, intent on the screen, her hair hiding her expression from him, body tilted away from the door.

'Pizza's up.' Joe walked to the other end of the boardroom, put the boxes on the table and lifted the lids.

Twisting away from the screen, she narrowed her eyes and stared at the pizza.

Joe frowned. 'Has Richard called? Is something wrong?'

There must be some reason for her obvious withdrawal.

'Nope and nope.'

'Come on, Imo.' Two sisters had taught him exactly when *nope* meant *Yes—I'm really pissed off.*

'I'm fine.'

'Great. Then would it be OK if we keep talking?'

Pulling out a slice of pizza, he took a bite.

'Mmm…'

She gave a roll of her eyes and an exasperated sigh that blew her fringe upwards…but she rose from her seat and headed over with the instinctive grace that he loved to watch.

She picked up the box. 'There's nothing to talk about. You asked for my advice. I gave it. You won't listen to it. Topic closed.'

'I've got a proposition for you.'

'For *me*?' Eyebrows raised, she halted in mid turn away from the table.

'Yup. You come to Leila's wedding with me and I'll come to Steve's wedding with you.' He allowed his lips to quirk upwards in his most persuasive smile.

'That's a joke, right?'

'Nope.' He tilted his palms upward. 'It's the perfect solution.'

'I wasn't aware *I* had a problem.'

'Think about it, Imogen. You said you wanted to go to Steve's wedding and show everyone you're over him. What better way than to take a man with you? You can present me however you like. As a man you're enjoying a wild, uninhibited affair with or as a boyfriend—either way, it should give everyone the message that you're over him.'

'I may have a bona fide date of my own by then. Either a sex god or the perfect man.'

'Maybe you will.' The idea was not one he wanted to contemplate or encourage. 'But most likely you won't.'

Her eyes narrowed. 'Why's that?'

'Because it's going to take you at least a year to find a man who ticks all the boxes on your list. That or a miracle.'

'Really?' Her voice would have created ice in a desert.

'Anyway, the point is you can help me and I can help you. You come to Leila's wedding and you'll be showing people you're *already* over Steve. In style.'

For a second he thought he had her, and then she shook her head and redirected that laser look at him.

'So I can help you *how*, exactly?'

'It's simple. I take you, we pretend to be in love—that will make Leila believe I'm OK and I'll be safe from the line-up of women.'

It was genius. As long as he ignored the small voice

that pointed out that it would mean spending three days *and nights* with Imogen Lorrimer.

Not a problem. After all, they had already had one night together—he'd already broken Rule One. It was inconceivable that he would break Rule Two. Even if Imogen wanted to—and he was damn sure she didn't.

'So I'll be camouflage?'

There was an edge to her voice that indicated Imogen was failing to see the mastermind qualities of the idea. But he really couldn't see her issue. It had been her suggestion that had sparked the idea in the first place.

'Yes.'

She slammed the pizza box down on the table with a thunk. 'Can you not see how insulting that is?'

'Insulting to whom?'

'Me!'

Joe stared at her; her blue-grey eyes sparkled with anger and her hands were clenched into small fists. 'How do you figure that?'

'You really can't see it, can you? I stupidly told you about Steve and Simone, but you still don't get it.'

'So why don't you calm down and explain it?'

'Fine. You—' a slender finger was jabbed towards his chest '—still love Leila. You don't want Leila to know you're holding a torch the size of the Empire State Building for her but, believe you me, it's obvious—and she knows it. If I come with you everyone will watch you mooning over Leila and feel sorry for me for being second-best. Or however far down the list I come in your table of one-night stands. So, thanks—but no thanks. I am *not* coming along to be an object of pity.'

Anger that Imogen would believe he was such an insensitive jerk clawed at his chest. 'That is the most stupid analysis of the situation imaginable.'

'*Hah!* Face the truth. You are nothing more than an insensitive arrogant bastard with his head up his bum. Well, you can find some other sucker. Hell, seems like I've been second-best or not up to scratch all my life. I'm not doing it again. No freaking way!'

His vocal cords appeared to have stopped working in the face of her torrent of words. Before he could find so much as a syllable her phone buzzed.

Tugging it out of her pocket, she looked down at the screen and the angry flush leeched from her skin. 'It's Richard.'

Joe raked a hand over his face and attempted to locate his professional business head. 'Pick it up. And put him on loudspeaker.'

Imogen hauled in an audible breath, pressed a button and lifted the phone. She wrapped one arm around her stomach and said, 'Hi, Richard. Imogen speaking.'

Looking down, Joe realised his knuckles had whitened as he grasped the table edge—he couldn't remember the last time a business deal had mattered this much to him.

Imogen rocked to and fro on the balls of her feet, her face scrunched into creases of worry, and Joe felt his anger dissipate—to be replaced by a deep, almost painful hope that they'd won this proposal.

'I'm grand.' Richard's voice boomed. 'Thank you for your proposal. Crystal and I have discussed it, and Graham's, and...'

Joe watched as Imogen caught her lower lip in her teeth, felt his gut lurch in sympathy.

'Yours came in more expensive...'

Her shoulders slumped and Joe rose to his feet, striding around the table to take the phone, see if he could negotiate.

'But we absolutely loved the premise so we've decided to go with you.'

'*Yes!*'

He could feel the grin take over his face as he heard the words, saw the smile that illuminated Imogen's features as the conversation continued.

'Th...thank you so much, Richard. Absolutely. Yes. I'll get a contract across to you as soon as the office opens for business.'

Dropping the phone onto the table, she fist-pumped the air before doing a twirl—he could almost see the elation fizzing off her and it made his chest warm.

'Congratulations. You did good.'

'*We* did good. They loved it. I mean *really* loved it. You heard Richard—he said the idea was inspirational and that the sketches made him feel like he was living and breathing France. He also said that the proposal was balanced by a sensible and realistic budget that showed him we'd done our homework. *We* gave better value for money *and* showed a much better understanding of what they wanted.'

Another twirl and she ended up right next to him, so close that her delicate flowery scent assailed him. So close all he had to do was reach out and...

Her eyes widened as she looked up at him—and then she jumped backwards, shaking her head.

'I...I...need to let Peter and Harry know, and—'

'It's one a.m., Imogen. Best to wait until morning.'

'Of course... Um...well, thank you, Joe. I truly mean that.'

One long blink and then she smoothed her hands down her jeans, the rise and fall of her chest distracting him as she breathed deeply. Once, twice, thrice.

'Sorry I got a bit heated earlier. I hope that you work it out with Leila and the wedding goes all right.'

'Whoa. Not so fast.'

'What do you mean?'

'I mean we hadn't finished our conversation. I thought you'd just hit your groove, in fact.'

'Yes, well… Probably a good thing we were interrupted. Before I screeched along in my groove and got myself fired.'

Affront panged inside him. 'I wouldn't fire you because of a personal argument.'

Her nose wrinkled in obvious disbelief. 'Um…good to know. But as far as I am concerned the topic is over.'

'Think again. I am *not* still in love with Leila.' The idea was laughable, even if he didn't feel like cracking so much as a smile. 'You will *not* be seen as second-best.'

Imogen huffed out a sigh. 'It's not going to fly, Joe. You're kidding yourself if you truly believe you're not carrying a flaming torch for her. There is no other explanation. No girlfriend since Leila. Just one-night stands. An aversion to relationships. Going to her wedding to make her happy. Wanting her to believe you're OK. Willing to lie and undergo an elaborate charade rather than say no to her.'

For a second, shock had him bereft of speech—he could see exactly why Imogen had added up two and two and got approximately a million. But now what? It wouldn't be easy to convince her of her utter miscalculation without telling her a lot more than he wanted to share.

Joe drummed his fingers on his thigh as he weighed up just how badly he needed Imogen's cooperation. Damn it—he couldn't come up with a better solution to the whole Leila issue than to take Imogen to the wedding.

Bottom line: he needed her on board.

Though it was more than that—truth be told, he didn't want to feature in Imogen's brain as a man hung up on his ex. The idea of being lumped together with a git like Steve left an acrid tang. If he wanted to bring utter honesty to the table he could see that Imogen was hurt, and that made his skin prickle in discomfort.

So he would have to tell her the truth.

'I'm not holding a torch for Leila. Truth is, I owe her.'

'Owe her what?' Imogen's brow creased.

Guilt panged inside him at his past behaviour; discomfort gnawed his chest at the thought of the man he had been. *Come on, McIntyre. No truth...no lifeline at the wedding from hell.*

'Leila and I met nine years ago at uni.' A lifetime ago. 'We started going out.'

The cool surfing dude and the hot surfer chick. Tension shot down his spine.

'Then two years later my parents died in a car crash.'

Imogen stilled, her eyes widening in shock as she stretched her hand across the table. He let it lie. He needed to focus on getting the facts out—there was no need for sympathy along the way.

'Joe. I am so sorry. I had no idea. I can't even imagine what that must have been like. But it must have been devastating for you. For you all. Your sisters...'

'It was a difficult time.' Not that he had any intention of going into detail; the lid was not coming off *that* buried box of emotions. 'For me, for the twins, and for Leila as well.'

Imogen frowned. 'Difficult for Leila how?'

'I made it difficult. I had to grow up fast and I put pressure on her to do the same.'

'The twins?'

'Yes. It got complicated. Holly and Tammy were eleven; I was twenty-one.' Twenty-one with a promising surfing career ahead—not exactly parent-equivalent material. 'There were no relatives on the scene so Social Services intervened, questioned whether I could look after them or whether they would be better off in care.' The taste of remembered fear that his sisters would be wrested from him coated his throat. 'Obviously there was no way I could let them go but...that was tough for Leila to understand.'

Imogen scrunched up her nose in clear disapproval. 'So Leila jumped ship?'

'Yes. No discredit to her. She was twenty-one as well— she didn't want to settle down and raise two grieving, rebellious pre-teens who didn't even like her.'

Her shoulders hitched in a shrug. 'Hmm… Call me dim, but I don't get how that makes you owe her?'

'Because I didn't take her ship-jumping very well. I was desperate for us to stay together.'

He'd been a mess of confusion, frustration, fear and anger as he'd watched the life he'd thought he had unravel—as he'd realised everything he'd believed his parents to be had been an illusion. The idea that everything he'd thought he and Leila had was another fantasy had been hard to get a handle on.

'I thought love should conquer all and a woman should stand by her man. I believed that being in a stable relationship would help me in my case for winning custody of the twins.'

Her blue-grey eyes held an understanding he didn't merit.

'That seems more than reasonable, Joe. You must have been terrified and grieving and shocked. You needed your girlfriend's support.'

'Unfortunately I wasn't exactly firing on all cylinders, so I wasn't at home to reason. First I proposed marriage.' He gave a small mirthless laugh as he remembered his frenzied planning and his clumsy stupidity. The candlelit dinner, the violins, the ring bought with scraped-together money he'd ill been able to afford. 'Leila refused to marry me and I… Well, I reacted badly.'

Imogen rose and walked round the table to sit beside him, placed a warm hand over his and held on when he tried to pull away.

'Save your sympathy. Believe me, I don't deserve it. I

made Leila's life hell. I couldn't let it go. I begged, threatened, hounded her. I tried character assassination tactics and I made wild promises. The works.' Shame seared his gut, along with the bitter memory of his abject neediness. 'In the end she threatened me with a restraining order and I forced myself to back off before the custody case went down the pan. So, you see, I do owe her.'

Imogen's hand tightened over his. 'You're being pretty hard on yourself. You were in a bad place then, coping with a lot of emotions.'

'That didn't give me the right to stuff up someone else's life.'

'That's plain dramatic.'

'I wish. Leila has invited me to her wedding because her therapist has recommended it so she can have closure and truly move on in life with her husband. Turns out she's been racked with guilt all these years and it's prevented her from forming relationships. Even now she's had to work extremely hard in therapy to believe herself worthy of love.'

'Joe, this all sounds a bit screwy to me. Wouldn't it be more sensible for the two of you to meet up in private, not at her wedding? Talk it through?'

He rubbed the back of his neck. 'Apparently her wedding is symbolic for both of us. She's the injured party here—I'll do whatever it takes to help her to find closure. I did send her a letter years ago, to apologise and let her know I'd won custody of the twins. I guess she never got it. I guess I should have tried harder to make amends. But, whichever way I look at it, the least I can do is go to the wedding. Not because I have any feelings left for her but because I owe her. Question is: will you come with me?'

There was a million-squillion-dollar question if ever there was one. Could she survive three days in the Algarve with

Joe? Forget days—what about the nights? What about the posing-as-loving-girlfriend factor?

Emotions swirled round Imogen's stomach and questions whirled around her brain. Overriding everything was the instinct just to say yes. Because her heart was torn by what Joe had told her and the tragedy he'd gone through. Because her chest warmed with admiration for the way he had fought to look after his sisters, his decision to take on a responsibility far beyond his years. And because she was damn sure Leila wasn't as injured as all that—something was off…she was sure of it.

But somehow she had to retain perspective.

She released his hand and picked up a piece of pizza—more for show than out of hunger. 'I'm not sure lying to Leila is the way forward. You'd be better to talk it all through.'

A barely repressed shudder greeted this suggestion—she'd swear his gills had paled further.

'Wouldn't work. I've tried for the past three weeks to convince her I'm perfectly happy as I am and that she has no need to feel bad. I've got nowhere. Leila needs to see me gallop off into the sunset to my own Happy Ever After.'

Maybe he had a point—talking to Leila did sound pointless. She seemed determined to see things her way. Mind you, so did Joe—he seemed unable to see that his behaviour, whilst not right, had been motivated by grief.

'Fair enough. But why me? There must be women queuing up to go with you—especially to the wedding of the decade. You could take anyone.'

'I don't want to take *anyone*—I want to take you.'

Her heart skipped a beat. 'Why?'

'Because I don't exactly have a list of women I can ask to pose as my girlfriend. And if I hire someone I risk them going to the press—this wedding is big news. I trust you not to do that.'

There was a daft, puppy dog aspect of her that pricked up its ears at any approval. Gave his words a significance they didn't have. The man was her boss and he had the power to make or break Langley. To give him credit, she knew he wouldn't use that to sway her decision—but there was every chance he'd sack her if she ran round betraying him to the press. Hell, she wouldn't blame him.

'Imogen? Yay or nay?'

Think, Imo.

It was a stupid idea for so very many reasons. Such as… 'What about Paris?'

His face shuttered: features immobile, eyes hard. 'What about Paris?'

'Won't it be…awkward?'

'Nope. The past few days have been fine, haven't they?'

Only because they'd become so immersed in work that somehow the awkwardness, the anger and the coldness of the morning after had thawed. Even then 'fine' was probably an exaggeration. Because to her own irritation, her own self-contempt, despite her absorption in work desire had strummed, *flared*, clenched at her tummy muscles with each accidental brush of his hand.

She had managed to keep her cool, not betrayed that desire by so much as a glance, but even so three days and nights in Joe's company would be akin to taking up fire-eating as a new career without any training. It wasn't just stupid—it was crazy.

'Yes. But you're proposing we act as a couple at a wedding. It's a bit different from working together in a boardroom.'

'It won't be a problem.'

As if just because he said so it would be so.

'I've never broken my One Night Only rule and I have no intention of starting now. You were pretty clear that you didn't want a repeat performance either. We agreed one night; we've had one night. I can't see an issue.'

Yet for a fraction of a second his gaze skittered away as he rubbed his neck—and there was the hint of a tic pulsing in his cheek.

Curiosity rippled inside her, along with a thread of sympathy. 'Is your rule because of what happened with Leila?'

Joe snorted. 'Spare me, Imogen. My relationship decisions have nothing to do with Leila or our split. One-night stands suit me because my priority is my sisters. The last thing they need is me introducing anyone into our circle who may not remain in it. But celibacy isn't my chosen option. Equally I have no desire to hurt anyone. One night means there's no time for hopes to be raised or for a relationship to be a possibility.'

'Oh.' That all made perfect sense, and yet... 'How old are your sisters now?'

'Eighteen.'

His face softened and his lips tilted up into a smile of affectionate pride that touched her.

'They are off travelling for a year. Holly has a place lined up at uni and Tammy wants to get straight into the job market. She's already landed a job in television—' He broke off and shook his head. 'Sorry—you don't want to hear about the girls.'

'Actually, I do,' Imogen said. 'It sounds like you've done a marvellous job, and it's wonderful that you've encouraged them to follow their dreams.'

Live the dream.

Moving on fast... 'But now they're eighteen they won't be so affected by you having a relationship longer than a night with someone.'

'I know that. But now it's about what *I* want—and I don't want the hassle or the commitment of a relationship. I love my sisters, and I'll always be there for them, but right now I'm going to kick back and see what it's like to be not just fancy-free but footloose as well.'

That made perfect sense too—he'd had his twenties turned upside down, been emotionally and fiscally responsible for two grieving young girls. Of course he would avoid further commitment like the avian flu. Yet she couldn't help but wonder if he had been more affected than she realised by Leila.

'Anyway... What's your decision? Three days in the Algarve at the wedding of the year? Surrounded by sunshine and the rich and famous? Showing Steve and Simone and the world that Steve is a dim and distant memory?'

When in doubt, eat pizza.

As she chewed Imogen tried to think. Every sensible bone in her body told her to scream *aargghhh* and run the hell away. But she couldn't—she wasn't made that way. Joe might be a ruthless corporate machine, but it turned out he was a human being too. A man who had undergone tragedy and stepped up to the plate to take on a responsibility beyond his years. Her heart ached for him—for the loss of his parents and all the attendant consequences.

Plus, for reasons she couldn't fully fathom, the thought of abandoning him to the wedding—the thought of him being pursued by a line-up of women on the catch for him—had her teeth on edge. There was also the consideration that this wedding would garner publicity, and she'd be less than human if she didn't want to cock a snook at all the people pitying her for Steve's defection.

So what was holding her back, really? Fear that she'd rip all his clothes off? That wouldn't happen. She'd learnt her lesson in Paris—realised that lust truly was dangerous and that all her theories were bang on the nail.

Joe didn't tick any boxes on her tick-list and as such he was off-limits.

'I'll do it,' she said.

His lips curved up into a smile that creased his eyes and flipped her tummy.

'Provided we have separate rooms.' No need to test her resolve too much.

'Separate beds. Apparently I have been allocated a twin room in a villa. Leila and Howard are paying for everything for all their guests. I think separate rooms would defeat the purpose of the whole charade.'

'Fair point.'

Joe reached for his tablet. 'I'll email Leila. Explain that I met you recently and it was love at first sight. We spend three days making sure she believes we've fallen for each other. She swans off into the sunset with full closure achieved.'

It all sounded so simple, and yet a faint flicker of foreboding ignited inside her.

'This calls for a celebration,' Joe stated, and strode across the boardroom to the fridge. 'I bought a few bottles of champagne so the office could celebrate if we won the proposal. I think a toast is in order right now.'

Minutes later he handed her a glass of sparkling amber liquid and clinked his glass against hers. Only then did she realise the sheer error of letting herself get so close.

His sculpted chest was just millimetres from her fingers. His warm scent ignited a deep yearning. Images strobed in her brain. Paris. Champagne. Naked Joe. Naked Imogen.

His eyes darkened, his powerful chest rose and fell, and she wondered if his heart was pounding as hard as hers. Then his jaw clenched as he stepped backwards and raised his glass.

'To the Harvey project,' he said. 'And to the Algarve.'

CHAPTER TEN

IMOGEN STARED OUT of the window of the aeroplane and tried to relax. Before her muscles cramped from the strain of keeping the maximum distance from Joe. Why couldn't she focus on the glorious blue of the sky and the wisps of cotton wool cloud? As opposed to the glory of the toned body scant millimetres from her own and the wisps of ten days' worth of dreams that clouded her brain.

Ten days during which she had managed to avoid him at Langley—relieved that he had held a lot of meetings off site, relieved that he'd spent a lot time closeted with Peter and Harry, walking them through the changes he'd made.

Maybe this hadn't been the world's best idea after all. Mel thought she'd lost the plot *and* her marbles, but Imogen had assured her she was in no danger. The irony wasn't lost on her that she had been sucked into helping another man with his ex-girlfriend issues. But Joe wasn't Steve and the situation was different. Imogen wasn't interested in Joe—he had no long-term relationship potential and she certainly didn't trust this damned attraction that had her practically squirming in her seat.

'So,' he said. 'Peter tells me that the Paris apartment is going well?'

'Yup.' This would be the *other* reason why she'd been avoiding Joe. 'Gosh. Look at that cloud. It looks a bit like a dragon, don't you think?'

'Nope.' He turned his torso so that he faced her and didn't so much as glance out of the window. 'He also said that despite my interim report recommending that you work on the project you've refused.'

'That's right.' Realising she'd folded her arms across her chest, she pushed down the absurd defensiveness and met his gaze full-on. 'There's no need. Peter is so excited by Richard's apartment he's back on form, and he and Belinda are working flat-out. Harry is back part-time and keeping an iron fist on finance, just as your report stated. Plus, there's been an awful lot of admin work to do—especially with all the new procedures you've recommended. So I appreciate your suggestion but I've decided that isn't the way forward for me. From now on I'm a PA and nothing more.'

An ominous frown creased his brow. 'Why?'

'Because…'

Because her time with Joe had terrified her on all sorts of levels and she'd run screaming back into her comfort zone and barricaded all the doors.

'I want to concentrate on streamlining my job properly. Also I need to focus on other aspects of my life. Like finding a place to live, thinking about my future.'

The future she had been in danger of forgetting. The nice, safe, secure one with her tick-list man.

His lips tightened and his eyebrows slashed into the start of a scowl.

'*Anyhoo*,' she said brightly. 'All in all it has been a very busy few days, so I think I'll catch some sleep.'

As if.

But at least closing her eyes put an end to the conversation. It had been tough enough to explain her decision to Peter—almost torturous not to get involved in the project itself. But her resolve had been bolstered when she'd heard Belinda on the phone to her husband, explaining night after night that she had to work late, seen her harassed expression when her child-minder had let her down. All a timely reminder of what could happen if you let a job take over your life. That was not for her.

Forcing herself to breathe evenly and remain still, Imogen kept her eyes firmly closed for the seemingly endless remainder of the journey. Relief arrived when the plane finally began its descent and she could legitimately stretch her cramped muscles.

'Nice rest?' Joe asked, a quirk of his lips expressing scepticism.

'Lovely, thank you.' She could only hope her nose hadn't stretched a centimetre or so. 'I can't believe I'm in the Algarve!'

Still hard to believe even when they descended the steps and a definitely non-British sun kissed her shoulders with glorious warmth as they headed for the airport terminal.

Once they had successfully negotiated passport control, customs, and collected their luggage Imogen looked round. 'What happens now?'

'According to my email from the very efficient wedding planner there will be a car to take us to the villa.' Joe glanced round. 'There we go.'

Following the direction of his finger, Imogen saw a man in a chauffeur's cap and suit holding up a card emblazoned with. 'Leila and Howie's guests'.

As they approached they saw a few others headed the same way. Imogen eyed them, a lump of doubt forming in her tummy. 'They look very glam,' she whispered. 'I'm not sure I'll fit in.'

Joe shrugged. 'And that's a problem because…?'

Before she could answer they had reached the chauffeur, whose name-tag identified him as Len.

'Joe McIntyre and Imogen Lorrimer.'

Len scanned his list and then shook his head. 'You're down for a different car.' He glanced round and pointed. 'Luis will be looking after you.'

'Senhor McIntyre—Senhorita Lorrimer?'

Imogen smiled at the young man who beamed at them as he pushed an overlong lock of dark hair from his forehead.

'I am Luis. I am one of the wedding planners and I will do my best to answer any questions you have about the timetable and I will deal with all your requirements. But first come this way and I will take you to your wonderful accommodation for your stay in the Algarve. All, of course, courtesy of the bride and groom.'

He paused for breath and then smiled again.

'The car is this way. I will take you the motorway route as you will want time to get ready for the ceremony. But there will be lovely scenery towards the end of the trip.'

Imogen glanced at Joe as they climbed into the four-wheel drive car. What was he thinking? It was impossible to tell from his expression but he must be feeling something. The one love of his life, the woman who had driven him to desperation—even if he was over her, even if he hadn't seen her for seven years—was getting married.

None of her business—she was sucked in enough; she couldn't risk getting further involved. That way led madness.

It was best if she concentrated solely on the scenery for the rest of the journey. So as the car glided down the motorway and then wound its way along bendy valley roads she inhaled the sweet breeze and soaked in the greens of the verdure outside until Luis said, 'Nearly there.'

Her vision didn't yield so much as a hut, let alone a villa, and Imogen frowned as Luis turned down a dirt track. 'Wow. So the villa is really secluded, then?'

'Villa?' Luis said. 'No, no—did no one email you?'

'No,' Joe growled. 'Should they have?'

'Yes. You see, all the singletons have been assigned the

villas. You have been given a yurt. You will *love* it. Full of luxury and romance. It is five-star.'

The scenery became so much irrelevant colour and the brilliant sunshine faded as Imogen struggled for breath. 'A *yurt*?' she coughed out.

'Do not worry. This is a state-of-the-art yurt. All mod-cons. Leila and Howard have had them specially put up for the occasion. You will be able to fall asleep together, gazing up at the stars.'

Tension ricocheted from Joe's body and no doubt collided with hers; in fact their mingled tension could probably power a rocket. All the way to the ruddy stars.

'Here we are,' Luis said cheerfully, apparently oblivious to the atmosphere as he parked the car and turned to look at them. 'Howard was very particular about your accommodation, so I hope I can report back to him that you are happy. Yes?'

Oh, hell and damnation. They were supposed to be a loved-up couple and Imogen had no doubt that Howard Kreel would much rather that was *exactly* what they were. It couldn't be much fun for the groom, having his bride's ex-boyfriend there for 'closure'.

This was clearly her cue to be adoring, when in actual fact the desire to strangle Joe with her bare hands was making her palms itch. 'Of course we're happy,' she said. 'How would it be possible *not* to be happy? Don't you agree, sweetheart?'

'Absolutely,' Joe said, with a credible attempt at enthusiasm and an overdose of heartiness. As if Joe had ever been *hearty* in his life. 'Imogen and I are sure to appreciate every second of our stay.'

'Excellent.' Luis sprang out of the car and opened Imogen's door. 'Then I'll take you on a guided tour of the site and leave you to it.'

Imogen tried to appreciate the fairytale beauty of the

site—she really did. It was a good few steps up even from a *glamp*site. Lord knew how much it must have cost to convert the area so spectacularly. Tipis and luxury tents dotted the area—all individually decorated and all, Luis assured them again, equipped with a variety of mod-cons. Two large wooden huts had also been constructed.

'There is the bar and the dining area. Meals and refreshments will be available all day.'

In addition to what money could buy was the wealth of nature's offerings—the colourful flowers, the vibrant vegetation, the lap of water from a small brook that wound its way down a rocky precipice and then meandered through the lush lime-green meadow.

And there in a secluded corner...

'Here we are,' Luis announced, gesturing at a pink canvas palace. 'You have guaranteed privacy. All the details about the wedding and the reception and the available activities are in a folder inside. The coach will arrive at four to take you to the beach ceremony.'

'Fabulous. Thank you *so* much, Luis,' Imogen trilled, forcing her lips upward, keeping the smile...aka rictus... in place as she watched his departing back.

Two more strides and Luis had climbed into the four-seater.

'Not! This is *not* fabulous, Joe. Look at it. It's got *turrets*! It's the yurt of love. What happened to the twin beds in a villa?'

'Yes, well, I obviously got upgraded from singleton to one of the loved-up people.' He thrust a hand through his hair. 'Let's not panic until we've actually looked inside.'

'Fine.' Imogen tugged the canvas door open. 'Um...'

Pink canvas walls were draped with beaded curtains and gauzy material. There were tasselled cushions, luxury pile rugs, an overstuffed sofa, a dressing table...and an enormous sleigh bed.

Below a porthole.

With a view of the stars.

For a fleeting second she wished that there could be a rerun of Paris—another rash decision to break the rules. But she knew that wasn't possible. Once was fine—could be chalked up to a magical experience. Twice… That was way too dangerous and she wouldn't go there. Couldn't go there for the sake of her own sanity.

She was *not* going to end up bedazzled, befuddled and controlled by lust.

Turning to Joe, she swept her hand towards the bed. '*Now* can I panic?'

Joe exhaled heavily and forced his features to neutral. What had he ever done to deserve this? A twin room in a populated villa would have been tough, but manageable. Worst-case scenario: he'd have stayed up in the lounge playing video games. All night.

There was nowhere to go in a yurt.

Chill. He needed to chill. He was a ruthless corporate businessman, for goodness' sake—not an adolescent.

Plus he had no one to blame but himself; this whole jaunt had been *his* damn fool idea. Now he would just have to suck it up.

'No need…' He stopped and cleared his throat, forced more words past the knot of panic in his throat. 'No need to freak out. I'll sleep on the sofa; you can have the bed.'

Rocking back on his heels, he swept a final glance around the tent and rubbed the back of his neck.

'I guess you need to change, so I'll leave you to it.'

Fresh air—that was what he needed. Fresh air and exercise. Perhaps if he walked a very, very long way he'd walk off the desire that urged him to turn round, rip open the door of the yurt and throw Imogen down onto the bed. Walk off the desire.

Master plan, McIntyre. But it was the only one he had…
It didn't work worth a damn.

An hour later, as he approached the yurt, anticipation unfurled in his chest. And when he stepped into the pink canvas bubble he stopped in his tracks. Because Imogen looked so beautiful she robbed his lungs of air. Her dark hair rode her shoulders in sleek glossy waves; a floaty floral dress gave her beauty an ethereal edge.

She rose from the dressing table and faced him, her lips tilted in an almost shy smile as she spread out her arms and gave a twirl, the orange and red flowers of the dress vibrant as they swirled around her.

'Do you think this is all right?' she asked. 'I chose it myself—no help from Mel, no ulterior motive. Just because I like it. But now I'm worried that it's not glam enough.'

'I don't think that's a problem,' he managed. Though his blood pressure might be approaching the turreted roof.

'You sure?'

'One hundred per cent. You look beautiful. I promise.'

Silence enveloped them; awareness hummed in the air. Time to distract himself.

Keeping his movements casual, he headed for the sofa and picked up a leatherbound folder.

'That must be the itinerary Luis mentioned,' Imogen said, her voice slightly high as she sat down.

'Yup.' He stared down at the words and forced his brain to make sense of them. 'So, as we know, after the ceremony there's a Bond-themed party on a yacht. We'll need to take a change of clothes with us. Then tomorrow there are various activities we can do. Leila and Howard will have left for their honeymoon, but they want all their guests to stay and have fun.'

'Activities?' Imogen looked up and there was genuine enthusiasm on her face as she no doubt worked out a way to avoid his company for the day. 'That sounds like a great idea. What sort of activities?'

Joe scanned the list. 'Sightseeing, beach yoga, surfing and…'

'And what?'

'There's an art class run by Michael Mallory, who is a lecturer at one of London's top art colleges. You should do that.'

Imogen narrowed her eyes. 'You don't give up, do you?'

'No. I've seen how talented you are—seems a shame for it to go to waste.'

'That is not your decision to make.'

'Agreed… But I just don't get why you are being so damn stubborn about this.'

For a second unease pricked his conscience. Why did it matter so much to him? Hell, it was way better to have this conversation right now than dwell on all the other things they could do in the Yurt of Love.

'Now is as good a time as any for you to tell me. No excuses—no need to nap.'

'I *did* need a nap.'

'Rubbish! No one sleeps with their body completely still and radiating tension. You were ducking out of a proper explanation of why you refused to go along with my report and help out on Richard's apartment. And please spare me the *I can't do any art because I need to move* crap.'

'It's the truth.' One defiant swivel and she presented her back to him, leaning forward to pick up a lipstick and peer into the heart-shaped gilded mirror. 'So I'll give the lesson a miss.'

'Shame.' Joe leant against the cushioned back rest and picked up the folder again. '"Michael Mallory: esteemed lecturer and mentor to Justin Kinley, Myra Olsten and Becca Farringham, all of whom exploded on to the art scene after graduation. Michael has planned an intense day in which you will learn how to express your artistic instincts and find your own definite artistic voice. This kind of near one-on-one tuition is an incredible chance to learn from a master and—'''

'Stop!' Imogen spun on the chair to face him, her chest rising and falling as she jabbed a mascara wand in the air. 'Just stop—OK?'

'Why? I'm just telling you what you're missing.'

'I get it. OK? I get what I'm missing and I'm good with it.'

Only she wasn't. Not by a long shot. He could see the sparkle of tears in her eyes even as she blinked fiercely. Sense her anger and frustration as she clenched her hands round the edge of her seat and inhaled deeply.

'Imo, sweetheart. You're *not* good with it.'

He stood, strode over the canvas floor and dropped to his haunches in front of her, covering her hands with his.

'Tell me. C'mon. I'm sorry I went on at you but I've seen your talent. That proposal—you made the sketches come alive. I could see the glitter of the mirror, feel the softness of the sheets, smell the freshly baked baguettes.'

'They were just a few pencil and charcoal sketches.'

'They were a lot more than that.' He shook his head. 'I don't get it, Imogen. Why don't you take the project further? I've seen how absorbed you've been, how much it matters to you.'

He had seen her frustration if it hadn't been perfect— the way she'd thrown crumpled bits of paper at the bin— seen the ink streaks on her forehead, the forgotten cups of tea and coffee, the food he'd forced her to eat.

'And that's exactly the problem!' she said.

'Meaning?'

For a moment she hesitated, and then a small reluctant smile tugged at her lips. 'I'm guessing you won't let up until I explain?'

'Nope.'

She leant back against the dresser and inhaled an audible breath. 'I told you my parents' marriage is less than stellar?'

Joe nodded.

'I didn't explain why. The main reason is my dad. He's an artist, and he's dedicated his life to his art even though he's barely sold anything. It's an obsession with him—more important than my mum, more important than me. Mum did *everything*. Worked at any job she could get to pay the bills and put food on the table. She wanted to study, to go to uni, but somehow it never happened. It couldn't because Dad wouldn't go and get a job, it was always, "When I get recognised, then it will all change."'

Her shoulders hitched in a shrug.

'Mum couldn't even leave me with him when she was at work, because he got so absorbed in his work he forgot me. It consumed him. I don't want that in my life.'

His throat tightened as he saw the pain in her eyes. So much made sense now: her desire for a job that didn't challenge her, her need for a partner who pulled his weight.

'Just because your father lost perspective it doesn't mean you would.'

'Not a risk I'm willing to take. And even if I were I couldn't do that to Mum. She had such high hopes for me. She wanted me to be a lawyer or an accountant. Make something of my life...do all the stuff she missed out on. When it turned out I couldn't achieve that she was devastated... I can't disappoint her even more.'

'But surely what your mum wants most for you is for you to be happy? You should talk to her about this. You can't live your life for your parents.'

Imogen shook her head. 'I'm not. Sure, Mum steered me away from art at every turn—but I don't blame her for that. I don't want to be bitten by the bug. Mum *does* want me to be happy and so do I. I know what I want from my life—I want to be secure, settled and comfortable. I want a nice husband and two point four kids. Maybe a Labrador and a white picket fence. The happy bonus is that I won't make my mother miserable, watching her daughter follow the same road as her husband.'

'The less than happy price is that you miss out on something you love.'

'Then it's a price I'm willing to pay.'

'Even to the point of not taking up art as a *hobby*?'

'I can't.' A small shake of her head as she looked at him almost beseechingly. 'I've realised that these past weeks. I did love doing Richard's proposal, I did enjoy working on projects for Peter, but you saw what happened. I became obsessed.'

'That was one proposal—with a deadline. And you don't have a family yet.'

'Doesn't matter. I have to draw a line under it now.' As if suddenly realising his hands still covered hers, she pulled them away. 'Do you understand?'

'Yes, I understand.'

Her words pulled a nerve taut. Years ago, after his parents' death, that had been his exact decision. With two grief-stricken sisters to look after and a company to try and sort out—responsibilities that had surpassed his own dreams—he'd drawn a line under his surfing career. He'd taken his board out one last time—and the memory of the cool breeze, the tang of salt, the roll of the waves was etched on his soul in its significance.

'But I don't agree.'

He rose to his feet and looked down at her. Lord knew he did know how she felt—maybe that was why he was reacting so strongly to Imogen's decision. But he'd had no choice. His sisters were his priority—that was an absolute, and he had no regrets as to his decision. But this...

this was different, and he wished—*so* wished—there was some way to show Imogen that.

'Your talent—your art—is a fundamental part of you that you're shutting down.'

'Maybe. But by shutting it down I get to be the person I want to be.' Her lips curved into a small smile. 'It's truly lovely of you to care, and I appreciate it, Joe, but I made this decision long ago—it's the sensible option. And I'm all about the sensible.'

Turning, she picked up the abandoned mascara wand and leant forward to peer at her reflection.

Only she *wasn't* 'all about the sensible'. He'd seen Imogen Lorrimer at her least sensible and she'd been vibrant and alive and happy.

It's truly lovely of you to care.

Her words echoed round his brain and set off alarm bells. Caring was not on his agenda. Time to back off—Imogen's life was hers. He'd had his say and now it was time to join the Sensible Club.

'Have it your way,' he said.

CHAPTER ELEVEN

IMOGEN SWALLOWED PAST the gnarl of emotion in her throat; she didn't even *know* Leila or Howard, and yet the sight of them repeating their vows had tears prickling the backs of her eyelids.

In a gown that clung to her in diaphanous folds of ivory and lace Leila radiated bridal joy—her smile could probably illuminate the whole of the Algarve. But it wasn't that which touched Imogen most—it was the way Howard looked at his bride. Such love, such adoration, such pride that it was little wonder Imogen's chest ached.

Hollywood, eat your heart out. Imogen, get a grip.

Maybe she was overreacting like this because the setting was so damn movie-like: the golden sand, the lap of waves and the glow of the setting sun that streaked flames of orange across the dusky sky.

What she needed to remember was that this was a moment of time—not a happy-ever-after. Look at her parents: she had pored over their wedding photos as a child, in an attempt to work out how such rosy happiness could have evaporated into screaming and bitterness.

Her parents' dreams had crumbled to dust, their radiance no more than sex and foolish hope. Proof-positive that a marriage based on lust did not work—a marriage between two incompatible people did not work. But a marriage based on a tick-list would. Imogen was sure of it.

There was a collective gasp as Howard lifted his wife's veil and kissed her. As Leila slid one slender arm around his neck Imogen cast a surreptitious look at Joe. Did he mind? Was he revisiting the past, wondering what would have happened if Leila had agreed to marry him all those years ago?

Surely not. He didn't look like a man harbouring thoughts of the past—if anything he looked faintly bored. Unless, of course, it was all a façade—Joe was hardly a man to wear his heart on the sleeve of his grey suit, and that was even assuming he *had* one.

'You OK?' she asked under cover of the applause that had broken out as Howard and Leila continued their lip-lock.

'Why wouldn't I be?'

'You loved her once—whatever your reasons, you wanted to commit a lifetime to her.'

Broad shoulders hitched. 'I'm happy for her—happy that she is happy. That the damage I did has been mitigated. No more than that.' He glanced around. 'Come on. It's the receiving line. So don't forget to turn on the adoring look.'

'I think you've forgotten something.'

'What?'

'It's a two-way street. You have to look adoringly at me too.'

And she had to remember that this was fake. Needed to dismiss the wistfulness that wisped through her brain at the thought that Leila and Simone got the real McCoy version of the adoring look and she was stuck with the false one.

Joe raised his eyebrows, a small smile playing on his lips, and all thoughts of wistfulness blew away, to be replaced by far more dangerous memories of the havoc those lips could cause.

'You think I can't do adoring?' he asked.

'I'm finding it hard to imagine.'

'Watch and learn, Imogen. Watch and learn.'

His cool broad fingers grasped hers and Imogen bit her lip to hold in her gasp. It was their first contact in days and her skin reacted like a parched plant in the depths of the Sahara to rain.

A little flicker of envy ignited in her as they approached Leila—even the stunning photos that graced the celebrity mags hadn't done her justice. Long blonde hair shimmered under her veil, exotic green eyes lit up as they rested on Joe, and her smile demonstrated the slant of perfect cheekbones and the curve of glossy provocative lips.

'J!' she exclaimed in a melodious yet husky voice that fitted the setting perfectly.

Any second now birds would swoop from the sky and land on her and everyone would break into song.

Not that Imogen cared. Much. So who knew why a mixture of jealousy and mortification seared her insides as Leila threw her arms around Joe before stepping back and raising a hand to cup his jaw?

'It's so very good to see you, J. I do appreciate you coming.'

Imogen tried not to clench her nails into Joe's palm and made an attempt to access the voice of reason. Leila was the bride—no way was she hitting on Joe. Or should she say *J*? *All* ex-girlfriends didn't have an agenda to win back their boyfriends. This was closure. Yet…damn it… she wasn't imagining that proprietorial look on Leila's face.

Joe stepped back and put an arm around Imogen's waist, squeezed her against him. 'Good to see you too, Leila— and congratulations. This is Imogen.'

Imogen blinked—was that *Joe's* voice? Low and tender and…well…*adoring*? As if he were introducing someone special and precious?

The bride's perfect smile froze a touch—she was sure of it.

'Imogen. I am so happy to meet you. You and I must have a proper girl-to-girl chat at the reception.'

Well, wouldn't *that* be fun? 'Super,' Imogen said, managing a smile as they moved along to stand in front of Howard.

'Joe. My man.' The groom slapped Joe on the back with what looked like excessive force. 'Thanks for coming along, dude,' he said. 'It means a lot to Leila—which is why I told her of *course* I didn't mind. Oh, and from one surfing dude to another—make sure you take your board out while you're here.'

Joe's lean body tensed next to hers and Imogen glanced up at him. Surfing dude? Joe was a *surfing dude*? Could Howard be mixing him up with someone else? There was nothing in Joe's face to indicate his thoughts; his features could have been carved from granite.

'Imogen.' Howard grasped her hands. 'It is so very nice to meet you and to know that Joe is in good hands. Hope you like the yurt?'

'It's—' Before Imogen could reply she saw Leila's head turn.

'But I put Joe and Imogen in the villa, sweetie.'

'I changed the plan, sugar puff. Paid a bundle for that yurt—shame for it to go to waste.'

A small frown creased Leila's brow before she smiled her radiant smile. 'Wonderful idea.'

'It's incredible,' Imogen chipped in, before they moved along to where the bride's and groom's parents awaited.

'Phew…' She whistled as they walked away from the line. 'I don't think you're exactly Mr Popular—with Howard's family or Leila's.'

'No big surprise, given the way I treated Leila.'

Imogen frowned. 'I'm not sure that's the problem.'

'What do you mean?'

'I get the idea they're worried that Leila still has feelings for you. To be honest, if I was your real girlfriend so would I be.'

Come to that, even as his fake girlfriend she wasn't happy about the idea.

Joe shook his head. 'That doesn't make sense. This is Leila's wedding day—she hasn't seen me in seven years. And, believe me, she can't possibly have any good memories of how we parted.'

'I suppose.'

Joe had a point—maybe her imagination had gone into overdrive. So affected by Steve's defection to Simone that she found bugbears where there weren't any. But...

She shrugged. 'Well, bear it in mind as a possibility.'

Before Joe could answer Luis waved at them and headed over. 'It was a beautiful ceremony, yes?'

'Absolutely.'

'And now your change of clothes is in the beach huts. If you come this way, and once you have changed please head for the yacht. Women this way—men that way.'

Joe stepped onto the garlanded deck of the yacht and blinked at the dazzling array of glittering disco balls and spinning lights that strobed the deck with multicoloured lights. Men in tuxedos and women in various Bond girl costumes chattered, their voices mingling with the Bond-themed music. As he scanned the crowd for Imogen he realised that he had no idea what she would be wearing. Not that it mattered—he would know her by her stance, her glorious shape, the sweep of her dark hair.

'You must be Joe,' a breathy voice proclaimed.

Before he could sidestep her a curvy petite woman had launched herself at him on a wave of overpowering perfume.

'Oh, my! You're every bit as gorgeous as Leila said. I'm Katrina. Part of your line-up. I know you've come with some other woman, but I wanted you to see what you're missing, sugar.'

Was she for real? 'No need, thanks. I'm—'

'Oh, come on, darlin'…no man can resist me. Just one little kiss.'

As Katrina pressed her over-glossed lips to his Joe looked over the top of the petite blonde's head to see Imogen walking straight towards them, her gown a swirl of Bohemian tangerine-orange. Her smile dropped from her lips and she faltered for a heartbeat as she took in the scene. Then her lips tightened, and if she could have lasered him with her glare he'd be dead by now.

Taking Katrina firmly by the arms, he hoisted her away from him.

'I'm taken,' he finished.

Katrina turned on one stiletto heel and gave a little giggle. 'Dear me. Caught red-handed. Catch you later, Joe honey.'

'Why don't you chase after her, *Joe honey*?' Imogen asked.

The cool sarcasm caught him on the raw. Surely she didn't believe he'd instigated that interlude?

'Don't mind me.'

'I don't want to chase after her. That was Katrina. One of the line-up you're here to protect me from.'

'Didn't look to me as though you needed protection at all.' Imogen emitted a mirthless laugh as she gestured to his pants pocket. 'Apart from the type that comes in foil packets. And no doubt you've got plenty of those handy in your wallet.'

A flash of anger stabbed him as he leant back against the railings. Did she really think so little of him?

'You don't think you're overreacting a touch?'

'I'm the one who found you with a woman draped all

over you, her tongue practically stuck down your throat. And you think I'm overreacting?'

'Yes, I do. Nice imagery. Even better point: Katrina *was* draped over me—believe me, short of dodging her and letting her fall flat on her face there wasn't much I could do.'

'Oh, please. That is ridiculous—a big, strong man like you couldn't defend himself? I'm sure you have plenty of moves to avoid women of all shapes and sizes, and Katrina is hardly wrestler material. From where I was standing you looked pretty happy.'

Shaking her head so that the orange flowers woven into her hair vibrated, she hoisted her palms in a get-away-from-me gesture.

'I cannot *believe* I could have been so stupid as to come to this wedding with you. I actually bought that whole spiel you gave me.'

What the hell…?

'Spiel? It wasn't a spiel. I told you the truth.' Which hadn't exactly been a picnic for him.

'*Hah!* I just had the dubious pleasure of witnessing "the truth".'

Frustration mixed with bewilderment and he expelled a sigh. 'Imogen. If I wanted to get involved with Katrina why would I have brought you to the wedding at all?'

'Maybe you hadn't realised how attractive Katrina would be. Maybe you're regretting bringing me.' Imogen's blue-grey eyes narrowed and she clicked her fingers. 'Or maybe this is all a ploy to make Leila jealous. What are you hoping for, Joe? That she'll realise that she still loves you?'

For a second sheer disbelief froze him to the spot. Then… 'Enough!'

Propelled by sheer anger, Joe stepped forward and pulled her into his arms.

'Stop it!' Slamming her palms on his chest, she leant

back against his hold. 'No need to kiss *me*. Leila already believes we are an item.'

'Never mind that,' he growled. 'I'm going to show you what a real kiss is—and then you can understand that I was *not* kissing Katrina.'

The idea that she really believed he was such a bastard made his blood simmer in his veins and he sealed her mouth in one harsh swoop. He revelled in the lushness of her lips, the taste of mint and strawberry. Her body stilled and then she tangled her fingers in his hair. The angry stroke of her tongue against his sent a shudder through him and he pulled her tight against him, so she could feel his body's instant savage reaction.

OK. Stop now, Joe. Whilst you can. Point made.

Breaking the kiss, he stared down at her as their ragged breaths mingled in the evening breeze. '*That's* a real kiss,' he rasped. 'Do you really believe I'd bring you here as my guest and then go off with someone else? *Really?*'

Her slim shoulders lifted in a shrug. 'Why wouldn't you? If it was a tactic in your strategy to win Leila back, I'm sure you are more than ruthless enough to do just that.'

'What strategy? I do not want to win Leila back. Even if I did I'm not a complete bastard. I have too much respect for you to treat you as a pawn. I am at this wedding for all the reasons I told you. I have no interest in Katrina. I am *not* Steve. You are not second-best. It's your call whether you believe me or not.'

Before she could answer he saw Luis, wending his way through the tables towards them. 'Ah, here you are,' he said with a smile. 'Leila sent me to find you. She'd like a chat with Imogen.'

Joe bit back the urge to tell Luis to tell Leila to take a hike; he and Imogen were in the midst of an important conversation. It mattered to him that Imogen believed him.

Imogen, on the other hand, practically leapt towards

Luis, clearly relieved to be let off the conversational hook. 'Of course. I'll come straight away.' As Luis started to thread his way through the crowds she turned and murmured, 'Don't worry, Joe. I'll stick to my part of the bargain. *Whatever* your motivations for wanting me to.'

CHAPTER TWELVE

'ALONG HERE,' LUIS said, and led Imogen away from the thronged deck, where people shimmied and twisted to the beat of the music. Imogen followed on automatic, still processing what had just happened with Joe; trying to work out what to believe.

Instinct bade her to accept Joe's version of events, but her instincts were hardly the most reliable—she'd trusted Steve implicitly and that hadn't exactly ended well. Worse, it could be that her instincts had been skewed by that kiss, her brain deceived by a heady cloud of lust. Her lips—hell, her whole body—still buzzed from the aftershock.

The noise from the deck faded as she followed Luis down some stairs and into a private corridor. *Come on, Imogen—get prepared.* She'd told Joe she'd still play her allocated role—convince Leila that she was Joe's much-loved girlfriend.

Her brain whirled. Did Joe have a point? Why would he have kissed Katrina if he wanted this charade to play out? Because he wanted Leila to realise that he wasn't really in love with Imogen and that he was available? Her temples ached as she tried to work it out.

Luis pushed a door open. 'In here.'

For a mad moment Imogen expected him to announce her, but instead he simply flashed a smile and withdrew. Still, the feeling of being a subject granted an audience, or in this case summoned, persisted.

The spacious conference room was dominated by a

sleek oval cherrywood table, with Leila enthroned at one
end on an ornate chair. She'd removed her veil, and also
the train of her dress, so that now she was encased in a
lace concoction that hit mid-thigh and moulded her model
figure to perfection.

Suddenly the tangerine Bohemian look seemed a fashion disaster—maybe the black diamanté evening dress
would have been better. She shook her head—why was she
even thinking about this now? Maybe it was the slightly
patronising I-am-more-beautiful-than-you-can-ever-be-
and-we-both-know-it look in Leila's green eyes. Shades
of Simone's cornflower-blue orbs, with their I-am-more-
exciting-alluring-and-interesting-than-you-and-Steve-has-
always-loved-me expression.

'Imogen. Thank you for seeing me in private.'

'No problem.' Choking back a sudden surge of hollow
laughter, she tried to smile as she sat down.

'Howard and I are leaving tonight, and before I go I
need to make sure Joe is in good hands.'

'Right. I see.' Or rather... 'Well, actually—no, I don't.
Joe's happiness is not your responsibility.' Unless, of
course, Joe's strategy was working and Leila was having
second thoughts.

The blonde woman settled back on the chair and shook
her head. 'You see, that's where you're wrong. I dashed
Joe's hopes to the ground years ago—spurned his love—
so I do feel that his happiness is very much my responsibility. He *loved* me so much. I was his world and then I
rejected him.'

Hurt touched Imogen and she gritted her teeth, unable
to help wondering what it must feel like to have Joe—correction, to have *any* man—think she was his world.

'I feel so awful that I broke his heart like that... And
when he looked at me today I saw all that love as though
it had never gone away...could be rekindled in a trice...'

The leaden realisation that she had been right plummeted in Imogen's tummy. Joe *did* still love Leila—she had been right on the money.

Wait. The word lit up her brain in neon and her gut screamed at her to listen to it as her brain replayed his words. *'I have too much respect for you to treat you as a pawn. I am at this wedding for all the reasons I told you.'*

She replayed their conversation over pizza in the Langley boardroom. His voice as he told her the truth about his past: the tragedy and its outcome. The guilt over Leila; his need to make amends.

Finding her voice, she met Leila's emerald-green eyes, tried to read her expression. 'Do you *want* to rekindle Joe's love? Do you still love him?'

'No. Not at all. Howie is the man for me. But now I know for sure Joe still has feelings for me I wanted to talk to you, so we can come up with a strategy to help him get over me.'

The hell with this. There was every possibility that she'd regret this, but somehow it wasn't possible for Imogen to believe that Joe had lied to her. Ruthlessness was one thing; dishonesty was another. Steve had lied to her. Joe hadn't. Not once.

'I think he *has* got over you.'

The words were liberating and oh, so right.

Green eyes blinked at her in sheer incomprehension. 'Darling, I know you want to believe that, but it's simply not true. I saw the look in his eyes when he saw me. I—'

'So did I. Joe told me he's over you and I believe him.'

'Then why hasn't he had a relationship since me?'

'Because he's spent the last seven years bringing up his sisters. You know that.'

'Don't I just? Those twins are devil children. I never understood how he could pick them over me. Without the twins maybe I could have stuck it out. Though I don't

know… I remember the first time he dressed up in a suit to
go and sort out his dad's company. He didn't look like my
Joe any more. He'd changed so much. No more surfing—
just dull, dull, dull business stuff. No more photo shoots,
no more magazine articles, no more parties and travel…
Joe could have been a surfing champion—famous, rich,
having a life of freedom and fun. With me. He *knew* that
was what I wanted, but he couldn't see sense.'

Surfing again. So it was true. Only Joe had been more
than a 'surfing dude'—he'd been a champion, with a glittering career ahead of him. Her heart rended at the image
of corporate, suited and booted Joe riding the waves, free
and laid-back and happy, before tragedy struck.

'He chose the twins over me. And when I told him I
couldn't marry him he heaped abuse on my head. I know
it was because he was driven to distraction by my refusal
and his love for me, but it *hurt*, Imogen. So much.'

For a few seconds Imogen could only open and close
her mouth as sheer disbelief silenced her vocal cords. Joe
had given up so much and then achieved so much, without
complaint, regret or martyrdom. And this idiot couldn't
see *any* of that. Could only see how the world revolved
around *her*.

Drawing breath, Imogen tried to do as Joe had asked.
'Joe does feel terrible about how he treated you. He did
actually write you a letter, apologising and…'

'*Hah!* I got that letter…'

Imogen stilled, a layer of anger laving the inside of her
tummy. 'You *got* that letter? Why didn't you contact Joe?'

'What was the point?' Leila shook her head. 'His letter
was full of the twins and how he'd won custody. It was too
late for him to change his mind. Otherwise I'd have given
him a second chance. If he'd seen reason it may not have
been too late for us to recapture our love and—'

'Rubbish. You didn't love Joe. You wanted to hang onto

his board shorts and be carried to fame and fortune. And you didn't care what happened to the twins as long as you got what you wanted.'

'That's not true. If he'd loved me he would have put me first. That's what love is. I was trying to show him how to be happy.'

'Joe asked you to marry him. Spend your life with him. If you loved him wouldn't you have at least thought about it? Even if it was just to help him with the twins?'

Leila threw up her arms. 'Those damned twins.'

'They were people, Leila. Children—*grieving* children. How could Joe have lived with himself if he'd abandoned them?'

'Hooey.'

'Hooey?'

'Yes. Hooey.' Leila nodded in emphasis. 'Joe and I could have had a wonderful future together. He would have made a fortune—not just from surfing but from advertising and endorsements. We would have been as big as any of these football celebrity couples. We could have had it all—hell, by now we could have been on reality TV, with millions in the bank.'

'Is that what Joe wanted?'

'Of course. He loved surfing—and I'd have handled all the other stuff. But then he went and blew it.'

Anger was on a slow burn now, along with a feeling of wonder as to why Joe thought he owed Leila *anything*. 'It wasn't his fault his parents died.'

'No, but he didn't have to let it change everything.'

'But it *did* change everything!'

OK, so she'd yelled, but it had been either that or give in and shake some sense into Leila.

'Leila, you need to wake up and smell the coffee—or iced tea, or whatever. Just for a minute can you *please* try and look at this from a different perspective?'

For a second guilt prodded Imogen. Less than an hour ago she'd been just as bad as Leila, willing to condemn Joe because of her own fears and inadequacies. She had judged him unfairly. Now she could make amends. By standing up for him. And maybe she could achieve something more. Because whether he liked it or not Joe had been affected by his relationship with Leila. Maybe this was Imogen's chance to achieve closure for him. And if that meant bursting Leila's bubble then she'd enjoy every second.

'If Joe had done what you wanted and surfed off into the sunset with you what would have happened to his sisters?'

'Well…they…they would have been fine. He could have visited them, kept in touch. They could have come to stay with us every so often.'

'Visited them where, Leila?'

Red stained the blonde's cheeks. 'There must have been other relatives.'

'Nope.'

'The care system. Or…' Discomfort creased Leila's face.

'You didn't think, did you?' Imogen leant forward and slammed a palm down on the table, hearing the frustration sharpen her voice. 'Or rather you just thought about yourself. If it had been me all those years ago I'd have married him to help him through. I'd have stood by him. He's a good man. Who feels terrible about the way he behaved to you all those years ago. He believes he blighted your life. *Did* he?'

The green eyes skittered away. 'I would dream about his anguished face…his words of anger would echo in my eardrums.'

'Leila. This is real life. *Please*. There is a good man up there, beating himself up because he thinks he did you damage. A man who gave up his dream to look after his sisters. A man who built a new life for them and him.'

A man she had accused unfairly and owed an apology to herself. But that could come later—now her chest ached as she held her breath and hoped that her words had had some effect.

There was a long silence as Leila's glossy painted mouth opened and closed, and to Imogen's surprise she saw the green eyes swim with tears.

'Oh, hell,' Leila said. 'Double hell. Now my mascara is running.' A small sniff and suddenly she looked a whole lot more accessible. 'You're right.' She gusted out a sigh. 'I'm behaving appallingly. I've always felt terrible about the way I left Joe. I was young and shallow and, truth be told, I don't believe Joe and I really loved each other. I loved being a surfer chick and he loved having a hot blonde girlfriend.'

'That's OK.' Surprise and a sudden leap of elation at the knowledge that her instincts had been right after all fizzed in Imogen's tummy.

'But that doesn't mean I should have deserted him. And now—because I don't want to face what an outright bitch I was, and I certainly don't want Howard to know—I've rewritten history to suit myself. Without giving Joe a thought. I'm sorry.'

Imogen shook her head. 'It's not me you owe the apology to.'

'You think I should talk to Joe?'

'Yes, I do.' Imogen smiled—whatever her faults, it had taken guts for Leila to acknowledge the truth and want to make amends. 'That way you can both have closure.'

'And I can get on with doing what I'm best at. Being adored and fêted and looked after.'

'I think that's the bride's prerogative. Truly, Leila, I wish you and Howard very happy.'

'We will be, darling. And, Imogen?'

'Yes?'

'I'm sorry I tried to put you in the villa and gave you all those evil vibes. I know what it looks like, but I'm really not interested in Joe. I love my husband. It's just...'

'Just what?'

Leila sighed. 'I suppose I was so caught up in this story I'd concocted, about being the woman Joe would never be able to get over, that it was a bit of a shock to hear about you and then see that he is genuinely happy. But I'm glad he's found real love—truly.'

'Leila, I—'

'No, really. I know he doesn't love easily, but I can see how much he adores you. I'm glad he's found the happiness that I have. I *do* love Howie, so very much. And that's why I'll tell him the unvarnished truth. *After* the honeymoon!'

Leila winked and rose to her feet, and Imogen couldn't help but smile as she followed her out of the room.

Once back on deck, Imogen found a secluded spot and leant against the railings as Leila approached Howard, had a quiet word with him, and then kissed him with a long, lingering embrace before she headed over to Joe. Minutes later the two of them headed off the deck.

Imogen turned and faced out to sea, hoping that the long overdue conversation would help Joe to cut himself a little slack. The sound of the waves lapping against the yacht made her heart suddenly ache. Giving up surfing must have been tough for Joe, and it made his insistence that she try out that art lesson make way more sense.

For a while she lost herself in a daydream, trying to imagine a younger, more carefree Joe, master of the waves, travelling to different competitions, sponsored, fêted, and doing something he loved.

But he'd given that dream up—and done so without martyring himself or making his sisters feel bad. He'd done what Eva Lorrimer had been unable to do—how could she not admire him for that?

The hairs on the nape of her neck rose to attention: a sure sign that Joe was in the vicinity.

'Hey.'

The warmth of his body was right next to her as he leant back against the rails so he was looking directly at her.

'Hey.' She smiled at him tentatively 'How did it go?'

Joe opened his mouth and closed it again, poleaxed by the sheer beauty of her smile. The reddish-orange of her kaftan dress was vivid in the dusk, her eyes bright with a warm, questioning look.

'It was…great.' He felt as though he'd shed a weight he'd barely even known he carried. 'Thank you. Leila told me what you said in there. If you hadn't championed me we'd both have gone on looking back from a skewed angle. Now we've sorted out the good memories and got the bad ones into perspective—and that feels good. So I'll say it again. Thank you.' He paused. 'I take it I'm off the Katrina hook as well?'

'Yes.' She blew out air and brushed her fringe from her forehead. 'I'm sorry. It's just that's exactly what Simone did to get Steve back. Turned up at some party with another man on her arm. He made a beeline for her. Worst thing is, I trusted him—thought he was aiming for closure. Turned out the only place he was aiming for was the bedroom, and I didn't realise. He two-timed me for months and I didn't have a clue. When Steve finally told me the truth he told me I was monochrome, grey, whilst Simone lit up his world.' Slim shoulders hitched. 'But it doesn't mean I should have painted you the same colour!'

'Then he must have been blind. You aren't grey and you aren't monochrome. You're Imogen Lorrimer, smart and beautiful—hell, you practically light up the yacht. I promise.'

For a long moment she stared at him, and his heart

twisted as he saw doubt wrestle with her desire to believe him. His feet itched with the urge to get hold of Steve and kick him round the town for what he'd done to Imogen, undermining whatever self-belief her mother had left her with.

'Thank you.'

'You're very welcome.'

Awareness flickered into being. The strains of music and the raised voices faded and all there seemed to be in the world was Imogen—so beautiful, so damned kissable. *Snap out of it, Joe.*

He forced a smile to his lips. 'Hey, we could start a mutual admiration society.'

Imogen blinked as if to break the spell. 'I'll drink to that.'

'I can take a hint. Hold that thought.'

Joe glanced around and waved at a passing waiter, who came over with a champagne-laden heart-shaped tray, decorated with a photograph of Leila and Howard, arms around each other on a beach.

Seconds later they clinked crystal flutes. 'To mutual admiration,' Imogen said.

A silence fell. Not awkward; more thoughtful.

And then... 'Joe?'

'Yes.' His gaze skimmed over her pensive features, over the delicate curve of her neck, the glorious thick dark hair that waterfalled past her shoulders.

'Why didn't you ever mention that you were a surfing champion?'

He stilled. Even knowing that Leila must have mentioned it, he still didn't want to talk about it. 'It's never come up in conversation.'

'It must have been tough to give it up.'

'It was.'

'Like shutting down a fundamental part of yourself?' she asked, quoting his own words back at him.

Dammit. That was what happened when you started to care about other people. It came back to bite you on the bum.

'Yes.'

'Do you regret it?'

'No.'

Clearly the monosyllabic answers weren't doing the trick. Her expression showed a mix of compassion and admiration, and Joe didn't want either.

'I mean it. Holly and Tammy are way, *way* more important to me than being a surfing pro. It was never a question in my mind that there was any choice. And I've never regretted it. Not once. My sisters are two wonderful people, we've built up a cache of incredibly happy memories over the years and we'll continue to do so. I have a career that I love and that I believe has value. Maybe I lost something, but I gained more. Life is what you make it.'

He'd known that all those years before—been determined never to look back and have regrets.

Blue-grey eyes surveyed him and then she stepped forward. Standing on tiptoe, she brushed a feather-light kiss across his cheek before almost leaping backwards.

'I was right. You're a good man.'

Emotions mixed inside him—the desire to pull her into his arms and kiss her properly along with a residue of embarrassment.

'Hey, there were days when it was hard. Don't make me into a saint because I'm not.'

Days when, surrounded by the collapse of the family business, facing the fact that his parents had not been the people he'd believed them to be, trying to help the twins through their grief, all Joe had wanted was his old life back. He had craved the feel of the waves under him, the powerful exhilaration of meeting the challenge of the swell. He'd yearned for the freedom of the sea instead of the net of responsibilities that had sometimes threatened to drown him.

'When did you last surf?' she asked.

'Just after my parents died.'

Her hand rose and one slender finger twirled a tendril of hair. 'I'll do you a deal,' she said.

'What sort of deal?'

'I'll go to that art class tomorrow if you'll go surfing.'

Whoa. 'I'm not sure that's a good idea.'

'Why not?'

'I haven't been on a board in years. I drew a line under it long ago.'

'Then maybe it's time to rub it out. I understand why you gave it up years ago, and I understand how back then you were scared to surf because it would be too painful. But maybe now you could take it up again.'

I'm too old and too unfit to go back to a professional surfing life, even if I wanted to. Which I don't.'

'Then what's the problem with just surfing because you enjoy it? For you?'

She laid a hand on his arm, her touch heating his skin even through the thick material of his tux.

'It's OK to feel sad that you had to give up something you loved, lived and breathed. It doesn't make your love for the twins any less, and it doesn't make you a bad person if sometimes you resented what fate did to you. Going surfing won't turn you to the dark side.'

How did she *do* that? Understand those deep, dark feelings of guilt and helplessness he'd experienced back then. Discomfort touched him. This was too much, too close, too…*something*. He needed to make a choice. Imogen had offered up a deal: art class in return for a surf session. So he needed to put his man pants on and get on with it.

'OK. Deal. I'll go surfing tomorrow and you'll go to the art class.'

'Deal,' she said.

Joe felt a little light-headed as silence blanketed them once more. This time it was a different silence. The kind that bound them together somehow. His muscles ached with the need to hold her in his arms.

As if on cue, behind them the strains of the music changed from an electro carnival beat to the pure sound of a haunting, melodic song of love and yearning.

The hell with it. He gazed down at her and the words fell from his lips: 'Let's dance.'

It was an awesomely bad idea, but for the life of him he couldn't bring himself to care. No more thinking—right now he wanted to dance with this woman and no other under the starlit sky. Stupid? Probably. But that was the way it was.

Without a word she pushed away from the railings, stood up straight and stepped towards him.

It felt ridiculously right to tug her into his arms, bringing her lush curves flush against him. Biting back a groan, he slid his hand round the slender span of her waist to rest on the flare of her hip.

A shiver ran through her body and she pressed against him, her breasts against his chest, her hair tickling his chin. As lyrics about desire and vows and promises were crooned onto the evening breeze they swayed together, their bodies a perfect fit.

Imogen looped her arms around his neck, her fingers brushing his nape, and this time he couldn't hold back the groan as his pulse-rate rocketed. His hands rested on the curve of her bottom and she looked up at him, lips parted, eyes wide and dark with desire.

How he craved her—with a longing that hollowed his

gut in an intense, deep burn of heat. There was only so much flesh and blood could stand, and his had stood it.

'Let's go,' he said.

Rational thought tried to intervene.

'Unless you want to stay for the photographs? The paps will be here soon.'

'I don't care. Let's go.'

There was no hesitation in her voice—just an acknowledgement that her need was as great as his.

She swallowed. 'Though we should say goodbye to Leila...'

'We'll write a thank-you note.'

Impossible to wait, to make the time to find the bride and groom amongst the crowds. He clasped her hand, interlaced his fingers in hers and pulled her towards the steps leading off the yacht.

Imogen pushed the door of the yurt open, her heart hammering against her ribcage and her whole body one great big mass of need. Following behind her, Joe shoved the door closed and she turned to face him, terrified he'd change his mind even as she knew he wouldn't.

He was no more capable of stopping this—whatever *this* was—than she was.

Every one of her senses felt heightened. Dizziness swirled in her head, and her legs were like blancmange. Staring at Joe, she thought he looked so defined, so focused, against the backdrop of pink canvas. The strength of his jaw, the angle of his cheekbones, the sinful line of his mouth...

Two steps and she was right up close as he leant back against the door and pulled her into his arms. Reaching up, she cupped his jaw, the roughness of his six o'clock shadow tantalising her fingers.

His hand was thrust into her hair and he angled her

face for his kiss before his lips locked over hers in fierce demand. A demand she met without hesitation—met and matched—her entire being consumed by a need only this man, only Joe, could fulfil.

Her greedy fingers tugged at the buttons of his shirt and they pinged to the canvas floor. Not that it mattered. All that mattered was that she could now run her hands over the sculpted muscles of his chest.

He groaned as she stroked his skin, ran a thumb over his nipple. 'I want you, Imo. So bad.'

Joe broke their lip-lock to trail a sizzling stream of kisses along her neck, unerringly finding the sensitive spot that drove her frenzied. She arched her back to give him better access, and then gave a gasp as he scooped her up and resumed their kiss.

He tantalised and tormented her with his tongue as he strode over to the bed and lowered her down, stood above her. The sinful smile that tugged at his lips made her ache with a sudden poignant want as she etched this moment onto her memory. Joe looked younger, carefree, gorgeous, with his brown hair spiked and mussed from her fingers, his eyes dark and dilated with a heat that made her squirm.

As if her movement spurred him on, he shrugged himself out of his shirt, shucked off trousers and boxers.

Her gaze ran over his magnificent body.

'You like?' he asked.

'I want,' she replied and, sitting up, she reached to pull him down onto the bed.

CHAPTER THIRTEEN

IMOGEN ADJUSTED HER sketchpad on the easel, dug her flip-flop-clad toes into the warm crunch of sand and tried to concentrate.

The lecturer was fully living up to his promise—Michael Mallory was brilliant, and in any other circumstances she would be riveted.

Chill out, Imo. So what if Joe hadn't been there when she'd woken up that morning? It was no biggie that he hadn't even left a note. They'd had a deal—she would paint and he would surf. So maybe the waves only worked at a certain time of day…he'd had to rush. Maybe he hadn't been able to find a pen or paper. Maybe he'd written a note and a stray dog had crept into the yurt and eaten it. There were endless possibilities. There was no need for her tummy to be knotted with a sense of dread.

Instead she needed to enjoy the moment and anticipate later. After what they had shared last night—after falling asleep wrapped in each other's arms, her head on his chest, his strong arm encasing her—there was no need for doom and gloom. Later they'd swap stories, have a meal, maybe a glass or two of wine and then…to bed.

And what happens after that, Imo?

Nothing. Nothing happens. Get a grip.

This was lust—pure and simple.

Only…was it more than that? Hadn't they shared things on an emotional level? Could Joe tick the boxes on her list?

'OK,' Michael said. 'Listen up, if you haven't already.'

Imogen jumped and stared at the tall, lanky man who was suddenly standing right in front of her.

He stroked his beard and frowned down at her. 'Yes, that means you. Here is your assignment. You have two hours and then report back here.'

Imogen glanced down at the piece of paper and then around her, realising that the rest of the class had already dispersed.

'Sorry,' she muttered.

'Redeem yourself by producing a worthwhile exercise,' he returned.

Determination seethed inside her. Joe had gone surfing reluctantly, this she knew, and he'd done it so that she could reap the benefits of this class. It was time to do exactly that.

'I will.'

'Good. I've assigned you a place—go there and come back with a land or seascape with a difference. It doesn't have to be technically perfect—draw from your heart and dig deep into your soul.'

Picking up her sketchpad and pencils, she set off. Twenty minutes later she'd reached her destination. It was incredible—a tiny cove of rich golden sand at the foot of a cliff-face that swept the skyline.

As Imogen walked forward her mouth dropped open at the rock formations—arches and shapes that almost defied nature, rock pools galore. Other than herself, the place was completely deserted. It was if she'd gone through a portal and entered another world.

Ah!

That was how she would draw this scene—she would make it slightly alien, use the rock formations to indicate a time portal…subtly distort things… Her brain popped and fizzed with ideas.

Making her way to a handy clump of rocks, she opened her sketchpad and started to draw…

* * *

'Imogen?'

A shadow fell over the sketchbook and she whipped her head up so fast she heard her neck crack.

'Joe.'

'Sorry to interrupt.'

His voice was cool and formal—the tone one you'd use with someone you'd just met and were thoroughly indifferent about. Not someone you'd tangled the sheets with just hours previously.

'That's fine. It's probably good—I'd lost track of time.'

Feeling at a sudden disadvantage, she scrambled to her feet, clutched the sketchbook to her chest. The dreaded leaden feeling returned with a vengeance at the look in his brown eyes—cold with a hint of wariness. She took in his clothes—despite the blaze of the midday sun he wore a crisp white shirt and a lightweight jacket over chinos.

'Didn't pack your Hawaiian shorts?' she asked.

'No.'

'So when are you hitting the waves?'

'That's what I came to tell you.' His voice was even, his features unreadable except for the tension in his jaw. 'I'll have to take a rain check—I have to leave. Now. I've changed my flight but you should stay here—finish the class, soak up some rays.'

'Why do you have to leave?' *Please tell me there's an emergency. Nothing life-threatening but a genuine valid reason for you to go.* 'A work crisis? Do the twins need you?'

'Is that what you want me to say?'

Hell, yeah. Right now Imogen wanted to dig a hole in the sun-scorched sand and bury her head deep, deep down. But she wouldn't do that—that was what she'd done with Steve: refused to see the truth, painted an illusory fictitious relationship world.

'I want you to say the truth.'

'The truth is that after last night I think it's best to cut this interlude short.'

Anger imploded in her: a molten core of volcanic rage. 'Really? That's what you think? Jeez, Joe. What happened to respect? To what you said last night about respecting me? Is this how you show it? Slinking off after sleeping with me? Wham-bam, thank you, ma'am?'

Joe flinched, his mouth set in a grim line.

'That's not how it was. It's not how it is.'

'Then tell me how it is.'

'I don't *know*, goddammit.' He rammed his hands into his pockets and rocked back on his heels. 'I'm not sure what happens after a second one-night stand. It's a situation I've managed to avoid for the past seven years.'

Freaking fabulous. What was she? The flu?

'So this is your answer. Hell, Joe, I'm surprised you even bothered to come out here to tell me you were going. I'd have worked it out soon enough.'

'I didn't want to do that. I don't want us to end badly.'

'Then don't go. Don't run away.'

Joe's guts twisted. Anger at himself pounded his temples. Imogen was hurt; he could see it in the way she hugged that sketchbook to her like some sort of magical shield.

Of course she's hurting, dumb-arse. Your behaviour puts you up for the Schmuck of the Year award.

He should never have let this situation happen. Yet last night he hadn't given Rule Two a thought. Not one. Everything had been obliterated by his need for Imogen—his need to possess her, hold her and savour every centimetre of her. To gaze at the stars and dream.

Madness.

Even looking at her now—so graceful, standing so tall, her eyes challenging—his hands were desperate to break free from his pockets and hold her. The simple sundress she wore exposed her sun-kissed shoulders and the curve of her toned bare arms. So beautiful his heart ached. The sooner he got on that plane the better. And it would be Rule Three all the way. 'No Looking Back'.

'I'm not running away. It's more of a strategic retreat.'

Her lips didn't so much as quiver, and he knew himself the words weren't funny—even if there was an element of truth in them. He knew with a bone-deep certainty that he couldn't spend another night with Imogen.

'I'm leaving because it's best for both of us. Things are getting complicated, and the best way forward now is to draw a line before they complicate further.'

'I thought we were through with drawing lines?'

'Not this one. We got carried away by chemistry again last night; that wasn't meant to happen and I will not risk being driven by lust again.'

Her arms squeezed the sketchbook even tighter as her face leeched of colour and Joe knew she was thinking of her parents' disastrous lust-driven relationship. Which was good—that was what he wanted: for Imogen to be on the same page as he was, in agreement that this had to stop here.

'You want a relationship that isn't based on lust. You want a man who ticks all your boxes and I don't tick any. So it's way better to cut your losses right here and now and go and find him.' His hand fisted in his pockets; the thought of Imogen with another man made him want to hit something—preferably the man. 'It's best for *you*.'

Just like that her shell-shocked face changed, and he knew he'd said the wrong thing as her mouth smacked open in outrage. Eyes narrowed, she stepped forward.

'And what gives you the right to make that decision for me?' Imogen asked. '*I* know what's best for me—not you. All my life people have known what's best for me.

My mother, Steve, and now you. And you've known me all of a few weeks.'

The sarcastic cut of her voice slashed at him and flamed his own emotions to anger. 'You said it yourself, Imogen. That it should only be one night.'

'Then something changed,' she flashed back, before exhaling a sigh. 'Last night *did* happen and I refuse to regret it. Or at least I didn't regret it until now. You know what, Joe? You don't really respect me. Because if you did you would have asked me what I think, how I feel, what I want, what *I* think is best for me. I accept that you need to go, but it's because it's best for *you*. Don't kid yourself or try to kid me you're doing it for me.'

He opened his mouth and then closed it again. Imogen was right. Yet... 'Imogen, I do truly believe this is best for you, but if I'd asked you before I booked that flight what would you have said?'

For a second her gaze dipped away from him, and then she jutted her chin out and met his eyes. 'I'd have suggested we stay here until tomorrow, as planned. I draw, you surf, we have another night. Tomorrow we go home and go our separate ways.'

It sounded so reasonable, so tempting, so....terrifying.

'And what if that slid into one more night? One more week...?'

'Would that be so bad?'

Her voice was small and tight, and Joe hated himself even as he knew what his answer had to be. Everything was sliding out of control, complications abounded, and he needed to get both himself and Imogen out of the line of fire.

'Yes, it would. You're looking for a man who wants a relationship, a white picket fence, a family. I'm not that man. I do *not* tick the boxes.'

'How do you know you couldn't?'

The very thought made his head reel with images of his parents, presenting their perfect married image to the world, supposedly living out their happy-ever-after behind the picket fence. They'd had it all—love, a family, a successful business.

Yet the whole time it had been nothing but a façade.

Joe remembered piecing together the reality of his father's affairs—so many of them with employees and clients. Remembered finding the paperwork showing that his mother was filing for divorce. The family company had been a hotbed of scandal and corruption: funds embezzled, nothing as it was supposed to be, business relationships and personal relationships all a quagmire to be waded through.

The realisation had dawned that everything he'd grown up with had been an illusion. And then it had turned out everything he'd believed he and Leila had was nothing more than another mirage. His whole life had been askew and off-kilter, viewed through the wrong perspective.

He would never put himself in that position again. This thing—whatever it was with Imogen—was meant to fit his rules; Imogen had agreed, goddammit.

'There is no way I can ever tick your boxes. It is not going to happen. Not now, not ever. I do not want complications in my life. You do not want a relationship based on lust.'

'Is that all you think we have?'

'Yes.'

'You really believe that, Joe?

'I—'

'And do you really believe that having a family and growing old together is just one big complication? Are you really such a coward that you'll always run away from any chance of getting close?'

'Yes, yes and yes again.' Better a coward, than a fool,

enmeshed in an emotional quagmire it would be nigh on impossible to break free from.

Imogen shook her head. 'Then you'd best go. Have a safe flight home.'

'Enjoy the art class.'

It was a monumentally stupid comment, but he was having difficulty unsticking his feet from the sand. Having difficulty doing the thing he needed to do.

'I hope this doesn't make you drop out of it.'

'Don't worry, Joe. Your conscience can rest. I keep my promises. See you around.'

The bitter taste of cowardice and confusion coated his tastebuds as she swivelled and started to walk away from him.

Without so much as a glance back.

He needed to do the same.

It was the only way forward.

CHAPTER FOURTEEN

Three days later

'How ARE YOU feeling, hun? Ready to go in there and freeze his balls?'

Imogen managed a smile at Mel's words, truly appreciating her best friend's attempts to cheer her up. Mel had been a rock—had plied her with tea and wine and chocolate and tissues as needed, listened to her rant and pretended not to notice when she cried.

Though who knew why she'd shed a single tear for a man who had made it more than plain that he wanted nothing more to do with her? Humiliation still burned inside her that she hadn't just let him go and feigned indifference. Honestly—she might as well stencil 'Doormat—Use Me' on her forehead.

Yet there had been a moment on that sun-kissed Algarve beach when the grim, haunted expression on Joe's face had twisted her heart—made her want to help with whatever inner demons tormented him.

Hah! More fool her. Inner demons, her foot—Joe had just been terrified that she would go emotional on him. Become a complication to his footloose and fancy-free existence.

Well, she'd show him. Joe had called a meeting at Langley with Peter and Harry, and Peter had asked her to minute it.

Pride straightened her spine. 'I am ready to go in and be arctically professional.'

Mel grinned at her. 'That's my girl. Well, you look the part.'

'Thanks to you! This dress is perfect.'

Imogen smoothed the skirt of the sculpted jersey dress with satisfaction. The demure yet tantalising rounded half-zip neckline, the way the Italian fabric clung to her body, dipped to just above the knee, made her feel professional from the sleek chignon atop her head to her perfectly pedicured pale pink toenails that peeped from a pair of killer heels.

'Show me "The Look".'

Hand on hip, Imogen focused on projecting icy disdain.

'Brilliant!' Mel clapped her hands together. 'Trust me, bits of him will shrivel! Go get 'em, Imo.'

Easier said than done. By the time she'd trekked the tube journey to work the thought of seeing Joe was filling her with a swirl of conflicted emotions. *Come on, Imo*. It was imperative that she crush any lingering stupid hopes, push down the insane lurch of anticipation.

As she approached the boardroom her heart pounded against her ribcage so loudly she'd probably deafen Joe rather than freeze him. Bracing herself, she pushed the boardroom door open and entered. Channelled every bit of her inner ice princess.

The Langley brothers sat on one side of the mahogany table facing Joe, who had his hands flat on the table edge, his gaze directed on Peter.

'You have got to be joking!' Peter Langley leapt to his feet, looking about to vault the table and throttle Joe.

'Peter. Sit down.' Harry half rose and grabbed Peter's arm.

Imogen cleared her throat. 'Sorry I'm late,' she said.

'You aren't.' Harry attempted a smile. 'We started early.

Peter and I just want to know which way the land lies. Come in, Imogen. We'd better minute this.'

'Sure.' Within seconds she'd seated herself at the table, notepad in hand, as foreboding prickled her neck. Something bad was clearly going down.

Yet even her apprehension couldn't prevent her brain from absorbing Joe's appearance. The immaculate charcoal-grey suit with a hint of pinstripe, the bright white shirt, dark blue tie. Professional from the spikes of his hair to the tips of his no doubt shined-up leather shoes. His face was neutral—no trace of any emotion whatsoever. It should be impossible to believe that this man had turned her life upside down, only—*dammit*—it wasn't. Her whole being was on alert, and it was taking every ounce of willpower to keep herself from staring.

'I'm ready,' she said.

Peter waved a hand. 'Go ahead, Joe. Explain your decision.'

'Langley is doing well, but progress has to be sustained and more. Ivan Moreton has come forward with a very lucrative buy-out offer.'

'*Ivan Moreton*?' Disbelief vied with horror.

'Yes.' The syllable gave nothing away. 'The deal he is offering is more than fair. In order to avoid the buy-out Langley needs to meet the criteria set out here over the next two months.' He pushed a bound report across the table. 'Again, I'll go through it for the record.'

As Imogen listened to the points, anger began to simmer. Glancing across at Peter and Harry, she could sense their worry and her tummy twisted in sympathy.

Head back down, she minuted the discussion until the three men had finished. Waited as Joe rose to his feet and shook hands first with Peter and then with Harry.

'You've got my number—any questions, just call. Otherwise I'll be back in two months to review the situation. I'll see you then.'

Hurt threaded through her building rage—Joe's glance had barely even skimmed over her, his brown eyes indifferent. Had he really managed to edit her out of his memory banks that easily—just another one-night stand to join the ranks? Just an anonymous employee in a company he was grinding in his corporate mill?

Well, hell, she was a lot more than that—and she would not just stand aside and let him do this. Forget freezing him—instead her palms itched with the desire to grab him by the lapels of that tailored suit and shake him until his teeth rattled. Her hands clenched into fists, all thoughts of professional cool forgotten

'Excuse me, Joe. Could I have a word before you go? In private.'

Just great. Exactly what he'd hoped to avoid. The meeting had been bad—for once knowing that his decision was financially sound and correct was not enough. Nowhere near enough. As for the effort of keeping his gaze averted from Imogen—his eyeballs positively ached.

Joe concentrated on maintaining his expression at strictly neutral. 'Of course.'

The Langley brothers exchanged glances. 'Stay in here,' Peter suggested. 'Harry and I need to go and come up with a plan of campaign for the next few months. Imogen, when you're done here could you please join us in my office?'

'Sure.'

She rose to her feet as they left the boardroom, and Joe braced himself to withstand the sheer force of her beauty and her anger.

'What can I do for you, Imogen?' he asked, sitting back at the table.

She slammed her palms down on the mahogany table-top. 'You can explain what the hell *that* was all about.'

'Meaning…?'

'Meaning I thought you said that you didn't like to close companies down.'

'I don't—and if you read the minutes you just took you'll see that I didn't.'

'Huh. Those criteria are nigh on impossible.'

'No, they aren't. They are difficult, I grant you, but they are doable.'

'Provided Harry doesn't have another heart attack and Peter doesn't relapse into another breakdown from the stress.'

Her voice caught and, heaven help him, guilt shoved him hard in the chest.

'How could you do this, Joe? It's wrong.'

'I have no choice—Ivan Moreton's offer is very generous.'

'Of course it is. That's because there is nothing Ivan wants more than to take this company down. He loathes Peter and Harry. You must realise that?'

Joe rubbed a hand over his face. 'Yes, I do. But that dislike gives Langley a profitable way out. He's even promised to keep the majority of staff.'

'So he can rub their noses in his triumph. Plus, he knows damn well neither Peter nor Harry would ever work for him.'

Something tugged in his chest; face flushed, eyes sparking, Imogen looked so beautiful he wanted to help. Wanted to give her whatever she wanted. Which was exactly why it was time to close this interview down. Before he did something stupid. *Again.*

Rising to his feet, he shook his head. 'This meeting is over, Imogen. I've given Langley a chance.'

For a second a doubt assailed him. *Had* his decision

been strictly business? Somewhere deep down had he reasoned that even if he'd refused to give Imogen a chance he could at least offer the company she loved one?

'I suggest you go out there and take it.'

A small frown creased her brow as her blue-grey eyes surveyed him.

He held out a hand. 'Goodbye, Imogen. And good luck.'

Her fingers lay in his for one brief final moment. 'Goodbye, Joe.'

Two months later

Imogen drew in a deep breath and looked around her tiny new studio apartment with approval. Spick and span, with nothing that even the most exacting parent could complain about. Fresh flowers on the small foldaway table, which was open and beautifully laid, complete with ice bucket for the champagne currently in the fridge. Hell, this would be a celebration even if it killed her. If it wasn't, and her parents went loopy, then she'd just drink the damn bottle herself.

Heaven knew she deserved it after the past months—but it had been worth every single lost moment of sleep as she and all of the Langley team had pulled together and managed to meet every criterion on Joe's list. Now Peter and Harry had met with Joe and Langley was safe—the knowledge was a constant warm glow inside her.

But that wasn't the reason for this lunch. Apprehension fizzed in her veins and as if on cue the doorbell rang. Her heart beating a nervous rhythm against her ribcage, she crossed the floor and pulled the door open.

'Hey, Mum. Hey, Dad.'

Panic roiled in her tummy at the sheer enormity of what she'd done and what she had to tell them. Even so, the certainty that she was right calmed her—Joe had been correct. She couldn't live her life for her parents, no matter how much she loved them. Any more than he would expect his sisters to follow a path of *his* choosing just because he had chosen to take responsibility for them.

Instead he'd encouraged them to live their dreams, and he spoke of them with love—never disappointment. Eva hadn't ever been able to do the same, and whilst that was perhaps wrong, what had also been wrong was Imogen's compliance in that. That was why Joe had urged her to embrace art.

Joe. Why did anything and everything always come back to Joe?

'Imogen? What's the matter? We haven't come all this way just to watch you daydream.'

Eva Lorrimer's querulous voice pulled her into the present.

'Sorry, Mum.' Imogen hauled in breath—no point dressing this up. 'Thank you for coming. I've got some fantastic news. I've been accepted into art college.'

Silence plummeted as Eva opened and closed her mouth, whilst Jonathan Lorrimer shifted from foot to foot.

'Is this some sort of joke?' Her mother had gone pale, her forehead pinched.

'No, Mum. It's for real. It's a top London college and I can start in January.' Imogen tried for a laugh...winced at the strangled gargle she achieved. 'So you know what to get me for Christmas.'

Eva shook her head. 'How could you be so stupid, Imogen? After everything I went through for you...'

Guilt surfaced, along with a hefty dose of self-doubt, but then she pushed her shoulders back and adhered her feet to the carpet. Joe might not be in her life, but he had taught her something life-changing. That life was for living and it was *her* life to live.

'Mum!'

To her surprise the interruption worked and Eva stopped talking.

'I know I've never managed to achieve what you wanted me to achieve, but that doesn't mean I'm stupid. Just because maths and science aren't my thing it doesn't make me useless.' She could feel a weight lift from her shoulders, was liberated by the words.

'I... I...' Eva rallied. 'I never thought that—I just wanted what was best for you. I wanted you to make something of yourself.'

'And I have done that. I'm proud of my work at Langley.'

'Being a PA is a good steady job...'

'It is—and I'm a good PA. But I've been more than that at Langley and now I want to pursue my dream, Mum. Not yours, but mine.'

'And end up penniless, knocking on my door for help?'

'No! I've thought all this through. Langley is safe now, and I've arranged with Peter to keep working there part-time. I've got a manageable student loan. I'll show you the figures, if you like. I can make this work *and* pay my own way. I'm so excited—please be excited for me.'

'I'm excited for you.'

Swivelling on her trainer-clad foot, Imogen surveyed her father with surprise.

'Truly I am, Imo. I may not have made it yet, but if you've been accepted into art college then maybe I can live vicariously through you. Well done, poppet.'

Poppet. He hadn't called her that for so many years. Not since those rare times when he'd sat with her as a child and shown her how to draw. Until either Eva had put a stop to it or he'd disappeared back to his studio, leaving her to fend for herself. But at least now he could find it in himself to be happy for her, rather than begrudge her a success he hadn't had, and she was grateful for that.

'Thanks, Dad.'

'*Tchah!* Well, *I'm* not excited for you, Imogen.' Eva sniffed. 'I can't stop you, and I won't try, but I still think you're making a grave mistake. You'll get caught up in this art malarkey and the rest of your life will pass you by. When will you have time to meet a nice man to settle down with?'

The question hurt, and she blinked hard as an image of Joe shot into her head. *Nice. Settle down.* Not words she associated with Joe—but it didn't matter. Like it or not, he'd insinuated himself into her heart and it was proving hard to prise him out. But she would—even if she had to get a chisel.

'You lost Steve, and now—'

'Steve loves Simone. And next week we can all dance at their wedding and wish them well.'

And she meant it—the thought of attending no longer had the sting it had held before. Steve and Simone were happy—that much was clear from the one conversation she'd had with Steve after he had voluntarily reimbursed her for the cost of the cruise. Further evidence had been provided by the stream of happy photos that Simone flooded social media with on a daily basis.

True, her stomach still dipped at the idea of being pointed out as the poor little ex, but she'd manage. At least she would be able to foil the sympathetic stares and prurient curiosity with her college news.

'So,' she said firmly. 'How about we open the champagne?'

One day later

Exhilaration shot through Joe's veins at the familiar feel of the surfboard under his feet. He felt weightless, suspended in time and nature, at one with the elements.

The power of the sea was both awe-inspiring and thrilling. Sheer adrenalin pumped in his blood as he caught the wave, and the screech of a seagull blended with the pounding in his ears, the tang of the sea spray on his skin causing sheer joy.

Just like the way he felt when he was with Imogen.

One week later

OK. She could do this. Imogen gazed out of the window as the train pulled in to the old-fashioned Devon station and she tried to block out her parents' bickering voices.

'Don't see why any of us are coming to this damned wedding at all,' Jonathan muttered. 'Though I suppose if you feel you need to go, Imo, the least we can do is come to give you some moral support.'

Eva sighed. 'I've explained time and again that we are going to this wedding because Steve was once part of our lives and he is the son of one of my oldest acquaintances.'

'The same acquaintance who looks at me as though I'm something she stepped in,' Jonathan grumbled as he lugged a suitcase onto the platform.

'Guys…'

Some things would never change—she would probably be playing peacemaker between her parents for ever. Yet it could be worse; she might have lost her parents in a tragedy like Joe had…

Not again. No thoughts of Joe, today of all days.

Raising her voice to drown out her thoughts, Imogen waved placating hands at her parents. 'For whatever reasons we are all here now, so let's just get on with it. At least the scenery is gorgeous, the church is beautiful, and maybe we can find time for a proper cream tea.'

A taxi ride later and Imogen scanned the churchyard, bracing herself for the sight of friends and acquaintances all waiting to pounce.

Instead…

She blinked and dropped her knuckles from her eyes in the nick of time. Rubbing her eyes was not an option—not with the amount of make-up she had on. It must be a hallucination, but however many times she blinked the man remained there.

Solid and real—he looked just like Joe.

Hallucinating—that was what she was doing.

The hallucination headed purposefully towards them, dressed to kill in the same dark grey suit he'd worn to Leila's wedding. Her nerves skittered, her tummy somersaulted—maybe it really was Joe.

'Hello, Imogen.'

'Joe. Um…what are you doing here?'

He raised his eyebrows. 'I'm here for the wedding, of course.'

Gathering her wits together, she managed an introduction, saw her mother's eyes scan from her face to Joe's and braced herself again. But to her surprise Eva tugged on her husband's arm.

'Come on, Jonathan. Let's get inside. Imo and her friend can follow us. I want a chance to talk to Clarissa.'

Her brain fried, scrambled and poached all at the same time—and if that wasn't bad enough all she wanted to do was launch herself at his chest and hold on for dear life.

Once her parents were out of earshot Imogen forced her vocal cords to obey her brain's command. 'So you're real?'

His eyebrows rose as his lips quirked upward. 'Last time I checked.'

Her whole being drank him in. She noticed that his hair was longer…even spikier. There was a touch of strain about his eyes, and as he rubbed his neck in that oh, so familiar gesture she would have sworn he was nervous.

'Is everything OK?'

'It is now. You're looking good.'

'Thank you. You too.' Hauling in breath, she asked the million-dollar question. 'Why are you here? Really?'

'I'm keeping my part of the bargain. You come to Leila's wedding, I come to Steve's—remember?'

Imogen hauled her senses into line. 'I kind of assumed all deals were off due to unexpected complications.'

'Nope.' His gaze latched on to hers with a seriousness that made her tingle all over. 'I've been surfing. All deals are back on.'

He'd gone surfing. Imogen's heart skipped in the sure knowledge that he'd done that out of honour. But that didn't change anything.

'I'm glad,' she said simply. 'And I appreciate this, but I'll be fine on my own.'

'OK.'

A curl of disappointment rippled inside her.

'I'll see you in there, then,' he continued.

'Huh?'

'I scored myself an invite of my own.'

'How?'

'I gate-crashed the wedding rehearsal and threw myself on Simone's mercy. I think she was quite pleased to see me.'

'You did what? What did you tell them?'

'I told them the truth. That I needed to see you. We need to talk. A bit more privately. There's a bench round the corner. We've got a bit of time before the ceremony.'

Imogen hesitated.

'Please.'

The word disarmed her. Joe was used to giving orders—plus he'd come all this way—plus... Plus she wanted to be with him, wanted to make the most of every minute, and wouldn't a proper closure be better than the way it had ended? No doubt that was why he was here.

'OK. But we can't be long.'

She followed him through the picturesque graveyard, tried to concentrate on the old gravestones, the feeling of history and peace, the autumnal smell in the air, the red-brown leaves on the trees.

'Here we go. It's secluded enough here and out of the wind. I checked.'

'How forward-thinking of you,' Imogen managed as she attempted to try and think through a haze of misplaced happiness. It was as though there had been a bit of her missing and now she was whole. She needed to get a grip.

'Isn't it?'

His eyes raked over her as she sat down and spread the swirl of her turquoise dress out so that he couldn't get too close. Close would be a bad idea. The man was uptight, rule-orientated, cold. A man who thought three nights was a commitment he couldn't deal with. But despite herself she craved the warmth of his body.

Her memory was flooded with the way he'd held her, the way he'd shown her so much about herself, the way he'd made love to her.

'Joe, it's OK. I'm OK. You don't have to explain anything. Everything has worked out fine. As you know, better than anyone, Langley is safe. I'm not going to melt down or be permanently affected by the time we had together or the way you behaved. Though, for the record, it sucked.'

'You're right. It did. And I'm sorry.'

The flare of hope she hadn't even realised she'd harboured died. He was here to apologise—nothing more.

'Apology accepted. Now, please don't feel you have to stay. Steve and I are good. We've worked out our differences. I can more than manage on my own.'

The words were true but oh, how she wished it wasn't like this. Her heart ached; her chest was banded with pain.

'So I guess this is goodbye. Again.'

* * *

This was *so* not the way it was supposed to play out—hard to understand how he who could grasp control of any boardroom meeting—anywhere, any time—couldn't manage this situation.

Panic sheened the nape of his neck with moisture. Imogen was saying goodbye—he'd obviously blown any available bridge sky-high.

'No.'

Was that croak his voice? Time to step up—because no way was he losing this woman without at least a fight.

'No,' he repeated firmly. 'It's not.'

'There is nothing more to say.'

'That's where you are so very wrong. There is a load more to say. But first I need to say the most important thing.'

'What's that?'

'I love you.'

Joe wasn't sure what he'd expected, but the sceptical rise of her eyebrows wasn't it—nor the determined shake of her head as she slipped her hands under her thighs.

'Don't, Joe…'

'Don't what?'

'Lie.'

'Lie?' She thought he was *lying*?

'It doesn't make sense. I haven't seen hide nor hair of you for two months. Last time I saw you, you couldn't even contemplate more than two nights with me—this is taking "absence makes the heart grow fonder" too far.'

He was making an incredible mess of this. Had he really thought she'd fall into his arms in a swoon of delight? He needed to make her believe him. This was his last chance.

'Imogen, I love you. I loved you back then and I love you now. That's a fact. Love isn't logical, and you can't put it in a tick-box. I panicked on that beach on the Algarve because for seven years I'd lived by my self-imposed rules and then you came into my life and changed everything. Broke down all the barriers I'd built to keep my life from complications.'

Imogen swept her fringe to one side as she contemplated his words. 'I'm not sure I want to feature in your life as an unwanted complication.'

'You won't.' He shoved a hand through his hair and tried to summon up coherence. 'I...I've done a lot of thinking over these past two months. And I've realised what I did after my parents died. I closed down.'

'That's understandable. It's part of the grieving process.'

'It was more than that. They left a mess behind them. Turned out their marriage was on the rocks and the family business was so far up the proverbial creek a hundred paddles wouldn't have been enough.'

He shrugged.

'I had no idea. I thought they had an idyllic marriage and the business was thriving. It was all an illusion. Tax evasion, fraud, infidelity, wrongdoing... My father was higher than a kite, funded by clients' money. Women... clients, colleagues, secretaries...he slept with them all. My mother turned a blind eye for the money, but the money was running out so she was filing for divorce. It was all very...complicated.'

'Oh, Joe.'

Her face was scrunched up in compassion as she twisted her body to face him, placed her hand on his thigh, her touch so warm, so right.

'I can't begin to imagine how confusing, how incredibly emotional it must have been for you. To have all your memories twisted—and you couldn't even ask them why. No wonder you decided the best way forward was no complications.'

He shifted his body to face her, amazed at how easy, how right it felt to share.

'All I wanted was to sort it all out, look after the twins and make sure I never let complication into my life again. So that's what I did. Then I met you and you changed everything; you've shown me how to feel again, to care, to love, and I don't care how complicated it is. I'll become the man you want me to be, Imogen, if I have to try all my life long. Give me that tick-list and I'll do my best.'

'No!'

The word hurt, slammed into him like a cannonball. But then she shifted along the bench, her warmth right next to him.

'There is no tick-list,' she said. 'I've shredded it and burnt the scraps.'

'Why?'

'Because you made me see what a stupid idea it was. How can someone conform to a tick-list? I tried to do that. For Steve. I tried to make myself fit his list and the result was a nightmare.' She laid her small hand on his thigh. 'I can *so* see why you closed down after your parents died. I didn't close down, but I built myself a comfort zone and I was too scared to leave it—too scared I'd repeat my parents' mistakes, too scared I'd be like my father and fail. Meeting you changed that, made me see how exhilarating it is to push the boundaries and go for what you want.'

She smiled at him—a smile that lit up his world.

'I've been accepted at art school.'

Happiness for Imogen and the world opening out to her warmed his chest. 'That's amazing news, sweetheart.'

'It all started from that art class. Mike, the lecturer, made me promise to keep in touch and he really encouraged me. He's been so supportive and…'

Jealousy and pain tackled him at the same time, twisted

his gut with a hurt he knew he had to conceal. 'So...you and this Mike guy...?'

'No! Don't be daft.'

Blue-grey eyes widened as she stared at him.

'Oh, Joe. Don't you get it? I love you.'

'You do?'

'Yes, I do. Every bit of you—from the spikes in your hair to the tips of your toes. I love how you've made me strive to live the dream, the way you make me feel protected and like I can do anything. I love how you talk about your sisters and I love how you give one hundred per cent of yourself to what you do. I just *love* you. Full-stop.'

He grinned at her, his heart full with the sheer joy of hearing the words. 'One thing you should know, though...'

'What's that?'

'I'm expecting plenty of lustful goings-on in our marriage, whatever you think.'

In one fluid movement she landed on his lap and cupped his face in her hands. 'Well, Mr McIntyre, that's lucky— because I wouldn't have it any other way.' Then she froze. 'Did you say marriage? You mean...?'

'If you'll have me. Imogen, I can't imagine anything better than being your husband and waking up every morning with you in my arms. I want it all—white picket fence, kids, the lot.' He pulled her closer, his arms round the slender span of her waist. 'Because what we have, Imogen, is way more than lust. We have liking and respect and love.'

She nodded. 'I know. That's why these past two months I've missed you so damn much. Talking to you...laughing with you. I've missed the way you need that first cup of coffee, the way your hair spikes up. I've missed your scowl and your smile. Your touch, your taste, your smell.'

'I know exactly what you mean, sweetheart. I've spent weeks trying to stick to Rule Three and not look back. But you—you've haunted my days and my nights. I'd wake up in the night and swear I could feel your hair tickling my chin. So many memories... I couldn't stop looking back, though God knows I tried. Filling my days with work and...'

'Your nights?'

'My nights were filled with fantasies of you. I love you, Imogen Lorrimer. You've made me see love can be real. Not an illusion. So, Imogen, if you want me in your life I oh, so definitely want you in mine. For ever. Will you marry me?'

'Absolutely, Joe. I am all yours. For ever.'

He smiled a smile that lit her world—a smile that made her feel like the most beautiful, wonderful, desirable woman in the world. A smile that spoke volumes, spoke of everlasting love and all-encompassing joy.

'Then let's live the dream, Imogen. Starting now.'

EPILOGUE

Dear Diary

In case you've forgotten me, as I've neglected you shamefully over the past few months, my name is Imogen Lorrimer—until tomorrow, when I will become Imogen McIntyre. Because tomorrow I am marrying Joe McIntyre, who I no longer have to dream is in my bed because he has taken to making a regular appearance there. Naked.

I love him.

Think sexy rumpled hair. That I love to run my fingers through. Think chocolate—the expensive kind—brown eyes that gaze at me with love in their depths. Oh, and a body that I plan to worship for the rest of my life.

Joe is kind and loving and altogether perfect. He has taken up surfing again and, believe me, watching Joe on a surfboard is a privilege. He's thinking of setting up some sort of surf school for teenagers in the future. Our long-term plan is to move out of London and settle in Cornwall—though first I want to finish college.

Which is utterly amazing—and Langley has been fantastic at being flexible so I can work and attend college. Mum is way happier about the whole art college scenario now I am marrying Joe. In fact I don't know how he's done it but he's even charmed her into

*admitting one of my pictures was 'not bad'. Which
from Mum is a compliment of the highest order.*

*Dad has found work in an art supply shop, and
whilst he still spends all his spare time in his studio, I have the feeling Mum and Dad are getting on
a little bit better.*

*Holly and Tammy are fantastic—it's like having
the siblings I always dreamed of. They are going to
be bridesmaids, with Mel as chief bridesmaid. So,
you see, life could not be better.*

*Tomorrow, dear diary, I will be walking down the
aisle towards Joe, and I know with all my heart and
soul that this is the man I will love for the rest of my
life. And that he will love me right back.*

For ever
Night-night
Imogen xxx

* * * * *

HER SECRET HUSBAND

BY
ANDREA LAURENCE

Andrea Laurence is an award-winning contemporary romance author who has loved books and has been writing stories since she learned to read and write. She always dreamed of seeing her work in print and is thrilled to be able to share her books with the world. A dedicated West Coast girl transplanted into the Deep South, she's working on her own "happily ever after" with her boyfriend and five fur-babies. You can contact Andrea at her website, www.andrealaurence.com.

To My Fellow Desire Divas
Jules Bennett & Sarah M. Anderson—

The day my editor announced my first sale to Harlequin
Desire on Twitter, I was greeted with congratulations
from a hundred people I've never met. You were two of
the first to welcome me as fellow Harlequin Desire
Authors and you've had my back ever since that day.
I never felt like the new kid in class. Thanks for the
support, the laughs and the Lego movie trailers.

One

"**Y**our dad's heart attack was pretty serious this time."

The doctor's words did little to make Heath Langston feel better about his foster father's condition. He stood outside Ken Eden's hospital room, listening to the doctor's prognosis. He felt helpless, which was not the way he liked it. He might be the youngest of the "Eden boys," but he owned his own advertising firm on Madison Avenue. He'd single-handedly developed one of the most successful ad campaigns of the last year. He was used to everyone, from his secretary to his business partner, looking to him to make decisions.

But this was serious stuff. Life and death. Not exactly his forte. Ken and Molly Eden's only biological child, Julianne, hadn't stopped crying since she arrived. Heath preferred to keep things light and he'd much rather see Julianne smile, but even he couldn't find anything to make a joke about right now.

The Edens' five children had rushed to their family farm in Cornwall, Connecticut, the moment they'd gotten the call about Ken's heart attack. Heath had gotten into his car and bolted from New York City, not knowing if his foster father would be alive by the time he got to the hospital. His biological parents had died in a car accident when he was only nine years old. He was a grown man now, the CEO of his own company, but he wasn't ready to face losing another parent.

Heath and Julianne were the last to arrive and were receiving the report the others had already heard.

"He's stable now, but we were lucky," the doctor continued. "That aspirin Molly gave him may have made all the difference."

Julianne's tiny figure stood in front of him. Despite the doctor's serious words, Heath couldn't keep his eyes from going to her. She took after Molly, being petite but powerful. Today, she looked even smaller than normal, with her shoulders hunched over and her head dipped down to focus her eyes on the floor. Her blond hair had been long and loose when she'd first arrived, but after sitting forever in the waiting room, she'd clipped it up into a messy twist. She shivered at the doctor's words and tried to snuggle deeper into her green cashmere sweater.

Heath put a reassuring hand on her shoulder. His brothers each had their fiancées to hold for support, but he and Julianne were both alone. His heart went out to her. He hated seeing his feisty, confident artist looking so broken. Although they'd grown up in the same house, she had never been a sister in his mind. She had been his best friend, his partner in crime, and for a short time, the love of his life.

Knowing they had each other in this dark moment made him feel better. Tonight, he hoped they could put their tumultuous past behind them and focus on what was more important. Since Julianne didn't pull away, she had to feel the same. Normally, she would give him a playful shove and artfully dodge the physical contact, but not today.

Instead, her body slumped against him for support, her back pressing into his chest. He rested his cheek against the gold strands of her hair and deeply breathed in the scent that was imprinted on his brain. She sighed, sending a tingle of awareness traveling along his spine. The sensation turned the doctor's voice into a muffled mutter in the distance. For a moment, there was only him and her. It wasn't the most appropriate of times, but he would revel in the contact.

Touching Julianne was a rare and precious experience. She had never been a very physically demonstrative person, unlike Molly, who hugged everyone she met, but she kept an even greater distance from Heath. No matter what had happened between them all those years ago and who was to blame, in a moment like this he regretted the loss of his best friend the most acutely.

"He's going to need open-heart surgery. After that, he'll have to stay in ICU a few days until we can move him to a regular room."

"How long until he'll be able to come home?" Julianne asked, making Heath feel guilty for where his mind had strayed. Even as they touched, she was focused on something more important than the two of them and their history together. It was enough for him to straighten up and put some distance between their bodies once again. He opted to focus on the doctor's answer instead.

The doctor frowned. "I don't like to set expectations on this kind of thing, but as I told the others, he's going to be with us a week at least. He might need to go into a rehab center for a while. Maybe he could be at home if there's a bed downstairs and a nurse could be brought in. After that, he's going to have to take it easy for a few months. No lifting, no climbing stairs. He won't be cutting down pine trees this Christmas, that's for sure."

That decided it. With everything else that was going on, Heath had already been thinking of taking a few months off to return to his foster parents' Christmas-tree farm. A body had been discovered on former family property last Christmas and it had recently been identified as Tommy Wilder, a foster child who had stayed briefly on the farm. Heath and the other Eden children knew that Tommy had been dead nearly sixteen years, but the police investigation was just now heating up.

Heath had been torn between wanting to keep up with every news story on television about Tommy and wishing he could just pretend the bully had never existed. Unfortunately, he knew well that ignoring issues wouldn't make them go away.

As much as he hated to admit it, it was time for Heath to come home and answer for what he'd done. It was just Ken and Molly on the farm now, and although they knew nothing about the truth behind Tommy's disappearance, they were having to deal with the police investigation on their own. According to his only biological brother, Xander, the stress of Sheriff Duke threatening to arrest Ken had put him into the hospital today.

It was bad enough that one person was dead because of Heath's mistakes. He couldn't bear it if someone else, especially someone innocent like Ken, also fell victim.

The doctor disappeared and he and Julianne made their way back to the waiting room area, where the rest of the family was assembled. His three brothers and their fiancées were scattered around the room. Some were reading magazines, others were focused on their phones. All looked tired and anxious. "I'll be coming to stay at the farm until Dad is better," he announced to the group. "I can handle things."

"I know it's only the beginning of October, but Christmas will be here before you know it," his oldest foster brother, Wade, pointed out with a frown furrowing his brow. "The last quarter of the year is always a nightmare. You can't take all that on by yourself."

"What choice do we have? All of you are busy. My business partner can run Langston Hamilton for a few months without me. And I've got Owen," Heath added, referring to the Garden of Eden Christmas Tree Farm's oldest and most faithful employee. "He can help me with the details. When Christmas comes, I'll hire some of the high school and college boys to bag and haul trees."

"I'm coming home, too," Julianne announced.

The whole family turned to look at her. She'd been fairly quiet since she had arrived from the Hamptons, but only Heath seemed to realize the significance of her decision. She was volunteering to come home, even knowing that Heath would be there. While she visited the farm from time to time, it was very rare that the boys were there aside from Christmas celebrations. Volunteering to spend months with Heath was out of character for her, but she wasn't exactly in a good headspace.

Despite how small and fragile she looked, there was a sternness in her eyes. Unfortunately, Heath knew that look well. The hard glint of determination, like emeralds, had set into her gaze, and he knew she wouldn't be dissuaded from her decision. Once Julianne's mind was made up about something, there was no changing it.

Even without Heath there, her coming to the farm was a big deal. Julianne was a sculptor. Both her studio and her boutique gallery were in the Hamptons. It wasn't the kind of job where you could just pick up your twelve-hundred-pound kiln and work wherever you like.

"What about your big gallery show next year?" Heath said. "You can't afford to lose two or three months of work to come down here."

"I'm looking to set up a new studio anyway," she said.

Heath frowned. Julianne had a studio in her home. The home she shared with her boyfriend of the last year and a half. It was a personal record for her and everyone thought Danny might be a keeper. Looking for a new studio meant looking for a new place to live. And possibly a new relationship.

"Has something happened with you and Danny?" their brother Brody asked, saving Heath the trouble of nosing into her love life.

Julianne frowned at Brody, and then glanced around at her protective older brothers with dismay. She obviously didn't want to talk about this now, or ever. "Danny and I are no longer 'Danny and I.' He moved out about a month ago. I needed a change of scenery, so I've sold the house and I'm looking for something new. There's no reason why I can't move back for a few months while Dad recuperates. I can help around the farm and work on my art pieces when we're closed. When Dad's feeling better, I'll look for a new place."

Heath and the other boys looked at her dubiously, which only made the color of irritation flush her pale, heart-shaped face. "What?" she said, her hands going to her hips.

"Why didn't you say anything about your breakup with Danny? And selling your house? You two were together a long time. That's a pretty big deal," Xander noted.

"Because," Julianne explained, "three of you guys have gotten engaged recently. It's bad enough that I'll be going stag to all of your weddings. I wasn't exactly looking forward to telling all of you that I've got yet another failed relationship under my belt. Apparently I'm doomed to be the old maid in the family."

"That's hardly possible, Jules," Heath said.

Julianne's cool, green gaze met his. "Point is," she continued, deliberately ignoring his words, "I'm able to come home and help, so I will."

Heath could tell by her tone that the discussion was over for now. Taking her cue, he turned to the rest of his siblings. "Visiting hours are about over, although you'll pay hell to get Mom from Dad's bedside. The rest of us probably need to say good-night and head back to the farm. It's been a long, stressful day."

They shuffled into Ken's hospital room, the dark, peaceful space ruined by the beep of Ken's heart monitor and the low rumble of the voices on his television. There was one light on over the bed, illuminating Ken's shape beneath the off-white blanket. He was nearly as pale as the sheets, but it was a big improvement over the blue-tinged hue his skin had taken on earlier. His light blond, nearly white hair was disheveled from constantly pulling out his oxygen tube and putting it over the top of his head like a pair of sunglasses. Molly had obviously forced it back into his nose recently.

She was sitting in a reclining chair beside him. It was the kind that extended into a bed and that was a good thing. Molly wasn't going anywhere tonight. Her normally cheery expression was still pasted onto her face, but that was more for Ken's benefit than anything. Heath could tell there wasn't much enthusiasm behind it. They were all struggling just to keep it together for Dad's sake.

Ken shifted his gaze from his favorite evening game show to the group of children huddled at his bedside. Heath realized they must look ridiculous standing there. Five rich, successful, powerful people moping at their father's hospital bed, unable to do anything to help. All their money combined couldn't buy Ken a new heart.

At least, not *legally*. Since they'd already done their fair share of dancing on the wrong side of the law and had enough police lurking around their property to prove it, they'd stick with the doctor's recommendations for now.

"There's not much happening here tonight," Ken said. He tried to cover the fact that speaking nearly winded him, but he had to bring his hand to his chest and take a deep breath before saying anything else. "You kids get on home and get some rest. I'll be here. I'm not going anywhere, anytime soon."

Julianne stepped to his side and scooped up his hand. She patted it gently, careful not to disturb his IV, and leaned in to put a kiss on his cheek. "Good night, Daddy. I love you."

"I love you too, June-bug."

She quickly turned on her heel and moved to the back of the group so others could take their turns. She'd let the tears on her cheeks dry, but Heath could see more threatening. She was trying to hold them in and not upset Ken.

One by one, the rest of them said good-night and made their way out to the parking lot. The hospital was a good distance from Cornwall, so they merged onto the highway and made the long, dark drive back to their parents' farm.

Wade and Tori returned to their nearby home, but the rest of the family continued on to the farm. The boys each parked at the bunkhouse, leaving an impressive display of luxury vehicles out front. Heath was last, pulling his Porsche 911 Carrera in between Xander's Lexus SUV and Brody's Mercedes sedan.

Twenty-five years ago, the old barn had been converted into a guest house of sorts, where the foster children who came to live at the Garden of Eden would stay. It had two large bedrooms and baths upstairs and a large common room with a small kitchenette downstairs. It was filled with old, but sturdy furniture and all the comforts teenage boys needed. Heath was the youngest of the four boys who had come to the farm and stayed until adulthood. These days they spent their time in multimillion-dollar mansions and apartments, but this farm was their home and when they returned, the boys always stayed in the bunkhouse.

Heath watched Julianne pull her red Camaro convertible up closer to the main house. The old Federal-style home was beautiful and historic, but it didn't have enough space for a large crew of children. Ken and Molly had a bedroom, their daughter, Julianne, had a room and there was one guest room.

She stood on the porch, fumbling with her keys and looking lost. Heath didn't like that at all. Normally, Julianne was a woman who knew exactly what she wanted from life and how to get it. But tonight she looked anything but her normally spunky self. Nearly losing Ken right after things went south with Danny must have been more than she could take.

Heath grabbed his overnight bag from the trunk of his Porsche and followed the group into the bunkhouse. He set his duffel bag on the old, worn dining room table and looked around. The downstairs common room hadn't changed much since he'd moved in, aside from the new flat-screen television Xander had purchased during his recent stay.

There was a sense of comfort in being back home with his family. He imagined that wouldn't be the same for Julianne, who would be returning to an empty house. Heath might not be the person she'd choose to stay with her tonight, but he wasn't going to argue with her about it. He wasn't leaving her alone.

"Hey, guys," he said to his brothers and their fiancées as they settled in. "I think I'm going to sleep in the big house tonight. I don't like the idea of Jules being alone. Not after the day we've had."

Xander nodded and patted him on the shoulder. "That's a good idea. We'll see you in the morning."

Heath picked up his bag, stepped out and then jogged across the grass and gravel to the back door.

Julianne knew she should go to bed; it had been a very long day with unexpected twists and turns, but she wasn't sleepy. She'd woken up worried about her work and the fallout of her latest failed relationship. Then the phone rang and her world turned upside down. Her previous worries were suddenly insignificant. She'd dropped everything, thrown some clothes in a bag and hit the road.

Even now, hours later, she was still filled with nervous energy. There was a restless anxiety in her muscles, the kind that urged her to go to her workshop and lose herself in the clay. Usually, immersing herself in her work helped clear her mind and solve her problems, but all the pottery in the world wouldn't fix this.

She settled for a cup of chamomile tea at the kitchen table. That might bring her brain down a few notches so she could sleep. She was sitting at the table, sipping the hot tea, when she heard a soft tap at the door. The door almost immediately opened and before she could get up, Heath was standing in the kitchen.

"What is it?" she said, leaping to her feet. "Did the hospital call? Is there a problem?"

Heath frantically shook his head, making one curl of his light brown hair dip down into his eyes. He held up his hands in surrender and she noticed the duffel bag on his shoulder. "No, no problem. Dad's fine," he insisted. "I just didn't want you to be alone in the house tonight."

The air rushed out of her lungs in a loud burst. Thank goodness Dad was okay. Her heart was still racing in her chest from her sudden panic as she slipped back down into her chair. She took a large sip of the scalding tea and winced. After the day she'd had, she didn't need Heath hovering nearby and the distracting hum of his presence in her veins. An hour after they had left the hospital, she could still recall the weight of his hand on her shoulder and the comforting warmth of his chest pressed against her. The contact had been innocent, but her eyes had fluttered closed for a moment to soak in the forbidden contact. She'd immediately snapped herself out of it and tried to focus on her father's health.

"I'll be okay alone," she said.

Heath dropped his bag onto the wooden floor and flopped in the chair across from her. "No, you won't."

She sighed and pinched the bridge of her nose between her thumb and middle finger. She could feel a headache coming on and that was the last thing she needed. Of course, she could take one of her migraine pills and knock herself out. That was one sure way to get to sleep tonight, but what if something happened to Dad?

When she looked up at her guest, she found herself getting lost in the light hazel depths of his eyes. Heath was always happy, always ready with a joke or a smile. But tonight, his expression was different. There was a softness, a weariness, that lined his eyes. He looked concerned. Worried. But not for Ken. At least not entirely. He was concerned about her.

As always.

Julianne wouldn't make light, even in her own mind,

of Heath's protectiveness of her. He had gone to extraordinary lengths to keep her safe. She knew that anytime, day or night, she could call him and he would be there. But not just because they were family and he cared about her. There was a great deal more to it than that and tonight was not the night she was willing to deal with it.

"Thank you," she said at last. She wasn't going to put up a fight and force him into the bunkhouse. She didn't have the energy to argue and frankly, it would be nice to have someone in the big, creaky house with her. No matter what had happened between them over the years, she always knew she could count on him to respect her boundaries.

"It feels weird to be in the house without Mom and Dad," he said, looking around at the large, empty kitchen. "Mom should be fussing at the sink. Dad should be tinkering with farm equipment outside."

He was right, but she didn't want to think about things like that. Those thoughts would require her to face the mortality of her aging parents. Dad would come home this time, but eventually, he wouldn't. She'd rather pretend they were immortal, like she had believed as a child. "Would you like some tea?" she asked, ignoring his words.

"No, I'm fine, thanks."

She wished he would have accepted the tea. That would have given her something to do for a couple of minutes. Instead, she had to sit idly and wait for the questions she knew were coming. They hadn't been alone together and able to really talk since before she had left for college eleven years ago. That had been by design on her part. There were so many thoughts, so many feelings she didn't want to deal with. Looking into Heath's eyes brought everything back to the surface. The burning attraction, the anxiety, the overwhelming feeling of fear...

"So, what happened with you and Danny? That seemed kind of sudden."

Julianne sighed. "We decided we wanted different things, that's all. I wanted to focus on my art and building my career. Things have really taken off and I want to strike while the iron is hot. Danny wanted to take our relationship to the next level."

A spark of interest flickered in Heath's light eyes, his full lips pursing with suppressed amusement. "He proposed?"

"Yes," she said, trying not to let the memories of the uncomfortable moment flood into her mind. She'd told him repeatedly that she wasn't interested in marriage right now, and kids were far, far on the horizon. And yet he'd asked anyway. He seemed to mistake her hesitation as her playing hard to get or using reverse psychology with him. She wished she knew why. She'd given him no signals otherwise. "I refused, as politely as I could, but he didn't take the rejection very well. After that, we decided if we weren't moving forward, we were stagnating. So he moved out."

Danny had been a great guy. He was fun and exciting and sexy. At first, he hadn't seemed interested in settling down. Given her situation, he was the perfect choice. She didn't want to get too serious, either. They wouldn't have even moved in together if he hadn't needed a new place on short notice. He must have seen that as a positive relationship step, when in fact it was simply practicality and economics. In time, it was just easier to stay together than to break things off and cause an upheaval.

"You didn't want to marry him?" Heath asked.

Julianne looked up at him again and shook her head in exasperation. That was a ridiculous question. He knew full well why she'd turned him down. "No, I didn't. But even if I *did*, what was I going to say to him, Heath?"

There was a long, awkward silence before Heath spoke again. "Jules?"

"Listen, I know I brought it up, but I really don't want to talk about it tonight." Julianne sipped the last of her tea and got up from the table. "With Dad and the stuff with Tommy, I can't take any more drama."

"That's fine," he said as he leaned back into the wooden chair and watched her walk into the kitchen. "But considering we're going to be spending the next few months together, you need to come to terms with the fact that we need to talk about it. We've swept the issue under the rug for far too long."

She knew when she made the decision to come home that this would happen. No matter how uncomfortable it might be, she knew they needed her help on the farm, so that was where she would be. There wasn't anywhere else for her anyway. She had sold her house. Closing was next week, and then she was officially homeless. She had to come back here. And she had to deal with her past once and for all.

Julianne looked over at the funny, charming man that had stolen her heart when she was too young and messed up to know what to do about it. Even now, the soft curve of his lips was enough to make a heat surge through her veins and a longing ache in her belly. It took almost no effort at all to remember how it felt when he'd kissed her the first time in Paris. The whisper of his lips along her neck as they admired the Sagrada Família in Barcelona...

Her parents thought they were sending their two youngest children on an exciting graduation trip through Europe. Little did they know what freedom and romantic settings would ignite between their daughter and their youngest foster child. Heath wasn't her brother. She'd known him before his parents died and had never thought of him like a brother. He was her best friend. But if she ever wanted him to be something more, she had to deal with the past.

"Agreed," she said. "Once Dad is stable and we have some time alone to talk, I'm ready to deal with it."

Heath narrowed his gaze at her and she knew instantly what he was thinking. He didn't believe her. She'd been feeding him excuses and dragging her feet for years. He probably thought she got some sort of sick pleasure from drawing all this out, but that was anything but true. She was stuck between not wanting to lose him and not knowing what do with Heath if she had him.

A lifetime ago, when they were eighteen and far, far from home, he'd wanted her. And she'd wanted him. At least, she thought she had. She was young and naive. Despite the attraction that burned at her cheeks when he touched her, she'd found she couldn't fully give herself to him in the heat of the moment.

"It's been easy to ignore while both of us were in school and building our careers," Heath said. "But it's time. Your recent breakup is one of several signs we can't disregard any longer. Whether you like it or not, eventually you and I are going to have to face the fact that we're still married."

Two

He'd laid his cards out on the table. This would end, and soon. After several minutes spent in silence, waiting for her to respond to his declaration, Heath finally gave up. "Good night, Jules," he said, pushing up from his seat.

With Ken's attack, he understood if she couldn't deal with this tonight, but he wasn't waiting forever for her. He'd already wasted too much time on Julianne. He picked his bag up off the floor, and carried it down the hall and up the stairs to the guest bedroom.

The guest room was directly across the hall from Julianne's room and next to the bathroom they would share. He could count on one hand how many times he'd slept in the big house over the years. It just wasn't where he was drawn to. The big house was beautiful and historic, filled with antiques and cherished knickknacks. Most anyone would be happy to stay here, but Heath always felt like a bull in a china shop when he was in the house.

As kids, the bunkhouse was the ideal boy zone. They could be rowdy because the furniture was sturdy but old, there were no breakable antiques and downstairs was all wood flooring, so they could spill and not stain the carpet. There was a big television, video games, a foosball table and an inexhaustible supply of soda and other snacks to fuel growing boys. Things had changed over the years, but being there with his brothers again would make it feel just the same.

Tonight, he made an exception and would stay in the big house for Julianne's sake, but it would be a mistake for her to confuse his gesture as weakness where she was concerned. Any love he had for her had fizzled away when she'd slammed her dorm room door in his face.

For years, he'd been as patient as he could stand to be. He knew now that he had been too nice. He'd given her too much space and let her get too contented. There was no incentive for her to act. That was going to change. He had no intention of being easy on her while they were here. Whatever it took, no matter how hard he had to push her out of her comfort zone, he would leave this farm a happily divorced man. Heath knew he shouldn't enjoy watching Julianne squirm, especially tonight, but he did.

Eleven years of marriage without his wife in his bed could do that to a guy.

He opened the door to the guest room and put his bag down on the white eyelet bedspread. The room was intricately decorated, like the rest of the house, with antique furniture, busy floral wallpaper, lacy curtains and shelves filled with books and framed pictures. As he kicked out of his Prada loafers, he noticed a portrait on the wall in a carved, wooden frame.

It was of Julianne. One of her elementary school pictures, although he couldn't be sure what year. Her golden hair was pulled up into a ponytail, a sprinkle of freckles across her nose. She was wearing a pink plaid romper with a white turtleneck underneath it. She looked just as he remembered her.

He had fallen in love with Julianne Eden the first time he'd seen her. They were in Mrs. Henderson's fourth-grade class together. The cheerful blonde with the curly pigtails and the bright smile had sat right next to him. Whenever he forgot his pencil, she would loan him one of hers. They were pink and smelled like strawberries, but he didn't care. He left his pencil at home on purpose just so he could talk to her.

He'd fabricated childish plans to marry Julianne one day. It seemed like a pipe dream at the time, but one day on the playground, she kissed him—his very first kiss— and he *knew* that she was meant to be his. He'd even made her a Valentine's Day card to tell her how he felt.

He never gave her the card. The weekend before their class party, his parents were killed in a car accident. Heath had been in the car at the time, but his injuries, while serious, had not been fatal. When he was finally discharged from the hospital, both he and his brother, Xander, had found themselves in the care of Family Services. The next thing he knew, they were living at the Christmas-tree farm on the edge of town and the beautiful golden-haired girl of his dreams was supposed to be his "sister."

He had outright rejected that idea right away. They might live in the same home, but not once in twenty years had he ever referred to her as "sis" or "my sister." She was Jules, usually; Julianne when he was speaking about her to the uninitiated.

He'd given up the dream of ever marrying his childhood love soon after coming to the Garden of Eden. Julianne never kissed him on the playground again. They were friends, but that was all. It wasn't until they were seniors in high school and the only kids left on the farm that things started to change between them. The trip to Europe had been the tipping point. Unfortunately, it hadn't tipped in his favor for long.

That seemed to be Julianne's M.O. Since they'd broken up, she had dated, but from what he could tell, never seriously and never for long. None of the brothers had ever met a boyfriend. She never brought one home to the farm. Danny had come the furthest, moving in with Julianne. She didn't really let any man get close, but Heath wasn't certain what was the cause and what was the effect. Did their marriage fail because she didn't do relationships, or did her relationships fail because she was married?

He had unpacked a few things and was halfway undressed when he heard a soft tap at his door. "Come in," he called out.

Julianne opened the door and stuck her head in. She started to speak, and then stopped, her gaze dropping from his face to his bare chest. He tried not to move, fighting the urge to puff up his chest and suck in his stomach. He liked to think he looked pretty good without all that, but it was such a reflex. He jogged the High Line every morning and lifted weights. As a child, he was always the smaller, scrappier of the boys, but no longer. He might be the shortest, at six feet, but he could take any of his brothers and look good doing it.

The dumbstruck Julianne seemed to agree. A crimson flush rose to her delicate, porcelain cheeks. Her full bottom lip hung, useless, until her tongue shot across it and her mouth slammed shut.

If Heath had known strutting around shirtless would get this kind of reaction from her, he would have done it a long time ago. Nothing made her more uncomfortable than the topic of sex. If he'd pushed the issue, perhaps he'd be happily single or happily married right now. Watching her reaction, he thrust his hands in his pockets. His Dolce & Gabbana slacks rode lower with the movement, exposing the trail of hair beneath his navel and the cut of his muscles across his hips.

Julianne swallowed hard and then shook her head and shifted her gaze away to the nearby armoire. "I'm s-sorry," she stuttered. "I didn't realize you were..."

"It's okay," Heath said with a sly smile, enjoying her discomfort. "I'm not bashful and it's nothing you haven't seen before."

She shook her head, sending a wave of the luxurious golden strands over her shoulders. "I don't remember you looking like *that*," she said, quickly bringing her hand up to cover her mouth. She looked embarrassed to share her observation aloud.

Heath glanced down at the display of his own body and shrugged. "I'm not eighteen anymore."

He supposed he would be struck just as hard to see her topless after all this time. Hell, he'd barely seen her naked back then. Sometimes when he was feeling particularly masochistic, he would allow himself to imagine what she looked like now beneath her sweaters and her jeans. The teenage girl he loved had become a very sexy and gifted woman. Any gangliness had been replaced with lush curves and soft, graceful movements. Beautiful and aggravating.

She stood awkwardly in the doorway, nodding, not looking at him, not saying anything for a few moments.

"Did you need something?" Heath prompted at last.

Her green gaze shifted back to his, her purpose suddenly regained. "Yes. Well, I mean, no. I don't *need* anything. I, uh, just wanted to say thank you."

"Thank you? For what?"

"For staying here with me tonight. I know you'd rather be laughing and chatting with Xander and Brody. You guys never get to see one another."

"I see them more than I get to see you," Heath said before he could stop himself. It was true. As children, they had been inseparable. She was his best friend. The marriage that should have brought them even closer together had driven them apart and he still didn't understand why. "I miss you, Jules."

A sadness crept into her eyes, a frown pulling down the corners of her mouth. "I miss you, too, Heath."

"Be honest. You avoid me. Why?" he asked. "Even if we divorced, I get the feeling that you'd still be uncomfortable around me."

"I'm not uncomfortable," she said, but not convincingly.

"Am I being punished for what happened between us?"

Julianne sighed and slumped against the door frame. "It's not about punishing you. And no, it's not about what happened in Europe, either. There are just things in our past that I don't like thinking about. It's easier to forget when I don't see or talk to you."

"Things in our past? Wait…" he said. "Are you blaming me for what happened with Tommy Wilder?"

"No!" she spoke emphatically, raising her palm up to halt him. "You are my savior. The one who protected me when no one else could."

"But you think of that horrible night when you look at me?" Heath was almost nauseated at the thought.

"No," she insisted again, but less forcefully. "If that were true, I never could've fallen for you. It's just easier for me to focus on the future instead of dwelling in the past. Our relationship is in my past."

"Not according to the public records office. It is very

much current and relevant. Ignoring things won't change them. It just makes it worse."

Julianne chuckled and crossed her arms over her chest. "Believe me, I know. I just don't know what else to do about it."

"We get divorced. We can't just stay married forever."

"It's worked okay so far."

Now it was Heath's turn to laugh. "Says the woman that just broke up with her boyfriend when he proposed."

"I didn't…" she began to argue, and then stopped. "This conversation has strayed from what I'd intended when I knocked. Thank you, again," she repeated. "And good night."

Heath watched her slip through the doorway. "Good night," he replied just as the door shut. Once he was certain she was settled in her room, he cast off the rest of his clothes and crawled into bed in his boxer shorts. The bed was soft and inviting, the sheets smelling like the lavender soap Molly used for linens and towels. The bed very nearly forced him to relax, luring him to the edge of sleep faster than he ever thought possible.

Things hadn't worked out between him and Julianne, but he wasn't stupid. He had long ago set aside any idea that their farce of a marriage might become something real. They'd never even consummated it. He'd thought she would come around eventually. It was her first time, perhaps she was just nervous. But then she left for her art program in Chicago without even saying goodbye. He chased after her, driving all night to figure out what was going on. He'd imagined a romantic moment, but instead, she'd told him their marriage was a mistake, he needed to forget it ever happened and practically shut her dorm room door in his face.

He'd been devastated. Then the devastation morphed

into anger. Then indifference. After that, he'd decided that if she wanted a divorce so badly, she could be the one to file. So he'd waited.

Eleven years.

As she'd mentioned, it hadn't been a problem. At least, logistically. He hadn't met a single woman that made him want to walk down the aisle again, but it was the principle of the thing. She didn't want him, and yet she was resistant to let him go. Julianne always seemed to have an excuse. They were broke. They moved around too much after school to establish residency. They were busy starting their businesses. Her appointment with her divorce attorney was rescheduled, and then rescheduled again.

After a while, he began to wonder if she would rather stay married and keep it a secret than file for divorce and risk people finding out she'd married *him*. Her big mistake.

He'd known her since they were nine years old and he still didn't understand what went on in that beautiful blond head of hers.

Julianne sat in a rocking chair on the back porch clutching a big mug of steaming coffee. She had barely slept last night and she desperately needed the infusion of caffeine to make it through today. She'd lain in bed most of the night thinking about Heath and how he was so close by. Her mind had wandered to their first trip together and how wonderful it had been. Even as young as they were, he'd known just how to touch her. With the backdrop of Europe, so romantic and inspiring, behind them, she thought she might be able to overcome the fear. She'd been wrong.

The familiar ache of need had curled in her belly, but she'd smothered her face in the pillows until it faded. It didn't matter how much she'd loved him back then. How much she wanted him. It didn't stop the fear from nearly strangling her with irrational panic. If she couldn't give herself to Heath, the one who protected her, the one she was closer to than anyone else… When it came down to it, she had been too messed up back then to be with anyone.

Heath was right, though. They needed to move on. She'd dragged her feet. Hoping the words would come easier after all this time, she made excuses. If the years had taught her anything, it was that the truth could be more painful than a lie. She lied for everyone's sake, including her own. To have a real, honest relationship with Heath, she would have to tell him the truth about their wedding night. And she just couldn't do it.

That meant that all there was left to do now was clean up the tattered remains of their relationship.

And there would be time for that soon. Other more pressing issues had to be addressed first, like arranging her move and seeing her father through his heart surgery, but even those could wait until after she'd had her coffee and settled into her day. It was early. The sun had just come up. Heath was still asleep and there was no sign of life from the bunkhouse. For now, it was just her, the cool air and the pine forest that spread out in front of her.

At one time in her life, those trees had been her sanctuary. Whenever something was troubling her, she could walk through row after row, losing herself in them. And then Tommy Wilder came to the farm. She never imagined someone could hurt her so badly and not kill her. The physical scars healed, but the emotional ones lingered. The trees had turned their backs on her that day, and she'd refused to go out there any longer. The boys had gladly picked up her share of chores in the field and she took on more responsibility in Molly's Christmas store. Her mother thought that it was Julianne's budding artistic spirit that drove her out of the trees and into the shop.

That was so far from the truth. It was actually the other way around. Her refuge in the shop had fueled an artistic creativity in her she didn't know she had. She started helping Molly decorate and make wreaths, but soon she was painting the windows and molding Nativity scenes out of clay. She was keeping so many painful, confusing things inside; it was easy to give her mind over to the intricacies of her art. It was only her good fortune that she was talented at what she did and was able to turn her therapy into a career.

The rumble of car tires across the gravel caught her attention. A moment later, Molly's Buick rounded the house and parked beside her Camaro.

Julianne got up and walked to the stairs to meet her. "Morning, Mama. Is Daddy doing okay?"

Molly nodded. "He's fine. Feeling well enough to shoo me home for a while. His surgery is tomorrow morning, so he wants me to take a break now, while I can."

That sounded like Daddy. He hated to be fussed over, just like she did. "I've made some coffee."

"Thank goodness," Molly said, slowly climbing up the stairs. "That sludge at the hospital hardly qualified."

They went inside and Julianne poured her a large mug with a splash of cream and one spoon of sugar. She joined her mother at the kitchen table, where she and Heath had had their uncomfortable conversation the night before. Looking at the weary, worn-out woman across from her, Julianne knew she just couldn't let her parents find out she'd eloped with Heath right out of high school.

It wasn't because of *whom* had she married, or even *how*. If Julianne hadn't been such a mess and things worked out, Molly wouldn't have been happy about them eloping, but she would have come around. The problem was explaining what went wrong between them and why she wasn't willing to work things out. Everyone would want to know how they could marry and break up in an instant. She couldn't even tell *Heath* that. How could she tell her parents, who had no clue that Tommy had ever laid a hand on her, much less ruined their daughter?

Julianne refused to be anything other than the cool and confident daughter of Ken and Molly. She supposed it was growing up as the only child of parents who desperately wanted more children. They loved her without question, but at the same time, they were always vocal about their disappointment in having only one. When they started taking in foster children, it made it even harder to get attention. At first, she tried to excel in school to prove to them that she was good enough to make up for being the only one. She was well-behaved, polite and never caused the tiniest problem for her parents.

It had worked. To a point. They were always quick to praise her, but her parents continued to bring in foster children. Perfection became her way to stand out and get noticed. It wasn't until after the incident with Tommy that she threw an uncharacteristic fit and demanded her parents stop bringing in other children and pay attention to her for once. It was selfish. And she felt horrible doing it. But she couldn't risk another boy coming to the Garden of Eden who might look at her the way Tommy did.

"Are you doing okay this morning?" Molly asked her.

"Yeah. Heath stayed in the guest room so I wouldn't be alone. We talked last night and a couple of us are going to come stay here for a few months. Through the New Year, at least, to help with Christmas and such."

Molly's chin shot up—her mother was ready to argue—but she stopped herself and nodded. They both knew she couldn't run the farm alone. Her petite frame and increasingly stiff fingers couldn't haul Christmas trees twice her size. Having the kids here would take the pressure off of her and keep Ken resting the way he should. "Which of you are coming up?"

"Heath and I. He's taking a few months away from the advertising agency. I've sold my house in Sag Harbor and I'm moving here until Dad is better, then I'll find some-place new."

"What about you and, uh…" Molly's voice trailed off.

Her mother couldn't remember the name of her boy-friend. That said volumes about her ill-fated relationship history. "Danny," Julianne offered. "We've broken it off."

"Oh," Molly said. "I'm sorry to hear that."

"Liar," Julianne said, smiling into her coffee mug as she took a sip.

Molly shrugged, but didn't argue with her on that point. "I've been speaking with a private medical care company about bringing your father home to recuperate instead of putting him in a nursing home. They recommended mov-ing a bed downstairs, and they could provide a live-in nurse for a few weeks."

"That sounds perfect." She wanted her father to have the best possible care, but she hated the idea of him in a nursing home, even if temporarily.

"Well, except that you'd have to stay in the bunkhouse. We'd need to move one bed downstairs and have the other for the nurse. Is that okay?"

"Absolutely," Julianne responded, although the idea of close quarters with Heath didn't thrill her. Last night was bad enough. "It will give me some room to store my equip-ment, too."

"Speaking of which, what about your studio? And your gallery showing? You have to keep working, don't you?"

"The store is fine without me. My place in the Hamp-tons does too well to move and my staff there run it beautifully. As for my studio, I'm thinking I can work here and it wouldn't impact the show. Since I'm staying out there, maybe I can use part of the bunkhouse."

"You know," Molly said, "the storage room there hasn't been used in ages. We could clean that out and you could use it."

"Storage room?"

"Yes. You know what I'm talking about. In the bunkhouse, under the staircase. It's about twelve by twelve, I'd say, with a window and its own door to the outside. That's where we used to hide your Christmas presents when you all were small. Right now, I think it might just have some boxes of the boys' old toys and sporting equipment."

Honestly, she hadn't given much thought to the nook under the stairs. Her time in the bunkhouse was usually spent watching television or messing around with the boys, not surveying the property. "Now I remember. If it's as big as you say, that would be perfect."

"If Heath is staying," Molly continued, "perhaps he can help you get the space ready. There should be some time before the holiday rush begins."

"What am I helping out with?" Heath stumbled sleepily into the kitchen in jeans, a casual T-shirt and bare feet. His light brown hair was tousled. It was a far cry from his expensive tailored suits and perfectly styled hair, but it impacted Julianne even more powerfully. This morning, he looked more like the Heath she'd fallen in love with. The successful, powerful advertising executive was a stranger to her.

"We need you to help clean out the old storage room in the bunkhouse," Molly answered.

He located a mug and made his own cup of coffee. "The one where you hid our Christmas presents?"

A light flush of irritation rose to Molly's cheeks. Julianne had her mother's same pale, flawless complexion. It was always quick to betray their feelings. They blushed bright red at the slightest provocation.

"You knew about that?" Molly asked.

Heath smiled and took a step farther from his mother under the guise of looking in the cabinet for something to eat. "We've always known, Mom. We just didn't have the heart to tell you."

"Well, hell," Molly said, smacking her palm against the table. "Just as well we turn it into a studio, then."

"Mom says that Dad's surgery is tomorrow," Julianne added, steering the conversation in another direction.

Heath pulled down a box of cereal and nodded. "Once we're certain that he's doing okay after surgery, I'll probably head back to New York for a few days and get my things. I need to make arrangements with work and such, but I can probably be back up here in two or three days."

Julianne nodded. She had plenty of things to take care of, too. "Same here. I've got to close on the house. Most of my things are already boxed up. I'll put what I can in storage somewhere and bring the rest."

"How are you going to get all your stuff into that little bitty sports car?" Heath asked.

"The Camaro is bigger than your Porsche," she countered.

"Yeah, but I'm not hauling all your sculpting supplies and tools. What about your kiln?"

"I'm selling it locally," Julianne said, although she didn't know why he was so concerned. "I wanted a new one anyway, so I'll get it delivered here."

Heath frowned at her and crossed his arms over his chest in irritation. She tried not to focus on the way the tight fabric stretched across his hard muscles when he moved, but her eyes were instantly drawn to it. She followed the line of his collar to the lean cords of his neck and the rough stubble along his jaw. Her gaze stopped short when she noticed his amused smirk and arched eyebrow. He'd caught her. At that, she turned her attention back to her coffee and silently cursed herself.

"You need movers," he persisted. "And a truck. I can get you one."

Julianne scoffed at the suggestion. This was so typical of the way the last few years had gone. They avoided the big issues in their relationship and ended up quibbling about stupid things like moving trucks. She supposed to others, they seemed like bickering siblings, when in fact they were a grumpy, married couple. "I might need a truck, but I don't need you to pay for it. I'm capable of handling all that myself."

"Why won't you—"

"We'll discuss it later," she interrupted. She wasn't going to argue with him in front of Molly. She eyed her mother, who was casually sipping her coffee and sorting through her mail.

As if she could feel the tension in the room, Molly set down her stack of bills and stood up. "I'm going to go take a shower," she announced. She took the last sip of her coffee and went upstairs, leaving the two of them alone.

Heath took Molly's seat with a bowl of cereal in one hand and a mug of coffee in the other. "It's later."

"You paying for my movers looks suspicious," she complained. And it did. She made decent money. She didn't need someone to handle it for her, especially Heath playing knight in shining armor.

"I wasn't planning on paying for it. My agency handles the Movers Express account. The CEO owes me a favor. I just have to make a call. Any why is it suspicious? If Wade or Xander offered the same thing, you'd take them up on it without question."

"Because I understand their motives," Julianne said.

Heath's brows went up in surprise. "And what are my motives, Jules? Do you think I'll demand my rights as a husband in exchange for it? Sex for a moving truck? That's certainly a new one on me. Shoot. I should have made that part of the deal up front." His light hazel eyes raked over her, a devious smile curling his lips. He leaned across the table and spoke in a low, seductive tone. "I saw the way you were looking at me just now. It isn't too late to rene-gotiate, Jules."

The heat of his gaze instantly warmed the blood pump-ing through her veins. He very quickly made her aware of every inch of her body and how she responded to him. She wished he didn't have that power over her, but the moment she'd looked at him as something more than a friend, it was like a switch had flipped and she hadn't been able to reverse it. She also hadn't been able to do anything about the attraction.

"Yes, it is," she said, dropping her gaze to her coffee mug in the hopes she could suppress her stirring libido. "Way, way too late."

"Well then, I guess I'm just trying to be nice."

He made her reluctance to accept his offer seem child-ish. "Of course," she said, but a part of her still wondered. There were too many undercurrents running between their every interaction. Whenever Heath was nice to her, when-ever he did something for her, she couldn't help but won-der why. He had every reason to be angry with her. She'd treated him terribly, practically throwing his love back in his face.

On their trip to Europe, they had lain on the grass at the base of the Eiffel Tower and watched the lights twinkling on the hour. There, he'd confessed to her that he had been in love with her since the fourth grade. Swept up in the moment, she told him that she loved him, too. Their relationship had begun in Paris. The marriage started and ended in Gibraltar just three days later. She'd pushed him away for his own good, but he'd never understand that. All he saw was that she turned her back on him and wouldn't tell him why.

For a while he was angry with her. He didn't talk to her for their entire freshman year of college. Then he avoided her, doing internships instead of coming home for the summer. Their interactions were short, but polite. It took years, but eventually, he went back to the funny, easygoing Heath she'd always loved.

The light banter and humor covered up their issues, however. They had both been apart for so long, most days it was easy to ignore what happened between them on the graduation trip. But now they were looking at months together. In close quarters.

Julianne had the feeling that the pressure cooker they'd kept sealed all this time was about to blow.

Three

Ken's surgery went perfectly the next day. He spent twenty-four hours in ICU, and then he was moved to a regular room. Once he was off the ventilator and able to talk, Ken demanded everyone go home and stop hovering over him like it was his deathbed.

As instructed, Brody and his fiancée, Samantha, drove back to Boston. When Ken had his attack, Xander had been in Cornwall to move his ten-year-old son and new fiancée, Rose, to D.C. to live with him. He'd sent them along without him, so he gathered up the last of their things and met up with them back in D.C. Wade and Tori lived nearby and agreed to watch the farm while Heath and Julianne went home to make arrangements and make the transition to their new, temporary home.

Heath had offered to drive with Julianne and help with her move, but of course, she'd declined. He didn't know if she just didn't trust him, or if she felt too guilty to accept things from him after she'd broken up with him. He liked to think it was guilt.

The drive to Manhattan was quick, about two and a half hours. He called his business partner as he reached Chelsea and asked Nolan to meet him at his place to go over details while he packed. He found a metered spot on the street as he got off the phone. It was a great spot, considering how much he needed to load into the car. Some days he wasn't so lucky and wished he'd gotten a place with parking.

He hadn't been looking for a condo in this area when he first started shopping, but he'd fallen in love with the modern feel and large rooftop terrace that was bigger than his first New York apartment. Everything else, including parking, fell to the wayside. It was close enough to the office, near a subway stop and one of his favorite restaurants was a block up the street. He couldn't pass it up.

Heath had cleaned all the perishables out of his refrigerator and had his largest suitcase packed when he heard the buzzer for the outer door of the building. He hit the release to let Nolan in and waited there for him to come out of the elevator. "Hey, man. Thanks for coming by."

Nolan smiled and straightened his tie as he walked down the hallway. It was the middle of the week, so he was dressed more for work than Heath, who was in his jeans and NYU alumni sweatshirt.

"How's your dad doing?" Nolan asked.

Heath urged him inside and shut the door. "He's stable. I think he's going to pull through fine, but as I mentioned earlier, I'm going to be gone a few months while he recovers."

"Totally understandable. I think everything will go smoothly at the office. The only account I worry about with you gone is J'Adore."

Heath went to the refrigerator and pulled out two bottles of sparkling water. He opened them both and handed one over to Nolan. "The cosmetics account? Why do they worry you?"

"Well—" Nolan shrugged "—it has more to do with the owner's preference for *Monsieur Langston*."

"Oh," Heath replied. Now he understood. The French cosmetics company was a great account. They'd helped J'Adore break into the high-end American cosmetics market in the last year. Thanks to his company's marketing campaign, J'Adore was the trendiest new product line for the wealthy elite. The only issue was the owner, Madame Cecilia Badeau. She was in her late fifties, wealthy and eccentric, and she had Heath in her sights. For a while he was concerned they would lose the account if he didn't make himself...*available* to her.

"Thank goodness you're married, man," Nolan said, flopping down onto the sleek, white leather couch.

There was that. It was the first time he was thankful to have that stupid piece of paper legally binding him to Julianne. In order not to offend Madame Badeau, Heath had to tell her he was married. It came as quite a shock to her, as well as Nolan, who was also in the room at the time. They were the only other people who knew he and Julianne were married. He explained that Julianne traveled for her work and was always out of town when he was asked about her. Madame Badeau had immediately backed off, but she still insisted the account be personally handled by Heath.

"I think she'll understand that I've taken a leave of absence."

Nolan looked at him, his dark brows pointedly drawn together with incredulity. "I sincerely hope so, but don't be surprised if you get a call."

"After a month on the farm, I might be happy to answer." Heath hadn't spent more than a few days back at the Garden of Eden Christmas Tree Farm since he'd graduated from college. Avoiding Julianne had meant avoiding his family, although he was beginning to think that was the wrong tactic. He was out of sight, out of mind with her. From now on, he was going to be up close and personal.

"Are you going to be running that huge place all by yourself?" Nolan asked.

"No," Heath said, sliding onto the other end of the couch. "Julianne is going back for a while, too."

Nolan sputtered, obviously trying not to choke on his sip of water. "Julianne? Your *wife*, Julianne?"

Heath sighed. "Technically, yes, but I assure you it means nothing. I mean, I told you we never even slept together, right?"

"I still don't know what you could've done to ruin a marriage within hours of your vows."

Heath had wondered that same thing a million times. One moment, he had achieved his life's dream and married his glorious Julianne. The next, she was hysterically crying and screaming for him to stop touching her. The moment he let her go, she ran into the bathroom of their hotel room and didn't come out for two hours.

"I don't know. She never would tell me what changed. She was happy. The perfect, beautiful blushing bride. She responded to me, physically. Things were going fine until they weren't. All she would ever say was that she was sorry. She thought she could be with me, but she just couldn't do it."

"Was she a virgin? My high-school girlfriend was a nervous wreck our first time."

"That's what I thought. I never asked her directly, that felt weird, but that was my assumption. I kept thinking she'd warm up to the idea. She didn't." When he'd first told his partner about his crazy marriage, Heath hadn't elaborated and Nolan had been kind enough not to press him for details. Now, facing months with Julianne, he was glad he had someone to talk to about it.

Nolan scoffed. "What about when you got home?"

"I was trying not to push her. She asked not to tell anyone about the marriage right away and I agreed. I thought she needed time, and we had a few weeks before we both went to school. One morning, I came in from the fields and her car was gone. She'd left early to go to Chicago and didn't tell me or say goodbye."

"What did you do?"

"I followed her up there. She wouldn't even let me into her room. I'd never seen such a hard, cold expression on her face before that day. She told me getting married was a mistake. She was so embarrassed, she couldn't bear to tell anyone about it. Then she told me to go home and forget it ever happened."

"Do you think there's more to it than what she told you?"

"Some days, yes, some days, no. I do think she was ashamed to tell people that she married me. Especially our parents. She's always been too concerned with what people think. Jules had to have Molly and Ken's approval for everything. Maybe she didn't think she would get it for our marriage."

"Or?"

That was the big question. Something just didn't add up. If she had been so concerned about their parents finding out what happened, she either wouldn't have married him at all or she would have panicked when they returned home and had to face telling them. But she had panicked on their wedding night without any warning that his eighteen-year-old self could pick up on. They had kissed and indulged in some fondling in the days before the wedding and again that night. It wasn't until all the clothes came off that the mood shifted.

Then there was fear in her eyes. Sudden terror. And he'd barely touched her, much less hurt her. He'd had eleven years to live that night over and over in his mind and still didn't know what he did wrong.

"I have no idea. I just know that whatever the issue is, she doesn't want to talk about it."

"Why are you two still married, then? You're not still in love with her, are you, Heath?"

"I'm not," Heath assured him. "That boyhood crush died a long time ago, but it's more complicated than that."

"Enlighten me."

"At first, I thought she would change her mind. We had broken up, but I was certain she would realize she was overreacting about the sex and after being apart for a while she would miss me and decide she really did love me and want to be with me." He sighed, remembering how many nights he'd lain in bed naively fantasizing about her revelation. "But she didn't. She just pretended it never happened and expected me to do the same. She wouldn't talk about it."

"Then divorce her," Nolan suggested. "Be done with it."

Heath shook his head. "I know that I should, but there's no way I'm letting her off the hook that easily. I definitely think it's time to wrap the whole thing up between us, but she left me. I'm going to make her finish the job."

Nolan didn't look convinced. "That hasn't worked so well for you so far."

"I just think she needs a little incentive. Something to push her to make a move."

"What have you got in mind?" Nolan asked, his eyes

lighting up with his wicked imagination. He was the perfect business partner for Heath. They were both devious to a fault, but Heath had the creativity and Nolan had the business smarts.

He could still picture her flushed cheeks and stuttering speech when she was faced with his half-naked body. That really was the key. "I'm going to go back to the house and help Jules set up her new studio there. I'll do everything I need to around the farm. But I'm not going to pretend like nothing ever happened between us. I'm not going to sit on my hands and ignore that we're still attracted to one another."

"You're still into her? After everything that has happened? That's kinda twisted, man."

Heath shrugged. "I can't help it. She's even more beautiful than she was back then. I've always been attracted to her, and if she was honest with herself, she'd have to admit she's still got a thing for me, too. I'm going to try to use it to my advantage. Sex was always our problem, so I intend to push the issue and make her so uncomfortable, she will be all too happy to file for divorce and put this behind her. By the time I come back to New York, I expect to be a free man."

Nolan nodded slowly and put his bottle of water onto the coffee table. "And that's what you want, right?"

Heath wasn't sure what his business partner meant by that. Of course he wanted this to be over. And it would be. There was no way that Julianne would take him up on his sexual advances. She'd run, just like she always did, and he could finally move on. Just because he was still attracted to Julianne didn't mean that anything would come of it.

"Absolutely." Heath smiled wide, thinking of all the ways he could torture his bride over the next few weeks.

When it was all said and done, he would get his divorce and they would finally be able to move on.

But he sure as hell wasn't going to make it easy on her.

No one was around when Julianne arrived in her small moving truck. She wouldn't admit it, but Heath had been right. She needed help moving. There was more than she could fit in the car, so she decided to skip the storage rental and just bring it all with her. By the time she had that realization, she was already in Sag Harbor staring down the piles of stuff she didn't remember accumulating, so she ended up renting a truck one-way and towing her Camaro behind it the whole way.

She pulled the truck up behind the bunkhouse, where it would be out of the way until she could unload everything. Her clothes and personal things could go into her bedroom, but all the supplies for her studio would have to wait. She'd scoped out the storage room before she left and knew it would take time to clean it out. She'd considered doing it then, but Heath had insisted she wait until he was back from New York and could help her.

She opened the door to the storage room to give it a second look. The room was dim, with only the light coming in from one window, so she felt around until she found a light switch. A couple of fluorescent bulbs kicked on, highlighting the dusty shelves and cardboard boxes that filled the space. Molly was right—with a little elbow grease it would be the perfect place for her to work.

The hardwood floors continued into the storage room. There were several sturdy shelving units and open spaces for her to put her equipment. The brand-new, top-of-the-line kiln she ordered would fit nicely into the corner. She couldn't wait to get settled in.

Julianne grabbed her large rolling suitcase and threw

a duffel bag over her shoulder. She hauled them slowly up the stairs and paused at the landing between the two bedrooms. She wasn't sure which one to use. She'd never slept in the bunkhouse before. Whenever she came home, she used her old room, but that was going to be unavailable for a few weeks at least until Dad was able to climb the stairs again. She reached for the doorknob on the left, pushing the door open with a loud creak.

It was a nice, big space. When she was younger the rooms had been equipped with bunk beds that would allow the Edens to take in up to eight foster children at a time. Wade, Brody, Xander and Heath had stayed at the Garden of Eden until they were grown, but there were a dozen other boys who came and went for short periods of time while their home situations straightened out.

She was relieved to see the old bunks had been replaced with two queen-sized beds. They had matching comforters and a nightstand between them. A large dresser flanked the opposite wall. She took a step in and noticed the closet door was ajar and a suitcase was lying open inside it. And a light was coming from under the bathroom door. Heath was back. She hadn't noticed his car.

Before she could turn around, the bathroom door opened and Heath stepped out. He was fresh from the shower. His hair was damp and combed back, his face pink and smooth from a hot shave. The broad, muscular chest she caught a glimpse of a few days before was just as impressive now, with its etched muscles and dark hair, only this time his skin was slick. He had a towel wrapped around his waist, thank goodness, but that was the only thing between her and a fully naked Heath.

Once upon a time, the sight of her naked husband had launched her into a complete panic attack. The cloud of confused emotions and fear had doused any arousal she might have felt. Eleven years and a lot of therapy later, only the dull ache of need was left when she looked at him.

Heath wasn't startled by her appearance. In fact, her appraising glance seemed to embolden him. He arched an eyebrow at her and then smiled the way he always seemed to when she was uncomfortable. "We've really got to stop meeting like this."

A flush rushed to her cheeks from a mix of embarrassment and instant arousal. She knew Heath could see it, so that just made the deep red color even worse. "I'm sorry. I've done it again." Julianne backed toward the door, averting her eyes to look at anything but his hard, wet body and mocking grin. "I parked the moving truck out back and didn't realize you were here. I was trying to figure out which room I should use."

"You're welcome to use this one," Heath said. He sat down on the edge of one of the beds and gave it a good test bounce. "That would prove interesting."

"Uh, no," she said, slipping back through the doorway. "The other room will be just fine."

Her hands were shaking as she gripped the handle of her luggage and rolled it to the opposite bedroom. When she opened the door, she found it to be exactly the same as the other one, only better, because it didn't have her cocky, naked husband in it.

She busied herself hanging up clothes in the closet and storing underthings in the dresser. Putting things away was a good distraction from the sexual thoughts and raging desire pumping through her veins.

Julianne was setting out the last of her toiletries in the bathroom when she turned and found Heath in her doorway, fully clothed.

"Do you need help bringing more things in?"

"Not tonight. Tomorrow, maybe we can work on clearing out the storage room and then I can unload the rest of my supplies there. There's no sense piling up things in the living room. I don't have to return the truck for a few days."

"Okay, good," he said, but he didn't leave.

Julianne stood, waiting for him to speak or do something, but he just leaned against her door frame. His hazel gaze studied her, his eyes narrowing in thought. A smile curled his lips. She had no idea what he was actually thinking, but it was unnerving to be scrutinized so closely.

Finally, she returned to putting her things away and tried to pretend he wasn't inspecting her every move. There was something about the way he watched her that made her very aware of her own body. It happened every time. He didn't have to say a word, yet she would feel the prickle of awareness start up the back of her neck. Her heart would begin pounding harder in her chest. The sound of her breath moving rapidly in and out of her lungs would become deafening.

Then came the heat. What would start as a warmness in her cheeks would spread through her whole body. Beads of perspiration would start to form at the nape of her neck and the valley between her breasts. Deep in her belly, a churning heat would grow warmer and warmer.

All with just a look. She tried desperately to ignore him because she knew how quickly these symptoms would devolve to blatant wanting, especially if he touched her. Eleven years ago, she was too frightened to do anything about her feelings, but she'd come a long way. There was nothing holding her back now. Whether or not Heath still wanted her, he seemed happy to push the issue. How the hell would she make it through the next few months with him so close by? With no brothers or other family here to distract them?

"I'm surprised you're staying in the bunkhouse," Heath said at last.

"Why is that?" Julianne didn't turn to look at him. Instead, she stuffed her empty duffel bag into her luggage and zipped it closed.

"I would've thought you'd want to stay as far away from me as possible. Then again," he added, "this might be your chance to indulge your secret desires without anyone finding out. Maybe you're finally ready to finish what we started."

Julianne turned to look at him with her hands planted on her hips. Hopefully her indignant attitude would mask how close to the truth he actually was. "Indulge my secret desires? Really, Heath?"

He shoved his hands into the pockets of his gray trousers and took a few slow, casual steps into the room. "Why else would you stay out here? I'm sure things in the big house are much nicer."

"They are," she replied matter-of-factly. "But Daddy will be coming home soon and there won't be a room for me there. Besides, being out here makes me feel more independent. My studio will be downstairs, so it's convenient and I'll be less likely to disturb Mom and Dad."

"Yes," he agreed. "You can stay up late and make all the noise you want. You could scream the walls down if you felt inclined."

Julianne clenched her hands into fists at her sides. "Stop making everything I say into a sexual innuendo. Yes, I will be staying out here with you, but that's only because it's the only place to go. If there were an alternative, I'd gladly take it."

Heath chuckled, but she could tell by the look on his face that he didn't believe a word she said. "You're an awfully arrogant bastard," she noted. "I do not want to sleep with you, Heath."

"You say that," he said, moving a few feet closer. "But I know you better than you'd like to think, Jules. I recognize that look in your eye. The color rushing to your cheeks. The rapid rise and fall of your breasts as you breathe harder. You're trying to convince yourself that you don't want me, but we both know that you hate leaving things unfinished. And you and I are most certainly unfinished."

He was right. Julianne was normally focused on every detail, be it in art or life. She was an overachiever. The only thing she'd found she couldn't manage was being a wife. Just another reason to keep their past relationship under the covers.

A tingle of desire ran down her spine and she closed her eyes tightly to block it out. Wrong choice of words.

"Were you this arrogant when we eloped?" she asked. "I can't fathom that I would've fallen for you with an ego this large."

Heath looked at her, the smile curling his lips fading until a hard, straight line appeared across his face. "No, I wasn't this arrogant. I was young and naive and hopelessly in love with a girl that I thought cared about me."

"Heath, I—"

"Don't," he interrupted. He took another step forward, forcing Julianne to move back until the knobs of the dresser pressed into her rear end. "Don't say what you were going to say because you and I both know it's a waste of breath. Don't tell me that you were confused and scared about your feelings for me, because you knew exactly what you were doing. Don't bother to tell me it was just a youthful mistake, because it's a mistake that you refuse to correct. Why is that, I wonder?"

Julianne stood, trapped between her dresser and Heath's

looming body. He leaned into her and was so close that if she let out the breath she was holding and her muscles relaxed, they might touch. Unable to escape, her eyes went to the sensual curve of his mouth. She didn't care for what he was saying, but she would enjoy watching him say it. He had a beautiful mouth, one that she'd secretly fantasized about kissing long before they'd gone to Europe and long after they came back.

"Maybe," he added, "it's because you aren't ready to let go of me just yet."

It was just complicated. She'd wrestled with this for years. She wanted Heath, but the price of having him was too high for both of them to pay. And yet giving up would mean letting go of the best thing that ever happened to her. "Heath, I—"

"You can lie to everyone else," he interrupted. "You can even lie to yourself. But you can't lie to me, Jules. For whatever reason, the time wasn't right back then. Maybe we were just too young, but that's no longer the case. You want me. I want you. It's not right or wrong, black or white. It's just a fact."

His lips were a whisper away from hers. Her own mouth was suddenly dry as he spoke such blunt words with such a seductive voice. She couldn't answer him. She could barely think with him this close to her. Every breath was thick with the warm scent of his cologne and the soap from his shower.

Heath brought his hand up to caress her cheek. "It's time for you to figure out what you're going to do about it."

Julianne's brow drew down into a frown. "What I'm going to do about it?"

"Yes. It's pretty simple, Jules. You either admit that you want me and give yourself freely and enthusiastically to your husband at last. Or…you get off your hind end and file for divorce."

Julianne's mind went to the last discussion she'd had with her attorney. He could draw up the paperwork anytime. It was a pretty cut-and-dried arrangement with no comingled assets. She just had to tell him to pull the trigger. It was that simple and yet the thought made her nearly sick to her stomach. But what was her alternative? Staying married wouldn't solve their problems. And if marriage meant sleeping with Heath, there would just be sex clouding their issues.

"Why can't this wait until we're both back in New York and can work through the paperwork privately? Don't we have enough going on right now? I'm not really interested in either of your options."

A wicked grin curled Heath's full lips, making her heart stutter in her chest. "Oh, you will be. There's no more stalling, Jules. We've both lived in New York long enough to have addressed it privately, if that was what you really wanted. If you don't choose, I'll make the decision for you. And if *I* file for divorce, I'll go to Frank Hartman."

Frank Hartman was the family attorney and the only one in Cornwall. Even if Heath didn't spread the news she had no doubt that their parents would find out about their marriage if he filed with him. That would raise too many questions.

"Your dirty little secret will be out in the open for sure. I'll see to it that every single person in town finds out about our divorce." His lips barely grazed hers as he spoke, and then he started to laugh. He took a large step back, finally allowing her a supply of her very own oxygen.

"You think on that," he said, turning and walking out of her bedroom.

Four

Heath stumbled downstairs the next morning after pulling on some clothes. He could smell coffee and although still half-asleep, he was on a mission for caffeine. He'd slept late that morning after lying in bed for hours thinking about Julianne. After he'd walked out of her room, he'd shut his door, hoping to keep thoughts of her on the other side. He'd failed.

It would take a hell of a lot more than a panel of wood to do that. Not after being so close to her after all this time apart. Not after seeing her react to him. She was stubborn, he knew that, but she'd gotten under his skin just as he'd gotten under hers.

Part of him had enjoyed torturing her a little bit. He wasn't a vindictive person, but she did owe him a little after what she'd done. He wasn't going to get a wife or an apology out of all this. He'd just be a lonely divorced guy who couldn't tell the people he was closest to that he was a lonely divorced guy. His brothers, whom he typically turned to for advice or commiseration, couldn't know the truth. Poor Nolan would end up with the burden of his drama. He could at least watch her squirm a little bit and get some satisfaction from that. The whole point was to make her so uncomfortable that she would contact her lawyer.

But what had bothered him the most, what had kept him up until two in the morning, had been the look in her eyes when he'd nearly kissed her. He'd been close enough. Just the slightest move and their mouths would have touched. And she wanted him to kiss her. She'd licked her lips, her gaze focused on his mouth with an intensity like never before. It made him wonder what she would have done if he had.

He hadn't kissed Julianne since their wedding night. Heath never imagined that would be the last time he would kiss his wife. They'd been married literally a few hours. Certainly things wouldn't go bad that quickly. Right?

With a groan, he crossed the room, his gaze zeroing in on the coffeepot, half the carafe still full. He poured himself a cup and turned just in time to see Julianne shuffle into the kitchen with a giant cardboard box in her arms.

Despite the chilly October weather outside, she had already worked up a sweat moving boxes. She was wearing a thin tank top and a pair of cutoff jean shorts. Her long blond hair was pulled up into a messy bun on the top of her head with damp strands plastered to the back of her neck.

Heath forced down a large sip of hot coffee to keep from sputtering it everywhere. Man, she had an amazing figure. The girl he'd married had been just that—a girl. She'd been a tomboy and a bit of a late bloomer. She had still been fairly thin, a tiny pixie of a thing that he sometimes worried he might snap when he finally made love to her.

Things had certainly changed since the last time he'd run his hands over that body. He'd heard her complain to Molly about how she'd gained weight over the years, but he didn't mind. The tight little shorts she was wearing were filled out nicely and her top left little to his imagination. His brain might not be fully awake yet, but the rest of his body was up and at 'em.

"What?"

Julianne's voice jerked him out of his detailed assessment. He was staring and she'd caught him. Only fair after her heavy appraisal of him over the last few days. "You're going to hurt yourself," Heath quickly noted. He tried leaning casually against the kitchen counter to cover the tension in his body.

Her cool green gaze regarded him a moment before she dropped the box by the staircase with a loud thud and a cloud of dust. It joined a pile of four or five other equally dusty boxes. "I'm supposed to be helping you with that," he added when she didn't respond.

She turned back to him, rubbing her dirty palms on her round, denim-clad rear end. "I couldn't sleep," she said, disappearing into the storage room. A moment later she came back out with another box. "You weren't awake."

"I'm awake now."

She dropped the box to the floor with the others. "Good. You can start helping anytime then." Julianne returned to her chores.

"Good morning to you, too," he grumbled, drinking the last of his coffee in one large sip. Heath put his mug in the sink and walked across the room to join her in the storage room.

He looked around the space, surveying the work ahead of them. Clearing out the room would be less work than figuring out what to do with all the stuff. He plucked an old, flattened basketball out of one box and smashed it between his hands. Just one of a hundred unwanted things left behind over the years. They'd probably need to run a couple loads to the dump in Ken's truck.

"Is there a plan?" he asked.

Julianne rubbed her forearm across her brow to wipe away perspiration. "I'd like to clear the room out first. Then clean it so we can move my things in and I can return the truck. Then we can deal with the stuff we've taken out."

"Fair enough." Heath tossed the ball back into the box and picked it up.

They worked together quietly for the next hour or so. After the previous night's declarations, he expected her to say something, but he'd underestimated Julianne's ability to compartmentalize things. Today's task was cleaning the storeroom, so that was her focus. She'd used the same trick to ignore their relationship for other pursuits over the years. He didn't push the issue. They'd get a lot less cleaning done if they were arguing.

When the room was finally empty, they attacked the space with brooms and old rags, dusting away the cobwebs and sweeping up years of dust and grime. Despite their dirty chores, he couldn't help but stop and watch Julianne every now and then. She would occasionally bend over for something, giving him a prime view of her firm thighs and round behind. The sweat dampened her shirt and he would periodically catch a glimpse as a bead of perspiration traveled down into the valley between her breasts.

He wasn't sure if it was the hard work or the view, but it didn't take long for Heath to get overheated. As they were cleaning the empty room, he had to whip his shirt off and toss it onto the kitchen table. He returned to working, paying no attention to what was going on until he noticed Julianne was watching him and not moving any longer.

Heath paused and looked up at her. She had her arms crossed over her chest, suggestively pressing her small, firm breasts together. He might enjoy the view if not for the irritated expression puckering her delicate brow. "Is something wrong, Jules?"

"Do you normally run around half-naked or is all this just a show for my benefit?"

"What?" Heath looked down at his bare chest and tried to determine what was so offensive about it. "No, of course I don't run around naked. But I'm also not usually doing hard, dirty labor. Advertising doesn't work up much of a sweat."

Julianne was frowning, but he could see the slight twist of amusement in her lips. He could tell she liked what she saw, even if she wouldn't admit that to herself.

"It seems like every time I turn around, you're not wearing a shirt."

Heath smiled. "Is that a complaint or a pleasant observation?"

Julianne planted her hands on her hips, answering him without speaking.

"Well, to be fair, *you've* barged into my bedroom twice and caught me in various states of undress. That's not my fault. That's like complaining because I don't wear clothes into the shower. You make it sound like I've paraded around like a Chippendales dancer or something." Heath held out his arms, flexing his muscles and gyrating his hips for effect.

Julianne brought her hand to her mouth to stifle a giggle as he danced. "Stop that!" she finally yelled, throwing her dust rag at him.

Heath caught it and ended his performance. "You're just lucky I left my tear-away pants in Manhattan."

She shook her head with a reluctant smile and turned

back to what she'd been cleaning. They finished not too long after that, then piled their brooms and mops in the kitchen and went back in to look around.

"This isn't a bad space at all," Julianne said as they surveyed the empty, clean room. "I think it will make the perfect studio."

Heath watched her walk around the space, thinking aloud. "Is it big enough for all of your things?"

"I think so. If I put the new kiln over here," she said, "my big table will fit here. I can use this shelf to put my pieces on that are in progress. My pottery wheel can go here." She gestured to a space below the window. "And this old dresser will be good to store tools and supplies."

She seemed to have it all laid out in her mind. They just had to bring everything in. "Are you ready to unload the truck?"

Julianne shook her head and smoothed her palm over the wild strands of her hair. "Maybe later this afternoon. I'm exhausted. Right now, all I want to do is take a shower and get some lunch."

Heath couldn't agree more. "I'll probably do the same. But proceed with caution," he said.

"Caution?" Julianne looked at him with wide, concerned eyes.

"Yes. I *will* be naked up there. And wet," he added with a sly grin. "You've been forewarned."

Julianne was certain this was going to be the longest few months in history.

She'd quickly taken her shower and sat down on the edge of the bed to dry her hair. She could hear the water running in his bathroom when she was finished, making her think of his warning. He was wet and naked in the next room. She was determined to miss out on that event this time. Running into him once was an accident. Twice could be considered a fluke. A third time was stalking. Julianne wasn't about to give Heath the satisfaction of knowing she enjoyed looking at him. She did; he had a beautiful body. But she'd already gotten her daily eyeful of his hot, sweaty muscles as they worked downstairs.

That was more than enough to fire up her suppressed libido and set her mind to thinking about anything but cleaning. She shouldn't feel this way. It had been over a month since Danny moved out. Not a tragic dry spell by any means and she was more than capable of managing her urges. But somehow, the combination of Heath's friendly eyes, charming smile and hard body made her forget about all that.

It had been like that back in high school. She had gone years having Heath live with her family, trying to keep her attraction to him in check. Heath had been the first boy she'd ever kissed. She liked him. But somehow, once he came to the farm, it seemed inappropriate. So she tried to ignore it as he got older and grew more handsome. She tried to tell herself they were just friends when they would talk for hours.

By their senior year, they were the only kids left on the farm and it was getting harder for her to ignore the sizzle of tension between them. After what had happened to her five years earlier, she hadn't really dated. She'd kissed a boy or two, but nothing serious and nothing remotely close enough to hit her panic button. It was easy. Heath was the only one who got her blood pumping. The one who made her whole body tingle and ache to be touched. So she avoided him.

But it wasn't until they were alone in Paris that she let herself indulge her attraction. There, with the romantic twinkling lights and soft music serenading them, he'd told her he loved her. That he'd always loved her. This had to be the right thing to do. She loved him. He was her best friend. Heath would never hurt her. It was perfect.

Until her nerves got the best of her. Kissing was great. Roaming hands were very nice. But anything more serious made her heart race unpleasantly. Heath thought maybe she was saving herself for marriage and that would remove the last of her doubts. So they got married. And it only got worse.

Julianne sighed and carried the blow-dryer back into the bathroom. Funny how the thing that was supposed to bring them together forever—the ultimate relationship step—was what ended up dooming them.

It was easy to forget about her problems when her brushes with Heath were few and far between. They were both busy, and usually he didn't want to talk about their issues any more than she did. That did not seem to be the case any longer. She could tell that something had gotten into him, but she didn't know what. Perhaps Ken's second heart attack made him realize life was too short to waste it married to someone who didn't love him like she should. Or maybe he'd found someone else but hadn't told anyone about it yet.

That thought was enough to propel her out of the room and downstairs for some lunch. She didn't like thinking about Heath with someone else. That called for an edible distraction. It was a terrible habit to have, but she was an emotional eater. It had started after Tommy attacked her and it became a constant battle for her after that. Her therapist had helped her recognize the issue and to stop before she started, but when things weren't going well, it was nothing a cheeseburger and a Diet Coke wouldn't fix. At least for an hour or so.

At the top of the staircase, Julianne paused. She could

hear Heath's voice carrying from the kitchen. At first, Julianne thought he might be talking to her. She started down the stairs but stopped when she heard him speak again. He was on the phone.

"Hey, sweetheart."

Sweetheart? Julianne held her breath and took a step backward so he wouldn't see her on the stairs listening in. Who was he talking to? A dull ache in her stomach that had nothing to do with hunger told her she'd been right before. He hadn't mentioned dating anyone recently, but that must be what all the sudden divorce talk was about. Why would he tell her if he were seeing someone special? She was a slip of paper away from being his ex-wife, all things considered.

"Aww, I miss you, too." Heath listened for a moment before laughing. "I know it's hard, but I'll be back before you know it."

There was a tone to his voice that she wasn't used to hearing—an intimacy and softness she remembered from the time they spent together in Europe. This woman obviously had a special place in Heath's life. Julianne was immediately struck with a pang of jealousy as she listened in. It was stupid. They'd agreed that if they weren't together, they were both free to see other people. She'd been living with Danny for a year and a half, so she couldn't complain.

"You know I have to take care of some things here. But look on the bright side. When all this is handled and I come home, we can make that Caribbean vacation you've been dreaming about a reality. But you've got to be patient."

"Hang on, baby," Julianne muttered to herself with a mocking tone. "I gotta ditch the wife, then we can go frolic on the beach." And to think he'd been acting like he had been interested in something more between them. When he'd pressed against her, she was certain he still wanted her—at least short-term. He apparently had longer-term plans with someone else.

"Okay. I'll call again soon. 'Bye, darling."

Julianne choked down her irritation and descended the stairs with loud, stomping feet. When she turned toward the kitchen, Heath was leaning casually against the counter, holding his cell phone and looking pointedly at her. He had changed into a snug pair of designer jeans that hugged the thick muscles of his thighs and a button-down shirt in a mossy green that matched the color of his eyes. This was a middle-of-the-road look, a comfortable median between his sleepy casual style and his corporate shark suits. He looked handsome, put together and, judging by the light in his eyes, amused by her irritation.

"Something the matter?" he asked.

"No," she said quickly. There wasn't anything wrong. He could do whatever and whomever he wanted. That wasn't any concern of hers, no matter how spun up she seemed to be at the moment.

It was just because she'd never been faced with it before. That was it. Neither she nor Heath had ever brought anyone home to meet the family. They both dated, but it was an abstract concept that wasn't waved in her face like a red cape in front of a bull.

"I know you were listening in on my conversation."

She took a deep breath and shrugged. "Not really, but it was hard to ignore with all that mushy sweetheart nonsense."

The corners of Heath's mouth curled in amusement. "What's the matter, Jules? Are you jealous?"

"Why on earth would I be jealous?" she scoffed. "We're married, but it doesn't really mean anything. You're free to do what you want. I mean, if I wanted you, I could've had you, so obviously, I wouldn't be jealous."

"I don't know," Heath said, his brow furrowing. "Maybe you're starting to regret your decision."

"Not at all."

She said the words too quickly, too forcefully, and saw a flash of pain in Heath's light hazel eyes. It disappeared quickly, a smile covering his emotions the way it always did. Humor was his go-to defense mechanism. It could be maddening sometimes.

"You seem very confident in your decision considering you still haven't filed for divorce after all this time. Are you sure you want rid of me? Actions speak louder than words, Jules."

"Absolutely certain. I've just been too busy building my career to worry about something that seems so trivial after all this time."

Heath's jaw flexed as he considered her statement for a moment. He obviously didn't care for her choice of words. "We've never really talked about it. At least not without yelling. Since it's so *trivial*, care to finally tell me what went wrong? I've waited a long time to find out."

Julianne closed her eyes and sighed. She'd almost prefer his heated pursuit to the questions she couldn't answer. "I'd really rather not, Heath. What does it matter now?"

"You left me confused and embarrassed on my wedding night. Do you know how messed up it was to take my clothes off in front of a girl for the first time and have you react like that? It's ego-crushing, Jules. It may have been more than a decade ago, but it still matters."

Julianne planted her hands on her hips and looked down at the floor. This was no time for her to come clean. She couldn't. "I don't have anything more to tell you than I did before. I realized it was a mistake. I'm sorry I didn't correct it until that inopportune time."

Heath flinched and frowned at her direct words. "You seemed happy enough about it until then."

"We were in Europe. Everything was romantic and exciting and we were so far from home I could forget all the reasons why it was a bad idea. When faced with…" Her voice trailed off as she remembered the moment her panic hit her like a tidal wave. He was obviously self-conscious enough about her reaction. How could she ever explain to him that it wasn't the sight of his naked body per se, but the idea of what was to come that threw her into a flashback of the worst day of her life? She couldn't. It would only hurt him more to know the truth. "When faced with the point of no return, I knew I couldn't go through with it. I know you want some big, drawn-out explanation as though I'm holding something back, but I'm not. That's all there is to it."

"You are so full of crap. I've known you since we were nine years old. You're lying. I know you're lying. I just don't know what you're lying about." Heath stuck his hands in his pockets and took a few leisurely steps toward her. "But maybe I'm overthinking it. Maybe the truth of the matter is that you're just selfish."

He might as well have slapped her. "Selfish? I'm selfish?" That was great. She was lying to protect him. She'd left him so he could find someone who deserved his love, but somehow she was selfish.

"I think so. You want your cake and you want to eat it, too." Heath held out his arms. "It doesn't have to be that way. If you want me, I'm right here. Take a bite. Please," he added with emphasis, his gaze pinning her on the spot and daring her to reach out for him.

Julianne froze, not certain what to do or say. Part of her brain was urging her to leap into his arms and take what he had to give. She wasn't a scared teenager anymore. She could indulge and enjoy everything she couldn't have before. The other part worried about what it would lead to. Her divorce attorney's number was programmed into her phone. Why start something that they were on the verge of finishing for good?

"Maybe this will help you decide." Heath's hands went to her waist, pulling her body tight against him. Julianne stumbled a bit, colliding with his chest and placing her hands on his shoulders to catch herself. Her palms made contact with the hard wall of muscle she had seen so many times the last few days but didn't dare touch. The scent of his shower-fresh skin filled her nose. The assault on her senses made her head swim and her skin tingle with longing to keep exploring her newfound discovery.

She looked up at him in surprise, not quite sure what to do. His lips found hers before she could decide. At first, she was taken aback by the forceful claim of her mouth. This was no timid teenager kissing her. The hard, masculine wall pressed against her was all grown up.

In their youth, he had never handled her with less care than he would a fragile piece of pottery. Now, he had lost what control he had. And she liked it. They had more than a decade of pent-up sexual tension, frustration and downright anger between them. It poured out of his fingertips, and pressed into her soft flesh, drawing cries of pleasure mingled with pain in the back of her throat.

Matching his ferocity, she clung to his neck, pulling him closer until his body was awkwardly arched over hers. Every place he touched seemed to light on fire until her whole body burned for him. She was getting lost in him, just as she had back then.

And then he pulled away. She had to clutch at the countertop to stay upright once his hard body withdrew its support.

His hazel eyes raked over her body, noting her undeniable response to his kiss. "So what's it going to be, Jules? Are the two of us over and done? Decide."

There were no words. Her brain was still trying to process everything that just happened. Her body ached for him to touch her again. Her indecisiveness drew a disappointed frown across his face.

"Or," he continued, dropping his arms to his side, "do like you've always done. A big nothing. You say you don't want me, but you don't want anyone else to have me, either. You can't have it both ways. You've got to make up your mind, Jules. It's been eleven years. Either you want me or you don't."

"I don't think the two of us are a good idea," she admitted at last. That was true. They weren't a good idea. Her body just didn't care.

"Then what are you waiting for? End it before you sink your next relationship." Heath paused, his brow furrowing in thought. "Unless that's how you like it."

"How I like what?"

"Our marriage is your little barrier to the world. You've dated at least seven or eight guys that I know of, none of them ever getting serious. But that's the way you want it. As long as you're married, you don't have to take it to the next level."

"You think I like failing? You think I want to spend every Christmas here watching everyone snuggled up into happy little couples while I'm still alone?"

"I think a part of you does. It might suck to be alone, but it's better than making yourself vulnerable and getting hurt. Trust me, I know what it's like to get your heart ripped out and stomped on. Being lonely doesn't come close to that kind of pain. I'm tired of you using me, Jules. Make a decision."

"Fine!" Julianne pushed past him, her vision going red as she stomped upstairs into her room. He'd kissed her and insulted her in less than a minute's time. If he thought she secretly wanted to be with him, he was very, very wrong. She snatched her cell phone off the bed and went back to the kitchen.

By the time she returned, the phone was ringing at her attorney's office. "Hello? This is Julianne Eden." Her gaze burrowed into Heath's as she spoke. "Would you please let Mr. Winters know that I'm ready to go forward with the divorce paperwork? Yes. Please overnight it to my secondary address in Connecticut. Thank you."

She slammed her phone onto the kitchen table with a loud smack that echoed through the room. "If you want a divorce so damn bad, fine. Consider it done!"

Five

The rest of the afternoon and most of the next day were spent working. They focused on their chores, neither willing to broach the subject of their argument and set off another battle. The divorce papers would arrive at any time. They had things to get done. There was no sense rehashing it.

They were unloading the last of her equipment from the rental truck when Heath spied Sheriff Duke's patrol car coming up the driveway.

Julianne was beside him, frozen like a deer in the oncoming lights of a car. He handed her the box he'd been carrying. "Take this and go inside. Don't come out unless I come get you."

She didn't argue. She took the box and disappeared through the back door of the storage room. He shut the door behind her and walked around the bunkhouse to where Duke's Crown Victoria was parked beside his Porsche.

Duke climbed out, eyeballing the sports car as he rounded it to where Heath was standing. "Afternoon, Heath."

Heath shook his hand politely and then crossed his arms over his chest. This wasn't a social call and he wouldn't let his guard down for even a second thinking that it was. "Evening, Sheriff. What can I do for you?"

Duke slipped off his hat, gripping it in his left hand. "I just came from the hospital. I spoke with your folks."

Heath tried to keep the anger from leaching into his voice, but the tight clench of his jaw made his emotions obvious as he spoke. "You interviewed my father in the hospital after open-heart surgery? After he had a heart attack the last time you spoke? Did you try to arrest him this time, too?"

"He's not in critical condition," Duke said. "Relax. He's fine. Was when I got there and was when I left. The doctors say he's doing better than expected."

Heath took a deep breath and tried to uncoil his tense muscles. He still wasn't happy, but at least Ken was okay. "I assume you're not here to give me an update on Dad as a public service to the hospital."

A faint smile curled Duke's lips. "No, I'm not. Would you care to sit down somewhere?"

"Do I need a lawyer?" Heath asked.

"No. Just wanting to ask a few questions. You're not a suspect at this time."

"Then no, I'm fine standing." Heath wasn't interested in getting comfortable and drawing out this conversation. He could outstand the older officer by a long shot. "What can I help you with?"

Duke nodded softly, obviously realizing he wasn't going to be offered a seat and some tea like he would if Molly were home. "First, I wanted to let you know that Ken and

Molly are no longer suspects. I was finally able to verify their story with accounts of others in town."

"Like what?" Heath asked.

"Well, Ken had always maintained he was sick in bed all that day with the flu. I spoke to the family physician and had him pull old records from the archives. Ken did come in the day before to see the doctor. Doc said it was a particularly bad strain of flu that year. Most people were in bed for at least two days. I don't figure Ken was out in the woods burying a body in the shape he was in."

"He was sick," Heath added. "Very sick. Just as we've told you before."

"People tell me a lot of things, Heath. Doesn't make it true. I've got to corroborate it with other statements. We've established Ken was sick that day. So, how did that work on the farm? If Ken wasn't working, did the whole group take the day off?"

"No," Heath answered with a bit of a chuckle. Sheriff Duke obviously hadn't grown up on a farm. "Life doesn't just stop when the boss is feeling poorly. We went on with our chores as usual. Wade picked up a few of the things that Ken normally did. Nothing particularly special about it. That's what we did whenever anyone was sick."

"And what about Tommy?"

"What about him?" Heath wasn't going to volunteer anything without being asked directly.

"What was he doing that day?"

Heath sighed and tried to think back. "It's been a long time, Sheriff, but if I had to guess, I'd figure he was doing a lot of nothing. That's what he did most days. He tended to go out into the trees and mess around. I never saw him put in an honest afternoon's work."

"I heard he got into some fights with the other boys."

Heath wasn't going to let Duke zero in on his brothers

as suspects. "That's because he was lazy and violent. He had a quick temper and, on more than one occasion, took it out on one of us."

Sheriff Duke's dark gaze flicked over Heath's face for a moment as he considered his answers. "I bet you didn't care much for Tommy."

"No one did. You know what kind of stuff he was into."

"I can't comment on that. You know his juvenile files are sealed."

"I don't need to see his files to know what he'd done. I lived with him. I've got a scar from where he shoved me into a bookcase and split my eyebrow open. I remember Wade's black eye. I know about the stealing and the drugs and the fights at school. You can't seal my memories, Sheriff." Some days he wished he could.

Duke shuffled uncomfortably on his feet. "When was the last time you saw Tommy?"

"The last time I saw him…" Heath tried to remember back to that day. He spent most of his time trying not to think about it. The image of Tommy's blank, dead stare and the pool of blood soaking into the dirt was the first thing to come to mind. He quickly put that thought away and backed up to before that moment. Before he heard the screams and found Tommy and Julianne together on the ground. "It was just after school. We all came home, Molly brought us some snacks to the bunkhouse and told us Ken was sick in bed. We finished up and each headed out to do our chores. I went into the eastern fields."

"Did you see Tommy go into the woods that day?"

"No." And he hadn't. "Tommy was still sitting at the kitchen table when I left. But that's where he should've been going."

"Was he acting strangely that day?"

He had been. "He was a little quieter than usual. More

withdrawn. I figured he'd had a bad day at school." Tommy had also been silently eyeing Julianne with an interest he didn't care for. But he wasn't going to tell Duke that. No matter what happened between the two of them and their marriage, that wouldn't change. He'd sworn to keep that secret, to protect her above all else, and he would. Even if he grew to despise her one day, he would keep his promise.

"Had he ever mentioned leaving?"

"Every day," Heath said, and that was true. "He was always talking big about how he couldn't wait to get away. He said we were like some stupid television sitcom family and he couldn't stand any of us. He said that when he was eighteen, he was getting the hell out of this place. Tommy didn't even care about finishing school. I suppose a diploma didn't factor much into the lines of work he was drawn to. When he disappeared that day, I always figured he decided not to wait. His birthday was coming up."

Duke had finally taken out a notepad and was writing a few things down. "What made you think he ran away?"

This was the point at which he had to very carefully dance around the truth. "Well, Wade found a note on his bed. And his stuff wasn't in his room when we looked the next morning." The note and the missing belongings were well-documented from the original missing-persons report. The fact that they never compared the handwriting to any of the other children on the farm wasn't Heath's fault. "It all added up for me. With Ken sick, it might have seemed like the right day to make his move." Unfortunately, he'd made his move on Julianne when she was alone in the trees.

"Did he ever talk to you about anything? His friends or his plans?"

At that, a nervous bit of laughter escaped Heath's lips. "I was a scrawny, thirteen-year-old twerp that did nothing but get in his way. Tommy didn't confide in anyone, but especially not in me."

"He didn't talk to your brothers?"

Heath shrugged. "Tommy shared a room with Wade. Maybe he talked to him there. But he was never much for chatting with the rest of us. More than anything he talked *at* us, not *to* us. He said nothing but ugly things to Brody, so he avoided Tommy. Xander always liked to keep friendly with everyone, but even he kept his distance."

"And what about Julianne?"

Heath swallowed hard. It was the first time her name had been spoken aloud in the conversation and he didn't like it. "What about her?"

"Did she have much to do with Tommy?"

"No," Heath said a touch too forcefully. Sheriff Duke looked up at him curiously. "I mean, there was no reason to. She lived in the big house and still went to junior high with me. If they spoke, it was only in passing or out of politeness on her part."

Duke wrote down a few things. Heath wished what he'd said had been true. That Tommy hadn't given the slightest notice to the tiny blonde. But as much as Julianne tried to avoid him, Tommy always found a way to intersect her path. She knew he was dangerous. They all did. They just didn't know what to do about it.

"Were they ever alone together?"

At that, Heath slowly shook his head. He hoped the sheriff didn't see the regret in his eyes or hear it in his voice as he spoke. "Only a fool would have left a little girl alone with a predator like Tommy."

Heath had been quiet and withdrawn that night. Julianne expected him to say *something*. About what happened with Sheriff Duke, about their kiss, about their argument or the divorce papers...but nothing happened. After Duke left, Heath had returned to unloading the truck. When that was done, he volunteered to drive into town and pick up a pizza.

While he was gone, the courier arrived with the package from her attorney. She flipped through it, giving it a cursory examination, and then dropped it onto the kitchen table. She wasn't in the mood to deal with that today.

Heath's mood hadn't improved by the time he got back. He was seated on the couch, balancing his plate in his lap and eating almost mechanically. Julianne had opted to eat at the table, which gave her a decent view of both Heath and the television without crowding in his space.

There was one cold slice of pizza remaining when Julianne finally got the nerve to speak. "Heath?"

He looked startled, as though she'd yanked him from the deep thoughts he was lost in. "Yes?"

"Are you going to tell me what happened?"

"You mean with Sheriff Duke?"

"I guess. Is that what's bothering you?"

"Yes and no," he replied, giving her an answer and not at the same time.

Julianne got up and walked over to the couch. She flopped down onto the opposite end. "It's been a long week, Heath. I'm too tired to play games. What's wrong?"

"Aside from the divorce papers sitting on the kitchen table?" Heath watched her for a moment before sighing heavily and shaking his head. "Sheriff Duke just asked some questions. Nothing to worry about. In fact, he told me Ken and Molly are no longer suspects."

Julianne's brow went up in surprise. "And that's good, right?"

"Absolutely. The conversation was fine. It just made me think." He paused. "It reminded me how big of a failure I am."

It didn't matter what happened between them recently. The minute he needed her support she would give it. "You? A failure? What are you talking about?" Every one of her brothers was at the top of their field with millions in their accounts. None were failures by a long shot. "You're the CEO of your own successful advertising agency. You have a great apartment in Manhattan. You drive a Porsche! How is that a failure?"

A snort of derision passed his lips and he turned away to look at the television. "I'm good at convincing people to buy things they don't need. Something to be proud of, right? But I fail at the important stuff. When it matters, it seems like nothing I say or do makes any difference."

She didn't like the tone of his voice. It was almost defeated. Broken. Very much unlike him and yet she knew somehow she was responsible. "Like what?"

"Protecting you. Protecting my parents. Ken. Saving our marriage…"

Julianne frowned and held her hands up. "Wait a minute. First, how is a nine-year-old boy supposed to save his parents in a car crash that he almost died in, too? Or keep Dad from having another heart attack?"

"It was my fault we were on that road. I pestered my father until he agreed to take us for ice cream."

"Christ, Heath, that doesn't make it your fault."

"Maybe, but Dad's heart attack *was* my fault. The second one at least. If I'd come clean to the cops about what happened with Tommy, they wouldn't have come here questioning him."

He was being completely irrational about this. Heath had been internalizing more things than she realized. "And what about me? How have you failed to protect me? I'm sitting right here, perfectly fine."

"Talking with Sheriff Duke made me realize I should've

seen it coming. With Tommy. I should've known he was going to come for you. And I left you alone. When I think about how bad it could've been..." His voice trailed off. "I never should've left you alone with him."

"You didn't leave me alone *with* him. I was doing my chores just like you were, and he found me. And you can't see the future. I certainly don't expect you to be able to anticipate the moves of a monster like he was. There's no reason why you should have thought I would be anything but safe."

He looked up at her at last, his brow furrowed with concern for things he couldn't change now. "But I *did* know. I saw the way he was looking at you. I knew what he was thinking. My mistake was not realizing he was bold enough to make a move. What if you hadn't been able to fight him off? What if he had raped you?" He shook his head, his thoughts too heavy with the possibilities to see Julianne stiffen in her seat. "I wish he had just run away. That would've been better for everyone."

The pained expression was etched deeply into his forehead. He was so upset thinking Tommy had attacked her. She could never ever tell Heath how successful Tommy had been in getting what he'd wanted from her. He already carried too much of the blame on his own shoulders and without cause. Nothing that happened that day was his fault. "Not for the people he would have hurt later."

Heath shrugged away what might have been. "You give me credit for protecting you, but I didn't. If I had been smart, you wouldn't have needed protecting."

Julianne scooted closer to him on the couch and placed a comforting hand on his shoulder. "Heath, stop it. No one could have stopped Tommy. What's important is everything you did for me once it was done. You didn't have to do what you did. You've kept the truth from everyone all this time."

"Don't even say it out loud," he said with a warning tone. "I did what I had to do and no matter what happens with Sheriff Duke, I don't regret it. It was bad enough that you would always have memories of that day. I wasn't about to let you get in front of the whole town and have to relive it. That would be like letting him attack you over and over every time you had to tell the story."

It would have been awful, no question. No woman wants to stand up and describe being assaulted, much less a thirteen-year-old girl who barely understood what was happening to her. But she was strong. She liked to think that she could handle it. The boys had other ideas. They—Heath especially—thought the best thing to do was keep quiet. Unlike her, they had to live with the fear of being taken away. They made huge sacrifices for her, more than they even knew, and she was grateful. She just worried the price would end up being far higher than they intended to pay.

"But has it been worth the anxiety? The years of waiting for the other shoe to drop? We've been on pins and needles since Dad sold that property. If you had let me go to the police, it would be long over by now."

"See…" Heath said. "My attempt to protect you from the consequences of my previous failures failed as well. It made things worse in the long run. And you knew it, too. That's why you couldn't love me. You were embarrassed to be in love with me."

"What?" Julianne jerked her hand away in surprise. Where the hell had this come from?

Heath shifted in his seat to face her head-on. "Tell the truth, Jules. You might have been intimidated by having sex with me or what our future together might be, but the nail in the coffin was coming home and having to tell your parents that you'd married *me*. You were embarrassed."

"I was embarrassed, but not because of you. It was never about you. I was ashamed of how I'd let myself get so wrapped up in it that I didn't think things through. And then, what? How could we tell our parents that we eloped and broke up practically the same day?"

"You're always so worried about what other people think. Then and now. You'd put a stranger ahead of your own desires every time. Here you'd rather throw away everything we had together than disappoint Molly."

"We didn't have much to throw away, Heath. A week together is hardly a blip in the relationship radar." How many women had he dated for ten times as long and didn't even bother to mention it to the family? Like the woman on the phone packing her bags for the Caribbean?

"It makes a bigger impact when you're married, I assure you. What you threw away was the potential. The future and what we could have had. That's what keeps me up at night, Jules."

It had kept her up nights, too. "And what if it hadn't worked out? If we'd divorced a couple years later? Maybe remarried and brought our new spouses home. How would those family holidays go after that? Unbelievably awkward."

"More awkward than stealing glances of your secret, estranged wife across the dinner table?"

"Heath…"

"I don't think you understand, Jules. You never did. Somehow in your mind, it was just a mistake that had to be covered up so no one would find out. It was an infatuation run awry for you, but it was more than that for me. I loved you. More than anything. I wish I hadn't. I spent years trying to convince myself it was just a crush.

It would have been a hell of a lot easier to deal with your rejection if it were."

"Rejection? Heath, I didn't reject you."

"Oh, really? How does it read in your mind, Jules? In mine, the girl I loved agreed to marry me and then bolted the moment I touched her. Whether you were embarrassed of me or the situation or how it might look…in the end, my wife rejected me and left me in her dust. You went off to art school without saying goodbye and just pretended like our marriage and our feelings for each other didn't matter anymore. That sounds like a textbook definition for rejection."

Julianne sat back in her seat, trying to absorb everything he'd said. He was right. It would have been kinder if she'd just told him she didn't have feelings for him. It would have been a lie, but it would have been gentler on him than what she did.

"Heath, I never meant for you to feel that way. I'm sorry if my actions made you feel unwanted or unloved. I was young and confused. I didn't know what to do or how to handle everything. I do love you and I would never deliberately hurt you."

He snickered and turned away. "You love me, but you're not *in love* with me, right?"

She was about to respond but realized that confirming what he said would be just as hurtful as telling him she didn't love him at all. In truth, neither was entirely accurate. Her feelings were all twisted where Heath was concerned. They always had been and she'd never successfully straightened them out.

"Go ahead and say it."

Julianne sighed. "It's more complicated than that, Heath. I do love you. But not in the same way I love Xander or Brody or Wade, so no, I can't say that. There are other feelings. There always have been. Things that I don't know how to..."

"You want me."

It was a statement, not a question. She raised her gaze to meet his light hazel eyes. The golden starbursts in the center blended into a beautiful mix of greens and browns. Heath's eyes were always so expressive. Even when he tried to hide his feelings with a joke or a smile, Julianne could look him in the eye and know the truth.

The expression now was a difficult one. There was an awkward pain there, but something else. An intensity that demanded an honest answer from her. He knew she wanted him. To tell him otherwise would be to lie to them both. She tore her eyes away, hiding beneath the fringe of her lashes as she stared down at her hands. "I shouldn't."

"Why not? I thought you weren't embarrassed of me," he challenged.

"I'm not. But we're getting a divorce. What good would giving in to our attraction do?"

She looked up in time to see the pain and worry vanish from his expression, replaced by a wicked grin. "It would do a helluva lot of good for me."

Julianne was hard-pressed not to fall for his charming smile and naughty tone. "I'm sure you'd be pleased at the time. So would I. But then what? Is that all it is? Just sex? Is it worth it for just sex? If not, are we dating?"

"Running off with me was very much out of character for you," he noted. "You can't just do something because it feels good and you want to. You have to rationalize everything to the point that the fun is stripped right out."

"I'm trying to be smart about this! Fun or not, you want us to get divorced. Why would I leap back into your bed with both feet?"

"I didn't say I wanted us to get divorced."

That wasn't true. He'd had her pressed against the dresser when he'd made his ultimatum. He'd demanded it yesterday. The papers were three feet away. "I distinctly recall you—"

"Saying you needed to make a choice. Be with me or don't. No more straddling the fence. If you don't want me, then fine. But if you do…by all means, have me. I'm happy to put off the divorce while we indulge in our marital rights."

Julianne frowned. "Do you even hear yourself? Put off our divorce so we can sleep together?"

"Why not? I think I deserve a belated wedding night. We've had all of the drama of marriage with none of the perks."

"You just want to catch up on eleven years of sex."

"Maybe." He leaned in closer, the gold fire in his eyes alight with mischief. "Do you blame me?"

The low, suggestive rumble of his voice so close made her heart stutter in her chest. "S-stop acting like you've lived as a monk this whole time. Even if you did, eleven years is a lot to catch up on. We do still have a farm to run and I have a gallery show to work on."

"I'm all for making the most of our time together here. Give it the old college try."

Julianne shook her head. "And again, Heath, what does that leave us with? I want you, you want me. I'm not about to leap into all this again without thinking it through."

"Then don't leap, Jules. Test the waters. Slip your toe in and see how it feels." He smiled, slinking even closer to her. "I hear the water is warm and inviting." His palm flattened on her denim-covered thigh.

The heat was instantaneous, spreading quickly through her veins until a flush rushed to her cheeks. She knew that all she had to do was say the word and he would do all the things to her she'd fantasized about for years. But she wasn't ready to cross the line. He was right. She did strip the spontaneity out of everything, but she very rarely made decisions that haunted her the way she had with him. She didn't want to misstep this time. She had too many regrets where Heath was concerned. If and when she gave herself to him, she wanted to be fully content with making the right choice.

"I'm sure it is." She reached down and picked up his hand, placing it back in his own lap. "But the water will be just as warm tomorrow."

Six

Julianne rolled over and looked at the clock on the dresser. It was just after two in the morning. That was her usual middle-of-the-night wake-up time. She'd gone to sleep without issue, as always, but bad dreams had jerked her awake about thirty minutes ago and she'd yet to fall back asleep.

She used to be a fairly sound sleeper, but she woke up nearly every night now. Pretty much since Tommy's body was unearthed last Christmas. As much as they had all tried to put that day out of their heads, there was no escaping it. Even if her day-to-day life was too busy to dwell on it, her subconscious had seven to eight hours a night to focus on the worries and fears in the back of her mind.

As much as he wanted to, Heath couldn't protect her forever. Julianne was fairly certain that before she left this farm, the full story would be out in the open. Whether she would be moving out of the bunkhouse and into the jailhouse remained to be seen. Sheriff Duke smelled a rat and he wouldn't rest until he uncovered the truth. The question was whether the truth would be enough for him. A self-defense or justifiable homicide verdict wouldn't give him the moment of glory he sought.

With a sigh, Julianne sat up in bed and brushed the messy strands of her hair out of her face. Tonight's dream had been a doozy, waking her in a cold sweat. She had several different variations of the dream, but this was the one that bothered her the most. She was running through the Christmas-tree fields. Row after row of pine trees flew past her, but she didn't dare turn around. She knew that if she did, Tommy would catch her. The moment his large, meaty hand clamped onto her shoulder, Julianne would shoot up in bed, a scream dying in the back of her throat as she woke and realized that Tommy was long dead.

You would think after having the same nightmares over and over, they wouldn't bother her anymore, but it wasn't true. It seemed to get worse every time. Most nights, she climbed out of bed and crept into her workshop. Something about the movement of the clay in her hands was soothing. She would create beauty and by the time she cleaned up, she could return to sleep without hesitation or nightmares.

For the last week, she'd had no therapeutic outlet to help her fall back asleep. Instead she'd had to tough it out, and she would eventually drift off again around dawn. But now she had a functioning workshop downstairs and could return to the hypnotizing whirl of her pottery wheel.

She slipped silently from the bed and stepped out into the hallway. The house was quiet and dark. She moved quickly down the stairs, using her cell phone for light until she reached the ground floor. There, she turned on the kitchen light. She poured herself a glass of water, plucked an oatmeal raisin cookie from the jar on the counter and headed toward her new studio.

The fluorescent lights flickered for a moment before turning on, flooding the room with an odd yellow-white glow. Heath had worked very hard to help her get everything in place. A few boxes remained to be put away, and her kiln wouldn't be delivered for another day or two, but the majority of her new workshop was ready to start work.

Julianne finished her cookie and set her drink on the dresser, out of the way. One of the boxes on the floor near her feet had bricks of ready-to-use clay. She reached in to grab a one-pound cube and carried it over to her wheel. A plate went down on the wheel, then the ball of soft, moist gray clay on top of it. She filled a bucket with water and put her smoothing sponge in it to soak.

Pulling up to the wheel, she turned it on and it started to spin. She plunged her hands into the bucket to wet them and then closed her slick palms over the ball of clay. Her gallery showing would be mostly sculpted figurines and other art pieces, but the bread and butter of her shop in the Hamptons was stoneware pieces for the home. Her glazed bowls, mugs, salt dishes and flower vases could be found in almost any home in the area.

When she woke up in the night, vases were her go-to item. Her sculptures required a great deal of concentration and a focused eye. At three in the morning, the creation of a vase or bowl on her spinning wheel was a soothing, automatic process. It was by no means a simple task, but she'd created so many over the years that it came to her as second nature.

Her fingers slipped and glided in the wet clay, molding it into a small doughnut shape, then slowly coaxing it taller. She added more water and reached inside. The press of her fingertips distorted the shape, making the base wider.

Cupping the outside again, she tapered in the top, creating the traditional curved flower-vase shape. She flared the top, forming the lip.

With the sponge, she ran along the various edges and surfaces, smoothing out the rough and distorted areas. Last, she used a metal tool to trim away the excess clay at the base and turned off the wheel.

She sat back with a happy sigh and admired her handiwork. When she first started sculpting, a piece like that would have taken her five tries. It would have collapsed on itself or been lopsided. She would press too hard and her thumb would puncture the side. Now, a perfect piece could be created in minutes. She wished everything in her life was that easy.

"I've never gotten to watch you work before."

Julianne leapt at the sound of Heath's voice. She turned around in her rolling chair, her heart pounding a thousand beats a minute in her chest. She brought a hand to her throat, stopping just short of coating herself in wet clay. "You shouldn't sneak up on a girl like that."

He smiled sheepishly from the doorway. "Sorry. At least I waited until you were done."

Heath was leaning against the door frame in an old NYU T-shirt and a pair of flannel plaid boxer shorts, and for that, she was thankful. She would lose her resolve to resist him if he came down in nothing but a pair of pajama pants. As it was, the lean muscles of his legs were pulling her gaze down the length of his body.

"Did I wake you?" she asked.

"I don't recall hearing you get up, but I woke up for some reason and realized I forgot to plug my phone into the charger. I left it in the kitchen accidentally." He took a few steps into the workshop. "I can't believe how quickly you did that. You're amazing."

Julianne stood up from her stool and took her metal spatula out of the drawer beside her. Uncomfortable with his praise, she lifted the metal plate and moved the wet vase over onto the shelf to dry. "It's nothing."

"Don't be modest," he argued. "You're very talented."

Julianne started the wheel spinning again and turned away to hide her blush. "Would you like to learn to make something?"

"Really?"

"Sure. Come here," she said. She eyed his large frame for a moment, trying to figure out the best way to do this. "Since I'm so short, it's probably easiest if you stand behind me and reach over. I can guide your hands better that way."

Heath rolled the stool out of the way and moved to her back. "Like this?"

"Yes." She glanced back at the position she had deliberately put them in and realized how stupid it was. Perhaps she would be smarter to talk him out of this. "You're going to get dirty. Is that okay?"

He chuckled softly at her ear, making a sizzle of awareness run along the sensitive line of her neck. "Oh, no, I'd better change. These are my good flannel boxers."

Julianne smiled at his sharp, sarcastic tone and turned back to the wheel. No getting out of this now. "Okay, first, dip your hands in the water. You have to keep them good and wet."

They both dipped their hands in the bucket of water, then she cupped his hands over the clay and covered them with her own. "Feel the pressure I apply to you and match it with your fingers to the clay."

They moved back and forth between the water and the clay. All the while, Julianne forced herself to focus on the vase and not the heat of Heath's body at her back.

The warm breath along her neck was so distracting. Her mind kept straying to how it would feel if he kissed her there. She wanted him to. And then she would realize their sculpture was starting to sag and she would return her attention to their project.

"This feels weird," Heath laughed, gliding over the gray mound. The slippery form began to take shape, their fingers sliding around together, slick and smooth. "And a little dirty, frankly."

"It does," she admitted. On more than one occasion, she'd lost herself in the erotic slip and slide of the material in her hands and the rhythmic purr of the wheel. That experience was amplified by having him so close. "But try to control yourself," she said with a nervous giggle to hide her own building arousal. "I don't want you having dirty thoughts every time you see my artwork."

Heath's hands suddenly slipped out from beneath hers and glided up her bare arms to clutch her elbows. The cool slide of his clay-covered hands along her skin was in stark contrast to the firm press of heat at her back. It was obvious that she was not the only one turned on by the situation.

"Actually, the artwork isn't what inspires me...."

A ragged breath escaped her lips, but she didn't dare move. She continued working the vase on her own now, her shaky hands creating a subpar product. But she didn't care. If she let go, she would touch Heath and she wasn't sure she would be able to stop.

Easing back, Heath brushed her hair over the other shoulder and, as though he could read her mind, pressed a searing kiss just below her ear. She tipped her neck to the side, giving better access to his hungry mouth. He kissed, nibbled and teased, sending one bolt of pleasure after the other down her spine.

She arched her back, pressing the curve of her rear

into the hard ridge of his desire. That elicited a growl that vibrated low against her throat. One hand moved to her waist, tugging her hips back even harder against him.

"Jules…" he whispered, sending a shudder of desire through her body and a wave of goose bumps across her bare flesh.

She finally abandoned the clay, letting it collapse on itself, and switched off the wheel before she covered his hands with her own. Their fingers slipped in and out between each other, his hands moving over her body. "Yes?" she panted.

"You said the waters would be just as warm tomorrow. It's tomorrow," he said, punctuating his point with a gentle bite at her earlobe.

That it was.

Julianne had been wearing a flimsy little pajama set when he walked in, but Heath was pretty sure it was ruined. The thin cotton camisole and matching shorts were sweet and sexy at the same time. The clothes reminded him of the girl he'd fantasized about in high school, and the curves beneath it reminded him of the ripe, juicy peach of a woman she was now.

He couldn't stop touching her, even though he knew his hands were covered in clay. Gray smears were drying up on her arms and her bare shoulders. The shape of his hand was printed on the cotton daisy pattern of her pajamas. A streak of gray ran along the edge of her cheek.

And he didn't care.

It was sexy as hell. Julianne was always so put together and mature. He loved seeing her dirty. He was so turned on watching her skilled hands shape and mold the clay. He wanted those hands on himself so badly, he had to bite his own lip to keep from interrupting her before she was finished. Even now he could taste the faint metallic flavor of his own blood on his tongue.

When Julianne finally turned in his arms to face him, he had to stop himself from telling her she was the most beautiful thing he'd ever seen in his life. Messy hair, dirty face and all. He'd already made the mistake of telling her too much before. It was a far cry from a declaration of love, but he intended to play this second chance much closer to the vest.

Julianne looked up at him, her light green eyes grazing over every inch of his face before she put her hands on each side of his head and tugged his mouth down to hers. The instant their lips met, colored starbursts lit under his eyelids. A rush of adrenaline surged through his veins, making him feel powerful, invincible and desperate to have her once and for all.

Their kiss yesterday hadn't been nearly enough to quench his thirst for her. It had only made his mouth even drier and more desperate to drink her in again. She was sweet on his tongue, her lips soft and open to him. The small palms of her hands clung to him. The moist, sticky clay felt odd against his skin as it started to dry and tighten, but nothing could ruin the feel of kissing her again.

It was like a dream. He'd stumbled downstairs, half-asleep, to charge his phone. He never expected to find her there at her wheel, looking so serene and focused, so beautiful and determined. Having her in his arms only moments later made him want to pinch himself and ensure he really was awake. It wouldn't be the first dream he'd had about Julianne, although it might be the most realistic.

Julianne bit on his lip, then. The sharp pain made him jerk, the area still sensitive from his previous self-inflicted injury. He pulled away from her, studying her face and coming to terms with the fact that she was real. After all these years she was in his arms again.

"I'm sorry," she said, brushing a gentle fingertip over his lip. "Was that too hard?"

Heath would never admit to that. "You just startled me, that's all."

Julianne nodded, her gaze running over the line of his jaw with a smile curling her lips. Her fingertip scraped over the mix of stubble and clay, making the muscles in his neck tighten and flex with anticipation. "I think we need a shower," she said. "You're a very, very dirty boy."

A shower was an awesome idea. "You make me this way," he replied. With a grin, Heath lifted Julianne up. As tiny as she was, it was nothing to lift her into the air. She wrapped her legs and arms around him, holding him close as he stumbled out of the workshop and headed for the stairs.

When they reached the top of the staircase, her mouth found his again. With one eye on his bedroom up ahead, he stumbled across the landing and through the door. He prayed there weren't any clothes or shoes strewn across the floor to trip him and he was successful. They reached into the bathroom and he pulled one hand away from a firm thigh to switch on the lights.

He expected Julianne to climb down, but she clearly had no intention of letting go of him. Not even to take off their clothes. She refused to take her mouth off of his long enough to see what she was doing.

She reached into the shower, pawing blindly at the knobs until a stream of warm, then hot, water shot from the nozzle. Julianne put her feet down onto the tiles and then stepped backward into the stall, tugging Heath forward until he stumbled and they both slammed against the tile, fully dressed. Their clothes were instantly soaked, and were now transparent and clung to their skin.

Her whole body was on display for him now. Her rosy nipples were hard and thrusting through the damp cotton top. His hands sought them out, crushing them against his palms until her moans echoed off the walls. His mouth dipped down, tugging at her tank top until the peaks of her breasts spilled out over the neckline. He captured one in his mouth, sucking hard.

The hot water ran over their bodies as they touched and tasted each other. Most of the clay was gone now, the faint gray stream of water no longer circling the drain. Their hair was soaking wet, with fat drops of water falling into his eyes as he hovered over her chest. It was getting hard to breathe between the water in his face and the steam in his lungs, but he refused to let go of Julianne long enough to change anything.

A rush of cold air suddenly hit his back as Julianne tugged at his wet shirt. She pulled it over his head and flung it onto the bathroom floor with a wet *thwump*.

"I thought you were tired of me running around without my shirt on," he said with a grin.

"You said it was okay in the shower, remember?"

"That I did." Leaning down, he did the same with her top and her shorts. She was completely exposed to him now, her body a delight for his eyes that had gone so long without gazing upon it. He wanted to take his time, to explore every inch and curve of her, but Julianne wasn't having it. She tugged him back against her, hooking her leg around his hip.

Lifting her into his arms once again, he pressed her back into the corner of the shower, one arm around her waist to support her, the other hand planted firmly on her outer thigh. The hot spray was now running over his back and was no longer on the verge of drowning them.

Julianne's hands reached between them, her fingers finding the waistband of his boxers and pushing them down. He wasn't wearing anything beneath. Without much effort, she'd pushed the shorts low on his hips and exposed him. He expected her to touch him then, but instead, she stiffened slightly in his arms.

"Heath?"

Julianne's voice was small, competing with the loud rush of the shower and the heavy panting of their breaths, but he heard her. He stopped, his hands mere inches from the moist heat between her thighs.

She wasn't changing her mind again, was she? He wasn't sure he could take that a second time. "Yes?"

"Before we…" Her voice trailed off. Her golden brown lashes were dark and damp, but still full enough to hide her eyes from him. "I don't want to tell anyone about us. *This*. Not yet."

Heath tried not to let the hard bite of her words affect him. She kept insisting she wasn't embarrassed of him and yet she repeatedly went out of her way to prove otherwise. He wanted to ask why. To push her for more information, but this wasn't exactly the right moment to have an in-depth relationship discussion. What was he going to say? He was wedged between her thighs, his pants shoved low on his hips. Now was not the time to disagree with her. At least not if he ever wanted to sleep with his wife.

"Okay," he agreed and her body relaxed. He waited only a moment before sliding his hand the rest of the way up her thigh. His fingers found her slick and warm, her loud cry more evidence that she wanted him and was ready to have him at last. He grazed over her flesh, moving in sure, firm strokes, effectively ending the conversation.

Julianne arched her back, pressing her hips hard into his hand and crying out. Her worries of a moment ago vanished and he intended to plow full steam ahead before she changed her mind, this time for good.

Heath braced her hips in his hands, lifting her up, and then stopping just as he pushed against the entrance to her body. He didn't want to move at this snail's pace; he wanted to dive hard and fast into her, but a part of him kept waiting for her to stop him. He clenched his jaw, praying for self-control and the ability to pull away when she asked.

"Yes, Heath," she whispered. "Please. We've waited this long, don't make me wait any longer."

Heath eased his hips forward and before he knew it, he was buried deep inside her. That realization forced his eyes closed and his body stiff as a shudder of pleasure moved through him. Pressing his face into her shoulder, he reveled in the long-awaited sensation of Julianne's welcoming heat wrapped around him.

How many years, nights, days, had he fantasized about the moment that had been stolen away from him? And now he had her at last. He almost couldn't believe it. It was the middle of the night. Maybe this was all just some wild dream. There was only one way to test it.

Withdrawing slowly, he thrust hard and quick, drawing a sharp cry from her and a low growl of satisfaction from his own throat. He could feel Julianne's fingers pressing insistently into his back, the muscles of her sex tightening around him. He was most certainly awake. And there was no more reason to hold back.

Heath gripped her tightly, leaning in to pin her securely to the wall. And then he moved in her. What started as a slow savoring of her body quickly morphed into a fierce claiming. Julianne clung to him, taking everything he had to give and answering his every thrust with a roll of her hips and a gasp of pleasure.

Everything about this moment felt so incredibly right. It wasn't romantic or sweet. It was fierce and raw, but that was what it needed to be. After eleven years of waiting... eleven years of other lovers who never quite met the standard Julianne had set. He was like a starving man at a buffet. He couldn't get enough of her fast enough to satiate the need that had built in him all these years.

Yet even as he pumped into her, his mind drifted to that night—the night they should have shared together in Gibraltar. They should have been each other's first. It would have been special and important and everything he'd built up in his mind. Instead, he'd given it up to some sorority girl whose name he barely remembered anymore. He didn't know who Julianne finally chose to be her first lover, but even all these years later, he was fiercely jealous of that man for taking what he felt was his.

He was going to make himself crazy with thoughts like that. To purge his brain, he sought out her mouth. He focused on the taste of her, instead. The slide of her tongue along his own. The sharp edge of her teeth nipping at him. The hollow echo of her cries inside his head.

His fingers pressed harder into the plump flesh of her backside, holding her as he surged forward, pounding relentlessly into her body. Julianne tore her mouth from his. The faster he moved, the louder Julianne's gasps of "yes, yes" were in his ear. He lost himself in pleasure, feeling her body tense and tighten around him as she neared her release.

When she started to shudder in his arms, he eased back and opened his eyes. He wanted to see this moment and remember it forever. Her head was thrown back and her eyes closed. Her mouth fell open, her groans and gasps escalating into loud screams. "Heath, yes, Heath!" she shouted.

It was the most erotic sound he'd ever heard. The sound went straight to his brain, the surge of his own pleasure shooting down his spine and exploding into his own release. He poured into her, his groans mixing with hers and the roar of the pounding water.

At last, he thought as he reached out to turn off the water. He'd waited years for this moment and it was greater than he ever could have anticipated.

Seven

He signed them.

Well, if that wasn't the cherry on top, Julianne didn't know what was. She didn't know exactly when it happened, but as she sat down at the kitchen table the next morning, she noticed the divorce papers were out of the envelope. She flipped through the bound pages to the one tabbed by her attorney. There she found Heath's signature, large and sharply scrawled across the page beside yesterday's date.

Well, at least he had signed it *before* they had sex.

That didn't make her feel much better, though. She had already woken up feeling awkward about what happened between them. She'd crept out of his bed as quietly as she could and escaped to the safety of downstairs.

Their frantic lovemaking in the middle of the night certainly wasn't planned. Or well-thought-out. It also wasn't anything she intended to repeat. He'd caught her in a vulnerable moment. Somehow, at 3:00 a.m., all the reasons it seemed like a bad idea faded away. Well, they were all back now. Eleven years' worth of reasons, starting with why they'd never had sex in the first place and ending with that phone call to his "sweetheart" the other night. They weren't going to be together. Last night was a one-time thing.

But even then, coming downstairs and finding their signed divorce papers on the table felt like a slap across the face somehow.

This was why she'd asked him to keep this all a secret. There was no sense in drawing anyone else into the drama of their relationship when the odds were that it would all be over before long. No matter what happened between them last night, they were heading for a divorce. He'd said that he didn't want a divorce, he wanted her to choose. Apparently that wasn't entirely true. For all his sharp accusations, he seemed to want to have his cake and eat it as well.

With a sigh, she sipped her coffee and considered her options. She could get upset, but that wouldn't do much good. She was the one who had the papers drawn up, albeit as a result of his goading. She couldn't very well hold a grudge against him for signing them after she'd had them overnighted to the house.

As she did when she got stuck on one of her sculptures, she decided it was best to sit back and try to look at this situation from a different angle. She and Heath were getting a divorce. It was a long time coming and nothing was going to change that now. With that in mind, what did sleeping with Heath hurt? She'd always wanted him. He'd always wanted her. Their unfinished wedding night had been like a dark cloud hovering overhead for the last eleven years.

When she thought about it that way, perhaps it was just something they needed to do. Things might be a little awkward between them, but they hadn't exactly been hunky-dory before.

Now that they'd gotten it out of their system, they could move forward with clear heads. But move forward into what? The divorce seemed to be a hot-button issue. Once that was official and they stopped fighting, what would happen? There was a chemistry between them that was impossible to deny. Now that they'd crossed the line, she imagined that it would be hard not to do it again.

What if they did?

Julianne wasn't sure. It didn't seem like the best idea. And yet, she wasn't quite ready to give it up. Last night had been…amazing. Eleven years in the making and worth the wait. It made her angry. It was bad enough that Tommy had attacked her and she had the shadow of his death on her conscience. But the impact had been so long-lasting. What if her wedding night with Heath had gone the way it should have? What if they'd been able to come home and tell their parents and be together? She felt like even long after he was dead, Tommy had taken not only her innocence, but also her future and happiness with Heath.

Back in college when her mind went down into this dark spiral, her therapist would tell her she couldn't change the past. All she could do was guide her future. There was no sense dwelling on what had happened. "Accept, acknowledge and grow" was her therapist's motto.

Applied to this instance, she had to accept that she'd had sex with Heath. She acknowledged that it was amazing. To grow, she needed to decide if she wanted to do it again and what the consequences would be. Why did there have to be negative consequences? It was just sex, right? They could do it twice or twenty times, but if she kept that in perspective, things would be fine. It didn't mean anything, at least not to her. Since he had signed the divorce papers first, she'd have to assume he felt the same way.

In fact... Julianne reached for the divorce decree and the pen lying there. She turned back to the flagged page and the blank line for her signature. With only a moment's hesitation, she put her pen to the paper and scrawled her signature beside his.

"See?" she said aloud to the empty room. "It didn't mean anything."

There. It was done. All she had to do was drop it back in the mail to her lawyer. She shoved the paperwork back in the envelope and set it aside. For a moment, there was the euphoria of having the weight of their marriage lifted from her shoulders. It didn't last long, however. It was quickly followed by the sinking feeling of failure in her stomach.

With a groan, she pushed away her coffee. She needed to get out of the bunkhouse. Running a few errands would help clear her mind. She could stop by the post office and mail the paperwork, pick up a few things at the store and go by the hospital to see Dad. Her kiln wouldn't be delivered until later in the afternoon, so why not? Sitting around waiting for Heath to wake up felt odd. There was no reason to make last night seem more important than it was. She would treat it like any other hookup.

She found it was a surprisingly sunny and warm day for early October. That wouldn't last. The autumn leaves on the trees were past their prime and would drop to the ground dead before long. They'd have their first snow within a few weeks, she was certain.

She took advantage of the weather, putting the top down on her convertible. There would still be a cold sting to her cheeks, but she didn't mind. She wanted the wind in her hair. Pulling out of the drive, she headed west for the hospital. With all the work on her studio, she hadn't been to see her father for a couple days. Now was a good time. Molly's car was at the house, so Dad was alone and they could chat without other people around. Even though her father didn't—and couldn't—know the details of what was bothering her, he had a calming effect on her that would help.

She checked in at the desk to see what room he was in now that he was out of intensive care, and then headed up to the fourth floor. Ken was sitting up when she arrived, watching television and poking at his food tray with dismay.

"Morning, Dad."

A smile immediately lit his face. He was a little thinner and he looked tired, but his color was better and they'd taken him off most of the monitors. "Morning, June-bug. You didn't happen to bring me a sausage biscuit, did you?"

Julianne gave him a gentle hug and sat down at the foot of his bed. "Dad, you just had open-heart surgery. A sausage biscuit? Really?"

"Well…" He shrugged, poking at his food again. "It's better than this stuff. I don't even know what this is."

Julianne leaned over his tray. "It looks like scrambled egg whites, oatmeal, cantaloupe and dry toast."

"It all tastes like wallpaper paste to me. No salt, no sugar, no fat, no flavor. Why did they bother saving me, really?"

Julianne frowned. "You may not like it, but you've got to eat healthier. You promised me you'd live to at least ninety and I expect you to hold up your end of the bargain."

Ken sighed and put a bite of oatmeal in his mouth with a grimace. "I'm only doing this for your sake."

"When do you get to come home? I'm sure Mom's version of healthy food will be better tasting."

"Tomorrow, thank goodness. I'm so relieved to skip the rehab facility. You and I both know it's really a nursing home. I might be near death, but I'm not ready for that, yet."

"I'm glad. I didn't want you there, either."

"Your mother says that you and Heath are both staying in the bunkhouse."

"Yes," she said with a curt nod. She didn't dare elaborate. The only person who could read her better than Heath was her dad. He would pick up on something pretty easily.

"How's that going? You two haven't spent that much time together in a long while. You were inseparable as kids."

Julianne shrugged. "It's been fine." She picked up the plastic pitcher of ice water and poured herself a glass. Driving with the top down always made her thirsty. "I think we're both getting a feel for one another again."

"You know," he said, putting his spoon back down on his tray, "I always thought you two might end up together."

The water in her mouth shot into different directions as she sputtered, some going into her lungs, some threatening to shoot out her nose. She set the cup down, coughing furiously for a few moments until her eyes were teary and her face was red.

"You okay?" he asked.

"Went down the wrong way," she whispered between coughs. "I'm fine. Sorry. What, uh…what makes you say something like that?"

"I don't know. You two always seemed to complement each other nicely. Neither of you seem to be able to find the right person. I've always wondered if you weren't looking in the wrong places."

This was an unexpected conversation. She wasn't entirely sure how to respond to it. "Looking in the family is frowned on, Dad."

"Oh, come on," he muttered irritably. "You're not related. You never even lived in the same house, really. It's more like falling for the boy next door."

"You don't think it would be weird?"

"Your mother and I want to see you and Heath happy. If it turns out you're happy together, then that's the way it is."

"What if it didn't work out? It's not like I can just change my number and pretend Heath doesn't exist after we break up."

Ken frowned and narrowed his eyes at her. "Do you always go into your relationships figuring out how you'll handle it when they end? That's not very optimistic."

"No, but it's practical. You've seen my track record."

"I have. Your mother told me the last one didn't end well."

He didn't know the half of it. "Why would dating Heath be any different? I mean, if he were even remotely interested, and I'm certain he's not."

Her father's blue-gray eyes searched her face for a moment, then he leaned back against the pillows. "I remember when you were little and you came home from school one day all breathless with excitement. You climbed into my lap and whispered in my ear that you'd kissed a boy on the playground. You had Heath's name doodled all over the inside of your unicorn notebook."

"Dad, I was nine."

"I know that. And I was twelve when I first kissed your mother at the junior high dance. I knew then that I was going to be with her for the rest of my life. I just had to convince her."

"She wasn't as keen on the idea?"

Ken shrugged. "She just needed a little persuading. Molly was beautiful, just like you are. She had her choice of boys in school. I just had to make sure she knew I was the best one. By our senior year in high school, I had won her over. I proposed that summer after we graduated and the rest is history."

Julianne felt a touch of shame for not knowing that much about her parents' early relationship. She had no idea they'd met so young and got engaged right out of school. They were married nearly ten years before they finally had her, so somehow, it hadn't registered in her mind. "You were so young. How did you know you were making the right choice?"

"I loved your mother. It might not have been the easy choice to get married so young, but we made the most of it. On our wedding day, I promised your mother a fairy tale. Making good on that promise keeps me working at our marriage every day. There were hard times and times when we fought and times when we both thought it was a colossal mistake. But that's when you've got to fight harder to keep what you want."

Julianne's mind went to the package of paperwork in her bag and she immediately felt guilty. The one thing she never did was fight for her relationship with Heath. She had wanted it, but at the same time, she didn't think she could have it. Tommy had left her in shreds. It took a lot of years and a lot of counseling to get where she was now and, admittedly, that wasn't even the healthiest of places. She was a relationship failure who had just slept with her husband for the first time in their eleven-year marriage.

Maybe if things had been different. Maybe if Heath's parents hadn't died. Or if Tommy hadn't come to the farm. Maybe then they could have been happy together, the way her father envisioned.

"I'll keep that in mind when I'm ready to get back in the saddle," she said, trying not to sound too dismissive.

Ken smiled and patted her hand. "I'm an old man who's only loved one woman his whole life. What do I know about relationships? Speaking of which—" he turned toward the door and grinned widely "—it's time for my sponge bath."

Julianne turned to look at the door and was relieved to find her mother there instead of a young nurse. "Well, you two have fun," she laughed. "I'll see you tomorrow at the house."

She gave her mom a quick hug and made her way out of the hospital. Putting the top up on the convertible, she drove faster than usual, trying to put some miles between her and her father's words.

He couldn't be right about her relationship with Heath. If he knew everything that had happened, her father would realize that it just wasn't meant to be. They would never be happy together and she had the divorce papers to prove it.

Julianne cruised back into town, rolling past Daisy's Diner and the local bar, the Wet Hen. Just beyond them were the market and the tiny post office. No one was in line in front of her, so she was able to fill out the forms and get the paperwork overnighted back to her lawyer's office.

It wasn't until she handed over the envelope and the clerk tossed it into the back room that her father's words echoed in her head and she felt a pang of regret. She hadn't fought. She'd just ended it. A large part of her life had been spent with Heath as her husband. It wasn't a traditional marriage by any stretch, but it had been a constant throughout the hectic ups and downs of her life.

"Ma'am?" the clerk asked. "Are you okay? Did you need something else?"

Julianne looked up at him. For a brief second, the words *I changed my mind* were on the tip of her tongue. He would fetch it back for her. She could wait. She wasn't entirely certain that she wanted this.

But Heath did. He wanted his freedom, she could tell.

She'd left him hanging for far, far too long. He deserved to find a woman who would love him and give him the life and family he desired. Maybe Miss Caribbean could give him that. That was what she'd intended when she broke it off with him originally. To give him that chance. She just hadn't had the strength to cut the last tie and give up on them.

It was time, no matter what her dad said. "No," she said with a smile and a shake of her head. "I'm fine. I was just trying to remember if I needed stamps, but I don't. Thank you."

Turning on her heel, she rushed out of the post office and back out onto the street.

Heath was not surprised to wake up alone, but it still irritated him. He wandered through the quiet house and realized at last that her car was not in the driveway. It wasn't hard to figure out that last night's tryst had not sat well with her. As with most things, it seemed like a good idea at the time.

They had been on the same page in the moment. It had been hot. More erotic than he ever dared imagine. They fell back to sleep in each other's arms. He'd dozed off cautiously optimistic that he might get some morning lovin' as well. That, obviously, had not panned out, but again, he was not surprised.

Frankly, he was more surprised they'd had sex to begin with. He dangled the bait but never expected her to bite. His plan had always been to push their hot-button issue, make her uncomfortable and get her to finally file for divorce. He never anticipated rubbing clay all over her body and having steamy shower sex in the middle of the night. That was the stuff of his hottest fantasies.

Of course, he'd also never thought she would cave so

quickly to the pressure and order the divorce paperwork the same day he demanded it. He expected spending weeks, even months wearing her down. She had already held out eleven years. Then the papers arrived with such speed that he almost didn't believe it. He'd wanted movement, one way or another, so he figured he should sign them before she changed her mind again.

Sleeping with her a few hours later was an unanticipated complication.

Heath glanced over at the table where he'd left the papers. They were gone. He frowned. Maybe she wanted this divorce more than he'd thought. He'd obviously given her the push she needed to make it happen, and she'd run straight to the post office with her prize.

He opted not to dwell on any of it. He signed, so he couldn't complain if she did the same. What was done was done. Besides, that's not why he was here anyway. Heath had come to the farm, first and foremost, to take care of things while Ken recovered. Dealing with Julianne and their divorce was a secondary task.

Returning to his room, he got dressed in some old jeans, a long-sleeved flannel shirt and his work boots. When he was ready he opted to head out to the fields in search of Owen, the farm's only full-time employee. It didn't take long. He just had to hop on one of the four-wheelers and follow the sound of the chain saw. They were in the final stretch leading up to Christmas-tree season, so it was prep time.

He found Owen in the west fields. The northern part of the property was too heavily sloped for people to pick and cut their own trees. The trees on that side were harvested and provided to the local tree lots and hardware stores for sale. Not everyone enjoyed a trek through the cold to find the perfect tree, although Heath couldn't fathom why. The tree lots didn't have Molly's hot chocolate or sleigh rides with carols and Christmas lights. No atmosphere at all.

Most of the pick-and-cut trees were on the west side of the property. The western fields were on flat, easy terrain and they were closest to the shop and the bagging station. He found Owen cutting low branches off the trees and tying bright red ribbons on the branches.

At any one time on the farm there were trees in half a dozen states of growth, from foot-tall saplings to fifteen-year-old giants that would be put in local shopping centers and town squares. At around eight years with proper trimming, a tree was perfect for the average home; full, about six to seven feet tall and sturdy enough to hold heavier ornaments. The red ribbons signified to their customers that the tree was ready for harvest.

"Morning, Owen."

The older man looked up from his work and gave a wave. He put down the chain saw and slipped off one glove to shake Heath's hand. "Morning there, Heath. Are you joining me today?"

"I am. It looks like we're prepping trees."

"That we are." Owen lifted his Patriots ball cap and smoothed his thinning gray hair beneath it before fitting it back on his head. "I've got another chain saw for you on the back of my ATV. Did you bring your work gloves and some protective gear?"

Heath whipped a pair of gloves out of his back pocket and smiled. He had his goggles and ear protection in the tool chest bolted to the back of the four-wheeler. "It hasn't been so long that I'd forget the essentials."

"I don't know," Owen laughed. "Not a lot of need for work gloves in fancy Manhattan offices."

"Some days, I could use the ear protection."

Owen smiled and handed over the chain saw to Heath. "I'm working my way west. Most of this field to the right will be ready for Christmas. Back toward the house still needs a year or two more to grow. You still know how to tell which ones are ready for cutting?"

He did. When he was too young to use the chainsaw, he was out in the fields tying ribbons and shaping trees with hedge clippers. "I've got it, Owen."

Heath went off into the opposite direction Owen was working so they covered more territory. With his headset and goggles in place, he cranked up the chain saw and started making his way through the trees. It was therapeutic to do some physical work. He didn't really get the chance to get dirty anymore. He'd long ago lost the calluses on his hands. His clothes never smelled of pine or had stains from tree sap. It was nice to get back to the work he knew.

There was nothing but the buzz of the saw, the cold sting of the air, the sharp scent of pine and the crunch of dirt and twigs under his boots. He lost himself in the rhythm of his work. It gave him a much-needed outlet as well. He was able to channel some of his aggression and irritation at Julianne through the power tool.

His mind kept going back to their encounter and the look on her face when she'd asked him to keep their relationship a secret. Like it had ever been anything but a secret. Did she think that once they had sex he would dash out of the house and run screaming through the trees that he'd slept with her at last? Part of him had felt like that after finally achieving such an important milestone in their marriage, but given he'd signed the divorce papers only a few hours before that, it didn't seem appropriate.

It irritated him that she wouldn't just admit the truth.

She would go through the whole song and dance of excuses for her behavior but refused to just say out loud that she was embarrassed to be with him. She wanted him, but she didn't want anyone to know it.

Up until that moment in the shower, he'd thought perhaps that wasn't an issue for them anymore. She might not want people to know they eloped as teenagers, but now? Julianne had been quick to point out earlier in the night just how "successful" he was. He had his regrets in life, but she was right. He wasn't exactly a bad catch. He was a slippery one, as some women had discovered, but not a bad one.

And yet, it still wasn't enough for her. What did she want from him? And why did he even care?

He was over her. Over. And he had been for quite some time. He'd told Nolan he didn't love her anymore and that was true. There was an attraction there, but it was a biological impulse he couldn't rid himself of. The sex didn't change anything. They were simply settling a long overdue score between them.

That just left him with a big "now what?" He had no clue. If she were off mailing their divorce papers, the clock was ticking. There were only thirty or so days left in their illustrious marriage. That was what he wanted, right? He started this because he wanted his freedom.

Heath set down the chain saw and pulled a bundle of red ribbons out of his back pocket. He doubled back over the trees he'd trimmed, tying ribbons on the branches with clumsy fingers that were numb from the vibration of the saw.

He didn't really know what he wanted or what he was doing with his life anymore. All he knew was that he wasn't going to let Julianne run away from him this time.

They were going to talk about this whether she liked it or not. It probably wouldn't change things. It might not even get her back in his bed again. But somehow, some way, he just knew that their marriage needed to end with a big bang.

Eight

Julianne returned to an empty bunkhouse. The Porsche wasn't in the driveway. She breathed a sigh of relief and went inside, stopping short when she saw the yellow piece of paper on the kitchen table. Picking it up, she read over the hard block letters of Heath's penmanship.

There's a sushi restaurant in Danbury on the square called Lotus. I have reservations there tonight at seven.

With a sigh, she dropped the note back to the table. Heath didn't ask her to join him. He wasn't concerned about whether or not she might have plans or even if she didn't *want* to have dinner with him. It didn't matter. This was a summons and she would be found in contempt if she didn't show up.

Julianne knew immediately that she should not have run

out on him this morning. They should have talked about it, about what it meant and what was going to happen going forward. Instead, she bailed. He was irritated with her and she didn't blame him. That didn't mean she appreciated having her evening dictated to her, but the idea of some good sushi was a lure. She hadn't had any in a while. Daisy's Diner wasn't exactly known for their fresh sashimi.

She checked the time on her phone. It was four-thirty now and it took about forty-five minutes to drive to Danbury. She'd never been to Lotus, but she'd heard of it before. It was upscale. She would have just enough time to get ready. She hadn't exactly gone all-out this morning to run some errands around town, so she was starting from scratch.

Julianne quickly showered and washed her hair. She blew it dry and put it up in hot rollers to set while she did her makeup and searched her closet for something to wear. For some reason, this felt like a date. Given they'd filed for divorce today, it also felt a little absurd, but she couldn't stop herself from adding those extra special touches to her makeup. After a week surrounded by nothing but trees and dirt, the prospect of dressing up and going out was intriguing.

Except she had nothing to wear. She didn't exactly have a lot of fancy clothes. She spent most of her time covered in mud with a ponytail. Reaching into the back of the closet, she found her all-purpose black dress. It was the simple, classic little black dress that she used for various gallery showings and events. It was knee length and fitted with a deep V-neck and three-quarter sleeves. A black satin belt wrapped around the waist, giving it a little bit of shine and luxury without being a rhinestone-covered sparklefest.

It was classic, simple and understated, and it showed off her legs. She paired it with pointy-toed patent leather heels and a silver medallion necklace that rested right in the hollow between her collarbones.

By the time she shook out the curls in her hair, relaxing them into soft waves, and applied perfume at her pulse points, it was time to leave.

She was anxious as she drove down the winding two-lane highway to Danbury. The fall evening light was nearly gone as she arrived in town. The small square was the center of college nightlife in Danbury and included several bars, restaurants and other hangouts. Lotus was at a small but upper-end location. She imagined it was where the college kids saved up to go for nice dates or where parents took them for graduation dinners and weekend visits.

Julianne parked her convertible a few spots down from Heath's silver Porsche. He was standing outside the restaurant, paying more attention to his phone than to the people and activities going on around him.

She took her time getting out of the car so she could enjoy the view without him knowing it. He was wearing a dark gray suit with a platinum dress shirt and diamond-patterned tie of gray, black and blue. The suit fit him immaculately, stretching across his wide shoulders and tapering into his narrow waist.

Heath had a runner's physique; slim, but hard as a rock. Touching him in that shower had been a fantasy come true after watching those carved abs from a distance day after day. Her only regret had been the rush. Their encounter had been a mad frenzy of need and possession. There was no time for exploring and savoring the way she wanted to. And if she had any sense, there never would be. Last night was a moment of weakness, a settling of scores.

It was then that Heath looked up and saw her loitering beside the Camaro. He smiled for an instant when he saw her but quickly wiped away the expression to a polite but neutral face. It was as though he was happy to see her but didn't want her to know. Or he kept forgetting he shouldn't be happy to see her. Their relationship was so complicated.

Julianne approached him, keeping her own face cautiously blank. She had been summoned, after all. This was not a date. It was a reckoning. "I'm here, as requested," she said.

Heath nodded and slipped his phone into his inner breast pocket. "So you are. I'm mildly surprised." He reached for the door to the restaurant and held it open for her to go inside ahead of him.

She tried not to take offense. He implied she was flaky somehow. After eleven years of artfully dodging divorce, it probably looked that way from the outside. "We've got weeks together ahead of us, Heath. There's no sense in starting off on the wrong foot."

The maître d' took their names and led them to their table. As they walked through the dark space, Heath leaned into her and whispered in her ear. "We didn't start off on the wrong foot," he said. The low rumble of his voice in her ear sent a shiver racing through her body. "We started off on the absolutely right foot."

"And then we filed for divorce," she quipped, pulling away before she got sucked into his tractor beam.

Heath chuckled, following quietly behind her. They were escorted to a leather booth in the corner opposite a large column that housed a salt water fish tank. The cylinder glowed blue in the dark room, one of three around the restaurant that seemed to hold the roof up overhead. The tanks were brimming with life, peppered with anemones, urchins, clown fish and other bright, tropical fish. They were the only lights in the restaurant aside from the individual spotlights that illuminated each table.

They settled in, placing their drink orders and coming

to an agreement on the assortment of sushi pieces they'd like to share. Once that was done, there was nothing to do but face why they were here.

"You're probably wondering what this is about," Heath said after sipping his premium sake.

"You mean you're not just hungry?" Julianne retorted, knowing full well that he had bigger motivations than food on his mind.

"We needed to talk about last night. I thought getting away from home and all *those people*," he said with emphasis, "that you worry about seeing us together might help."

Julianne sighed. He'd taken it personally last night when she asked to keep their encounter a secret. She could tell by the downturn of his lips when he said "those people." He didn't understand. "Heath, I'm not—"

He held up his hand. "It's fine, Jules. You don't want anyone seeing us together. I get it. Nothing has changed since we were eighteen. I should just be happy we finally slept together. Unfortunately, finding you gone when I woke up put a sour taste in my mouth."

"And going downstairs to find you'd signed the divorce papers left a bitter taste in mine."

Heath's eyes narrowed at her for a moment before he relaxed back against the seat. "I signed those last night after you left me on the couch, alone and wanting you once again. I assure you that making love to you in the shower at three a.m. was not in my plan at the time."

Julianne shook her head. "It doesn't matter, Heath. We both know it's what we need to do. What we've needed to do for a very long time. I'm sorry to have drawn it out as long as I have. It wasn't very considerate of me to put you through that. The papers are signed and mailed. It's done. Now we can just relax. We don't have to fight about it anymore. The pressure is off and we can focus on the farm and helping Dad recuperate."

He watched her speak, his gaze focused on her lips, but he didn't seem to have the posture of relief she expected. He had started all this after all. He'd virtually bullied her into filing. Now he seemed displeased by it all.

"So," she asked, "are you upset with me because I did what you asked? Because I'm confused."

Heath sighed. "I'm not upset with you, Jules. You're right, you did exactly as I asked. We filed. That's what we needed to do. I guess I'm just not sure what last night was about. Or why you took off like a criminal come morning."

Julianne looked at him, searching his hazel eyes. Having a relationship with him was so complicated. She wanted him, but she couldn't truly have him. Not when the truth about what had happened that night with Tommy still loomed between them. She didn't want anyone else to have him, either, but she felt guilty about keeping him from happiness. Letting him go didn't seem to make him happy. What the hell was she supposed to do?

"We shouldn't read too much into last night," she said at last. "It was sex. Great sex that was long overdue. I don't regret doing it, despite what you seem to think. I just didn't feel like psychoanalyzing it this morning, especially with our divorce papers sitting beside my cup of coffee."

"So you thought the sex was great?" Heath smiled and arched his brow conspiratorially.

"Is that all you got out of that?" Julianne sighed. "It was great, yes. But it doesn't have to change everything and it doesn't have to mean anything, either. We're attracted to each other. We always have been. Anything more than that is where we run into a problem. So can't it just be a fun outlet for years of pent-up attraction?"

Heath eyed her for a moment, his brows drawn together

in thought. "So you're saying that last night wasn't a big deal? I agree. Does that mean you're wanting to continue this…uh…*relationship?*"

When she woke up this morning, it didn't seem like the right thing to do. It would complicate things further in her opinion. But here, in a dark restaurant with moody lighting and a handsome Heath sitting across from her, it wasn't such a bad idea anymore. They were getting a divorce. The emotional heartstrings had been cut once and for all. If they both knew what they were getting into, why not have a little fun?

"We're both adults. We know that it's just physical. The things that held me back in our youth would not be in play here. So, perhaps."

The waiter approached the table with two large platters of assorted sushi. Heath watched only Julianne as things were rearranged and placed in front of them. The heat of his gaze traveled like a warm caress along her throat to the curve of her breasts. She felt a blush rise to her cheeks and chest from his extensive inventory of her assets.

When the waiter finally disappeared, Heath spoke. "You want us to have a fling?"

That's what she'd just suggested, hadn't she? Maybe that was what they needed. A no-strings outlet for their sexual tension. Perhaps then, she could sate her desire for Heath without having to cross the personal boundaries that kept them apart. He never needed to know about the night with Tommy or what happened during their botched honeymoon. She could make it up to him in the weeks that followed.

And why not? They were still married, weren't they?

Julianne smiled and reached for her chopsticks. She plucked a piece from the platter and put it into her mouth. Her eyes never left his even as she slipped her foot out of her shoe and snaked it beneath the table in search of his leg. His eyes widened as her toes found his ankle beneath the cuff of his suit pants. She slid them higher, caressing the tense muscles of his calves. By the time she reached his inner thigh, he was white-knuckling the table.

She happily chewed, continuing to eat as though her foot had not just made contact with the firm heat of his desire beneath the table. "You'd better eat. I can't finish all this sushi on my own," she said, smiling innocently.

"Jules," he whispered, closing his eyes and absorbing the feeling as her toes glided along the length of him. "Jules!" he repeated, his eyes flying open. "Please," he implored. "I get it. The answer is yes. Let's either eat dinner or leave, but please put your shoe back on. It's a long drive home in separate cars. Don't torture me."

The next few weeks went by easily. The uproar of the move and chaos of being thrown together after so long apart had finally dissipated. Dad was home and doing well under Nurse Lynn's care. Jules had a fully operational workshop with her new kiln. She had three new gallery pieces in various stages of completion that were showing a lot of potential and nearly a full shelving unit of stoneware for her shop. During the day, she worked with Molly in the Christmas store preparing for the upcoming holiday rush. They made wreaths, stocked shelves and handled the paperwork the farm generated. In the evenings, she worked on her art.

Heath had done much the same. During the day, he was out in the fields working with Owen. He'd sent out some feelers for teenagers to work part-time starting at Thanksgiving and had gotten a couple of promising responses. When the sun went down, he worked on his computer, try-

ing to stay up-to-date with emails and other business issues. Things seemed to be going fine as best he could tell.

Most nights, Julianne would slip into his bed. Some en-
counters were fevered and rushed, others were leisurely
and stretched long into the early hours of the morning.
He'd indulged his every fantasy where she was concerned,
filling his cup with Julianne so he would have no regrets
when all of this was over.

He usually found himself alone come morning. Julianne told him she woke up with bad dreams nearly every
night, although she wouldn't elaborate. When she did wake
up, she went downstairs to work. When she returned to
bed, she went to her own room. It was awkward to fall
asleep with her almost every night and wake up alone
just as often.

Despite the comfortable rhythm they'd developed, moments like that were enough to remind him that things
were not as sublime as they seemed. He was not, at long
last, in a relationship with Julianne. What they had was
physical, with a strong barrier in place to keep her emotions in check. She was still holding back, the way she
always had. Their discussions never strayed to their marriage, their past, or their future. She avoided casual, physical contact with him throughout the day. When nightfall
came, they were simply reaping the benefits of their marriage while they could.

Given Heath had spent eleven years trying to get this
far, he couldn't complain much. But it did bother him from
time to time. When he woke up alone. When he wanted
to kiss her, but Molly or Nurse Lynn were nearby and she
would shy away. When he remembered the clock was ticking down on their divorce.

At the same time, things at the bunkhouse had certainly
been far more peaceful than he'd ever anticipated going

into this scenario. It was one of those quiet evenings when his phone rang. He'd just gotten out of the shower after a long day of working outside and had settled in front of his laptop when the music of his phone caught his attention from the coffee table.

Heath reached for his phone and frowned. It was Nolan's number and picture on the screen of his smartphone. He was almost certain this wouldn't be a social call. With a sigh, he hit the button to answer. "Hey."

"I'm sorry," Nolan began, making Heath grit his teeth. "I had to call."

"What is it?" And why couldn't Nolan handle it? He couldn't voice the query aloud. Nolan was running the whole show to accommodate Heath's family emergency, but Heath couldn't help the irritation creeping up his spine. He had enough to worry about in Connecticut without New York's troubles creeping in.

"Madame Badeau called today. And yesterday. And last week. For some reason, she must think your assistant is lying about you being out of the office. She finally threw a fit and insisted to talk to me."

Heath groaned aloud. Thank goodness only Nolan and his assistant had his personal number. The older French woman refused to use email, so if she had his personal number, she'd call whenever she felt the urge, time difference be damned. "What does she want?"

Nolan chuckled softly on the line. "Aside from you?"

"Most especially," Heath responded..

"She wants you in Paris this weekend."

"What?" It was *Wednesday*. Was she insane? He held her advertising account; he wasn't hers to summon at her whim. "Why?"

"She's unhappy with the European campaign we put together. You and I both know she approved it and seemed happy when we first presented it, but she's had a change of heart. It's a last-minute modification and she wants you there to personally oversee it. She wants the commercial reshot, the print ads redone—everything."

That wasn't a weekend task. Heath smelled a rat. Surely she wasn't just using this as an excuse to lure him to Paris. He'd told her he was married. She seemed to understand. "Why can't Mickey handle this?" Mickey was their art director. He was the one who usually handled the shoots. Redoing the J'Adore campaign fell solidly into Mickey's bucket.

"She didn't like his vision. She wants you there and no one else. I was worried about this. I'm sorry, but there's no dissuading her. I told her about your leave of absence for a family emergency, but it didn't make any difference to her. All she said was that she'd send her private jet to expedite the trip and get you back home as quickly as possible. A long weekend at the most, she insisted."

As much as Heath would like to take that private jet and tell Cecilia what she could do with it, they needed her account. It was hugely profitable for them. If she pulled out after they had spent the last two years making J'Adore the most sought-after cosmetic line in the market, it would be catastrophic. Not only would they lose her account, but others would also wonder why she left and might consider jumping ship. It was too high-profile to ruin. That meant Heath was going to Paris. Just perfect.

"So when is the plane arriving to pick me up?"

"Thursday afternoon in Hartford. Wheels up at four."

"I guess I'll pack my bags. I didn't really bring a lot of my suits to work on the farm. Thankfully it's only for a few days."

"You need to pack Julianne's bags, too."

"What?" he yelled into the phone. "How the hell did she get involved in this discussion?"

"Just relax," Nolan insisted, totally unfazed by Heath's tone. "When I was trying to talk her out of summoning you, I told her that your father-in-law had a heart attack and you and Julianne had gone to the farm. I thought reminding her about your wife and the serious situation you were dealing with would cool her off a little. I lost my mind and thought she would be a reasonable person. Instead, she insisted you bring Julianne to Paris as well."

"Why would I want to bring her with me?"

"Why wouldn't you want to bring your sweet, beloved wife with you to Paris? It's romantic," Nolan said, "and it would be suspicious if you didn't want to bring her. Between you and me, I think Madame Badeau wants to see her competition in the flesh. What can it hurt? Maybe she'll back off for good once she sees Julianne and realizes she's not just a made-up relationship to keep her at arm's length."

Heath groaned again. He'd never met a woman this aggressive. Had his mother not died when he was a child, she would be a year younger than Cecilia. It didn't make a difference to her. She was a wealthy, powerful woman who was used to getting what she wanted, including a steady stream of young lovers. Heath was just a shiny toy she wanted because she couldn't have him.

"Do you really think it will help to take her?"

"I do. And look at the bright side. You'll get a nice weekend in Paris. You'll be flying on a fancy private jet and staying in a fabulous hotel along the Seine. It's not the biggest imposition in the world. You're probably tired of staring at pine trees by now. It's been almost a month since you went up there."

Heath *was* tired of the trees. Well, that wasn't entirely

correct. He was tired of being cooped up here, pacing around like a caged tiger. If it weren't for the nights with Julianne to help him blow off steam, he might've gone stir-crazy by now. Perhaps a weekend away would give him the boost he needed to make it through the holidays. It was early November, so better now than in the middle of the holiday rush.

"Okay," he agreed. "You can let her know we'll be there."

"Thanks for taking one for the team," Nolan quipped.

"Yeah," Heath chuckled, ending the call.

Paris. He was going to Paris. With Julianne. Tomorrow. Even after the happy truce they'd come to, going to Paris together felt like returning to the scene of the crime, somehow. That's where he'd told her he loved her and kissed her for the first time since they were nine years old. They'd left Paris for Spain, and then took a detour to Gibraltar to elope.

With a heavy sigh, Heath got up from the kitchen table and tapped gently at the door to Julianne's studio. Now he had to convince her to go with him. And not just to go, but to go and act like the happy wife *in public*, one of the barriers they hadn't breached. To fool Madame Badeau, they had to be convincing, authentic. That meant his skittish bride would have to tolerate French levels of public affection. It might not even be possible.

The room was silent. She wasn't using her pottery wheel, but he knew she was in there.

"Come in."

Heath twisted the knob and pushed his way into her work space. Julianne was hovering over a sculpture on her table. This was an art piece for her gallery show, he was pretty certain. It was no simple vase, but an intricately detailed figure of a woman dancing.

Julianne's hair was pulled back into a knot. She was wearing a pair of jeans and a fitted T-shirt. There was clay smeared on her shirt, her pants, her face, her arms—she got into her work. It reminded him of that first night they'd spent together, sending a poorly timed surge of desire through him.

"I have a proposition for you, Jules."

At that, Julianne frowned and set down her sculpting tool. "That sound ominous," she noted.

"It depends on how you look at it. I need to take a trip for work. And it's a long story, but I need you to come with me. Do you have a current passport?"

Julianne's eyebrows lifted in surprise. "Yes. I renewed last year, although I haven't gone anywhere. Where on earth do you have to go for work?"

"We're going to Paris this weekend."

"Excuse me?"

Heath held up his hands defensively. "I know. I don't have a choice. It's an important account and the client will only work with me. She's a little temperamental. I know it sounds strange, and I hate to impose, but I have to take you to Paris with me. For, uh…public companionship."

A smile curled Julianne's lips. "I take it the French lady has the hots for you?"

He shook his head in dismay. "Yes, she does. I had to tell her I was married so she'd back off."

"She knows we're married?" Julianne stiffened slightly.

"I had to tell her something. Rebuffing her without good reason might've cost us a critical account. I had to tell my business partner, too, so he was on the same page."

Julianne nodded slowly, processing the information. She obviously didn't care for anyone outside of the two of them and their lawyers knowing about this. It was one thing for family to find out, but who cared if a woman halfway across the globe knew?

"She's insisting I come to Paris to correct some things she's unhappy with and to bring you with me on the trip. I think she wants to meet you, more than anything. It would look suspicious if I didn't bring you. We're supposed to be happily married."

"What does that mean when we get there?"

Heath swallowed hard. They'd gotten to the sticking point. "Exactly what you think it means. We have to publically act like a married couple. We need to wear our rings, be affectionate and do everything we can to convince my client of our rock-solid romance."

Heath looked down and noticed that Julianne was tightly clutching her sculpting tool with white-knuckled strength. "No one here will find out," he added.

Finally, Julianne nodded, dropping the tool and stretching her fingers. "I haven't seen you look this uncomfortable since Sheriff Duke rolled onto the property." She laughed nervously and rubbed her hands clean on her pants.

He doubted he had looked as concerned as she did now. "I can probably get Wade to step in and help while we're gone. Things are in pretty good shape around here. So can I interest you in an all-expense-paid weekend in Paris? We leave tomorrow. My personal discomfort will simply be a bonus."

Julianne nodded and came out from behind her work table. "I get to be a witness to your personal discomfort *and* experience Paris for free? Hmm…I think I can stand being in love with you for a few days for that. But," she added, holding up her hand, "just to be clear, this is all for show to protect your business. Nothing we say or do can be considered evidence of long-suppressed feelings for one another. By the time we get home, the clock will be up on the two of us. Consider this trip our last hoorah."

Nine

"Did you remember to bring your wedding ring?"

Julianne paused in the lobby of J'Adore and started searching in her purse. "I brought it. I just forgot to put it on. What about you?"

Heath held up his left hand and wiggled his fingers. "Got it."

Julianne finally located the small velvet box that held her wedding band. The poor, ignored gold band had been rotting in her jewelry box since the day they returned from their trip to Europe. They'd bought the bands from a small jewelry shop in Gibraltar. With a reputation for being the Las Vegas of Europe, there were quite a few places with wedding bands for last-minute nuptials. They hadn't been very expensive. They were probably little more than nickel painted over with gold-colored paint. Had they been worn for more than a week, the gold might have chipped off long ago, but as it was, they were as perfect and shiny as the day they'd bought them.

She slipped the band onto her finger and put the box away. It felt weird to wear her ring again, especially so close to the finalization of their divorce. Part of her couldn't help thinking this ruse was a mistake. It felt like playing with fire. She'd been burned too many times in her life already.

"Okay, are you ready? This is our first public outing as a married couple. Try to remember not to pull away from me the way you always do."

Julianne winced at his observation. She *did* pull away from him. Even now. Even with no one here having the slightest clue who they were. It was her reflex to shy away from everyone who touched her, at least at first. He seemed to think it was just him instead of a lingering side effect of her attack. She just didn't care to be touched very much. She wanted to tell him that it wasn't about him, but now was not the time to open that can of worms. "I'll do my best," she said instead. "Try not to sneak up on me, though."

Heath nodded and took her hand. "Let's go and get this over with."

They checked in at the front desk and were escorted to the executive offices by Marie, Madame Badeau's personal assistant. The walls and floors were all painted a delicate shade of pink that Heath told her was called "blush" after the company's first cheek color. When they reached the suite outside Madame Badeau's offices, the blush faded to white. White marble floors, white walls, white leather furniture, white lamps and glass and crystal fixtures to accent them.

"*Bonjour,* Monsieur Langston!"

A woman emerged from a frosted pair of double doors. Like the office, she was dressed in an all-white pantsuit. It was tailored to perfection, showing every flawless curve of the older woman's physique. This was no ordinary woman approaching her sixties. There wasn't a single gray hair in her dark brown coiffure. Not a wrinkle, a blemish, or a bit of makeup out of place. This woman had the money to pay the personal trainers and plastic surgeons necessary to preserve her at a solid forty-year-old appearance.

Heath reluctantly let go of Julianne's hand to embrace Madame Badeau and give her kisses on each cheek. "You're looking ravishing, as always, Cecilia."

"You charmer." The woman beamed at Heath, holding his face in her hands. She muttered something in French, but Julianne hadn't a clue what she said.

And then the dark gaze fell on her. "And this must be Madame Langston! Julianne, *oui?*"

At first, Julianne was a little startled by the use of the married name she'd never taken. She recovered quickly by nodding as the woman approached her. She followed Heath's lead in greeting the woman. "Yes. Thank you for allowing me to join Heath on this trip. We haven't been back to Paris since he confessed his love for me at the base of the Eiffel Tower."

Cecilia placed a hand over her heart and sighed. "Such a beautiful moment, I'm sure. You must have dinner there tonight!" The woman's accent made every word sound so lovely, Julianne would've agreed to anything she said. "I will have Marie arrange it."

"That isn't necessary, Cecilia. I'm here to work on the spring J'Adore campaign. Besides, it would be impossible to get reservations on such short notice."

Cecilia puckered her perfectly plumped and painted lips with a touch of irritation. "You are in Paris, Heath. You *must* enjoy yourself. In Paris we do not work twenty-four hours a day. There must be time for wine and conversation. A stroll along the Seine. If you do not make time for that, why even bother to be in Paris at all? *Non*," she said, dismissing his complaint with the elegant wave of her hand. "You will dine there tonight. I am good friends with the owner. Alain will make certain you are accommodated. Is eight o'clock too early?"

Julianne remembered how late Parisian evenings tended to go. Eating dinner at five in the evening was preposterous to them. "That would be lovely," she responded, before Heath could argue again. The last time she was in Paris, they couldn't even afford the ticket to the top, much less dining in their gourmet French restaurant. She would take advantage of it this time, for certain. "*Merci, madame*," she said, using two of the five French words she knew.

Cecilia waved off Marie to make the arrangements. "Quickly, business, then more pleasure," she said with a spark of mischief in her dark eyes. "Heath, your art director has made the arrangement for a second photo shoot today. It should only take a few hours. While we are there, perhaps your *belle femme* would enjoy a luxurious afternoon in the spa downstairs?"

Julianne was about to protest, but the wide smile on Heath's face stopped her before she could speak. "That's a wonderful idea," Heath said. "Jules, the J'Adore spa is a world-famous experience. While I work this out, you can enjoy a few hours getting pampered and ready for dinner this evening. How does that sound?"

She thought for certain that Heath wouldn't want to be left alone with Cecilia, but this didn't seem to bother him at all. Perhaps her appearance had already made all the difference. "*Très bien*," Julianne said with a smile.

Cecilia picked up the phone to make the arrangements and she and Heath settled at her desk to work on some details. Julianne sat quietly, sipping sparkling water and taking in the finer details of the office. A few minutes later, Marie reappeared to escort her to the spa.

Remembering her role as happy wife, Julianne returned to Heath's side and leaned in to give him a passionate, but appropriate kiss. She didn't want to overdo it. The moment their lips met, the ravenous hunger for Heath she'd become all too familiar with returned. She had to force herself to pull away.

"I'm off to be pampered," she said with a smile to cover the flush of arousal as one of excitement. "I'll see you this evening. *Au revoir*," she said, slipping out of the office in Marie's wake.

They returned to the first floor of the building, where a private entrance led them to the facility most customers entered from the street to the right of the J'Adore offices. Marie handed her over to Jacqueline, the manager of the spa.

"Madame Langston, are you ready for your day of pampering?" she said with a polite, subdued smile.

"I am. What am I having done?"

Jacqueline furrowed her brow at her for a moment in confusion, and then she laughed. "Madame Badeau said you are to be given all our finest and most luxurious treatments. You're doing *everything, madame*."

Heath hoped everything went okay with Julianne. Had he not sent her to one of the finest day spas in the world, he might have been worried about working and leaving her alone like that. He'd thought perhaps that he would need her to stay with him all the time, but the moment Cecilia laid eyes on Julianne, the energy she projected toward him shifted. He knew instantly that she would no longer be in pursuit of him, although he wasn't entirely sure what had made the difference.

It wasn't until they were going over the proofs of the photo shoot several hours later that she leaned into him and said, "You love your Julianne very much, I can tell."

At first, he wanted to scoff at her observation, but he realized that he couldn't. Of course he would love his wife. That's how marriages worked. He tried to summon the feelings he'd had for her all those years ago so his words rang with an authenticity Cecilia would recognize. "She was the first and maybe the last woman I'll ever love. The day she said she would marry me was the happiest and scariest day of my life."

That was true enough.

"I see something between you two. I do not see it often. You have something rare and precious. You must treat your love like the most valuable thing you will ever own. Don't ever let it get away from you. You will regret it your entire life, I assure you."

There was a distance in Cecilia's eyes when she spoke that convinced Heath she knew firsthand about that kind of loss. But he couldn't see what she thought she saw in his relationship with Julianne. There might be passion. There might be a nostalgia for the past they shared. But they didn't have the kind of great love Cecilia claimed. A love like that would have survived all these years, shining like a bright star instead of hiding in the shadows like an embarrassing secret. Perhaps they were just better actors than he gave them credit for.

The conversation had ended and they'd finished their day at work. Julianne had texted him to let him know a car was taking her back to their hotel and she would meet him there to go for dinner. Cecilia had booked them a room at the Four Seasons Hotel George V Paris, just off the Chámps Élysées. He arrived there around nightfall, when the town had just begun to famously sparkle and glow.

Perhaps they could walk to the Eiffel Tower. It wasn't a long walk, just a nice stroll across the bridge and along the Seine. The weather was perfect—cool, but not too cold.

He opened the door of their hotel room, barging inside. He found Julianne sitting on the edge of their king-sized bed, fastening the buckle on the ankle strap of her beige heels. His gaze traveled up the length of her bare leg to the nude-colored lace sheath dress she was wearing. It hugged her every curve, giving almost the illusion that she was naked, it so closely matched the creamy ivory of her skin.

Julianne stood up, giving him a better view of the dress. She made a slow turn, showcasing the curve of her backside and the hard muscles of her calves in those sky-high nude pumps with red soles. The peek of red was the only pop of color aside from the matching red painted on her lips. "What do you think?"

"It's…" he began, but his mouth was so dry he had difficulty forming the words. "Very nice."

"When I got done a little early, I decided to go shopping. It's a Dolce & Gabbana dress. And these are Christian Louboutin shoes. I honestly can't believe I spent as much money as I did, but after all that pampering, I was feeling indulgent and carefree for once."

"It's worth every penny," Heath said. In that moment he wanted to buy her a hundred dresses if they would make her beam as radiantly as she did right now. "But now I'm underdressed. Give me a few minutes and I'll be ready to go."

Heath didn't have a tuxedo with him, but he pulled out his finest black Armani suit and the ivory silk dress shirt that would perfectly match her dress. He showered quickly to rinse away the grit and worries of the day and changed into the outfit.

"I was going to suggest we walk since it's so nice, but I'm thinking those shoes aren't meant for city strolls."

"Even if they were, Marie arranged for a car to pick us up at seven forty-five. Perhaps we can walk home." Julianne gathered up a small gold clutch and pulled a gold wrap around her shoulders.

Heath held out his arm to usher her out the door. In the lobby, a driver was waiting for them. He led them outside to the shiny black Bentley. They relaxed in the soft leather seats as the driver carried them through the dark streets and across the bridge to the left bank where the Eiffel Tower stood.

The driver escorted them to the entrance reserved for guests of the Jules Verne restaurant. The private elevator whisked them to the second floor in moments. Heath remembered climbing the over six hundred stairs to reach this floor eleven years ago. The lift entrance tickets were double the price, so they'd skipped it and walked up. The elevator was decidedly more luxurious and didn't make his thighs quiver.

They were seated at a table for two right against the glass overlooking Paris. Out the window, they could see the numerous bridges stretching over the Seine and the glowing, vaulted glass ceiling of the Grand Palais beyond it. The view was breathtaking. Romantic. It made him wish he'd been able to afford a place like this when they were kids. Proposing from the lawn had been nice, but not nice enough for their relationship to last. Caviar and crème fraîche might not a good marriage make, but it couldn't have hurt.

They both ordered wine and the tasting menu of the evening. Then they sat nervously fidgeting with their napkins and looking out the window for a few minutes. Pretending to be a couple in front of Cecilia was one thing. Now they were smack-dab in the middle of one of the most romantic places on earth with no one to make a show for.

They'd spent the last few weeks together. They shared a bed nearly every night. But they hadn't done any of that in Paris, the city where they fell in love. Paris was the wild card that scared Heath to death. He'd done a good job to keep his distance in all of this. Julianne's remoteness made that easier. He liked to think that in a few short days, he would be divorced and happy about that fact.

But Paris could change everything. It had once; it could do it again. The question was whether or not he wanted it to. He shouldn't. It was the same self-destructive spiral that had kept him in this marriage for eleven long years. But that didn't keep him from wanting the thing he'd been promised the day they married.

As the first course arrived, he opted to focus on his food instead of the way the warm lighting made her skin look like soft velvet. He wouldn't pay attention to the way she closed her eyes and savored each bite that passed her lips. And he certainly would ignore the way she occasionally glanced at him when she thought he wasn't looking.

That was just asking for trouble and he had his hands full already.

"We have to stay and watch the lights."

Julianne led Heath out from beneath the Eiffel Tower to the long stretch of dark lawn that sprawled beside it. The first time they had been here, they'd laid out on a blanket. Tonight, they weren't prepared and there was no way she would tempt the fabric of her new dress with grass stains, so she stopped at one of the gravel paths that dissected the lawn.

"We've seen them before, Jules."

She frowned at him, ignoring his protests. They were

watching the lights. "It's five minutes out of your busy life, Heath. Relax. The moment it's over, we'll head back to the hotel, okay?"

With a sigh, he stopped protesting and took his place beside her. It wasn't long before the tower went dark and the spectacular dance of sparkling lights lit up the steel structure. It twinkled like something out of a fairy tale. Heath put his arm around her shoulder and she slipped into the nook of his arm, sighing with contentment.

Heath might be uncomfortable here because this was where their relationship had changed permanently, but Julianne was happy to be back. This had been the moment where she was the happiest. The moment she'd allowed herself to really love Heath for the first time. She'd been fighting the feelings for months. Once he said he loved her, there was no more holding back. It had been one of those beautiful moments, as if they'd been in a movie, where everything is perfect and romantic.

It was later that everything went wrong.

The lights finally stopped and the high beams returned to illuminate the golden goddess from the base. Julianne turned and found Heath looking at her instead of the tower. There was something in his eyes in that moment that she couldn't quite put her finger on. She knew what she wanted to see. What she wanted to happen. If this *had* been a movie, Heath would have taken her into his arms and kissed her with every ounce of passion in his body. Then he would have said he loved her and that he didn't want a divorce.

But this was real life. Instead, the light in his eyes faded. He politely offered her his arm and they turned and continued down the path to the sidewalk that would lead them back to the Seine. Julianne swallowed her disappointment and tried to focus on the positives of the evening instead of the fantasy she'd built in her head.

As they neared the river, the cool night air off the water made Julianne shiver. The gold wrap was more decorative than functional.

"Here," Heath said, slipping out of his coat and holding it for her. "Put this on."

"Thank you," Julianne replied, accepting the jacket. "It's quite a bit cooler than it was when we went to dinner." She snuggled into the warm, soft fabric, the scent of Heath's skin and cologne comingling in the air surrounding her. It instantly brought to mind the hot nights they'd spent together over the last few weeks. The familiar need curled in her belly, urging her to reach for him and tell him to take her back to the hotel so she could make love to him.

Despite the night chill, her cheeks flooded with warmth. She no longer needed the coat, but she kept it on anyway. As much as she craved his touch, she wasn't in a hurry to end this night. The sky was clear and sparkling with a sprinkle of stars. The moon hung high and full overhead. After the emotionally trying few weeks they'd had, they were sharing a night together in Paris. She wouldn't rush that even to make love to Heath.

They stopped on the bridge and looked out at the moon reflecting on the water. It was such a calm, clear night, the water was like glass. In the distance, she could hear street performers playing jazz music. Heath was beside her. For the first time in a long time, Julianne felt a sense of peace. Here, there were no detectives asking questions, no family to accommodate, no unfinished art projects haunting her and no dead men chasing her in her dreams. It was just the two of them in the most romantic city in the world.

"Do you remember when we put the lock on the Pont des Arts bridge?"

Heath nodded. The bridge was farther down the Seine near the Louvre. It was covered in padlocks that had couples' names and dates written on them. Some couples came on their wedding day with special engraved locks. Others bought them from street vendors on the spur of the moment, like they had. The man had loaned them a marker to write "Heath and Julianne Forever." They'd put the lock on the bridge and threw the key into the river before heading to the train station and leaving Paris for Spain. The idea was that you were sealing your relationship forever. Perhaps that was why she couldn't fully let go of him.

"I wonder if it's still there."

"I doubt it," he said. "I read that they cut locks off or remove entire panels of the fence at night. It's been eleven years. I'm sure our lock is long gone."

Julianne frowned at the water. That wasn't the answer she was looking for. A part of her was thinking they would be able to walk down to the bridge and find it. That they might be overcome with emotions at seeing it firmly clasped to the fence, never to be unlocked, and they would finally be able to triumph over the obstacles that were keeping them apart.

Yes, because that's exactly what she needed to do when her divorce was virtually finalized. But if she were honest with herself, if she let her tightly clamped down emotions free like she did that night in Paris all those years ago, she had to admit nothing had changed. She still loved Heath. She had always loved him. It was her love for him that had forced her to push him away so he could have a real chance at happiness. And it was her love for him that wouldn't let her cut the cord that tied them together. She didn't need a lock to do that.

Heath had accused her of commitment-phobia, of using their marriage to keep men away. But that wasn't the whole truth. The whole truth was that she could never love any of those men. How could she? Her heart belonged to Heath and had since elementary school.

"That makes me sad," she admitted to the dark silence around them. "I was hoping that somehow our lock would last even though we didn't. Our love should still be alive here in Paris, just like it was then."

Heath reached for her hand and held it tight. He didn't say anything, but he didn't have to. The warm comfort of his touch was enough. She didn't expect him to feel the same way. She'd thrown his feelings back in his face and never told him why. He'd asked for a divorce, so despite their mutual attraction and physical indulgence over the last few weeks, that was all he felt for her. He'd carried the torch for her far longer than he should have, so she couldn't begrudge him finally putting it down. Telling Heath she had feelings for him *now*, after all this time, would be like rubbing salt in the wound.

Instead of focusing on that thought, she closed her eyes and enjoyed the feel of Heath's touch. In a few weeks, even that would be gone. Carrying on their physical relationship after the divorce wasn't a good idea. They were divorcing so Heath could move on with his life. Find a woman who could love him the way he deserved to be loved. Maybe take his mystery woman to the Caribbean. For that to happen, she couldn't keep stringing him along. She had to let him go.

She needed to make the most of the time they had left and indulge her heart's desires. And tonight, she intended to indulge in the fancy, king-sized bed of their hotel suite. She wanted the passionate, romantic night in Paris that she couldn't have when they were young and in love.

Julianne opened her eyes and turned to look at Heath. His gaze met hers, a similar sadness there although he hadn't voiced it. He probably thought they were mourning their marriage together in the place where it started. That was the smart thing for her to do. To appreciate what they had and to let it go once and for all.

She pressed her body to his side and with the help of her stilettos, easily tilted her head up to whisper into his ear. "Take me home."

Ten

Heath opened the door to their suite and Julianne stepped inside ahead of him. In a bucket by the seating area was a bottle of Champagne with a note. Julianne plucked the white card from the bottle and scanned the neat script.

"Madame Badeau has sent us a bottle of Champagne. She's not quite the cougar you warned me about, Heath."

Heath was slipping out of his coat jacket and tugging at his tie when he turned to look at her. "She told me earlier tonight that she could see we had a rare and precious love."

Julianne's eyes widened at him, but he didn't notice. He was too busy chuckling and shaking his head.

"Boy, did we have her fooled. I think she's finally given up on me."

She swallowed the lump in her throat and cast the card onto the table. A woman she'd known less than a day could see what Heath refused to see. "Spoils to the victor," she replied, trying to keep the bitter tone from her voice. "Open it while I change."

He walked over to take the bottle from her. When she heard the loud pop of the cork, she moved the two crystal flutes closer to him and took a few steps away to watch as he poured.

As many times as they had been together over the last few weeks, there hadn't been much fanfare to their love-making. No seduction. No temptation. It hadn't been as frantic as that first night in the shower, but they wanted each other too badly to delay their desires. But tonight she wanted to offer him a night in Europe they'd never forget, this time, for all the right reasons.

Heath set down the bottle and picked up the flutes filled with golden bubbly liquid. His gaze met hers, but instead of approaching him, she smiled softly and let her gold wrap fall to the floor. She reached for the zipper at her side, drawing it down the curve of her waist and swell of her hip. His gaze immediately went to the intimate flash of her skin now exposed and the conspicuous absence of lingerie beneath it.

Julianne knew the exact moment he realized she hadn't been wearing panties all evening. He swallowed hard and his fingers tightened around the delicate crystal stems of the glasses. His chest swelled with a deep breath before his gaze met hers again. There was a hard glint of desire there. He might not love her any longer, but there was no question that he wanted her. The intensity of his gaze stole the breath from her lungs.

Drawing in a much-needed lungful of cool air, she turned her back to Heath and strolled into the bedroom. Her fingertips curled around the hem of her dress, pulling it up and over her head. Her hair spilled back down around her shoulders, tickling her bare shoulder blades. She tossed the dress across the plush chaise and turned around.

Heath had followed her into the bedroom. He stood just

inside the doorway, clutching the glasses in an attempt to keep control. She was surprised he hadn't snapped the delicate stems in half. Julianne stalked across the room toward him, naked except for her gold jewelry and the five-inch heels she was still wearing. She stopped just in front of him. She reached past the glasses to the button of his collar. Her nimble fingers made quick work of his shirt, moving down the front until she could part the linen and place her palms on the hard, bare muscles of his chest.

He stood stone still as she worked, his eyes partly closed when she touched him. He reopened them at last when she took one of the glasses from him and held it up for a toast.

"To Paris," she said.

"To Paris," Heath repeated, his voice low and strained. He didn't drink; he just watched Julianne as she put the Champagne to her lips and took a healthy sip.

"Mmm..." she said, her eyes focused only on him. "This is good. I know what would make it better, though."

Leaning into Heath, she held up her flute and poured a stream of the Champagne down his neck. Moving quickly, she lapped at the drops that ran down his throat and pooled in the hollow of his collarbone. She let her tongue drag along his neck, meeting the rough stubble of his five o'clock shadow and feeling the low growl rumbling in his throat.

"You like that?" she asked.

Heath's arm shot out to wrap around her bare waist and tug her body close. Startled, Julianne smacked hard against the wall of his chest, pressing her breasts into him. She could feel the cool moisture of the Champagne on his skin as it molded to hers. When she looked up, he had a wicked grin across his face.

"Oh, yeah," he said. He took a sip of Champagne and then brought his lips to hers. The bubbly liquid filled her own mouth and danced around her tongue before she swallowed it.

Their mouths were still locked onto one another as Heath walked her slowly back toward the bed. With his arm still hooked around the small of her back, he eased Julianne's body down slowly until she met with the cool silky fabric of the duvet.

He pulled away long enough to look longingly at her body and whip off his shirt. Then he poured the rest of the Champagne into the valley between her breasts. He cast the empty flute onto the soft carpet with a thud and dipped his head to clean up the mess he'd made. His tongue slid along her sternum, teasing at the inner curves of her breasts and down to her ribcage. He used his fingertip to dip into her navel and then rub the Champagne he found there over the hardened peaks of her nipples. He bathed them in the expensive alcohol, then took his time removing every drop from her skin.

Julianne arched into his mouth and his hands, urging him on and gasping aloud as he sucked hard at her breast. Her own empty Champagne flute rolled from her hand across the mattress. She brought her hands to his head, burying her fingers in his thick hair and tugging him closer. He resisted her pull, moving lower down her stomach to the dripping golden liquid that waited for him there. His searing lips were like fire across her Champagne-chilled skin. She ached for him to caress every part of her and he happily complied.

Heath's hands pressed against her inner thighs, easing them apart and slipping between them and out of her reach. She had to clutch handfuls of the luxurious linens beneath them to ground herself to the earth as his mouth found her heated core. His tongue worked over her sensitive skin, drawing a chorus of strangled cries from her throat. He was relentless, slipping a finger inside of her until she came undone.

"Heath!" she gasped, her body undulating and pulsing with the pleasure surging through her. She hadn't wanted to find her release without him, not tonight, but he didn't give her the option. She collapsed back against the mattress, her muscles tired and her lungs burning.

She pried open her eyes when she felt the heat of Heath's body moving up over her again. He had shed the last of his clothing, his skin gliding bare along hers.

A moment later, his hazel eyes were staring down into her own. She could feel the firm heat of his desire pressing against her thigh. Eleven years ago this moment had sent her scrambling. The need and nerves in Heath's loving gaze had twisted horribly in her mind to the vicious leer of her attacker. Now there were only the familiar green and gold starbursts of the eyes she fantasized about.

She reached out to him, her palms making contact with the rough stubble of his cheeks. She pulled his mouth to hers and lost herself in him. Instead of fear, there was a peace and comfort in Heath's arms. When he surged forward and filled her aching body with his, she gasped against his mouth but refused to let go. She needed this, needed him.

Julianne drew her legs up, cradling his hips and drawing him deeper inside. She wanted to get as close to him as she could. To take in Heath and keep a part of him there inside her forever. The clock was ticking on their time together, but she could have this.

As the pace increased, Heath finally had to tear away from her lips. He buried his face in her neck, his breath hot and ragged as he thrust hard and fast. Her body, which had been exhausted mere moments ago, was alive and tingling with sensation once again. Her release built inside, her muscles tightening and straining like a taut rubber band as she got closer and closer. Heath's body was equally tense beneath her fingertips, a sheen of perspiration forming on his skin.

"I've never...wanted a woman...as much as I want you, Julianne."

His words were barely a whisper in her ear amongst the rough gasps and rustling sheets, but she heard them and felt them to her innermost core. Her heart stuttered in her chest. It wasn't a declaration of love, but it was serious. She couldn't remember the last time he'd used her full name when he spoke to her. And then it hit her and she knew why his words impacted her so greatly. When he'd said their wedding vows.

I take thee, Julianne Renee Eden, to be my lawfully wedded wife from this day forward.

The words from the past echoed in her mind, the image of the boy he was back then looking at her with so much love and devotion in his eyes. No one had ever looked at her like that again. Because no one had ever loved her the way he did. She might have ruined it, but she had his love once and she would cherish that forever.

"Only you," she whispered. "I've only ever wanted you."

There was the slightest hesitation in his movement, and then he thrust inside of her like never before. For a moment, she wondered what that meant, but before she could get very far with her thoughts, her body tugged her out of her own head. The band snapped inside and the rush of pleasure exploded through her. She gasped and cried into his shoulder, clutching him tightly even as he kept surging forward again and again.

"Julianne," he groaned as his whole body shuddered with his own release.

With Heath's face buried in her neck and their hearts beating a rapid tattoo together, she wanted to say the words. It was the right moment to tell him that she loved him. That she wanted to throw their divorce papers out the window and be with him. To confess the truth about what had happened on their wedding night and explain that it wasn't a lack of loving him, but that she was too damaged to give herself to anyone. It had taken years of therapy to get where she was now. She couldn't have expected him to wait for her.

But she knew telling him the whole truth would hurt him more than his imagined insults. All the boys carried a burden of being unable to protect her, but Heath most of all. If Heath knew that the end for Tommy had come too late…that he had already pillaged her thirteen-year-old innocence before he arrived, he would be devastated. Their marriage would no longer be his biggest regret; that moment would replace it and he would be reminded of it every time he looked at her.

Julianne wanted Heath to look at her with desire and passion. She didn't dare ask for love. But if he knew the truth, he would see her as a victim. He would know the full extent of the damage Tommy had caused and that would be all he would see. Could he make love to her without thinking about it?

Julianne squeezed her eyes shut and her mouth with them. She couldn't tell him. She couldn't tell anyone. No matter how much she loved Heath and how badly he deserved to know the truth, the price of voicing the words was too high. She'd rather he believe she was a flighty, spoiled little girl who couldn't decide what she wanted and stomped on his heart like a ripe tomato.

Heath rolled onto his side and wrapped his arm around her waist. He tugged her body against his, curling her into the protective cocoon to keep her warm. Even now, without realizing it, he was trying to protect her. Just like he always had.

Heath could never ever know that he'd failed that day.

The drive back to Cornwall from Hartford was long and quiet. Heath wasn't entirely sure what was going on with Julianne, but she'd barely spoken a word since they'd departed Paris earlier that morning. How was it that their relationship didn't seem to work on U.S. soil?

They pulled up at the bunkhouse and stumbled inside with their bags. It had been a long day, even traveling by private jet. The sun was still up but it was late into the night on Parisian time.

Heath was pulling the door shut behind him when he nearly slammed into Julianne's back. She had stopped short, her bags still in her arms, her gaze fixed firmly on the kitchen table.

"What is it?" he asked, leaning to one side to look around her. She didn't answer, but she didn't have to. Molly had brought in an overnighted package and left it on the table for them. The same type of packaging the divorce papers had originally arrived in. That only brought one option to mind. The thirty-day waiting period was up. A judge had signed the papers and her lawyer had mailed them.

They were divorced.

Just like that. After eleven years, their relationship was possibly better than it had ever been and they were divorced. Heath took a deep breath and closed his eyes. He wanted this. He had asked for this. He'd harassed her and demanded his freedom. And now he had what he wanted and he'd never felt so frustrated in his life.

He unceremoniously dropped his bags to the floor and

walked around Julianne to pick up the envelope. It had her name on it, but he opened it anyway. There was probably a similar envelope being held at the front desk of his building, waiting for him to return to Manhattan.

A quick glance inside confirmed his suspicions. With a sad nod, he dropped the papers back to the table. "Welcome home," he said with a dry tone.

"The time went by quickly, didn't it?"

He looked up, surprised at her first words in quite a while. "Time flies when you're having fun."

Julianne's eyes narrowed at him, her lips tightening as she nodded. She didn't look like she was having fun. She also didn't look pleased with him although he had no clue what the problem was.

"Julianne…" he began, but she held up her hand to silence him.

"Don't, Heath. This is what we wanted. I know the last few weeks have muddied the water between us, but it doesn't change the fact that we shouldn't be married. We aren't meant to be together long-term. As you said, we were having fun. But fun is all it was, right?"

Heath swallowed the lump in his throat. That was his intention, but it had started to feel like more. At some point, he had forgotten about the divorce and just focused on being with her. Was he the only one that felt that way? It didn't seem like it at the time. It seemed like she had gotten invested as well. Perhaps that was just Paris weaving its magic spell on their relationship again. "Fun," he muttered.

Julianne brushed past him and pulled her wedding ring off her finger. They were both still wearing them after their weekend charade for Madame Badeau. She placed it on top of the paperwork. "We won't need these anymore."

Even as she said the words, Heath got the feeling that

she didn't mean them. She was unhappy. Her, the girl who slammed the door in his face and told him to move on. When he finally tries, she takes it personally.

"So now what?" he asked. Heath wasn't sure how to proceed from here. Did getting a divorce mean their fling was over? They still had the crush of the Christmas season ahead of them. He wasn't looking forward to the long, cold nights in bed without her.

"I think it's time for me to move back into the big house," she said, although she wouldn't look him in the eye.

"Why?"

"When I spoke with Mom yesterday, she said the live-in nurse would be leaving tomorrow. They were able to move Dad's bed back upstairs since he's getting around well. That means I can have my room back."

"Your studio is out here."

She nodded. "But under the circumstances, I think it might be better if we put some distance between us."

Heath's hands balled into angry fists at his side. It was his idea to move forward with the divorce and yet it still felt like Julianne was breaking up with him all over again. "Why is it that whenever our relationship gets even remotely serious, you run away?"

Her eyes met his, a flash of green anger lighting them. "Run away? I'm not running away. There's nothing to run from, Heath. As I understand it, we were just having some fun and passing the time. I don't know if that qualifies as a relationship."

She was lying. He knew she was lying. She had feelings for him, but she was holding them back. Nothing had changed with her in all these years. She loved him then, just as she loved him now, but she refused to admit it. She always pulled away when it mattered. Yeah, he hadn't confessed that he had developed feelings for her, but what fool would? He'd done it once and got burned pretty badly.

"Why do I get the feeling that you're always lying to me, Jules? Then, now, I never get the whole story."

Her eyes widened. She didn't expect him to call her on it, he could tell. She sputtered a moment before finding her words again. "I-I'm not always lying to you. You know me too well for me to lie."

"You'd think so, and yet you'll look me in the eye and tell me we were just 'having fun.' We've had a lot of sex over the last few weeks, but that's the only barrier I've broken through with you, Jules. You're still keeping secrets."

"You keep your secrets, too, Heath."

"Like what?" he laughed.

"Like the reason why you really wanted a divorce."

Heath had no clue what she was talking about. "And what exactly did I say that was a lie?"

"It may not have been a lie, but you have certainly kept your relationship with that other woman quiet while you were sleeping with me the last few weeks. Now you're free to take her to the Caribbean, right?"

"What woman?"

"The so-called Sweetheart you were gushing at on the phone that day."

"You mean my sixty-three-year-old secretary?" He chuckled, although it wasn't so much out of amusement as annoyance. "I knew you were listening in on my phone call."

"You laid it on pretty thick. Do you really expect me to believe your sweetheart is a woman older than Mom?"

"You should. She likes to be flirted with, so I call her all sorts of pet names. I told her if she held down the fort while I was gone that I would give her a bonus big enough to cover the vacation she wants to take to the beach with her grandkids. Without *me*," he added. "Do you really think I would've pursued something with you while I had a woman on the side?"

Julianne's defiant shoulders slumped a bit at his words. "Then why did you really want the divorce, Heath? You came in here demanding it out of nowhere. I thought for sure you had another woman in mind."

"There's no other woman, Jules. How could there be? I'm not about to get serious with any woman while I'm married to you. That's not fair to her. Just like it wasn't fair to your almost fiancé. You just play with men's minds but you have no intention of ever giving as much as you take. You're right. It's a good thing this was just 'fun' to pass the time. It would be foolish of me to think otherwise and fall for your games twice."

"How dare you!" she said. "You don't know anything about my relationships. You don't know anything about what I've gone through in my life."

"You're right," he said. "Because you won't tell me anything!"

"I have always been as honest as I could be with you, Heath."

"Honest? Really. Then tell me the truth about what happened on our wedding night, Jules. The truth. Not some made-up story about you changing your mind. You were in love with me. You wanted me. The next minute everything changed. Why?"

Julianne stiffened, tears glazing her eyes. Her jaw tightened as though she was fighting to keep the flow of words inside. "Any question but that one," she managed to say.

"That's the only question I want answered. Eleven years I've spent wondering how you could love me one minute and run from me the next. Tell me why. I deserve to know."

Her gaze dropped to the floor. "I can't do that."

"Then you're right, Jules. We shouldn't be married. I'm glad we've finally gotten that matrimonial monkey off our backs. Maybe now I can move on and find a woman who will let me into her life instead of just letting me be a spectator."

"Heath, I—"

"You know," he interrupted, "all I ever wanted from you was for you to let me in. Over the years, I've given you my heart, my soul. I've lied for you. Protected you. I would've gone to jail before I let anyone lay a finger on you. And hell, I still might if Sheriff Duke comes back around. I'd do it gladly. Even now, although I really don't know why. I just don't understand you, Jules. Why do you keep me at arm's length? Even when we're in bed together, you've kept your distance, kept your secrets. Is it me? Or do you treat all men this way?"

Julianne looked back up at him and this time, the tears were flowing freely. It made his chest ache, even as he fought with her, to see her cry that way. But he had to know. Why did she push him away?

"Just you," she said. Then she turned and walked upstairs alone.

<u>Eleven</u>

Julianne sat on the edge of the bed staring at the bags she'd already packed. This morning, she would move back into the big house where she belonged. It broke her heart and made her cry every time she thought about it for too long, but she had to do it. They were divorced. No matter how much she loved him, Heath deserved to be happy. He deserved his freedom and a chance with a woman who could give him everything he wanted.

As much as she wanted to be, Julianne would never be that woman. She would always have her secrets. She would always have a part of herself that she held back from him. Even if she told him it was for his own good, he wouldn't believe her.

After the last few weeks together, she could tell he was confused. It was easy to feel like things were different when they were together so much, but that wouldn't last forever. They'd end up caught in the same circular trap where they'd spent the last eleven years. But she could get them out of it, even if he didn't seem to like it at the time.

He wanted his freedom and she would give it to him.

With a sigh, she stood up and extended the handle of her roller bag. She was nearly to the door of her room when she heard a loud banging at the front door.

She left her luggage behind and went downstairs. The low rumble of male voices turned into distinguishable words as she reached the landing.

"I'm going to have to bring her in for questioning."

"Why? You've asked a million questions. What do you want with her?"

Sheriff Duke was lurking in the door frame, looking larger and more threatening than ever before. "I need to talk to her. We also need a hair sample."

Heath glanced over his shoulder to see Julianne standing at the foot of the stairs. He cursed silently and turned back to the doorway. "Ask her your questions here. And get a warrant for the hair. Otherwise, you have to arrest us both."

"I can't arrest you just because you ask me to, Heath."

"Fine. Then arrest me because I killed Tommy."

Duke's eyes widened for a moment, but he didn't hesitate to reach for his handcuffs. "All right. Heath Langston, you're under arrest for the murder of Thomas Wilder. You have the right…"

The sheriff's voice faded out as the reality of what was happening hit her. Sixteen years' worth of karma was about to fly back in their faces. And to make things worse, Heath had confessed. Why had he confessed?

Duke clamped the cuffs on Heath's wrists and walked him to the back of the squad car.

"Don't say anything, Jules," she heard Heath say before the door slammed shut.

Returning to face Julianne, Duke started his speech again and reached for his second pair of cuffs. She stood silent and still, letting him close the cold metal shackles around her wrists. He took her to the other side of the squad car and sat her there beside Heath.

The ride into town was deadly silent. Anything they said could be used against them, after all. It wasn't until they were led into separate interrogation rooms that the nervous flutter of her stomach started up.

An hour went by. Then two.

She didn't have her watch on, but she was fairly certain that nearly four hours had passed before Sheriff Duke finally came in clutching a file of paperwork. Her stomach was starting to growl, which meant lunchtime had come and gone.

He settled down at the table across from her. No one else was in the room, but she had no idea how many people were gathered on the other side of the one-way glass panel. He flipped through his pages, clicked the button on his pen and looked up at her.

"Heath had a lot to say, Julianne."

She took a deep breath. "About what?" she replied as innocently as she could.

"About killing Tommy."

"I'm not sure why he would say something like that."

"I'm not sure, either. He had a pretty detailed story. If I didn't know better I'd lock him up right now and be done with it."

"Why don't you?"

A smirk crossed the policeman's face and Julianne didn't care for it. He was too pleased, as though he had everything figured out. He was probably already planning to use this big case to bolster his reelection.

"Well, as good a tale as he told me, it just doesn't match

up with the evidence. You see, Heath told me that he found Tommy on top of you and he hit him on the back of his head with a rock to stop him, accidentally killing him."

Julianne didn't blink, didn't breathe, didn't so much as shift her gaze in one direction or another.

"Problem is that the coroner says Tommy was killed instantly by a blow to his left temple."

"I thought they said on the news that Tommy had the back of his head bashed in." She tried to remember what she had seen on television. That's what the reports had said. Only she knew that injury came second. She didn't know if he was already dead by then or not.

"He did. But we don't release all the critical information to the news. Like the hair we found."

"Hair?" She hadn't heard anything about hair, either.

"You'd think that after all these years that any evidence would be destroyed, and most of it was, but we were lucky. Tommy died with a few strands of long blond hair snagged on the ring he was wearing. Hair and bone are usually all that's left after this length of time. It was as though he'd had a handful of a woman's hair in his hand shortly before he died."

"There are a lot of blondes in Cornwall."

"That's true, but Heath has already stated he saw Tommy on top of you, so that's narrowing it down for me."

"You said you didn't believe his story."

"I said it didn't match the coroner's report. And it doesn't. So that made me think perhaps he was protecting you. That made a lot of the pieces click together in my mind. Why don't you just save me the trouble and tell me the truth, Julianne. You don't really want me to charge Heath with Tommy's murder do you?"

"It wouldn't be murder," she argued. "It would be self-defense."

"Not exactly. He wasn't being threatened, just you. It might have been accidental, but his lawyers will need to prove it. There's nothing that says he didn't come up on Tommy in the woods and bludgeon him for no reason."

Julianne swallowed the lump in her throat. She wouldn't let Heath take the blame for this. She just couldn't. He'd always told her it wouldn't come to this, but if it did, he wouldn't be charged because he was protecting her. The sadistic gleam in Sheriff Duke's eyes made her think Heath might be wrong about that. Heath wouldn't spend a single day in jail protecting her. This had all gone on far too long. Keeping him out of prison was far more important than protecting his ego.

"I'm the one that killed Tommy. He..." She fought for the words she'd only said aloud a few times in her therapist's office. "He raped me," she spat out.

Sheriff Duke's eyes widened for a moment and he sat back into his chair. He didn't speak, but he reached over to check his voice recorder to make sure it caught everything.

She took a moment trying to decide where to go from there. "I was doing my chores after school. Same as any other day. The next thing I knew, Tommy was there, watching me. I was startled at first, but I thought I would be okay. Until he pulled out a switchblade and started walking toward me. I ran, but he grabbed my ponytail and yanked me back. I fell onto the ground and he was on top of me in an instant.

"He was so large. Bigger than my brothers. I was only thirteen and smaller than other girls my age. There was no way to fight him off. He had the knife at my throat so I couldn't scream. I kicked and fought at first, but he grabbed a fistful of my hair and yanked hard enough to bring tears to my eyes. He said if I didn't keep still, he'd cut my throat and leave my body naked for my daddy to find me."

Julianne's hands started trembling. The metal of the handcuffs tapped against the tabletop, so she pulled her arms back to rest in her lap. Her eyes focused on the table instead of the man watching her.

"I knew in the pit of my stomach that I was dead. No matter what he said, he wasn't going to let me run to my parents or the police. He would finish this and me before he was done. I tried to keep my focus and ignore the pain. It would've been so easy to tune everything out, but I knew that I couldn't. I knew that eventually, he'd get distracted and I would have my one and only chance to escape.

"I was able to slowly feel along the ground beside me. At first, there was nothing but pea gravel. I could've thrown that in his eyes, but it would have only made him angry. Then I found a rock. It was small but dense with a sharp edge I could feel with my fingertips. He still had the knife at my throat and if it wasn't enough to knock him out, I knew it was all over, but I didn't care. I had to do it. I brought the rock up and slammed it into the side of his head as hard as I could."

Julianne had seen this image in her dreams a thousand times so it was easy to describe even after all this time. "His eyes rolled into his head and he collapsed onto me. I struggled as quickly as I could to push him up and off of me. When I was finally able to shove him off, his head flung back and struck a rock sticking up out of the ground. That's when he started bleeding. I panicked. I kicked the knife away from him and started pulling my clothes back on. That's when Heath found me.

"We kept waiting for Tommy to get up, but he didn't. That's when we realized that hitting his head on the rock must have killed him. There was so much blood on the ground. He told me to sit tight while he went for help. He came back with the other boys. The rest was a blur, but I heard him tell the others that he'd hit Tommy with the rock when he saw him attacking me. There were so many times that we should've stopped and gone to the house to call the police, but we were so scared. In the end, all they wanted to do was protect me. And they did. None of them deserve to get in trouble for that."

"What about the note Tommy left? And all his things that were missing?"

"We did that," she said, not mentioning one brother or another specifically. "We were running on adrenaline, reacting faster than we could think. We hid the body, destroyed all his stuff and tried to pretend like it never happened."

"That didn't exactly work out for you, did it?"

Julianne looked up at the sheriff. He didn't seem even remotely moved by her story. He tasted blood and no matter what she said, she was certain he wasn't going to just close the case based on her testimony. "It's hard to pretend you haven't been raped, Sheriff Duke."

"And yet you waited all these years to come forward. It seems to me like you're hiding something. I think—"

A loud rap on the one-way glass interrupted him. Duke's jaw tightened and he closed the folder with his paperwork. "I'll be back," he said. He got up and left the room.

Julianne wasn't certain what had happened, but she was relieved for the break. It took a lot out of her to tell that story. Whether or not he backed down and dismissed the charges as self-defense, she knew she would have to tell that story again. And again. A part of her was terrified, but another part of her felt liberated. This secret had been like a concrete block tied around her neck. She knew it had to feel the same way to the others.

Maybe, finally, they could all stop living with the dark cloud of Tommy's death over their heads.

They sure were slow to book him. Heath had spent hours waiting for the inevitable. He'd told them he killed Tommy. Certainly the wheels of progress should be turning by now.

Not long after that, the door opened and Sheriff Duke's deputy, Jim, came through the door. "You can go."

"What?" He stood up from his chair. "I can go?"

Jim came over and unlocked the handcuffs. "Yes." He opened the door and held it.

Heath was thoroughly confused, but he wasn't about to wait for them to change their minds. In the hallway, he found several people waiting there. He recognized the woman as Tommy Wilder's sister, Deborah Curtis. Brody had sent them all the background report on her when she came to Cornwall asking about her brother. She was standing there with a man wearing an expensive tailored suit. He carried himself like he was important somehow, like he was her lawyer. Heath froze on the spot. Was she here to confront him for killing her brother?

Another door opened off the hallway and Julianne stepped out with a disgusted-looking Sheriff Duke at her side.

"What is going on?" Heath asked.

Julianne shook her head. "I have no clue. Duke said I was free to go."

The man beside Deborah stepped forward. "My name is Pat Richards. I'm a prosecutor for the state of Connecticut. With the evidence I have, your testimony and that of Mrs. Curtis, the state has opted not to press charges. This situation was tragic, but obviously in self-defense. I can't in good conscience prosecute Julianne after everything she went through."

Heath frowned. "Prosecute Julianne? I'm the one that confessed to killing him."

Pat smiled wide and nodded in understanding. "A noble thing, for sure, but it wasn't necessary. The charges have been dropped. You're both free to go."

Sheriff Duke shook his head and disappeared down the hallway into his office with a slam of his door.

"He disagrees, I take it?"

The prosecutor chuckled. "He fancied himself the hero cracking a huge case. There's not much crime around here for him to tackle, and this would give him the boost for his reelection. But even without Mrs. Curtis's testimony of her own attack, there was nothing for us to go forward on."

"What?" This time the question came from Julianne.

Deborah stepped forward, speaking for the first time. "I want you to know that I don't harbor any ill will against you or your family. You took Tommy in when no one else would and did only what you had to do to defend yourself. I completely understand that. My brother started displaying violent tendencies before he was even twelve years old. My parents tried to control him. They punished him, they put him in therapy. They even considered one of the boot camps for troubled teens. But it wasn't until my father came home early from work one day and caught him... attacking me..."

Julianne gasped, bringing her hand to cover her mouth. "Oh, god." Heath wanted to go to her side, but he resisted. Despite what had happened, she might still be upset with him.

"Tommy didn't succeed," Deborah said, "but he would've raped me if my father hadn't come home. I didn't want to press charges, I was too embarrassed. After that, he wasn't allowed to be alone with me. His close call didn't stop him from getting in trouble, though. He was constantly getting picked up for one thing or another. He even did a few weeks in juvie. Eventually the state removed him from the home as a repeat juvenile offender and I tried to forget it ever happened." She shook her head. "I never dreamed he would try to do it again. I feel awful."

"Mrs. Curtis's story was so similar to Julianne's that there was no reason to believe she wasn't telling the truth. The forensic evidence supported her version of his death. There's not a grand jury that would indict her. Anything that happened after the fact is well past the statute of limitations." Pat looked down the hall at the sheriff's office and shook his head. "Sheriff Duke might not be happy, but the only real crime here was committed by the deceased a long time ago. As much as I'd like to, I can't charge a dead man with second-degree sexual assault."

The words hung in the air for a moment. Heath let them sink into his mind. Pat meant *attempted* sexual assault, right? Attempted. Julianne had sworn that Tommy hadn't... And yet, why would a traumatized young girl want to tell him something like that? She wouldn't.

And then it hit him like he'd driven his Porsche into a brick wall. In an instant, every moment made sense. Every reaction Julianne ever had. Their wedding night...

How could he have missed this? It was so obvious now that he felt like a fool. And a first-class ass. He'd believed what she told him despite all the signs indicating otherwise. All these years he'd been angry with her while she'd carried this secret on her own.

"I'm going to have a talk with the local child services agency. There is a major breach in conduct if they didn't share the information about Deborah's assault with Mr. and Mrs. Eden before they placed Tommy there. They might not have taken him in if they'd known." The phone on Pat's hip rang and he looked down at the screen. "If you'll excuse me," he said, disappearing through the double doors.

After a few silent, awkward moments, Deborah spoke again, this time to Julianne. "Mr. Richards and I were listening in the observation room while you told your story," she said. "You are so much braver than I ever could have been. I'm sorry I wasn't stronger. If I had been, I would've pressed charges or talked to people about what happened and this might never have happened to you."

Julianne approached Deborah and embraced her. The two women held each other for a moment. "This is not your fault. Don't you ever think that. I've kept this a secret, too. It's hard to tell people the truth, even though you didn't do anything wrong."

When Julianne pulled away, Deborah dabbed her eyes with a tissue and sniffed. "You know, I came back to Cornwall to track down Tommy, but I wasn't looking for a happy family reunion. My therapist had recommended I find him so I could confront my fears and move on. He had vanished, but I expected him to be in jail or working at a gas station in the middle of nowhere. This," she said, waving her hand around, "was more than I ever planned to uncover. But it's better, I think. I don't have to be afraid of Tommy anymore. He's never going to show up on my doorstep and he'll never be able to hurt me or my little girl. I'm happy I was able to help with your case, too. It makes me feel like I have more power and control over my life than ever before."

Heath stood quietly while the two women spoke. He had so many things he wanted and needed to say to Julianne, but now wasn't the time. They eventually moved down the hallway, making their way out of the police station.

He was relieved to step outside. It was cold, but the sun

was shining. It was like an omen; Noah's rainbow signaling that all of this was finally over. They no longer had to worry about the police coming after them. It was in the past now, where it belonged.

At least most of it. With the truth out, the papers would no doubt pick up the story. They needed to sit down with Mom and Dad and tell them what had happened before some woman cornered Molly at the grocery store. Hopefully Ken's heart could withstand the news now that the threat of his children's incarceration was behind them.

Heath whipped out his phone to text his brothers, but found that wasn't enough. He needed to call them. He and Julianne both, to share the news. He wished he could give Julianne time to prepare, but the truth was out. They had protected her as well as they could over the years, but now she would have to tell her story. First to her family, then to the public. Perhaps after all this time, the blow of it would soften. He couldn't imagine the tiny, thirteen-year-old Julianne talking to police and reporters about killing her attacker. Her *rapist*.

His stomach still ached painfully at that thought. If he had only come across the two of them a few minutes sooner. He might have stopped Tommy before he could have… He sighed and shoved his hands into his pockets. He already believed he failed to protect Julianne, but he had no idea the extent of the damage that was caused. And by keeping Tommy's death a secret, they had virtually forced her to keep the rape a secret as well, and hadn't even known it. Had their attempt to protect her only made it worse?

The bile started to rise in the back of his throat. She should have been taken to the doctor. To a therapist. She should've been able to cry in her mother's arms and she was never able to do any of that.

His knees started to weaken beneath him, so Heath moved quickly to sit on the steps. He would wait there until Julianne and Deborah were done talking. Maybe by then, he could pull himself together.

After a while, Deborah embraced Julianne again, and then she made her way down the sidewalk to her car. Julianne watched her walk away and then finally turned to look at him. It was the first time she'd done that since they'd all gathered inside the police station. She walked over to the steps and sat down beside him.

Minutes passed before either of them spoke. They had shared so much together, and yet when it came to the important things, they knew almost nothing about each other.

"Thank you," she said at last.

That was the last thing he ever expected her to say. "Why on earth would you be thanking me right now?"

"Thank you for loving me," she elaborated. "No matter what we've said or done to each other over the years, when it was important, you were there for me. You probably don't think so, but the truth is that you would have gone to jail for me today. You've spent the last sixteen years covering for me, even lying to your own brothers about what happened that day. You looked Sheriff Duke in the eye and told him you killed Tommy, consequences be damned. How many people are lucky enough to have someone in their life that is willing to do that for them?"

"That's what families do. They protect each other." He watched the traffic drift by the main thoroughfare for a moment. He couldn't turn to face her while he spoke or he might give away the fact that his feelings for her ran much deeper than that. No matter what happened between them, he would always love Julianne. He couldn't seem to stop. Knowing the truth only made it harder not to love her more. All his reasons for keeping her at arm's length were nullified. But they were divorced. What did that matter now?

"You went far beyond family obligation, Heath."

"Why didn't you tell me what happened, Jules? You could've told me the truth."

"No," she said, softly shaking the blond curls around her shoulders. "I couldn't. You had me on this pedestal. I couldn't bear for you to know how flawed I was. How broken I was."

"As though what happened was your fault?"

"It wasn't my fault. I know that. But it wasn't your fault, either. If you knew, you would've blamed yourself. And you'd never look at me the same way again. I didn't want to lose that. You were the only person in my life that made me feel special. Mom and Dad loved me, but I always felt like I wasn't enough for them. You only wanted me. I wanted to stay that perfect vision in your mind."

"By making me despise you? You made me stay up nights wondering what I'd done wrong. Christ, I *divorced* you."

Julianne turned to look at him with a soft smile curling her lips. "I tried to push you away, but you still loved me. All this time, that was the one thing I kept hoping would change. I couldn't tell you the truth, so I knew there would always be a barrier between us. I kept hoping you'd move on and find someone who could love you the way you deserved to be loved. The way you loved me."

He shook his head. He didn't want anyone else to love him. All he had ever wanted was for Julianne to love him. And the way she spoke convinced him that she did. Maybe she had all this time, but the secret she kept was too big. It was easier to keep away than be subjected to his constant needling about why she left him. But to push him into another woman's arms *because* she loved him? "I still don't understand what you're thinking sometimes, Jules."

"I know." She patted his knee and stood up. "Let's go home. We have some long conversations to have with the family."

He got up and followed her to the street. She was right. And he had one important conversation with Ken in mind that she wouldn't be expecting.

Twelve

It was over. Good and truly over.

Julianne slipped into her coat and went out onto the porch to gather herself. The last hour had been harder than confessing the truth to Sheriff Duke. Looking her parents in the eye and telling them everything had been excruciating. Not for her, but she hated to burden them with the truth.

They had taken it better than she expected. Ken got quiet and shook his head, but his color was good and he remained stable. When it was over he'd hugged her tighter than he'd ever hugged her in her entire life. Molly cried a lot. Julianne expected that she would continue to for a while. Her mother was a mother hen. Knowing that had happened to her children under her watch would eat at her for a long time. Maybe always. But Julianne assured her that she was okay, it was a long time ago, and it seemed to calm her.

As she stepped onto the gravel lot behind the house, Julianne looked out at the trees. She had loved being out there once but hadn't set foot in the fields in sixteen years. The boogeyman was long gone. Most of her own personal demons had been set loose today. She took a deep breath and headed for the north field. That was where she'd been that day. If she were going to face this, she needed to go there.

It didn't take long to find the spot, but it took a while to walk out there. The trees were different, always changing as they were harvested and replanted. There were no monsters in the trees, no men to chase her, but she could feel the change in the weight on her chest as she got closer. While Wade had hidden the body and Brody took her to shower and change, Heath and Xander had cleaned up the scene. The rock she'd hit him with was flung into the far reaches of the property. The pool of blood was long gone. But when she looked, she could still see it all.

That's when the first snowflake drifted past her face. One flake became ten, became a thousand. In only a few minutes' time, the tree branches were dusted with white and the bloodstain in her mind slowly disappeared beneath a layer of snow.

It was a perfect moment. A pure, white cleansing of her past. She tipped her face up, feeling the tiny prickles of flakes melting on her cheeks, and sucked in a deep, cold breath.

Over.

Julianne turned her back to the scene of her attack, putting it behind her with everything else, and started walking in the opposite direction, through the fields. For the first time since she was thirteen, she could enjoy the moment. The snow was beautiful, drifting slowly down into fluffy clumps on the branches. The flakes were getting fatter, some larger than nickels. They would have several inches sticking before too long.

She climbed up the slope of the back property, looking for her favorite place on the farm. Somehow she expected it to have changed, but when she finally reached it, everything was just as she remembered. There, jutting out of the side of the hill, was a large, flat rock. She had come out here to sit and think when she was younger. The household was always full of kids and this was a place she could be alone.

Julianne dusted off the snow and sat down on the rock, turning to face the slope of the property laid out in front of her. To the left, she could see the roofline and lights of Wade and Tori's house over the hill. In front of her was the whole of the Garden of Eden. Her own little paradise.

It was nearing sunset, but the fat, gray clouds blocked out the color of the sky. The light was fading, but she could still make out the rows of trees stretching in front of her. The big house, with glowing windows and black smoke rising from the chimney, lay beyond it. Then the dark shape of the bunkhouse with Heath's silver Porsche out front.

Heath. Her ex-husband. Julianne sighed and snuggled deeper into her coat. With Sheriff Duke's unexpected arrival, she hadn't had much time to process her new marital status. While they had come clean about Tommy, they had deliberately opted not to tell anyone about the marriage. That was too much for one day. It might not be something they ever needed to tell. What would it matter, really? It only impacted the two of them since they were the only ones aware of it. And since it was done…it would only hurt her family to find out now.

But, like anything else in her life, keeping her feelings inside made it harder to deal with it.

Maybe if she hadn't come back to stay in Cornwall she

would feel differently about her freedom. If she hadn't made love to him. If they hadn't gone to Paris together. If the last month and a half never happened she might feel relieved and ready to move on her with life.

But it *had* happened. She had let herself get closer to Heath than she ever had in the eleven years of their marriage and then it was all done. How was she supposed to just walk away? How was she going to learn to stop loving him? Eleven years apart hadn't done it. Was she doomed to another eleven years of quiet pining for him?

In the gathering darkness, Julianne noticed a dancing light coming up the main tree lane from the house. The snow had let up a little, making it easier to see the figure was walking toward her with a flashlight. She tensed. She was at a tentative truce with the trees, but she wasn't sure if adding another person would work. It didn't feel as secure as being here alone.

Then she made out the distinctive bright blue of the coat and realized it was Heath. She sighed. Why had he followed her out here? She needed some time alone to mourn their relationship and deal with a hellish day.

Heath stopped a few feet short of the rock, not crowding into her space. "Your rock has missed you."

At that Julianne chuckled. Even Heath remembered how much time she had spent sitting in this very spot when they were kids. "Fortunately, time is relative to a rock."

"I still feel bad for it. I know I couldn't go that long without you in my life."

The light atmosphere between then shifted. Her gaze lifted to meet his, her smile fading. "Life doesn't always work out the way you plan. Even for a rock."

"I disagree. Life might throw obstacles in your path, but if you want something with your whole heart and soul, you have to fight for it. Nothing that's easy is worth having and nothing worth having is easy. You, Julianne, have been incredibly difficult."

"I'm going to take that as a compliment."

He smiled. "You should. I meant it as one. You're worth every moment of pain and frustration and confusion I've gone through. And I think, perhaps, that we might have weathered the trials. In every fairy tale, the prince and the maiden have obstacles to triumph over and strengthen their love. I think the evil villain has been defeated. I'm ready for the happy ending."

It sounded good. Really, it did. But so much had happened. Could they really ever get back to a happy ending? "Life isn't a fairy tale, Heath. We're divorced. I've never read a story where the prince and his princess divorce."

"Yeah, but they have angry dragons and evil wizards. I'll take a divorce any day because things can always change. We don't have to stay divorced. We can slay this dragon, if you're willing to face it with me."

She watched as his hand slipped into his coat pocket and retrieved a small box. A jewelry box. Her heart stilled in her chest. What was he doing? They'd been divorced for two days. He wasn't really…he couldn't possibly want this after everything that had happened.

"Heath…" she began.

"Let me say what I need to say," he insisted. "When we were eighteen, we got married for all the wrong reasons. We loved each other but we were young and stupid. We didn't think it through. Life is complicated and we were unprepared for the reality of it. But I also think we got divorced for all the wrong reasons."

Heath crouched down at the foot of the rock, looking up at her. "I love you. I've always loved you. I never imagined my life or my future without you in it. I was hurt that you wouldn't open up to me and I used our divorce to punish you for it. Now, I understand why you held back. And I realized that everything you did that hurt me was also meant to somehow protect me.

"You said at the police station today that I was willing to go to jail for you. And you were right. I was willing to take on years of misery behind bars to protect you. Just as you were willing to give me a divorce and face a future alone in the hopes that I could find someone to make me happy."

"That's not the same," she insisted.

"A self-imposed prison is just as difficult to escape as one of iron and stone, Jules." He held up the box and looked her square in the eye. "Consider this a jailbreak."

"Are you honestly telling me that between Parisian jet lag, getting divorced, getting arrested and spending all day at the police station, you had the time to go to the jeweler and buy an engagement ring?"

"No," he said.

Julianne instantly felt foolish. Had she misinterpreted the whole thing? If there were earrings in that box she would feel like an idiot. "Then what is going on? If you're not proposing, what are you doing?"

"I am proposing. But you asked if I went to a jeweler and I didn't. I went to talk to Ken."

Julianne swallowed hard. "We agreed we weren't going to tell them about us."

"Correction. We agreed not to tell them we were married before. You said nothing about telling him that I was in love with you and wanted his blessing to marry you. No one needs to know it's round two for us."

She winced, torn between her curiosity about what was in the box, her elation about his confession of love and how her daddy had taken the news. "What happened?" she asked.

Heath smiled wide, easing her concerns. "He asked me

what the hell had taken so long. And then he gave me this."
He opened the hinge on the box to reveal the ring inside.

It couldn't be. Julianne's jaw dropped open. The large round diamond, the eight diamonds encircling it, the intricate gold lacework of the dull, worn band… It was her grandmother's wedding ring. She hadn't seen this ring since she was a small child and Nanna was still alive.

Heath pulled the ring from the box and held it up to her. "The last ring I gave you was cheap and ugly. This time, I have enough money to buy you any ring you'd like, but I wanted a ring that meant something. Ken told me that they had been saving this ring in the hopes that one day it would be your engagement ring. He knew how much you loved your nanna and thought this would be perfect. I was inclined to agree.

"Julianne Eden, will you marry me *again?*"

Heath was kneeling in the snow, freezing and holding his breath. Julianne took far too long to answer. Her expression changed faster than he could follow. At first, she'd stared at that ring like he was holding up a severed head. Then her expression softened and she seemed on the verge of tears. After that, she'd gone stony and silent. Waiting more than a beat or two to answer a question like this was really bad form.

"Yes."

And then his heart leapt in his chest. "Yes?"

Julianne smiled, her eyes brimming with tears. "Yes, I will marry you again."

Heath scrambled to slip the ring onto her finger. It flopped around a bit. "I'm sorry it's too big. We'll get it sized down as soon as we can get to a jeweler."

"That's okay. Nanna was Daddy's mother and I take after Mama's side of the family. We're much tinier people." She looked down at the ring and her face was nearly beaming. "I love it. It's more than perfect."

She lunged forward into his arms, knocking him backward into the snow. Before he knew it, he was lying in the cold fluff and Julianne was on top of him, kissing him. Not so bad, after all. He ignored the cold, focusing on the taste of the lips he'd thought he might never kiss again. That was enough to warm his blood and chase off any chill.

Julianne was going to marry him. That just left telling Molly. Even though he now knew that Julianne had never kept their relationship a secret out of embarrassment, the idea shouldn't bother him, but he still felt a nervous tremble in his stomach. A part of him was afraid to say the words. "It's getting dark. Are you ready to head back to the house and tell everyone?"

He expected her to dodge the way she always did, to make some excuse, to say that she wanted to celebrate with just the two of them for now. A part of him would even understand if she wanted to wait until tomorrow after all the drama of the day.

"Absolutely," she said, smiling down at him. "I'm thrilled to give them some good news for a change."

Relief flooded through him, and the last barrier to total bliss was gone. They got up and held hands as they walked back through the trees to the house. When they came in together through the back door, Molly was in the kitchen cooking and Ken was in the living room reading a book.

"Mom, do you have a minute?"

Molly nodded, more focused on the boiling of her potatoes than the clasping of their hands. "Yes, these need to go for a bit longer."

"Come into the living room," Heath said, herding her ahead of them to sit down next to Ken by the fireplace.

Heath and Julianne sat opposite them. He was still holding Julianne's hand for support. She leaned into him, placing her left hand over their clasped ones and inadvertently displaying her ring.

"Mom, Dad…" Heath began.

"What is that?" Molly asked, her eyes glued on Julianne's hand. "Is that an engagement ring? Wait. Is that Nanna's ring?" She turned to Ken with an accusatory glare. "You knew about this and you didn't tell me!"

Ken shrugged. If he got wound up every time Molly did, he would have had twenty heart attacks by now. "He asked for my blessing, so I gave him the ring. That's what you wanted, didn't you? Saving the ring for Jules was your idea."

"Of course it's what I wanted." Molly's emotions seemed to level out as she realized she should be more focused on the fact that Heath and Julianne were engaged. A bright smile lit her face. "My baby is getting married!" She leapt from her chair and gathered Julianne into her arms.

She tugged Heath up from his seat to hug him next. "I didn't even know you two were seeing each other," she scolded. "A heads-up would have been nice before you dropped a marriage bomb on me! Lordy, so much news today. Is there anything else you all need to tell us?"

Heath stiffened in her arms. He was never good at lying to Molly, but Julianne was adamant that their prior marriage stay quiet, no matter what. "Isn't this enough?" he said with a smile.

"Wonderful news," Molly said, her eyes getting misty and far off as her mind drifted. "We'll have the wedding here at the farm," she declared. "It will be beautiful. Everyone in town will want to come. Please don't tell me you want a small affair or destination wedding in Antigua."

Julianne smiled and patted Molly's shoulder. "We'll

have it here, I promise. And it can be as big and fabulous as you can imagine it."

"This time," Heath added, "I think we need to have a grand wedding with the big cake and a swing band."

"This time?" Molly said, her brow furrowed.

Julianne turned to look at him, her green eyes wide with silent condemnation. It wasn't until then that Heath fully realized what he'd said. Damn it. With a shake of her head, Julianne held out her hand, gesturing for him to spill the last of their secrets. They might as well.

"Uh, Mom…" he began. "Julianne and I, uh, eloped when we were eighteen."

Both he and Julianne took a large step backward out of the blast zone. Molly's eyes grew wide, but before she could open her mouth, Ken stood up and clasped her shoulders tightly. It made Heath wonder if it was Ken's subtle restraining of his tiny wife hidden beneath the guise of supportiveness.

Molly's mouth opened, then closed as she took a deep breath to collect her thoughts. "When did this happen?"

"While we were on our European vacation after graduation."

"You two immediately went off to separate schools when you got home," she said with a frown.

"Yeah, we didn't plan that well," Heath admitted. Even if they'd had the perfect honeymoon and had come home blissfully in love they still would have faced the huge obstacles of where they went from there. They were heading to different schools a thousand miles apart. Not exactly the best way to start a marriage, but an ideal way to start a trial separation.

"And how long were you two married? I'm assuming you're divorced now, considering you're engaged again."

This time Heath looked at Julianne. It was her turn to

fess up since they were married that long due to her own procrastination.

"Eleven years. Our divorce was final a couple days ago."

Molly closed her eyes. "I'm not going to ask. I really don't think I want to know. You think you know what's going on in your kids' lives, but you have no clue. You two were married this whole time. Xander and Rose had a baby I never knew about. And to think I believed all of you were too busy with careers and I might never see everyone settled down!"

"We would've told you, Mama, but we pretty much broke up right after we married. We've been separated all this time."

"I think I've had about all the news I can take for one day, good or bad. This calls for a pot of tea, I think. You can let go of me now, Ken." Molly headed for the kitchen, then stopped in the entryway. "I might as well ask...you're not pregnant, are you?"

Julianne shook her head adamantly. "No, Mama. I promise we are not pregnant."

"All right," she said. "You two wash up. It's almost time for supper."

Molly disappeared. Ken clapped Heath on the shoulder as he passed by. In a moment, they were alone with all their secrets out on the table.

"I think it was better this way, don't you?" Heath asked.

"You only think that because you're the one that spilled the beans."

Heath turned to her and pulled Julianne into his arms. "Maybe. But I am happy to start our new life together with no more secrets. Everything is out in the open at last. Right? You've told me all of it?"

Julianne nodded, climbing to her toes to place a kiss on his lips. "Of course, dear."

Heath laughed. "Spoken like a wife filled with secrets she keeps from her husband."

She wrapped her arms around his neck, a naughty grin curling her lips as she looked up at him. "This *is* my second marriage, you'll remember. I'm an old pro at this now."

"Don't think I don't know all your tricks, woman. It's my second marriage, too," Heath noted. "And last."

Julianne smiled. "It better be."

Epilogue

It was a glorious spring day in northwestern Connecticut. The sun was shining on the farm. The delicate centerpieces of roses, hydrangeas, lilies and orchids were warming in the afternoon light, emitting a soft fragrance on the breeze. It was the perfect day for a wedding on the farm; the second in the last six months, with two more on the horizon.

Molly was absolutely beaming. She'd been waiting years to see her children marry and start families of their own. All of them had been more focused on careers than romance, much to her chagrin, but things had turned around and fast. It seemed like each of them had gone from single to engaged in the blink of an eye.

Today was Brody and Samantha's big day. It was the ceremony that she'd lain awake nights worrying she might never see. Molly had always hoped that Brody would find a woman who could look beyond the scars. She couldn't have imagined a more perfect match for him than Sam.

She had thought for certain that Brody and Sam would opt for a wedding in Boston. He'd promised her a huge ceremony with half the eastern seaboard in attendance, but when it came down to it, Sam had wanted something far more intimate at the farm, which thrilled Molly. That didn't mean a simple affair, by any stretch—this was still Sam's wedding they were talking about. Her new daughter-in-law imagined an event that was pink and covered in flowers and Swarovski crystals.

All of "her girls" were so different, and Molly was so pleased to be able to finally say that. She had four daughters now, and each of their weddings would be unique experiences that would keep the farm hopping all year.

When Ken had his heart attack, Wade and Tori had postponed their plans for a fall wedding. Since Brody and Sam were already planning a spring ceremony, they opted to wait until the following autumn and keep with the rustic theme they'd designed. Xander and Rose were marrying over the long Fourth of July weekend in an appropriately patriotic extravaganza.

And as for Heath and Julianne...they hadn't gotten very far into planning their second wedding when it all got chucked out the window. They'd promised Molly a big ceremony, but when they realized they'd come home from Paris with more than just souvenirs, they moved up the timeline.

Molly stepped away from her duties as mother of the groom to search for her daughter in the crowd. Julianne was sitting beneath the shade of the tent, absent-mindedly stroking her round, protruding belly. The delicate pink bridesmaid gown Sam had selected for her daughter to wear did little to hide the fact that she was extremely pregnant. Although Julianne had sworn she had no more secrets, in only two months, Molly would be holding her second grandbaby and she could hardly wait.

Julianne and Heath had had the first of the weddings on the farm—a small family ceremony while everyone was home for Christmas. It was the polar opposite of to-day's circus. Brody and Sam had a band, dancing, and a catered sit-down meal.

A new song began and Brody led Sam onto the dance floor. They might as well have been the only people here since Brody couldn't take his eyes off of her. His bride was beaming like a ray of sunshine. Her white satin gown was stunning against the golden tan of her skin. The in-tricate crystal and bead work traveled down the bodice to the mermaid skirt, highlighting every amazing curve of Sam's body. Her veil was long, flowing down her back to pool on the parquet dance floor they set up on the lawn. She was stunning.

Brody, too, was looking handsome. Molly had always thought he was a good-looking boy, but the first round of reconstructive surgery with the specialist had done won-ders for his scars. There would be more surgeries in the future, but Molly could already see the dramatic change in the way he carried himself. She'd never seen Brody look happier than he did right now.

It wasn't long before Wade and Tori joined them on the dance floor. Then Xander and Rose. Julianne took a little convincing, but eventually Heath lured her out to dance, completing the wedding party.

The sight of all of them together brought a happy tear to Molly's eye. The last few years had been so hard with nearly losing Ken, the crippling financial burden of his medical bills and dealing with the police investigation. Even when all that was behind them, Molly and Ken had to work through their guilt over what had happened with

Tommy and how their children had suffered silently for all these years. It had been rough, but the Edens were made of stern stuff and they had survived and become stronger for it. The year of weddings at the Garden of Eden was a fresh start for the whole family.

Molly felt a warmth at her back, then the slide of Ken's arms around her waist. He hugged her to his chest, pressing a kiss against her cheek.

"Look at our beautiful family, Mama," he whispered into her ear.

Molly relished the feel of his still strong arms holding her and sighed with contentment. "It's hard to believe there was a time we thought we might not have any children," she said. "And here we are with a full house. And grandbabies."

"It's better than I ever imagined or could even have hoped for. I think the fairy tale I promised you on our wedding day is finally complete."

"Yes," Molly agreed. "We've reached our happily ever after."

* * * * *

MILLS & BOON®
By Request

RELIVE THE ROMANCE WITH THE BEST OF THE BEST

A sneak peek at next month's titles...

In stores from 15th June 2017:

- **Powerful & Proud** – Kate Hewitt

- **A Night in His Arms** – Annie West, Cat Schield & Kate Carlisle

In stores from 29th June 2017:

- **Bound by Passion** – Cara Summers, Katherine Garbera & Kate Carlisle

- **Single Mum Seeking...** – Raye Morgan & Teresa Hill

Just can't wait?
Buy our books online before they hit the shops!
www.millsandboon.co.uk

Also available as eBooks.

7/05